Sandy Barker is an Australian writer, traveller and hopeful romantic with a lengthy bucket list and a cheeky sense of humour.

Many of Sandy's travel adventures have found homes in her writing, including her debut novel, a contemporary romance set in Greece, which was inspired by her true-life love story.

sandybarker.com

 twitter.com/sandybarker
facebook.com/sandybarkerauthor
instagram.com/sandybarkerauthor

THE DATING GAME

SANDY BARKER

One More Chapter
a division of HarperCollins*Publishers* Ltd
1 London Bridge Street
London SE1 9GF
www.harpercollins.co.uk

HarperCollins*Publishers*
1st Floor, Watermarque Building, Ringsend Road
Dublin 4, Ireland

This paperback edition 2021
First published in Great Britain in ebook format
by HarperCollins*Publishers* 2021

2

A catalogue record of this book
is available from the British Library

ISBN: 978-0-00-850932-3

Printed and bound in the UK using 100% Renewable Electricity
by CPI Group (UK) Ltd

For my fellow Renegades, Andie, Nina, and Fi
I love you gals — thank you for being in my family of friends

A Note From the Author

Because this book is about the world of reality television, there are a *lot* of characters. But don't worry! I've got sneaky little reminders for you about who's who woven into the story—and if you get completely lost (it's not as bad as trying to remember all the characters from *Game of Thrones*, I promise), here are a couple of tips:

If you're reading on an e-reader, there's a function that will tell you about a character if you tap on their name. And I've also provided a cast of characters for you at the end of the book.

Happy reading!

Chapter One

'Okay, Abigail, time to sell off a little piece of your soul. Mama needs a new pair of shoes. Hah! Mama needs to pay her rent, more like.'

I don't often talk to myself out loud. All right, that's an abject lie, but sometimes I need a little pep talk, like when I sit down to write my columns for the online tabloid, Food for Your Mind—Hula Hoops and Jaffa Cakes, anyone? That's not its real name, of course, just a more accurate version of its actual name, which is (stupidly) Feed Your Mind. I'm not sure who came up with that, but it was pre-me and may indicate that they had loftier goals than photographs of celebs without makeup, gossip, and the trite tripe that I write, sarky recaps of reality television shows.

Last night was the premier of the latest season of *The Stag*, an archaic show about a single man seeking the love of his life—hah! more like fame, fortune, or someone to shag—amongst an array of women—the 'Does'—who are

1

so homogenous and awful, they all blend into one fake-tanned blob.

It's rumoured that each season, the winning Doe gets her happily ever after *and* a hefty 'dowry' somewhere in the vicinity of £50,000. If that's true, no wonder they clamber over the Stag like bargain hunters on Black Friday. It remains a rumour, however, as the Does are sworn to secrecy—and not just about the 'prize'. They film the show weeks in advance and every Doe, even those who are sent packing from Stag Manor after the first Pin Ritual, must remain tight lipped until the finale airs. I couldn't manage that for five minutes! Fortunately, I don't have to.

My mission, should I choose to accept it—and I do, because of that 'eking out an existence' thing—is to write witty recaps of each episode for our readers—far less taxing than keeping a slew of epic secrets. And my fans love my work, especially my recaps of *The Stag*. Sure, my posts about *Isle of Passion*, *The Incredible Chase*, and *I'm Super Famous, I Want Out!* go down a treat, but this is my opus, where I really get to sharpen my snarky, sarky teeth. *The Stag* has begun and hunting season is open! Brilliant—a tagline for my first post.

I do all this anonymously, of course. I am now somewhat famous—well, my alter-ego is. Apparently, Zoe Ball thinks I'm hilarious—*Zoe Ball!* So, not wanting to appear in my own online magazine, caught down at the local Tesco sans makeup and wearing last season's Lululemon knock-offs—the scandal!—I, Abigail (Abby) Jones, write my witty repartee under a much more exciting moniker. You see, I am *the* Anastasia Blabbergasted. It's quite a clever name, if I do say so myself.

And, besides my editor and my best friend, Lisa, no one knows. *No one.*

Right, enough of that, *Anastasia*. Time to stop faffing about and put that BA in Journalism to work!

The Stag Recap: Hunting Season is Open
by Anastasia Blabbergasted

The Stag has begun and it's hunting season! Ah, Staggy, so good to have you back.

The producers have really upped their game this year with our delectable stag, Jameson (a good thing his father's favourite tipple wasn't Glenlivet!), aka Jaimie. If Henry Cavill and Alex Pettyfer had a love child, it would be this 6'5", chiselled, Greek-god-in-an-outdoor-adventurer's-body.

And this season's ~~Playboy Mansion~~ Stag Manor certainly is a step up from the last one—quite literally; did you see that imposing staircase?—with not one pool, but two! If the mercury cracks 22°C (all appendages crossed), we're bound to see some serious water action. Cue the barely there bikinis, sarky comments about cellulite and breast implants, and the montage sequence of splashing about and squealing, poolside posing, and a slick of spray-on tan floating on the surface of the pool—not to

3

mention, many, *many* shots of those lovely Staggy abs!

So, the tried and tested format for the premiere is trotted out again (why mess with perfection?), with Jaimie waiting anxiously to meet and greet each Doe as they arrive in a limousine (nothing but the best for our girls). And how much does your heart twang for our little (big) Jaimie when he whispers to himself, 'I hope they like me,' just before the first Doe arrives? Aww, bless. Yes, this Staggy is straight out of a lusty romcom—even if he spells his name wrong (come on, the hint's right there in your name—it's 'Jamie', love).

Aside: Whoever designed that pathway from the limousine to Staggy is a maniacal sadist.

The brief: Nervous women wearing sky-high heels and floaty, drag-on-the-ground gowns will walk along this path at night-time. **The design:** Slippery flag-stones surrounded by gravel. May the odds (of not slipping and falling) be ever in your favour!

Another aside: We all agree there's only one limousine, right? And that the Does are lined up on the other side waiting in turn to 'arrive'?

Thought so.

And what about our Does! In assembling ~~Jaimie's harem~~ this bevvy of beauties, the producers have obvs scoured Britain for the brightest, most gregarious, most altruistic, and socially-aware young women (Greta, Malala—watch out!). Sorry, just checked my research—that was for *Britain's Got OBEs*.

This season's casting call was for women who are constantly told how special they are, even if completely unremarkable, and were raised by parents who allowed talking back and slamming doors during their teen years. Vacuous celebrity hunters, influencers, wannabes, wannabe influencers, pouters, flouters, and BLTs (bossy little things) were also encouraged to audition.

The producers then assembled a cast *so* diverse, they've even included a natural redhead! I didn't know until I saw this season's premier that hair colour was a protected class. Thank you for enlightening us, Marie-Alice! (Love a double-barrelled first name, BTW—*super posh*!)

As usual, for your viewing pleasure, I have categorised members of the beauteous bevvy as follows:

- (potential) Brides
- Villains
- Dark Horses
- Miscellaneous

- Filler

Let's start with the last category: **Filler**

Do not bother to learn these Does' names; do not seek out their online profiles; do not become invested in them in any way whatsoever (even if you drew one of their names in a sweepstake), because they are just there to fill up spaces on those ridiculously long sofas. (Quick question: where do you buy those, or are they custom made for Stag Manor?) One by one, the Filler Does will be picked off in early episodes, tearily departing Stag Manor sans one of Jaimie's pins as if they've (actually) spent more than five minutes alone with him. Case in point: Byeeee **Cassie** and **Helen** (oops, I learnt their names, but let's not bother with the other four).

The Villains!
Ah, yes, the ones Jaimie will be ~~told~~ asked to keep around (until it becomes FAR TOO OBVS that the producers are doing that), just to up the drama. This season's (wonder) Villains include:

- **Veronica** For the oldest Doe in the Manor, you sure do pout, shout, and carry on a lot – put your big-girl knickers on, Veronica—it's going to be a bumpy season!
- **Serena** In case you missed it (and really, how could you have?), Bond villainess, Serena, is a

'bossy little *thang*'. She described herself as 'the boss' so many times, I was able to decline the word in Latin by the time her meet and greet with Jaimie (or is that 'meet and *grate*'?) was over. Let's see … bossa, bossum, bossae, bossā

- **Donna** Is this girl a plant? Her acting is so bad, she's like a reject from a casting for *Emmerdale* extras. And I love a good swear, truly I do, but what's with using the F-word as a noun, adjective, *and* a verb, *Donna*? You'll definitely keep the censors busy.
- **Marie-Alice** (Or 'Marie Claire', as Serena calls her accidentally-but-really-on-purpose) is a #hotmess #trainwreck who will probably set feminism back 500,000 years. With all that airtime, the producers clearly love her, though Jaimie doesn't appear to be particularly impressed. And not that it *really* matters, but I'm not either.

Dark Horse

This season, the (only) one to watch is **Simone**! She doesn't seem to take herself—or this show—too seriously, and more than once she *may* have induced full-on snort laughter (don't judge me). Arriving at Stag Manor dressed as a llama?! Genius—the perfect way to stand out in a sea of pageant gowns. Not to mention that she's gorgeous, though seems to have no idea. Yes, our little (big) Jaimie's eyes lit up at the sight of Simone—a fascinating mix of mirth and lust—and she's my pick for Dark Horse. Or, rather, Dark *Llama*. Baaaa! (Llamas go 'baaaa', right?)

Miscellaneous

These are the (somewhat) odd Does who don't fit into any other category. They are *marginally* more interesting than the Filler Does, but definitely not Bride material:

- **Kerry** PLEASE CALM DOWN, KERRY! Nothing is *that* funny, love, not even Simone. And your laugh sounds like a donkey going through menopause—that will get old fast!
- **Natalie** Sweet, but she has one of those wide-eyed smiles that betrays she has no idea what's going on.
- **Daisy** No, Daisy, I'd bet *my* winged eyeliner that *you* will not get a one-on-one date—seriously, though, who bets on their eyeliner? Unborn child, absolutely, but *eyeliner*?

(potential) Brides

Only two that I can see: **Julia** and **Chloe**. These are the most real/lovely/I-would-be-friends-with-them-in-real-life Does of the lot. But as Julia is a mum of two and our little (big) Jaimie is a young man about town, how would that even *work*? Besides, did you *see* those fireworks between Jaimie and Chloe when they first met. I'm fairly certain I heard one of the crew bellow, 'Get a room!'

So, punters are already calling **Chloe** for the win! Huzzah.

But even if it is a(n almost) foregone conclusion, won't it be such fun to watch all the DRAMA unfold? Dah-duh-duhhhhh!

Til next time …

There, that should do it——£750 please. I know that may sound like a lot and it is considering it's for three hours of work——one for viewing and two for writing——but Feed Your Mind makes oodles of advertising money from Anastasia. She's a brand and she sells so aren't I entitled to my little piece?

The best weeks are when shows air concurrently. That keeps me busy, sure, but for someone who grew up in council housing, I like being able to put money away, build my nest egg. I'm not entirely sure what I'm saving for——perhaps the sense of security. My mum never had that chance when I was growing up. It was just the two of us and she worked three jobs and we lived payday to payday. I also give money to my mum, even though she tells me not to. I can't help it——I love my mum.

I live a modest existence. My one-bedroom flat is more of a bedsit, I only buy clothes and shoes from the sale section (more often than not, that's a *supermarket's* sale section), and I rarely splurge on anything——but it's enough.

And with Anastasia bringing in my 'bread and butter', I have time for what I love to do—what I *trained* to do—which is proper writing.

I am constantly pitching to (real) magazines and news organisations, mostly deep dives into societal issues. I've had some pieces published—on average two or three a year—though sometimes it strikes me that I left university a decade ago and have little to show for it.

But I hold onto my dream, to have my own column in a real magazine and to write under my own name—*only* my name. Until then, I will don the moniker of Anastasia Blabbergasted, providing light entertainment to readers across Britain, and try not to think too much about how I am (probably) contributing to the degradation of society.

Chapter Two

The ringing of my phone permeates my dream as an ice cream van, only it's blaring Duo Lipa's latest song—my ringtone—instead of 'Green Sleeves'. Just as I'm about to flag it down and ask for a 99, my eyes pop open.

Only two people would ever call me first thing in the morning: my mum and my editor, Prue. Prue van der Puttin—truly, that's her name. Though, sometimes I'll drop the 'van', the 'der', and one of the 't's because she can be a little, er, dictatorial.

Prue Putin, editor extraordinaire, able to leap errant commas in a single bound and reduce a grown man to tears with merely a glance. Cut-throat, curt, churlish and charm-less—that's our Prue!

I would never say this out loud, of course. I am not an idiot nor a masochist. Staying out of Prue's firing line is one of the core competencies of my job. It's why I am one of her 'darlings'. I cannot even imagine what it's like being in the *other* stable of staff writers—'those people', as she calls them.

All this flies through my head in a microsecond and I'm in such a rush to answer my phone that I knock over my water glass, drowning one of the 3-for-£5 books I picked up yesterday at The Works. Maybe it's salvageable—I hope so. I love a good romcom.

I glance at my phone screen—it's Prue, not Mum—and stab at the green button before it goes to voicemail and I have to grovel through a return call. 'Hello, Prue,' I say, a little breathless.

'Abigail,' she states, like I don't know my own name. 'I thought I was going to have to leave a message,' she adds peevishly. It's only now that I look at the clock. 7:18am. On a Saturday. And not that she knows this, but I was up late last night researching the positive impact of pets on people in aged care. Yet *she's* the one who gets to be peeved.

'So sorry, Prue. I was, er …' I'd rather tell her I was on the loo than the truth. Knowing Prue, she thinks it's a professional weakness to require sleep. She probably doesn't even need sleep, as I half suspect she's a vampire. She certainly could pass for one—her look is rather *dramatic*.

Pin-straight, jet-black hair in a blunt bob to her chin, a severe fringe, pale, luminescent skin, blood-red matte lipstick (always, even right after she's had her morning coffee), winged black eyeliner and lashings of mascara, and a wardrobe that's predominantly black with the occasional smattering of stark white. Think Mia Wallace from *Pulp Fiction*, only nearing fifty and without the dance moves. I haven't seen Prue's skin sparkle in the sunlight, but that's probably because I've never seen her outside of her windowless office.

It turns out I don't need to lie about being on the toilet because she cuts me off. 'Have you seen the feeds?' she asks, her public-school accent lingering on the long 'ee' sounds.

She means my Twitter, Instagram, and Facebook feeds. Well, *Anastasia's* social media feeds, in any case (practically no one follows Abby Jones). They must be blowing up for her to call this early—on a *Saturday*. And no, I haven't checked them because I've been asleep.

'Er, not yet. I was just about to—' The only thing I was just about to do was order an imaginary ice cream. And even if I were wide awake and it was a Tuesday, I rarely check those feeds. I don't even contribute to them—they're run by a pimply teenaged intern that Prue hired.

All right, that's not fair—they're probably perfectly nice and I have no idea if they have pimples or not. They are, however, fantastic at their job, saving me from buying *SEO for Dummies* and allowing me to focus on writing high-impact clickbait.

'They are on fire,' she says, pronouncing 'fire' as 'fy-ah'. 'Your latest piece on *The Stag*—just superb. One of your best, Abigail.'

'Oh, er, thank you.' Compliments are rare in Prueland—take 'em when you can get 'em.

'Mmm.' Prue speak for *'you're welcome'*. 'Anyway, I've received an email from the executive producer.'

'The producer? Of *The Stag*?' Oh god, this cannot be good. Did I cross a line? I've always worried this would happen, that I'd take it too far and get sued or something.

God, I hope I don't get fired. Or, as Prue would say, 'fy-ahed'.

'Yes, that's right.' My stomach lurches and I instantly regret the pot noodles I doctored with sriracha last night. They may just make a reappearance.

'They loved it. Absolutely lapped it up like kittens slurping from a giant bowl of cream.' Before the disturbing image can take hold, my mind starts screaming, *'Oh! My! God!'*

'Really? So, I'm not in any trouble or anything?'

She barks out a laugh, a sort of ack-ack-ack that sounds remarkably like a smoker's cough. 'No, no, nothing like that. On the contrary' —yes, she actually says things like that— 'they are *thrilled* with the buzz it's generating. They think it may just be their most watched season ever—largely due to your piece.'

I am staring open-mouthed at the pattern on my duvet, a swirling grey squiggle, when she drops an even bigger bombshell. '*And* they've asked if you will go on the show.'

What. The. Actual. Effing … What?

'Sorry, I didn't, er … they want me to be on *The Stag*? As what, a guest host or something?' My mind flits from one image to the next of me dolled up like Effie Trinket from *The Hunger Games* and running the Does through their paces.

'*No*,' she replies—it's obviously the most idiotic suggestion she's ever heard. 'They want you to be a *contestant*. Undercover. Get you behind the scenes so your recaps will be particularly juicy.'

This is bonkers. There's no way this is real. Prue is having me on and any moment now, she'll say, 'Just joking,' and ack-ack-ack at me again. Only she doesn't. 'And I haven't even told you the best part, Abigail. Next season, they are filming in Sydney—*Australia*.' She needn't have added that last part; I know very well where Sydney is. It's been on my bucket list since I learnt what one was.

Something occurs to me. 'They're flying sixteen Does and the Stag to *Australia*?' I ask, incredulous. I've always thought they must have a sizeable budget for *The Stag* but that will cost a mint!

'Actually, no. There will only be twelve Does for the Sydney season—and half will be antipodeans. *Now*,' she continues as my mind struggles to grasp all of this, 'they want to meet you, of course—to see what they're working with, that sort of thing. I've already mentioned that they'll want to consider a makeover—an *extensive* one.' Well, thank you, Prue. I roll my eyes, grateful she can't see me. 'So, be at my office first thing on Monday morning.'

This conversation is like being on a whirligig, but I finally come to my senses. I am definitely not going on *The Stag* as a contestant. Worst nightmare. Way worse than missing out on an imaginary ice cream. Me? On camera? As a contestant on *The Stag*? No. No. No. No. No.

'Er, Prue, I think I'll need to decline.'

There's silence—perhaps the most pregnant of all pauses since the dawn of time—and I send a silent plea to Cadmus, the Greek god of Writing, hoping he will somehow rescue me from what I know is coming.

'*Abigail*,' says Prue, her exasperation turning my name into a puff of air with consonants, 'you seem to be under the glaring misconception that this telephone call is to *ask* you if you will appear on a highly rated television show to, one—establish a partnership between my magazine and a television network, and two—boost our reach and, therefore, our readership, potentially *ten*-fold.'

Cadmus, you traitor.

'I assure you, that it is not. This is me calling to share some excellent news and to tell you that you absolutely *will* appear on the Sydney season of *The Stag* as a contestant. *If* they don't take one look at you and run screaming for the hills, that is.'

Ouch. That last part was unnecessary, but particularly Prue-like and an indication that I have irked her more than usual.

'Do you understand?'

'Er … yes. Yes, of course.' I hear myself say.

'Excellent. So, Monday. 9am—*sharp*. And Abigail?'

'Yes, Prue?'

'Dress to impress, will you? Or at least do your best.'

'Will do,' I say weakly. The line goes silent; she's hung up without saying goodbye—another Prueism.

I drop my phone into my lap and glance at the clock again. 7:26am. Eight minutes ago, I was asleep and now I'm going to be a contestant on *The Stag*. Well, possibly. As Prue said, they may take one look at me and run for the hills—'screaming' she'd said.

Or I may come to my senses and tell them all to sod right off. It's not like I need my job, right?

Oh, Cadmus, I am absolutely screwed.

'Hiya, Abs,' says my best friend, Lisa, as she opens the door to her flat. After my call with Prue, I waited until a reasonable hour—that's at least 10am for Lise—then texted to say I needed to see her. She invited me for brunch, so I've shown up with a paper bag brimming with croissants from the bakery downstairs. When Lisa invites me over for food, I have to bring it with me. 'Come on in. I've just put the kettle on.'

She pads into her kitchen-lounge-dining room and I follow, dumping the croissants on the bench, then seating myself at her table for two. 'You've tidied up,' I say, looking about her flat. It's considerably larger than mine but is essentially two rooms—this one at the front of the building, which overlooks the high street, and her bedroom at the back of the building, which has a rather charming view of the bakery's industrial bins and an alley. Sandwiched between the two rooms is a tiny but modern bathroom that runs the length of the hallway.

It's a rather nice flat—a little noisy sometimes—and if it weren't for the fact that Lisa is (what can only be described as) an utter slob, it would be lovely. When I said she'd tidied up, I meant that she'd washed her dishes and there were no takeaway containers littering her coffee table.

We've been best friends since I arrived at St Mary's College on a full scholarship in sixth form. Unlike me, she's from money—*serious* money—though you probably wouldn't know it if you met her. She has a (supposedly unassuming) job with the government, which I know nothing about and secretly suspect it's because she works for MI5 or MI6—probably the former as she doesn't travel much.

Though, whatever Lisa's job actually entails, it's not what her parents had in mind for her. Their little darling was supposed to be a barrister, or a Harley Street consultant, or the editor-in-chief of a fashion magazine, not a 'lowly public servant', as they say.

She's also chiselled some edges into her born-and-bred plum-in-the-mouth accent, giving it more of a contemporary London flavour. This is either part of her cover, or it's to disguise the fact that she's titled and grew up in the type of house where her father had a valet.

I called her 'milady' once. It did not go down well.

The only clues to her 'former life', as she refers to it, are her list of Facebook friends and the incredible fashion cast-offs she receives from her favourite aunty—Lisa's wardrobe is practically brimming with last season's designer wares. And, just quietly, if I had an aunty who lavished me with expensive gifts, she'd be my favourite too.

But to me, she is just 'Lise', a brilliant and lovely person—albeit a messy one—who, for some reason, decided on that fateful first day of school, we would be best friends. While others were carving a wide berth around me in the St Mary's dining hall as I looked about for somewhere to sit, she hooked her arm through mine and steered me towards a table in the corner. That's where I met our gang, the friends we had all the way through to sitting our A-levels. We disbanded after that and, though I am still connected with them on Facebook, we only catch up every now and then.

Lise, however, is my *person*, the sister I always longed for. I love her more than anyone else in the world, besides Mum, but I will never *ever* live with her. I value our friendship too much.

She plonks a mug of tea in front of me and it sloshes onto the table. At least the mug looks clean. One time she served me tea and right as I was about to take a sip, a mouldy blob floated to the surface. I didn't drink tea for at least a week after that.

She's back in the kitchen now, bustling about—probably looking for a clean plate for the croissants. I'm wrong. They arrive on the table still in the paper bag, which she rips open. 'Only my best serving platter for you, Abs,' she says, then laughs to herself. I sip the tea while she searches for some jam in her mini fridge.

'Strawberry or plum?'

'Bring both.' She does, along with her tea and finally sits down. That's the other thing about Lisa—once she's awake, she never stops moving—boundless energy. Like a puppy with purpose.

'Right, what's your news?' she asks through a mouthful of croissant.

'I'm going on *The Stag*, as a contestant.' I decided on the way over here that, just for fun, I'd come right out with my news. No preamble, no context. My plan backfires when she splutters and coughs, showering the table—and me—with chewed-up croissant.

I leap up and pat her on the back, but she shoos me away so I go to the kitchen to get something for the mess. I'm wiping down the table with a Nando's napkin when she says sternly, 'Abby, leave it. Just tell me what's going on.'

I sit and the whole tale tumbles out, unedited and

including my impression of Prue, which (as always) makes her laugh. By the time I wrap up with, 'And dress to impress, will you? Or at least do your best,' delivered less like Prue and more like Ursula the sea witch from *The Little Mermaid*, Lisa is in fits and I feel marginally better about this ridiculous situation.

Me on *The Stag*. Hah!

'So, speaking of,' says Lisa, 'what *are* you going to wear to this meeting?'

Right. Terrific question. I work from home and my social life is hardly what you'd call exciting—or even existent. I have precisely one decent pair of black trousers (thank you, Marks & Spencer), which are a little worse for wear and probably due for an upgrade, but they might do. But what to wear with them? A quick mental catalogue of my 'bargain bin' tops—Prue's patronising words echoing in my ear—brings me up flummoxed.

'What about that dress you wore to Pip's wedding?' asks Lisa. Pippa is her cousin. I've only met her a few times over the years, but Lisa insisted I go to Pippa's wedding last summer as her 'plus one'. I'd splurged on an extremely over-the-top dress—far fancier than anything I've ever owned or would buy again. And with the loan of matching shoes, clutch, and hat from Lisa—the accessory trifecta—I at least looked the part. Even so, I spent much of the wedding—from arriving at the church for the ceremony right through to the posed photographs and the reception—feeling like an imposter.

'You don't think it's too much? Too … er … posh?' I ask.

She shrugs. 'There's no such thing as being overdressed,

only underdressed. Besides, you look great in that dress and you want to make a good impression, right?'

'*Or*—and stay with me here—I show up looking like the dog's dinner, they realise they can't possibly make a silk purse from a sow's ear, they send me packing, and I'm off the hook. How does that sound?'

'Like you've used your quota of idioms,' she teases. I expel a sigh. 'Stop moping. This could be a brilliant opportunity for you.'

'I doubt it.'

'Well, you won't know until you show up—*looking your best*—and find out what they have to say. Wear the dress. You can borrow my matching shoes.' I frown at a croissant, picking at it and grinding flakes of the pastry into smaller flakes between my thumb and forefinger. 'And stop that. You're making a mess.'

My eyes lift to meet hers. She's smirking at her own messy expense and we both start sniggering. 'All right,' I say eventually. 'I'll go to the meeting and I'll wear my fancy dress with your fancy shoes. But I still hope they won't want a bar of me. Just the thought … Honestly, if I have to go on that wretched show, it will be my worst nightmare come true.'

'That's the spirit, Abs.' When I roll my eyes and shake my head, she just laughs.

Chapter Three

It's Monday morning! I've added the exclamation point, not for emphasis, but to distract myself from the growing terror that has seeped into every pore, every *cell* of my body.

I may be dressed up, but I am still me and this morning, I'd been left to my own devices when it came to hair and makeup. I could hardly expect my best friend to get up extra early on a *Monday*, get herself ready for work, then come over and doll me up—all before 8am. Right? Actually, I had expected that—or at least hoped—and then I'd remembered who my best friend is.

So here I am, squished into the lift with a dozen other people, wearing an OTT (now) slightly-too-tight and (in retrospect) definitely-too-short silk dress with billowing sleeves and Lisa's matching shoes (which I secretly love, and hope she won't miss too much when I 'forget' to return them).

My belongings—a pocket-sized packet of tissues, a Burt's Bees lip balm, my Oyster card, and my wallet—currently reside in my other loan from Lisa, an enormous handbag that would have cost more than a month's rent, gifted to her by that favourite aunty.

I've washed and dried my slightly wavy, mousy-brown hair and pulled it into a low ponytail, and I'm wearing as much makeup as I've mastered, which is practically none—mascara, cream blush, and the lip balm.

I will do.

The lift pings its arrival at my floor and I push through the tightly knit crowd, murmuring increasingly louder excuse-me's as I try to get to the door before it closes. How do people still not know how to let others out of a lift? By the time I reach the doors, they are starting to close and I shove my arm in the way to stop them. Only they don't. They close on my arm and I have a horrifying thought that I am going to be dragged up to the next floor, arm out and soon to be decapitated. An arm can be decapitated, right? Or is that only for heads?

A moment later the doors rebound off my arm, popping open long enough for me to retrieve it, but when they close again my stupid billowing shirtsleeve is caught between the giant jaws of death. Oh, my god. If this lift starts to move, my sleeve still trapped between the doors, my dress is going to be torn off me in front of all these strangers and they'll see me for who I really am—an average-looking woman in a six-year-old ill-fitting bra and a greying pair of knickers!

I hear someone stab repeatedly at a button, his voice permeating the thick crowd behind me (and I mean both dense and stupid, as they are all doing absolutely *nothing* to help me). My rescuer adds swearing to his efforts, 'Come on you bloody thing,' and—thank god—the doors finally slide open. I stumble out of the lift, double over, and blow out a heavy breath. Now is not the time to have a panic attack—well, I mean, it *is*. If one is prone to them, like I am, this is exactly the time one would be attacked by panic—but I am due to meet the producers of *The Stag* in a matter of minutes.

A pair of suede sneakers pops into view and I raise my gaze to see that they're part of a casual ensemble worn by the person I presume is my rescuer—slim-cut dark-denim jeans, a brown T-shirt that says, 'I aim to misbehave' (Oh, do you now?), and a canvas cross-body satchel. I right myself and my presumed rescuer smiles at me, a concerned look on his face. It seems as if he's about to pat my back in a 'there, there' sort of way, but he pulls his hand away and stuffs it into his pocket instead.

'Are you okay?' he asks, a thick Australian accent the perfect addition to his ensemble. He is a few inches taller than me, has a lean build, a mop of floppy dark-blonde, slightly-too-long-but-actually-sort-of-gorgeous hair, large green eyes that peer at me with concern, and the most perfectly shaped mouth I have ever seen. *Ever*.

Ding dong! I never quite understood Bridget Jones's reaction to seeing Mark Darcy at her parents' turkey curry buffet—until now.

'Er, yes, quite. Thank you.'

'You sure? Your cheeks are bright red,' he says.

Ding don't! He's probably trying to be nice, but I'm not one of those women who gets a natural blush of pink on the apples of her cheeks. When I blush—or *flush*, as in the case of a near-panic attack——my cheeks could be used to guide the aeroplanes landing at Heathrow. I press my palm against my left cheek——red hot. Just brilliant. If *The Stag* producers were going to be underwhelmed by me before, this could push them over the edge——or under it.

'Can I get you some water? Do you wanna sit down?' He looks around the Feed Your Mind lobby and indicates a row of fancy-looking but extremely uncomfortable chairs (I've sat out here waiting on Prue more times than I care to remember) and my feet are on the move before my mind catches up. I plonk onto one of the chairs while my rescuer approaches the reception desk, and focus on my breathing. In-two-three-four, out-two-three-four.

I watch the exchange at reception curiously. I can't make out what he's saying, but he seems to be gesturing far more dramatically than a retelling of my minor incident should require. The receptionist looks over at me, grimaces, nods curtly, and disappears——snarky little cow. Last time I was here, she was an intern whose sole job was to run to the nearest Costa four times a day for coffee——*and* she got my order wrong!

I glance at my watch. It's a hair before nine and I hate to be late——Prue will be livid. But I can't meet the producers when I'm this out of sorts. My rescuer makes his way back to me and cocks his head to the side. 'You're looking a bit better. She's gone to get you some water——and to tell them we're here.'

'Sorry, that *we're* here?'

'Yeah. Turns out we're both here for the same meeting. I'm Jack. I'm producing the show in Sydney.'

No, no, no, no, no, this cannot be happening. 'The show?' I ask weakly. Perhaps there is a slim chance that he's talking about a completely different television show that just happens to have a 9am meeting scheduled with my editor.

'Yeah, *The Stag*. You must be Anastasia, right?' I stare at him, mouth agape. 'But hey,' he lowers his voice 'that's not your real name, is it? I mean, I know "Blabbergasted" is made up—clever name, by the way—' I'm frowning at him, a mix of disbelief and mortification, but he trundles ahead with our one-sided conversation as though I'm doing my part. 'But what about Anastasia? Is that really you?'

'Sorry?'

'I just meant, what should I call you?' he asks.

'What? Call me?'

'Yeah—you know, when you're on the show?'

And then it strikes me.

Despite being caught in the lift doors, the near panic attack, and the inability to utter one audible indication that I have a formidable mind, the producer of *The Stag* has not run for the hills. Instead, he's taken it as a given that I will be on the show.

Apparently, I'm *Stag* material. And I don't know how to feel about that. Should I be pleased or insulted?

'Abby,' I say, my voice barely above a whisper. 'You can call me Abby.'

Jack smiles down at me. 'Abby, nice,' he says simply.

'They're ready for you,' says the receptionist, still riding her wave of superciliousness. 'And here.' She holds out a bottle of water, and Jack takes it from her and loosens the lid before handing it to me. It's a small gesture, but thoughtful, and I file it away under 'attractive *and* nice'.

'Thank you,' I say. I take a sip, swallow, and follow up with a slow, deep breath.

'You right now?' he asks.

'Yes, thank you.'

'We should probably get in there then,' he says, smiling.

'Oh, right,' I say, standing and smoothing down my dress. Even though I've been dreading this meeting for two days, I sense that having Jack there will make it all right, like I have an ally of sorts.

When we get to Prue's office, Jack pushes open the giant glass door and stands aside to let me pass. I'm basking in the glow of his lovely manners when I come face to face with a stout, sour-faced woman who eyes me up and down so mercilessly, I nearly turn on my heels and leave. No preamble, no 'hello, nice to meet you', just raw, naked scrutiny—she's a rancher and I'm a prize mare. It gets worse when her eyes narrow slightly as she scans my face and hair, then turns to Prue and says, 'I see what you mean about the makeover.'

'I beg your pardon,' my mind screams.

Jack rallies, standing by my side as he makes introductions. 'Roberta, this is Abby. Abby this is Roberta, the executive producer of *The Stag*.'

Right. So, this vile woman is the one who emailed Prue about my post, the one who hired Jack, and the one who (apparently) wants me to appear on the show as a Doe. So far, it is a big fat 'no' from me—as if the choice is mine. But if she keeps scowling at me like that, her lips pursed into a pallid cat's bottom, I may not need to worry. She certainly doesn't appear keen on me.

'Hello,' says Roberta. A tiny part of me is impressed. I had no idea that a cordial greeting could carry so much disdain, nor that it's possible to speak through pursed lips.

'Hello,' I say back, meeting her unwavering gaze. I may be wearing borrowed shoes, but I am a very clever woman and I write witty repartee for a living. I will not be intimated by this woman, even if she makes Prue look like Mary Effing Poppins.

Speaking of … Prue leaps up from behind her desk and comes to stand with the rest of us. I suppose, looking in, we might appear as though we're about to clasp hands and sing 'Kumbaya' or something. It's already the oddest meeting I've ever had and we're only two minutes in.

'And you must be Jack,' says Prue, reaching her hand across the circle. He shakes it and does a good job of behaving normally, despite the odd start to our little gathering.

'Yeah, I'm Jack. Good to meet you, Prue.'

'Roberta has told me excellent things about you,' she gushes, her mouth doing something I've never seen before—*smiling*. I'm suddenly struck with the realisation that Prue does have a chink in her armour, after all—and it's attractive, younger Australian men.

'So, now that we've all met, how about we sit down and discuss this incredible opportunity for Feed Your Mind? And for Abigail, of course,' she adds quickly. She indicates the sitting area of her office, where a two-seater sofa faces two side-by-side armchairs, a low coffee table in between.

Still reeling from Roberta's insult and even more so from seeing this unexpected side of Prue, I head straight to the sofa and collapse onto it. Jack sits next to me, the fabric of his jeans pressing against my bare thigh. I tug at the hem of my dress and wiggle away from him as surreptitiously as I can, breaking the contact. I do not need my tell-tale cheeks betraying how much I already like him——or how good I think he smells. It's like a freshly dried cotton sheet when you retrieve it from the washing line after a breezy, sunny day.

Roberta sits directly opposite me and looks me over again. 'There's enough to work with, at least,' she says tartly. High praise from Vile Demon Woman——huzzah!

Prue claps her hands together——another oddity——and says, 'Excellent. And as you know, Abigail is quite the writer. Having first-hand experience of all the behind-the-scenes machinations, she is bound to do a fabulous job of recapping the upcoming season.'

I glance over at Jack and we share a quick smile. His says, *'This is going to be great.'* Mine says, *'I have no idea who that woman is that's body-snatched my editor.'*

Roberta, however, doesn't seem to be listening to Prue. 'So, now that I've seen what we're working with——and that with a little spit and polish, you'll do——here's the run down. We start shooting the next season in September. You'll need a work visa for Australia and Jack will help you sort that out. You'll be on the show as yourself, of course, not Anastasia. And we will guarantee that you get to the top four Does, so you get a decent look behind the scenes, so to speak. And for the rest of the details, we can hammer those out at a later point, don't you think?'

I know the question is rhetorical, but no, I do *not* think. I want to know right this minute every single detail of this … this … My mind *wants* to grasp onto words like 'adventure', 'escapade', or 'jaunt', but settles on 'utter debacle waiting to happen'. And first and foremost, I will absolutely *not* be going on the show as myself.

'Er, no,' I say, lifting my chin to show how profoundly serious I am.

'I'm sorry?' says Roberta in that passive-aggressive way that we British have perfected. She's clearly not sorry about anything at all.

'First, I am not comfortable with committing to the show until I know exactly what it entails.' I'm bluffing, of course. This is a mandate from Prue and my job depends on me consenting, but I'm betting on Roberta not knowing that.

'And second, if I do decide to go on the show, I'll want a pseudonym. There is no way I'll agree to be a Doe as Abigail Jones. I write under that name, *my* name.' Prue knows this, I'm sure, although she's never raised it with me. 'There aren't many pieces out there—yet—but I want an Abigail Jones byline to *mean* something.' What I don't say is that I want my name to mean, 'serious investigative journalist' and 'brilliant writer', not 'dolly bird who went on *The Stag* for a free trip to Sydney'.

In my periphery, I see Prue look between me and Roberta, her eyes popped and her mouth agape, but I keep my eyes locked on my adversary's. Prue may kill me later, but right now, I'm standing my ground. And I'm not sure where this confidence is coming from—perhaps it's due to Jack's steady presence beside me.

'I see,' says Roberta through her teeth. Though, I doubt she does. She seems like the type of woman who surrounds herself with sycophants who wouldn't dare contradict her. The silence fills the room with a thick tension as we eye each other across the coffee table.

Prue starts to speak—likely to intervene and assure Roberta that I'm only joking—*I'm not*—but Roberta raises a hand and silences her, as though she's Obi Wan Kenobi. *'This is not the Doe you are looking for.'*

'Fine. You can have a pseudonym.' A win! 'But you'd best choose something close enough to your real name that you answer to it instinctively. It can be a little obvious otherwise—believe me. And I will not go down that path again.' My mind starts scanning over past seasons of the show, wondering which Does had false names.

'How about Abby?' asks Jack. I abandon my mental audit of Does and turn towards him. He's looking at me, those green eyes showing kindness and good humour, and I could absolutely get lost in them if we were somewhere other than my editor's office in this bizarre meeting. Instead, I latch onto what he's said.

'Abby,' I say, trying on my own name for size.

'Yeah, that's how you introduced yourself to me. And it's common enough—so is "Jones". Even if someone did find out your last name, it's unlikely they'd make the connection.'

'I like it.' He grins at me and I grin back.

'If you two are finished, I have somewhere else I need to be in twenty minutes,' says Vile Demon Woman.

'But what about everything else, all the other details?' I ask.

Prue leaps into the conversation with, 'Oh, I am sure it will all be *fine*, Abigail. It's such an *incredible* opportunity.' I've worked with her long enough to listen between the lines, and her pointed tone says everything her words don't. This is an incredible opportunity for Feed Your Mind and I am skirting the edges of ruining it.

Though, if I do want to play the 'what's in it for me?' card, I suppose I could write about the 'reality' of reality television. Roberta has already alluded to some of the cast members playing characters—or at least, alternate versions of themselves. There may be a story there, and likely that's just scratching the surface.

Roberta stands and Prue shoots lasers at me from her eyes—the kind that say, *'She's about to leave and your job is on the line, so hurry up and lock this in.'*

'Well, as it *is* such an incredible opportunity and we've sorted the matter of my name,' I say magnanimously, 'I'll do it.'

'Excellent. I'm pleased to hear that, Abigail,' says Roberta, her tone a complete about-face. She punctuates her words with the fakest smile I have ever seen—and that's after watching hundreds of episodes of reality television. This tactic probably works for her more often than not, but I think I just got the opener for my exposé—producer and Vile Demon Woman, Roberta Whatsername, wheedles her way through casting sessions, alternating between bullying and placating.

'And Jack can fill you in on anything else you want to

know,' she adds, sweetening the pot. And I won't lie, learning that I get to spend more time with Jack is the only good news I've had since Prue called me on Saturday morning.

Roberta turns to go and Prue scrambles to her feet. 'Let me see you out, Roberta,' she says, her voice dripping with niceness.

Roberta purses her lips in reply, then turns towards the door. 'Jack, Abby,' she says over her shoulder, a dismissive goodbye. Prue follows her, full grovel mode activated and at their departure, the air in the office goes from stifling to normal.

'You did great,' says Jack.

'Really?' I'm not convinced. The whole thing was over practically before it started and no doubt, I will spend hours agonising over what I *should* have said and done.

'Yeah, for sure. I've worked with Roberta on a few projects, and I've never seen anyone stand up to her like that.'

'Don't you?' I ask.

This incites a full-throated laugh, then, 'God no. These gigs pay good money and until my brother and I have our own production company, I do as I'm told. Yes, Roberta, no Roberta …'

'Three bags full, Roberta,' I say, completing the sentence.

'Exactly.' A frown scuppers across his face. 'I hope you don't think any less of me for it.'

'No, not at all,' I say, only realising the truth in my words as they leave my mouth. No matter how he earns a living, it's clear that he and Roberta are cut from very different cloths.

'Good, I mean, it really is about the money for me. Harry—that's my brother—we've committed to saving as much money as possible—at least for the next year or so and then we're hanging out our own shingle. We want to produce—films mostly. There's a great indie scene in Australia, and we know heaps of actors, directors, writers … It's gonna be amazing, but right now, we're just putting our heads down and taking the highest-paying gigs we can get.'

'I understand—truly. That's like Anastasia for me. She pays the bills—and earns me enough to save a little—but I don't love what I'm doing. Not yet anyway. It's a means to an end, that's all, just like this show is for you.'

'You really do get it,' he says simply.

'I really do.'

'Sooo,' he says, breaking into a smile and waggling his eyebrows, 'you're gonna be on *The Stag*!' I utter a guttural 'ugh' and he nudges my arm with his. 'Don't worry, it'll be great. Sydney's amazing, and you'll get to live in a mansion …'

'With a dozen other women. And isn't it dormitory style?'

'Uh, yeah …' He shrugs. 'Still …'

'Honestly, Jack, this all makes me feel a bit sick.'

'I get it. Look, how 'bout we go grab a coffee or something and you can pick my brain?'

'Really? Because I want to know *everything*—exactly what I'm signing up for, the logistics, how you see the subterfuge playing out ... especially that. That's the part I'm most worried about.'

'Then I'm all yours.' If only that were true. 'You can ask me anything.' Oh, if only *that* were true. If it were, I'd ask, *'Can't we just forget this bonkers plan and run off to Greece for a holiday instead?'*

What I actually say is, 'All right. That sounds good.'

We share another smile and just as we stand, Prue marches back into her office. 'Abigail Jones, what in the *hell* were you playing at?'

I glance at Jack, catching his surprise. *'You see?'* I say with my eyes, *'This is the real Prue.'* It must have been exhausting being as charming as she was for the entire duration of our micro meeting. I have no time to respond to her, however, because she launches at me with, 'You came remarkably close to ruining everything. How dare you put me on the back foot like that.'

Her bony forefinger aims right at me and, like a pin, it pricks my defences. 'You're right,' I concede——because she is.

Well, that takes the wind out of her sails. 'Oh,' she says benignly, followed closely by, 'Good, yes, quite right.' She skirts around her desk and sits primly on the edge of her office chair.

'Shall we go, Abby?' asks Jack, like we're late for a reservation or something.

'Absolutely, yes. Jack is going to answer all my questions about the show,' I say to Prue.

She nods. 'Very good. And, Jack, I imagine you will be in touch about Abigail's work visa?' she says pleasantly——the same woman who just chewed me up and spat me out right in front of him.

'Sure thing, yeah.' He shepherds me through the door, his hand lightly touching my back and for the first time today, I'm glad to be wearing a thin silk dress. When we're out of earshot, just near the lifts, he whispers to me, 'She's almost as bad as Roberta.'

'Oh, you have no idea,' I reply, and we both dissolve into quiet giggles as the lift doors open. I step inside, followed by Jack, and this time, I keep my billowing sleeves well away from the giant jaws of death.

Chapter Four

'Go back to Jack again. I want to hear more about the gorgeous Australian,' says Lisa.

'He's not …' Oh, who am I fooling? After spending several hours with Jack at the café across the road from Feed Your Mind, Jack is absolutely 'the gorgeous Australian'. My blossoming crush was solidified when he offered to buy my coffee *and* the blueberry muffin I was eyeing in the glass cabinet next to the till.

I called Lisa as soon as I got home. It went to voicemail, of course—with her being a super spy, she never answers my calls during work hours. She is now ensconced on my tatty (but loved) sofa, peering at me curiously over the rim of her wine glass. We're drinking fizz, which she insisted on bringing, even though I'm only fifty-seven per cent certain there's anything to celebrate, and most of that number is because of Jack and Sydney—and the thought of spending time with Jack *in* Sydney.

'Am I being ridiculous?' I ask.

She blinks at me and lowers her glass, nestling it between cupped hands. I only have one set of wine glasses, giant globes, and no matter what we're drinking, Lisa insists on filling them to the equator. There's almost half a bottle in each glass, but my thoughts of fizz and equators are simply a distraction. Despite having asked it, I don't want to ponder my own question——deep down, I already know the answer.

'How do you mean?' she prompts. I purse my lips and blow out a long breath, my gaze fixed on the stack of tabloid magazines I subscribe to for work. 'Abs?'

I leap off the sofa, taking my glass with me, and start pacing the (short) length of my lounge-dining-kitchenette. 'Two days ago, I was a staff writer at an online tabloid.'

'You still are,' she interjects. I flash her a shushing look and she raises a hand in apology——she knows better than to interrupt a 'talk it through' monologue. 'Continue.'

'Two days ago, I was a staff writer at an online tabloid,' I start again (it's always the best way), 'and now I'm supposed to embrace my tabloid writer status and dive even deeper into the muck.' She goes to say something but stops herself. 'But what if this Stag caper cements my position at Feed Your Mind and I can never, ever break away from there?' My voice pitches, sounding screechy and desperate, and I take a sip of fizz.

'All right, I know it's against the rules, but I'm going to stop you there,' she says. I cease pacing. 'Well, keep pacing if it helps.' It does so I do, looping my finger in the air to tell her to continue. 'So, you go, you write your recaps, you enjoy being schlepped about Sydney——because let's face it, those shows spare no expense when it comes to excursions—and you write the exposé you mentioned … I think that's the part you should focus on.'

'Really?'

'Abs, it's a *brilliant* idea. And just think, you could get picked up by *The Guardian*, or *The Conversation* or *The New Yorker*! Imagine the doors that could open and then you'd be able to leave Feed Your Mind. For good.'

'But what if it all blows up in my face?'

'What do you mean?'

I sigh out another long breath and deposit my glass on the table. 'Well, the plan is to pretend to be someone else, Doe Abby, while writing recaps as Anastasia Blabbergasted, while also writing an exposé as *me*, Abigail Jones the journalist. That's a lot of versions of myself to keep track of. What if I'm rubbish at all the role playing and deception? I'm not *you*,' I say, alluding to her spy status. She rolls her eyes, but I note that she doesn't correct me and I continue.

'But I mean it, Lise, what if I screw up and let something slip? Or worse? What if the Stag is gorgeous and lovely and I fall madly in love with him, only I'm not me, I'm Doe Abby and I can't write my exposé, because I've gone and done the one thing I wasn't supposed to do—fall in love with the Stag!'

'All right, now you're just catastrophising.' She's right. I'm whipping myself into quite a state, a sure-fire way to trigger a panic attack. I join her on the sofa and reach for my water bottle, downing a generous slug.

'And, Abs, you're forgetting something.' I look at her. 'Jack.'

Oh, right, Jack. Who needs the Stag when there's lovely,

lovely Jack, with the floppy hair, gorgeous green eyes, and that 'misbehaving' T-shirt? Oh dear, I am in massive trouble. 'And what about the makeover this Roberta woman is insisting on?' she asks.

'Hmm?' I heard her, I just don't want to tear my thoughts away from Jack.

'What does that entail exactly? Did Jack say?'

'I did ask, but he was a little vague on the details. He just said something about a spa day and hair and makeup. Honestly, Lise, every time I think about that part, I get an even squidgier tum. What if at the end of it I'm not *me* anymore.'

'It's probably just a little zhuzhing, that's all. I mean, you're already gorgeous,' she says, indicating the blob of insecurity that is me.

'I can't tell if you're taking the piss or not.' My mind? Incredible—a word I can say in four languages, by the way. My looks? Er, not so much.

'Abs, no! You're a natural beauty—I've told you that so many times! You've got perfect skin, those big brown eyes, curves for days—*and* your gorgeous, glossy hair. You know I'd kill for your natural highlights—instead, I pay squillions for mine.'

I eye her suspiciously, but don't detect a shred of insincerity. 'Will you come with me?' I ask.

'What, to the makeover?'

I nod. 'Just to make sure they don't go overboard.'

'Of course! I'd be happy to.' I'm awash with relief. 'I'll be your bodyguard—get it? Your *body*guard.' She waggles her eyebrows at me. It's a good thing I'm the writer in our relationship. Her jokes are dreadful.

'Oh! I've just remembered, Jack also said I'll meet with a personal shopper—and that I've got an allowance for clothes.'

'Well, *that's* not terrible. Just focus on that,' she says, taking another sip of fizz.

She's right. I'm in this come what may and I should think of it in terms of what I'll gain, not what could go wrong. There's Sydney, there's Jack, and it will be nice to have some proper clothes. So, several major concerns dispelled and I'm now hovering around eighty per cent sure that this is something to celebrate.

But what about the other twenty per cent? When will that get on board?

It's been two months since that fateful meeting in Prue's office and it's makeover day. Since receiving this (bizarre) assignment, I've oscillated so many times between calm acceptance and abject terror, that I've discovered a new form of motion sickness—*e*motion sickness.

And as Lisa and I wait for the town car to collect us, I've gone from a squidgy tum to a squidgy bum. I have literally run to the loo three times in the past half-an-hour.

'Good god, Abs, sit down, will you? You're making me dizzy.'

'Sorry,' I say, reaching for my water bottle.

'Are you all right? You look …' her eyes narrow '… not good—greenish.'

'I'm just nervous, that's all.'

'I promise I'm not going to let them do anything drastic.'

'No, not about that. I mean, yes, a little, but this makes it real. Lise, I'm flying to Australia next week. I'm really doing this.'

'It's not too late to back out,' she says, perhaps to be helpful. It's not.

'That's just the thing, though. There is no "out". I've signed the contract. And look.' I go to my desk and retrieve the dossier Roberta had couriered over a couple of days ago. I hand over a folder marked 'Confidential' across it in large red letters and watch as Lisa flicks through page and after page of Doe Abby's backstory, her brow creased.

'This is quite … uh …'

'"Comprehensive" is the word you're looking for,' I say.

She looks up at me and breaks into a grin—a completely different reaction to what I was expecting. 'Abs, this is brilliant.'

'What? How so?' I join her on my sofa and poke an unmanicured nail at a random detail. 'Look at this. Apparently, I grew up in a manor—a *manor*! They've essentially given me your background.'

'That's what I mean, Abs, if anything comes up that you're not quite sure of, you can message me—I'll be your de Bergerac.'

'Well, *obvs* I've already thought of that,' I say, my tone a little sarky (but isn't that what besties are for—loving us even when we're behaving badly?) 'But you're forgetting one thing.'

'What's that?'

'I'll be in a technology-free zone—*total blackout*. We're not allowed phone calls, text messages, media, *social* media, anything. For two months!' I screech.

'Oh, Cadmus, I will absolutely screw this up,' I think as I ride the pendulum back towards abject terror.

'Oh, but that's where *you're* wrong, my friend,' says Lisa. 'You are Abigail Effing Jones and you are not going on this stupid-pathetic-awful show because you want to win or "find love"' —her voice drips with cynicism— 'or any of that nonsense. You are there undercover. And, of *course*, you're going to have access to a phone or a laptop or something—how else do they expect you to write your recaps?'

For someone with a brilliant mind, I can be very dim. It's the one question I've never asked—how will I communicate with the outside world—or, at least with Prue?

'Give it,' I say, practically tearing the folder from Lisa's hands. I start flicking through all the pages—Doe Abby's bio and backstory, bios and backstories on all the other Does, each with photographs—this is pure platinum right here in my hands—and there it is, at the back, a single sheet of paper entitled, 'Provisions'. I lift it from the folder, the rest of the contents lying on my lap and threatening to spill onto the floor in an avalanche of private information.

I scan the one-pager and my eyes settle on words like 'private office', 'internet access', 'mobile telephone', and 'viewing privileges'.

As I said, I've been dim. I had it in my head that I'd

write my recaps on scraps of ill-gotten paper or some loo roll, then leave them in a pot plant for someone to retrieve, then send to Prue. I'm not sure who I was imagining that 'someone' would be—perhaps a spy-like person, someone like Lisa.

'See?' she asks, reading over my shoulder.

'You were right,' I admit, never one to stubbornly hold a position I know is wrong. But this just consolidates what I am already most fearful of. 'I'm going to be rubbish at all this sneaking about,' I add, glumly.

'You are not. You're the smartest person I know. You're so, so clever, and where do you think Anastasia comes from, anyway? That brilliant, sassy bitch is *you*, Abs. You've got this in the bag, no question.'

'But it says in there that I can ride a horse—a *horse*! You know I'm terrified of horses,' I say, my voice wavering. It's true. Lisa took me horse riding on her family estate once. Five minutes in, I was tossed into the air by a prize mare, resulting in a trip to A&E to see if I'd broken my ankle or merely sprained it.

'So what? It's *The Stag*. Even if there is any horse riding, it will probably be at a hobby farm or something. You know, with those horses that are trained to follow each other around a set trail. And besides, Jack knows this is all make-believe. He won't make you ride a horse if you tell him you're afraid, all right?' She runs a soothing hand up and down my back.

'Look, the car will be here soon,' she continues. 'This is supposed to be the fun part, Abs—a spa day, then meeting your personal shopper. Uh, *hellooo*, this is the *Pretty Woman* part. Do you really want to spend the day all tied up in knots?'

I look at my best friend, one of only two people in the world who I would do anything for, and I am overwhelmed by the kind (but tough) love I see in her eyes.

'Oh, fuck it,' I say, and she bursts out laughing; it's not often that I break out the profanity. 'Let's go and have a fabulous day and forget about all this nonsense.'

Her smile tells me that she knows this is bravado but she'll indulge me and go along with it—which is exactly why she's my best friend.

'You have ze skin of infant. *Perfection*.' Nadia is a striking, dark-haired, pale-eyed Russian woman with cheekbones you could use to cut diamonds. She's also my beauty therapist and after that comment, we're off to a good start.

She has my chin clasped between her strong fingers and is examining me—well, my face—intensely. Occasionally, she makes a guttural sound in the back of her throat, which I am taking as approval.

'Ve vill do deep cleanse, zen intense moisture, zen brows—make zose brown eyes pop. Zen mani-pedi, of course. Everyzing else—is makeup. I vill teach,' she adds with a wink. Oh, I am definitely Team Nadia. I wonder if I can talk Jack into flying her down to Sydney for the next couple of months.

'Oh, and bikini,' she adds, seemingly as an afterthought.

'Bikini?'

'*Da*, I do wax—make very tidy.'

Oh. I deflate a little. I've never had a bikini wax before. I've always been … er … *natural*.

'Now, lie back,' she commands.

I do, soon losing myself in the soothing motions of lathering and slathering as she gets to work on my face. I hear the occasional flicking of a magazine page—my only tether to the real world and a reminder that Lisa is right there with me—but I slip into an almost meditative state. Even the brow shaping doesn't impede my Zen. There's something almost comforting about the tugging sensation as Nadia runs the dual threads across my brow arches.

'Okay. Up now.' I blink my eyes open—that cannot have been an hour—and slowly sit up.

'Oh, Abs, your brows look amazing!' Lisa drops *In Style* into her lap and smiles at me encouragingly.

'Here.' No-nonsense Nadia hands me a mirror and I regard my reflection. My skin looks better than I've ever seen it and I have a natural flush in my cheeks that makes me look almost pretty. But my eyebrows! Lisa is right; they look great, framing my eyes perfectly.

'Is pop, yes?' asks Nadia, pursing her lips at me and nodding in admiration of her own work.

'Is pop,' I reply, mirroring her syntax.

She nods at me in approval. 'Mani-pedi now. Come.'

'Er, I was thinking, what if we did the bikini wax now?' She arches an eyebrow at me. 'It's just that I'm a little nervous about it and I've heard that it hurts … er … a bit. So, if we do that first, then the mani-pedi is like a reward, yes?'

A little scowl appears, disappearing almost instantly as she nods at me again. 'Strip,' she commands. 'Bottom half only.' My eyes fly to Lisa's in a panic. Surely, I can leave my knickers on and we can work around them? 'Everyzing,' adds Nadia confirming my fears.

'I'll excuse myself for this part, Abs,' says my best friend, *abandoning* me. But I suppose watching a stranger pour hot wax on my vulva and tear out my pubic hair is beyond the boundary of our friendship.

Fifteen minutes later, Nadia has 'made tidy' and I'm left wondering if there is a lollypop big enough to make up for that much pain. I cast my eyes about—no jar of lollipops, but I do have the mani-pedi to look forward to before hair with Günter. Oh, god, I hope he doesn't want to do anything drastic, like giving me a pixie cut. But that's why I brought Lisa, so she could step in if they try to turn me into 'not me'.

But this isn't about me, I remind myself. This is about creating Doe Abby and maybe *she* has a pixie cut. Gah!

'Oh, Abs,' says Lisa for the umpteenth time today, though I really don't mind. As my makeover progresses, each reveal has been more and more surprising—in a good way—and now I'm actually enjoying myself.

My time with Günter ended up being brilliant. He was a straight talker with warm, friendly eyes, and he took one look at my anxious grimace then assured me I had nothing to worry about. 'Your hair is *gorgeous*,' he said, 'great colour, good condition. I'm thinking just a light trim and adding some layers to frame your face. How does that sound?' I sighed with relief and grinned at him in the mirror, nodding vigorously.

When he spun me around an hour later, I eyed myself curiously in the large mirror, acknowledging that with Nadia's makeup and his expert styling, I looked pretty. Like me, but pretty.

This latest reveal is the work of Caitriona, my personal shopper. I'm wearing dark-wash jeans, a silky cream-coloured shirt with the sleeves rolled up, and heeled espadrilles. 'Perfect for a casual date,' says Caitriona. 'And you can dress up the shirt with those trousers you tried on earlier.'

I gaze at myself in the three-way mirror. Is it completely narcissistic that I've got a girl crush on Doe Abby? It's just that I've never looked this good in my life. And seeing how perfectly these jeans accentuate my curves, I have an epiphany. A good fit makes all the difference. Maybe after I get back from Sydney, I'll splurge on decent clothes once in a while——clothes that actually fit, rather than ten-pound 'mom jeans' from Sainsbury's.

'Right,' says Caitriona, as she scrolls the list on her iPad. 'I think that's everything.' I should hope so——we've been at this for hours and the 'yes' pile is enormous; I'm *so* glad *The Stag* is footing the bill. I have casual outfits, smart-casual outfits, dresses for day, dresses for evening, several pairs of shoes, a *swimsuit*. And if I thought finding the perfect *jeans* was a minor miracle (and it is), Caitriona found the holy grail of swimsuits——it looks good *and* it supports my boobs!

'Oh, wait,' she says, 'just bras and knickers left.'

My shoulders slump—I *hate* shopping for bras and knickers. Until now—bikini wax not included—my entire day has been like a movie makeover montage. Why did we save the worst part for last? Again—bikini wax not included.

'Come on, Abs. It'll be nice to have some pretty knickers, don't you think?'

'But why does it matter? I mean, who's even going to see them? It's not like …' I realise my gaff and close my mouth. Caitriona knows I'm a contestant on *The Stag*. I should at least *pretend* I have a chance of winning the Stag's heart.

'That's no way to think,' says Lisa, jumping in to cover for me. 'You have just as much of a chance as anyone else who's going on the show. And besides, having nice undergarments gives you confidence, right Caitriona? It's not just about who might see them, but how they make you *feel*.'

'Absolutely. And I promise, I'll make this as painless as possible. We'll get you fitted and kitted out in no time.'

I relent. But I am definitely asking for a lollipop after this.

Chapter Five

'D o you have everything?' asks my mum.

I can't believe she's taken time off work to say goodbye—especially as Heathrow is gigantic and could swallow up someone like Mum, someone who's only been here a couple of times in her life and never once to fly anywhere. It's a lovely gesture, but as she is an acute worrier—a trait she has passed down to me—I can tell that's why she came. She's wearing worry like a cloak.

'Yes, Mum,' I reply, infusing my tone with as much brevity as I can. I tap a palm against my new leather bag, part of my Doe trousseau. 'Passport, Kindle, travel calm, ear plugs, eye mask …' She's blinking at me, tears in her eyes. 'It's only a couple of months, Mum.'

She nods. Oh, god, I can practically see the lump in her throat and one starts growing in mine. 'You'll be absolutely fine. You'll be too busy keeping Aunty Lo out of trouble to even miss me.' Another lie—they're already piling up. Well,

I suppose there's some truth to this one. Aunty Lo—Lois—is my mum's closest friend. I've known her my whole life and in the absence of a 'proper' aunty, she's been as much a sister to my mum and an aunty to me as a blood relation. She's also the naughty one in the family and, hopefully, her escapades will be a good distraction for Mum in my absence.

'And, you have Lisa's number if you need anything—*anything*, Mum. You know she'll be right round to help, all right?'

'All right, love.'

'Oh, and please remember, Mum, this is highly confidential, me filming the show. You can't tell anyone, even Aunty Lo—not until it's about to air, all right?'

'I remember and I promise. But Abby …'

'What? Is there something else that's worrying you?'

'I … I'll miss you, love, that's all.'

I envelop her in a hug. 'I'll miss you too, Mum, but I'll call you—every week, I promise.' All the other Does will be in 'radio silence' with their loved ones, but (thankfully) this is one of the provisions of my contract.

Mum clings to me, her voice muffled by my shoulder. 'I just don't know why you're going all that way to find love,' she says.

Oh, right, the enormous lie I've told her.

I pull back and study the concern creasing her brow. I hate that I've lied to my mother—*again*. Not only does she not know I'm Anastasia Blabbergasted, she believes I make my living as a freelance copywriter for small businesses. The few times I've had pieces published under my own name, Mum has bragged about me to anyone who cared to listen—and, I'm sure, many who didn't.

I suppose that by lying all this time about my job, I'm more prepared than I thought to dive into this world of duplicity. But now I've lied again, telling her I'm going on *The Stag* because I adore the show and genuinely believe I might find love.

'It will be fine, Mum, I promise.'

'You are the most wonderful, most lovable person in the whole world, Abigail. You don't need to go across the world to fall in love. It *will* happen, my darling girl. You so deserve it.'

The lump is back, tightening my throat and making it near impossible to reply. But what can I say to that? She's tapped into something I've buried so deep, it rarely shows its ugly head. My father left us when I was a baby, never to be seen again, and in my darkest moments—those I won't even share with Lisa—I will probe into the part of me that genuinely believes that I am not worthy of love.

And yet, here is this incredible woman—a woman who took in extra ironing in the evenings so she could buy me a dress for prom, something not covered by my otherwise generous scholarship—and she loves me so unconditionally and so thoroughly, that perhaps it seems ungrateful of me to seek out love elsewhere.

Even if romantic love is something entirely different.

'Thank you, Mum,' I finally manage. 'I know I am loved—probably more so than any other daughter in the world ...' This makes her smile, although it's tinged with sadness. 'I just …' I just what? Damn this stupid, *stupid* lie! 'Look, they're calling my flight.' They aren't—that's another one. 'I'd best go through.'

'All right, love.' She gives me a quick squeeze and when she steps back, her lips are pressed together—perhaps resignation that her beautiful, clever, and lovable daughter (her words, not mine) is going on a reality television show to find the love of her life.

I give her a weak smile and say, 'I love you. You're the best mum ever. I'll talk to you soon.' She nods, then I turn and stride towards departures.

I hope flying business class takes the sting out of that goodbye.

Honestly, if there were no emotions attached to this assignment, it would be a dream come true. Paid travel to Australia—check. A makeover—check. An entirely new wardrobe—check. A rather gorgeous Australian man waiting at the other end of this flight—check.

But there *are* emotions. Guilt. Terror. Worry. Check, check, check.

Gah! I need to focus on the positives. I have a job, I have a home, I have a wonderful mother, and a best friend who may very well be on Her Majesty's Secret Service. I get to *write* for a living. It may not always be what I want to write, but it will be eventually (I have to believe that). And I'm going to Sydney, somewhere I've dreamt of going for years.

That's better—a #gratitudeattitude!

I suppose the only fly in my gratitude ointment is Jack. Well, not Jack himself, but I'm certain that fraternising with the show's producer would be (severely) frowned upon. And that's assuming Jack is remotely interested in me. I haven't seen him in person since the day we met, but emails and video chats have been enough to nurture my (let's face it, probably one-sided) crush. 'Crush'—such a juvenile word. But I suppose when it comes to love, I am a juvenile—or at least a novice.

I need to distract myself; navel gazing as a romantically stunted thirty-something has already lost its lustre.

Right, this is my first (and possibly only) time in a business-class lounge—perhaps there's a story here? I scan the room from my cosy spot in the corner, taking in all the amenities that (we) mere mortals could only imagine—a neat display of magazines and newspapers in multiple languages that rivals Waterstones, a fully stocked bar, signage for the beauty salon (although, this just brings back horrid memories of hot wax), lounge chairs and low tables and desks with office chairs, and a long buffet with cheeseboards, platters of charcuterie and antipasto, enormous bowls of fresh salads, and fruit platters.

Why would you ever want leave? It's nice enough right here.

Unfortunately, this vast array of luxury and excess doesn't spark even an inkling for a piece. I doubt that 'Nubile Newbie Noshes on Nummy Nibbles' will induce a bidding war between *The Guardian* and *The Atlantic*.

I head to the buffet and eye the stack of teeny plates with

disdain. Are they designed to encourage repeat trips or deprivation and starvation? I'm guessing the latter. I can only image the scandal of multiple trips. *I say, who let the hoi polloi in here? Did you see how many times she visited the buffet? Was it seven or eight?*

I take one of the teeny plates and (strategically) pile up a neat pyramid of cheese and olives, then make my way to the bar and slide onto a stool. The bartender nods discretely in my direction, telling me that she's seen me and will be with me momentarily. The fact that her eyes haven't bugged in horror tells me I must look like I belong and I send a silent thank you to Nadia, Günter, and Caitriona, my makeover dream team.

'Oh, hey!' I hear beside me.

My mind knows whose voice it is, but it also knows that he's not supposed to be here—he's supposed to be in Sydney, where he was the last time we spoke. I turn my head in his direction.

'Jack,' I say, my mouth ahead of my thoughts.

'You look great,' he says. And not as in, *'Wow, what an enormous difference your makeover has had—I hardly recognised you,'* but a simple compliment.

'Er, thank you,' I say, wishing I were more practised at being gracious. 'But I thought …' My voice trails off in confusion at seeing him here.

'Oh, yeah … Why am I here when I'm supposed to be there?' Jack grins, his perfect, *perfect* lips stretching wide, and I will neither confirm nor deny that my crush on him is galloping along, out of control, and very likely to trample

55

my inexperienced heart. 'Casting problem,' he says, answering his own question.

'Oh, right.'

'Yeah, normally we'd just go with the alternate, but she was no longer available—new job up in Scotland. Besides, we needed *two* new Does, not just the one.'

'Two?'

'Yep. Turns out that one of the originals was pregnant when she auditioned, only she didn't know it, and the other has shingles.'

'Oh, goodness. That poor woman.'

'Which one?' he asks. I hope he's joking.

'The woman with shingles,' I reply, and he winks. 'Oh, you *were* joking.'

'Yeah, 'course.' We share a laugh, which sets me at ease and then it's just me and Jack, the friendly ally who rescued me—from the giant jaws of death, yes, but also from Roberta's scrutiny and Prue's wrath. 'Besides, the pregnant woman is over the moon and all loved up with the baby's dad. We were hardly gonna hold her to the contract when we learnt all that.'

'Right. So, you've been back here scouring the country for Britain's finest, then?' I ask, Anastasia poking her head out.

'Yep. Found 'em too,' he says, clearly missing the slight snark in my tone. 'Oh, that reminds me.' He starts rummaging in his carry-on luggage. 'These are for you. Dossiers on the new Does.' He hands me a manilla folder with garish red letters screaming 'Confidential' across the middle—just like the one in my bag.

'Thank you. I suppose I'll brush up on the plane.'

'And then scrub your brain of everything you've already learnt about Angela and Paula.'

'Oh, no, *Paula*?' He nods. 'Shingles or pregnant?'

'Shingles.'

'That makes it all the worse, poor love. I really liked her, even just from her dossier. I thought we might become friends.'

'Yeah, it's pretty crap. She was cool.'

'I almost want to send her a get-well card or something, but how would that go? "Dear Paula, you don't know me, but I know you. In fact, I know practically every intimate detail of your life."' Jack's eyes dance with mirth and encouraged, I forge on.

'"We were due to be fellow Does on the upcoming season of *The Stag* and, with your volunteering at disadvantaged schools and your close relationship with your nan (she sounds lovely by the way), I was positive we were destined to become best friends. I now hear, from the powers that be, that you have befallen foul of the pox and are unable to make the filming of the show, which saddens me no end. Please don't ask me how I know all this about you because I *could* tell you, but then I'd have to kill you. Perhaps we will meet some day. 'Til then, sending my warmest regards for a speedy recovery. Love, Abby."'

'How about that?' I ask, lifting my chin smugly.

Jack chuckles softly. 'You're very funny.'

'Well, Anastasia is.'

'Sure, but she's just a side of you, right?' An echo of Lisa's voice rings through my mind. *'Where do you think*

Anastasia comes from, Abby?' It seems that Jack agrees with her.

'I suppose so. It's easy to forget that *I* am Anastasia, or that she's me, or however it works. You know, before all this preparation for *The Stag*, I hadn't realised how much I compartmentalise my life. Like when I write my recaps, I switch seamlessly into Anastasia. And these clothes, this look, that's Doe Abby—like putting on a costume if I were an actor in a film.'

'So, who did I meet that day at Feed Your Mind?'

'Oh, er … just me. Abby,' I say, punctuating my words with a slight shrug.

'Well, from what I can tell, I like all sides of you.' He holds my gaze and I shift slightly on my stool. It's a lovely thing to say, but I'm not used to compliments, especially from men with gorgeous green eyes and perfect lips.

But that's real Abby and now it's time for Doe Abby to come to the fore and stay there. 'Thank you, Jack,' says Doe Abby, confidently returning his gaze. Hmm, there's something rather intoxicating about playing a more assured, more attractive version of myself.

'So, what would you like?'

'You and me on a weekend away in Tuscany—no, make it a week,' I think.

Though I doubt that's what Jack's asking. 'Sorry, what?'

'To drink.' Jack nods his head towards the bartender who is looking at me expectantly.

'Oh,' I say, 'I'll have a gin and tonic, please. Lime, not lemon, if you have it.' Apparently, Doe Abby drinks G&Ts, even though I haven't had one in ages, and with *lime*. I'll have to add an addendum to her dossier. Abby Jones—lover of G&Ts, confident, sexy, frequents business club lounges and flirts with gorgeous Australian men—at your service.

So far, I quite like playing Doe Abby.

———————

'Hi again.' Jack is standing in the aisle next to my seat, smiling down at me. We'll be taking off soon, and I've just completed an inventory of the clutch-sized toiletries bag that was on my seat when I boarded. There are lots of lovely products in there and I was contemplating giving myself a mid-air facial when Jack showed up.

'Hello,' I reply, peering up at him. Any moment now, the flight attendants will start preparing the cabin for take-off and he really ought to be in his seat.

'So, there's actually an empty seat next to mine and I asked the flightie if you could move. She said you could after we take off, if you like.' It takes me half-a-second to figure out what a 'flightie' is but when I do, I move swiftly onto Jack's suggestion.

I'll admit that I was both disappointed and relieved when I learnt we wouldn't be sitting together. It's twenty-six hours from wheels up at Heathrow to touchdown in Sydney, including a four-hour layover in Dubai. That's either a lot of time to get to know someone, or too much time to spend with the man you have a crush on. What if I nod off and dribble in my sleep or *snore*?

Aside: I'm not sure that I do snore—this romantic novice has only had one long(ish)-term relationship. It was in my mid-twenties and he never mentioned it——me snoring, that is. He was called Angus, a burly Scottish bloke who did snore——*and* who farted in bed. He also had a penchant for barmaids with names like 'Cindy' and 'Cherie'. Not exactly a catch and Lisa tolerated him for approximately three months before convincing me to give him the flick.

All this flies through my mind as I weigh up my options——sit with the gorgeous Australian and potentially embarrass myself, or forgo this opportunity to get to know him, save myself from embarrassment, and give myself that facial?

Jack's smile is the decider.

'Er, yes, that would be lovely.' His smile gets wider and dozens of tiny wings take flight in my mid-section.

'Cool,' he replies, just as a flight attendant approaches.

'Sir, please take your seat.'

'Yeah, no worries.' To me he says, 'See ya in a bit.' He adds a wink and, in his wake, leaves anticipation tinged with a whisper of apprehension. Surely, he's just being nice. He's probably like this with all the Does; he's just a genuine, thoughtful man without guile or agenda. I mean, when I made that snarky comment about 'Britain's finest' earlier, it didn't seem to land in the slightest. Perhaps he's just not wired to be cynical or to run people down.

Like I am.

Well, like Anastasia is, in any case.

So, if Jack *is* just being nice, how do I reconcile the tummy flutters? It's been so long since anyone induced them, I'm not quite sure what to do. Not only would acting on these feelings be frowned upon by my editor and his boss, it would exceedingly complicate my time in Stag Manor—as if it's not going to be complicated enough.

As the engines rev and we speed off down the runaway and soar into the air, my stomach lurches and I can't tell for sure if it's the G-force or the start of something extraordinary.

Chapter Six

'*This is not a date, Abigail,*' I remind myself for the fourth time in two hours.

If it were, however, it would be the best date I've ever had—possibly the best date anyone has ever had—mostly because of the sparkling conversation which has flowed non-stop since I changed seats after take-off.

And that's not the only thing flowing. I'm also on my second glass of fizz—actual champagne, from *France*. When I'd asked for a top-up, Jack jokingly told the flight attendant to leave the bottle and she smiled, then returned with a full bottle sitting in an ice bucket. An ice bucket! On an aeroplane!

I will need to slow down, however, because everyone knows that alcohol goes to your head faster when you fly—or is that a made-up 'fact' we published on Feed Your Mind? Either way, I'm a little bit tipsy and in Jack's lovely, *lovely* company, the time is already flying (so to speak). Only twenty-four hours to go!

'So, it's just you and your brother? No other siblings?' I ask.

'Nah, just us. Mum says that after Harry was born—what with me only being a toddler and Dad away filming for months at a time—she was run off her feet. I mean, Dad helped out a bit when he was back in Sydney, but still …' He trails off, a crease between his brows. 'It's weird that, don't ya think, what they used to say about dads—that they were "helping" the mums? But really, if you have a child, you're not "helping out" your spouse, you're just being a parent, right?'

'Right,' I say, although I have no frame of reference for what a dad should or could or would do to be a good parent. That said, I put Jack's astute observation in the plus column of my 'Jack as a Potential Love Interest' balance sheet. I haven't even told Lisa I've been compiling it, but I suspect she knows.

'The stories my old man could tell …' Jack chuckles softly. 'Still does when he's had a few. He worked with Clint Eastwood once.'

'Really?'

'Yep. His first time as DOP—' He must catch the flicker of confusion on my face. 'Director of Photography,' he explains and I nod. 'Yeah, apparently, Clint had seen his work on this Australian film—you might have heard of it—*The Station*?' I shake my head. 'Anyway, he'd seen Dad's work and called him up and offered him the job. Dad thought it was one of his mates having a laugh at first, but no. It was legit.'

'That's brilliant,' I say, smiling.

'Too right. But if you ever meet my dad and he starts telling that story, get comfy. He can drag it out for at *least* an hour.'

I laugh and he joins in. The way he talks about his family … there's so much affection. His whole face lights up. And then I realise what he's just said. '*If you ever meet my dad* …' For all intents and purposes, we're colleagues—well, of sorts. There should be no reason that I would meet Jack's parents while we're filming in Sydney. Unless …

Maybe this *is* a date.

'*No, he's just being friendly, Abigail. It's a long flight,*' I reason.

'Anyway, I've been rabbiting on long enough. What about you—your family?' he asks.

Typically, this question gets my hackles up. A poor single mum juggling multiple jobs, an absent father, our postcode screaming 'council estate' … Most people either tilt their heads in that 'Oh, how I pity you' way, or there's an almost imperceptible shift in how they view me, like I'm suddenly lesser—lesser than them, certainly, but also lesser than the person they thought I was before my big revelation.

But I already know that Jack is not 'most people', so I opt for a good portion of the truth, omitting my father altogether and simply describing my mum as a 'single mum'. When I wrap up with, 'She came to the airport to see me off,' he replies, 'She sounds like an incredible woman.'

'She is. I'd do anything for my mum. I just …' I stare down at the thousands of bubbles rising to the top of my glass.

'It's the lying,' he says simply.

My head snaps in his direction. 'Yes. How did you know?'

He shrugs. 'I can tell you're a decent person and it must be rough having to lie to your mum.'

'She's worried that I think I'm unlovable.' The words are out of my mouth before I've even registered the thought. Why? *Why* would I tell Jack something like that, something so private, something that paints me in such a pitiful light? Stupid champagne. I frown at the glass and place it on the table between our seats, feeling the colour rising in my cheeks.

'Hey …' I absolutely do not want to look at Jack. I want to gather my belongings and go back to 10B and see out the rest of the flight in quiet humiliation from the back of the business-class cabin.

'Abby … Look, I can totally understand why she'd say something like that.' He can? I glance sideways at him, emboldened by the empathetic tone in his voice.

'How so?'

'This is the fourth one of these shows I've done—well, the first of the British version, but I've produced three seasons of *The Buck*—that's what we call it back home …' I already knew that—one of the many nuggets I discovered when researching Jack online. It was for my job, by the way—I'm not a creepy cyber-stalker. I promise.

'Anyway, this is the fourth time I've assembled a cast of Does, and you know what?' he asks rhetorically, 'from what I've seen, most Does legitimately want to find love. If you take that into account, along with what you've told me about how close you two are, it's not hard to see how she made the leap.'

I nod, realising he's right. My mum has only connected the dots I've given her. It still stings that I have caused her any angst, but I do not think I am unlovable. Not really, despite what my inner voice says from time to time. And I'll find a way to reassure my mum, even if I never tell her the truth about my appearance on *The Stag*.

I have a thought. 'So, what about the rest of the Does?'

'What's that?'

'If most of the Does want to find love, what about the others?' I ask.

'Oh, right. Yeah, they either come on the show as a lark or they just want to be on TV. For some, it's about getting an agent, or a role on *Neighbours*, or something.'

'And you know that upfront?'

'Well, not … *officially*.' His eyes twinkle with mirth. 'I'm sure they think they're doing a great job at being "sincere",' he says, adding the air quotes with the waggle of his forefinger, 'but it's pretty obvious.' He shrugs. 'Often, we end up casting a few of them to up the drama, you know?'

Ooh, insider information. Anastasia's ears prick.

'Not that I love that part of the gig, you know, fabricating drama for ratings …' His voice trails off and, noting his frown, I add another item to the plus column of that balance sheet. He has a conscience and this show is just a means to an end, a way to earn enough money to start a production company with Harry.

He shakes his head, as though clearing his thoughts, and flashes me a smile. I promise myself we'll explore his moral dilemma the next time he brings it up, but as he's just revealed a juicy nugget of information, my mind switches gear. Anastasia has work to do.

'So …' I retrieve the dossiers from my bag and set them on my lap. 'Tell me who's who.'

'You sure you don't want to figure it out for yourself? I've read your recaps. No doubt you'll have all the Does accurately pegged by the end of the first Soirée,' he says, referring to the show's staged cocktail parties.

'Absolutely not. Forewarned is forearmed. So, let's start with Tara.'

'If you say so. I'm topping you up, though,' he says, reaching for the chilled bottle.

'Sounds reasonable—you get me tipsy while I pump you for information.' Oh, god. I did not just say I was going to 'pump' the gorgeous Australian. His widened eyes tell me that I absolutely did say that. Bollocks.

He starts to say something, then shakes his head instead. 'You're lost for words, aren't you?' I ask unnecessarily. His head changes direction and his lips press together. 'Well, we can blame Doe Abby for that. She *is* a saucy one.'

'Oh, I bet she is,' he teases, a smile playing on his lips. Now *I'm* rendered speechless—*me*, the writer! Fleeting moments of vulnerability notwithstanding, this really is the most fun I've had with a man in ages. Perhaps ever.

'So, that just leaves me,' I say, laying my pen in my lap. I've taken copious notes on the other Does, annotating their dossiers with little gems that Jack has provided over the past couple of hours. And, having heard him describe each Doe—even those who *are* looking for fame and fortune rather than true love—I have to admire how respectful he's been. He and Roberta have stuck to the established formula for assembling the cast, but Jack has only revealed truths and observations—no conjecture and no gossip. I suppose all that will be left to Anastasia. It's only just occurring to me now, however, that it might be difficult to write about myself—well, Doe Abby—especially as I'm unsure where she'll fit in. 'What role will I play?' I ask.

'You should just be yourself,' he replies easily, like he's already thought it through. I blink at him, confused. Surely, I will be 'assigned' a particular role? 'I mean that', Jack continues. 'You just be you. Abby-you, not Anastasia-you. No doubt Tara and Kylie will provide enough "excitement" in the Manor without you having to switch on Anastasia,' he adds diplomatically. 'Also, that will help you keep it clear in your head, right?'

'How so?'

'Well, you will just be yourself—clever, funny, kind—and you only have to don Anastasia when you're writing your recaps.' My mind leaps about like a monkey swinging between the trees. *'Clever, funny, kind,'* he'd said—more pluses for the balance sheet.

But I latch onto something else—Jack thinks 'Anastasia mode' is only for writing recaps. Whereas, I suspect she will always be lurking just under the surface, ears pricking like they did earlier and ready to pounce on insecurities and gaffs, missteps, poor judgement, and shocking revelations. I haven't made a living from writing recaps for the past seven years by being 'kind'—just the opposite. Perhaps what will be harder than writing about myself is lampooning women who I will come to know, perhaps even befriend.

Bollocks.

This is too much to contemplate right now, so I set aside my qualms and redirect the conversation to the one topic we have yet to cover—well, the one show-related topic—the Stag himself. So far, all I know about him is his name—Daniel.

'So, why is there no dossier on Daniel?' I ask, lightly tapping the pile of paper on my lap.

He grins. 'I was wondering when you were going to ask about him.'

'Is that so?'

'It is.' He smirks at me, the first sign of smugness I've detected since I met him.

'Well?' I prod.

He captures his bottom lip between his teeth and narrows his eyes at me, clearly deciding something. 'Okay, look, I'm not sure how you're gonna feel about this, but … We thought there might be a chance that you'd actually fall for the Stag, so we wanted you to meet him cold—like the rest of the Does.'

'What?' I'd heard him—of course I had, he's sitting two feet away—but my mind is having trouble parsing his words and generating any meaning that makes sense.

'Yeah. It was Prue's idea and Roberta loved it, so …' The puzzle pieces slot into place and I am—at once—humiliated and infuriated.

'So, you've all been conspiring behind my back?'

'No, uh …'

'Right, I see things quite plainly now. Poor, miserable, lonely Abby—let's give her at least a fighting chance at finding true love. This may be the only one she ever gets,' I say, my voice viscous with derision.

'Abby, no. It wasn't like that.' I gather the dossiers from my lap and shove them into my bag.

'I should go back to my assigned seat now.'

'Wait,' he says. I'm halfway out of the seat when his hand clasps my wrist. 'Please, will you just wait?' I plop back down and scowl at him.

'Well?'

'I handled that badly.'

'You did—without question. On top of behaving like a massive … arrogant … condescending … *meanie*.' For someone who writes insults for a living, I am botching this terribly. Jack thinks so too—it's in the way his mouth quirks at the edges.

'How about this?' he says, his tone belying our status as adversaries. 'You let me explain my intentions behind this decision, and I'll let you have another crack at telling me off.'

His mouth quirks again, a sideways tug on those perfectly formed lips, and I feel my own mouth inverting into a smile. I pull it back into line, unwilling to concede so easily. 'Fine, explain,' I say, lifting my chin, my gaze steady. 'But tell me the truth because I'll know if you don't.'

He blows out a breath, seeming to appreciate the opportunity to redeem himself. 'Right, so this came up the week after we all met at Prue's office—a conference call with me, Roberta, and Prue, right? Roberta tasked me with creating the Doe dossiers for you and when I mentioned we'd need one on Daniel too, Prue said that she'd been thinking … that you—Abby—might fall for Daniel … for real … so we should hold off on his dossier.'

I frown. That doesn't sound like something Prue would say—she doesn't care one iota about me and my happiness.

'She said something to the effect of, "Won't that make the *best* recap if Abby actually falls in love with the Stag?" Or something like that. Anyway, Roberta thought it was a great idea—"compelling television," she said—and I … well, I was thinking about you, about how you're not keen on the whole thing, but agreed to do it anyway, and I figured that if you *did* like Daniel, maybe even fall for him, that at least you'd get something out of this—besides the pay check, I mean. So, yeah …' He shrugs.

'She calls me Abigail, not Abby,' I say quietly. It seems easier to call out this minor detail than to deal with the larger implications of Jack's explanation.

'What's that?' he asks, his confusion evident.

'Prue. She always calls me Abigail.'

'Right.' He rubs the back of his neck. 'But everything else is true, I promise.'

I believe him. How could I not? There was nothing cagey or duplicitous in his explanation—he'd even held eye contact the entire time. He hasn't lied to me, but I'm smacked with a horrible realisation. If Jack believes I might fall for this Daniel fellow—*and* helped execute this little plan—then he has no romantic designs on me whatsoever.

All this frisson I've felt between us has been imaginary, a conjuring from my own hopeful (hopeless) mind.

This is absolutely not a date—in any guise. This is a business meeting. 'All right,' I say quietly. 'I accept your explanation.'

'I'm really sorry, Abby. I didn't mean to upset you.'

'And your apology,' I add.

'So, we're good?'

'We are,' I say, thinking the exact opposite. I lean my head back against the seat and close my eyes. A *date*? What an idiot I am.

Chapter Seven

I can confidently say that I have never seen a sky this exact colour of blue before—cerulean—and with the puffs of snow-white clouds that dot the sky, as if carefully placed to create the perfect heavenly vista, my first foray into the city of Sydney is surreal. In a good way.

I CANNOT BELIEVE I AM HERE—a giant, big, fat enormous tick next to 'Sydney' on my bucket list. I've been pinching myself so much I now have a bruise on my forearm. I should probably stop doing that.

Jack and I saw out the rest of our journey steering clear of anything contentious and sticking to innocuous topics, such as our favourites—books, food, films. We also watched a film together, trying to synch our screens by pressing play at the same time, though we were always a half-a-second off.

Just after leaving Dubai, I even braved sleeping—turned away from him, of course, so he couldn't see if I did dribble in my sleep. And that bag teeming with toiletries had certainly come in handy to make myself presentable in the morning—though, when you're crossing multiple time zones, 'morning' is an arbitrary concept decided by the airline. It's simply when they choose to serve breakfast instead of dinner.

We arrived in Sydney late last night and after clearing customs and immigration, Jack helped me into a taxi, telling the driver where to take me, then caught one home. My hotel was a shiny new high-rise right in the heart of the city—and the view! *Nothing* could have prepared me for looking out my window to see the illuminated sails of the Sydney Opera House—they practically *glowed*—or the golden arcs of lights adorning that famous bridge.

I almost didn't want to climb into bed. I could have looked at that view for hours.

Fatigue from the travel—albeit, far less than I would have experienced had I flown economy—eventually won and at 1am, I had a quick shower and slipped into those crisp white sheets, succumbing to blissful sleep.

I am now in the back of a town car heading to Stag Manor. It's probably not the done thing to have the window down, but I do so I can properly take in my surroundings. And uncaring that I must look like a neophyte crossed with a Labrador, I am practically halfway out the window, tongue out, wide-eyed, and exclaiming at everything from the cafés with people squeezed around tiny tables on the footpath to stately, colonial-style homes, and eucalyptus-lined roads.

The roads and traffic even remind me a little of London—not a straight, nor a wide road in sight and like in London, the drivers seem to have a sixth sense about how to manoeuvre and merge lanes without causing collisions.

'First time?' asks the driver.

'In Sydney? Yes. It must be obvious,' I say, sitting back against my seat.

He smiles at me in the rear-view mirror. 'It's nice to be reminded that I live in the most beautiful city in the world.'

'I've wanted to come for ages. I don't think it's quite sunk in yet—that I'm really here,' I say, eyeing the bruise on my forearm.

'Holiday?'

'Er, something like that, yes.'

'Well, you're staying in a nice suburb—Point Piper's one of the nicest in all of Sydney.'

'Oh, right. Well, someone else made the arrangements, but that's good to hear.'

Stag Manor is traditionally an actual manor, a stiff and stuffy antique of a dwelling that's dusted off and spruced up for filming. I can only imagine what's waiting for me in one of the 'nicest suburbs in Sydney', especially as the roads are getting narrower and windier and the driveways, garden walls, and gates are getting grander.

'And here we are.' The driver pulls into the next driveway on the left, passing through an open gate, rounding a large, angular fountain, and stopping the car outside an enormous glass house. *'People in glass houses …'* The words pop into my mind unbidden and I marvel at the irony. I am about to live in a glass house and while there, I shall throw *many* a judgemental stone under the guise of 'popular journalism'.

I get out of the car while the driver retrieves my cases from the boot and look around. There are two large vans also parked in the driveway and half-a-dozen people, all dressed in black, buzz about with cables and equipment boxes—the production crew.

'Abby!' A familiar voice rings out and attached to it is a gorgeous man who induces tummy flutters. Jack, wearing a T-shirt that says, 'FREE HUGS', jogs down the front steps of the house and takes the handle of one of my cases.

'Oh, I can manage,' I say, even though dragging two cases up those steps might be a little tricky. I'm also wondering how many of those hugs I can request without seeming unprofessional.

'Nah. Come on. I'll show you around. Now, as promised, you're the first Doe here—it's a couple of hours 'til the others arrive,' he says. This had been arranged so he can show me the Control Room and where I'll write my recaps.

I call out a thank you to the driver and follow Jack, dragging my smaller wheeled case across the sharp gravel of the driveway—not an easy task and I'm glad Jack has come to rescue me. Oh, no, not 'rescue' per se ... er, 'help'—a much better word.

As I cross the threshold, it's like stepping into another world—one of sharp angles and hard shiny surfaces, of glass and so much sunlight, I need to squint. Shafts of it pour into the house through skylights and windows. From the entry, I can see through to the lounge room, and the entire back wall of the house is made of glass—giant floor-to-ceiling windows that are concertinaed open. There's a patio just outside the lounge room—though the line between inside and outside is blurred, as it's been set up for indoor–outdoor living—then a lush green lawn slopes away to a strip of sandy beach and the water, where pinpoints of light bounce off thousands of tiny peaks.

'Wowser,' I say inelegantly. 'I practically need sunglasses.'

'Yeah, it's bright in here—can be a nightmare for filming—but it's nice, eh?' 'Nice' is such an inadequate word, especially to describe this beautiful suburb and this spectacular house. Actually, even 'beautiful' and 'spectacular' won't do. I'll need to start brushing up on my superlatives so Anastasia can do Stag Manor justice.

'The bedrooms are upstairs,' Jack says. 'Can you manage that one?' he asks, pointing to my smaller case. 'Or I can get one of the crew to bring it up?'

'Jack!' a man calls out across the patio. 'Can you come down to the beach for a sec? I need your thoughts on the shot setups for the Pin Rituals,' he says as he enters the house and crosses to us.

'Yeah, sure. But first, this is Abby. Abby, this is my brother, Harry.'

'Oh!' we both say at the same time—a dual revelation that Jack has told each of us about the other.

Harry laughs. 'Okay, what has he told ya?'

'Only good things, I promise.' Harry eyes his brother suspiciously, then breaks into a broad grin. When he smiles, the resemblance between them is remarkable, though Harry is a little stockier than Jack and his hair is darker. He's also not quite as handsome—in my opinion, anyway.

'Well, I've heard all about you too.' He has? I'm desperate to know what 'all about' comprises. '*Abby is brilliant, Harry, and so, so funny. She's also gorgeous, a true natural*

77

beauty. When this show wraps up, I am going to sweep her off her feet and take her on holiday to the Maldives.' I'm not sure why every time I dream about going on holiday with Jack, it's to an entirely new location, but perhaps I should be writing these down——a bucket list of romantic getaways.

'And listen,' says Harry, lowering his voice. 'It's just me and Jack that *know*, okay?' It's immediately clear what he's saying and I nod. Then realisation hits. This is real. I am in Stag Manor and in a couple of hours, the other Does will arrive and then I'm *on*. I'm Doe Abby at all times for the next eight weeks——except those times when I will be sequestered away working.

I gulp, but before I can dwell on my predicament, Harry claps his hands together. 'Righteo. You right with your bags?' he asks me.

'Er, yes, thank you. Jack is helping me take them upstairs.'

'What? This scrawny one? He can't carry shit.'

'Hey! Thanks a lot.'

'Come on, race ya!' Harry picks up the larger of my two cases by the handle and runs up the stairs, depositing it on the landing. 'Told ya. Too slow, old man,' he calls over the railing.

'See what I have to put up with?' Jack says.

'Ah, ya love it,' Harry mocks as he runs back down the stairs. 'See you down at the beach——*soon*,' he adds before exiting through the lounge room. I realise I've watched the whole exchange with a grin on my face.

'So, now you've met my brother.'

'He's quite fun,' I say, smiling at him.

'Yeah, yeah, he's the charming one. I know.' Jack shakes his head and carries my smaller case upstairs. 'Come on, I'll show you to your room.' I do like Harry, but he is not the brother who has charmed me. Though I say nothing, of course, and follow Jack.

The room I'll share with Becca, one of the Australian Does, is halfway down a long hallway that has bedrooms on either side. The room is far more spacious than I'd imagined and even has its own en suite. We leave my cases for me to unpack later and go back downstairs, where Jack leads me outside to the annex, a detached section of the house where the Control Room is.

'So, this is where the magic happens,' he says, pushing the door open. He doesn't seem to realise what that insinuates and as I cast my eyes around the large, but cramped room—a bank of monitors and a large screen on one wall and an array of film equipment covering every flat surface—my mind conjures a particularly *adult* magic moment starring Jack and Abby.

'This is where we hold production meetings. It's also where you'll watch rough cuts of the episodes after Harry and I've edited them together—for your recaps,' he says. Right, yes, recaps. The reason I'm here.

After I draft them, each recap with go to Prue and Vile Demon Woman (a.k.a. Roberta) for critique, and I'll make revisions as requested. It's the first time I've worked this way—essentially having a client as well as an editor—and it makes me a little nervous. What if my recaps aren't up to scratch and Roberta sends me packing? Prue will be furious and my time with Jack will come to a screeching halt. He may not be interested in me romantically, but I can still be his friend, right? *Right?*

Next on the tour is the small room Jack's set aside at the back of the annex for my writing——my little 'hidey hole'——but he's called away by an impatient Harry before he can show it to me properly. At least I know where to find it, along with a loaned laptop and a mobile phone for contacting Mum——and Lisa, if I can pin her down. The reminder that I'll have *some* contact with the outside world for the next couple of months eases my nerves a little, and I head back to my room to unpack and wait for the other Does to arrive.

———————

This is real. This is real. This is real.

For two hours, as I've unpacked, then explored the rest of the house, these three words have been on a loop in my mind, and my nerves are now cranked up to eleven. I need to distract myself and reorganising my bras and knickers isn't doing the trick.

We were allowed to bring books into the Manor——up to five each——and I'm hoping the other Does will also bring some, so we can swap between us. I retrieve one from my cache of brand new romcoms and lie down on my bed.

Chapter One

Emmy-Lou didn't think she could be any later for her blind date, having been delayed on both the bus and the tube, but now she'd gone and stepped in a puddle.

It's no good. I feel for Emmy-Lou—there's nothing worse than being on your way somewhere, already late, and having a minor disaster like a wet shoe—but I can't concentrate, and I invert the book on my bed and look about the room.

There are two single beds, two bedside tables, two chests of drawers, one of which now holds my foldables and (organised by colour) bras and knickers, a wardrobe with sliding doors where I've hung my other clothes—and that's it. Though the furniture downstairs is 'luxury showroom' ready, as that's where the filming takes place, the furniture in here is flatpack. But it's clean, the mattress is comfortable, and the bedding is soft. It's 'nice'—this time the perfect use for an otherwise banal word.

'Oh, Abigail, what on *earth* are you doing here?' I ask myself aloud. I'm now grateful I opted to use my own name on the show. Imagine if someone had caught me talking to myself using a different one—hardly covert. I expel a long sigh and before it comes to a satisfying conclusion, a voice echoes about the entry.

'Bloomin' 'ell, will you get a load of this!' In the moment that follows, there's a murmur of agreement and a random selection of exclamations.

They're here. It's showtime, Doe Abby.

I leap off the bed and go to the railing that overlooks the entry. 'Hallo,' I call down. Five faces look up at me and I mentally attach headshots and dossiers with the living, breathing versions. These are the other British Does—Tara, Daphne, Ellie, Tabitha, and Elizabeth. I have to pretend I don't know any of this, of course, so I introduce myself.

'I'm Abby. I … er … got here earlier.' Bollocks. How did it not occur to me to have a reasonable explanation for arriving before the other Does? I'm already terrible at this. Deflect!

'Er, the bedrooms are up here,' I call down cheerily. In an instance of perfect timing, a production assistant arrives wielding an iPad like a clipboard to oversee their arrival and give out room assignments. However, there's no one to help carry their cases up the stairs and Daphne, who Roberta has chosen as a potential Bride, makes no secret of her displeasure.

Not long after the British Does start getting settled—each in a different bedroom as we're all sharing with an Australian—I hear the crunch of driveway gravel and peek out the window to see a large black minivan pull up. The Australians have arrived and I am about to meet my roommate, Becca. I put away my abandoned book in the top drawer of my bedside table and smooth the covers on my bed.

'Holy crap!' says one Doe as they enter the Manor—same sentiment as before, different vernacular. I return to my lofty spot to repeat my greeting, peering over the railing at six Does this time, and the same production assistant—I've learnt her name now (it's Carlie)—runs through the same routine to get them all sorted and situated while I return to my room and wait for Becca.

'Hey,' says a beautiful woman from the doorway. 'You

must be Abby. I'm Becca.' She drops her cases at the door, then crosses the room, holding out her hand to shake mine.

'Hi. I'm Abby.' She smiles at me and I mentally slap myself. She already knew my name—there was no reason to repeat it, but I am a little 'Doe-struck'. No headshot, no amount of desktop research could have prepared me for the stunning beauty that is Becca.

She's even more like a Victoria's Secret model in person than she is in her photographs—tall, tiny waist, perfect C-cups, legs for days, flawless light-brown skin, cascading dark-brown curls, and a beautiful face, even sans makeup, as she is now. I also know that she's studying for her master's degree in data analytics at the University of New South Wales and from her warm greeting—no guile, no distaste when she laid eyes on me—she's also friendly.

Becca is the total package and there is no way I will ever compete with her for the Stag's heart. It's a good thing I don't have to.

Becca chats at me as she settles in, giving me her potted history—most of which I already know—and asks me questions which I respond to as 'Doe Abby'. There is quite a lot of hullaballoo in the rest of the Manor—I can't remember the last time I heard this much squealing and exclaiming—and I realise that it will be a long time before I experience solitude again—or perhaps even five minutes of silence. This is real. This is real. This is real. I exhale a long, slow breath to calm myself.

'So, what do I do with these?' Becca asks, indicating her empty cases.

'Oh, Carlie will come collect them. They go into storage while we're here, so they're out of the way.'

'Cool. So, should we go check out the rest of the house?' she asks excitedly.

'Er, yes, absolutely.'

We're on the landing when we hear it—crying coming from one of the water-facing bedrooms further down the hallway. Becca and I exchange a quick look and change direction away from the stairs. When we get to the door of the room, it's ajar and I poke my head around it.

It's Elizabeth, though I haven't officially met her yet. She's sitting on the end of her bed, her head in her hands, and appears on the brink of a full-blown proper cry. Becca pushes the door open and we both go to her, kneeling on the floor.

'Hey, are you okay?' Becca asks. I know it's the thing you say, but it occurs to me how odd it is to ask when it's plainly not the case.

Elizabeth shakes her head. 'I can't believe I've done this,' she says, her voice muffled.

'What, come all this way to spend weeks locked up in a fancy dormitory with strangers, so you can meet another stranger, hoping he'll fall in love with you? That?' I ask.

It does the trick. She coughs out a laugh and lifts her head, her blotchy, tear-stained face breaking into a smile.

'Yes, exactly that.'

'Here,' Becca retrieves a folded tissue from her jeans pocket. 'It's clean, I promise.'

Elizabeth takes the tissue and wipes under her nose, then her cheeks. She is about to dissolve into tears again, and I place a firm hand on her knee. 'The good news is that you are not alone in this. And you already have two friends in the Manor. That's Becca and I'm Abby.'

She sniffles and nods. 'Elizabeth.'

'Hi,' says Becca.

'Hello, Elizabeth,' I say, and we share a smile. 'Now, do you want more good news, or the even better news?' I ask.

'Both.'

'Well, the other good news is that we're not filming until tomorrow night and, hopefully, by then we'll all be old hats at this.' She nods again, her eyes hopeful. Becca hands over a box of tissues she's found, and Elizabeth takes a handful to wipe her face properly.

'And the even better news is something I have to show you. Come on, up you get,' I say, standing and offering her a hand. She takes it and I walk her over to the window. 'Look.'

She blinks at the view—the *stunning* view of the patio, the lawn and garden, the beach, and the sparkling sunlit water of Sydney Harbour. 'Now, what do you think of that?'

'It's incredible,' she replies.

'Yeah, our room looks out over the driveway,' says Becca with a laugh. 'I'll swap ya?' she jokes.

Elizabeth laughs, which turns into a hiccup. 'We're going downstairs to look around,' I say. 'How about you come find us when you're feeling a bit better?'

'I'll be in the kitchen,' says Becca. 'I'm *starving*.'

Elizabeth bites her lip and a frown scuppers across her face. 'It's surreal for all of us,' I say.

'Yeah, totally,' says Becca. 'It's, like, really weird. But we're here now, so let's make the most of it, 'kay?' This is met with a quick nod and I sense that Elizabeth just wants to be alone now. 'See you downstairs,' I say, and we go.

'I really am starving,' Becca says quietly once we've left Elizabeth's room. 'God, I hope there's Vegemite,' she adds. 'I practically live on the stuff.'

'Lordy, she's crying already? Toughen up, you snivelly little git!' Becca and I stop and look at each other, her appalled expression mirroring mine.

We're outside Tara and Kylie's room. They've put the two Villains together and despite the absence of cameras, they're already behaving as the loathsome cows they've been cast as. They also look like they've stepped out of Gotham City—Batman's latest nemeses, a pigeon pair of acidic beauty. Tara with her jet-black hair, straightened to within an inch of its life, falling dull and lustreless down her back, and Kylie with the exact same hairstyle—only platinum blonde—and both wearing enough makeup to kit out a Mac counter. Beauty from a (heavily abused) bottle.

A cackle of laughter follows Tara's snide comment and Kylie dives right into the exchange, seeming to relish sparring with a fellow Villain. 'And she's such a mousy little thing. She'll be outta here at the first Pin Ritual, don't you worry.'

'Oh, I'm not worried. Have you *seen* the others? We're definitely two of the hottest girls here. And what about that Heffalump, the plain, chubby girl?' Tara snorts out a scoffing laugh.

My eyes drop to the floor and I feel a hand reach down and squeeze mine as my tum turns squidgy. *I* know I'm not Doe material, but I'd fooled myself into thinking the makeover was enough, that the others would see me as a peer.

'Oh, my god, she must come from a rich family or something. She probably bought her way in here. Daddy, please can you get me on *The Stag*,' whines Kylie. Oh, the irony of how far that is from the truth!

There's a tug on my hand and when I look at Becca, she's signalling for us to leave before we hear any more. But I am rooted to spot, my instincts for self-preservation having deserted me, and I steel myself to hear every last nasty thing they have to say about me.

'Too bloody right,' says Tara. 'We'll probably be the last two Does, don't you reckon?' It's not lost on me that they've not mentioned Daniel, the Stag, even once. This is a game to them—they're here to win rather than fall in love.

'Well, there's that hot chick from Brissie,' says Kylie. She's talking about Justine, a wannabe actress—and yes, she's pretty, but there's a lot of grooming that goes into that look and those are most certainly not the breasts that nature doled out.

'Oh, right, yeah. S'pose she could be top three with us.' Like *they* get to decide that! Hah! If only they knew.

'And maybe that stuck-up one—Becca,' says Kylie. I look at Becca and she's grimacing. She meets my eyes and jerks her head to indicate that *we really should leave now*. I agree. It's one thing for me to be in the firing line but calling Becca stuck-up when she seems so lovely is nothing short of jealousy. It's the impetus I need and this time when Becca tugs my hand, I follow. As we reach the top of the stairs, Tara's voice trails behind us.

'Yeah, who the blooming 'ell does she think she is, swanning about ...'

Becca and I reach the kitchen before we say anything to each other.

'They're just jealous of you,' I say.

'They're bitches,' Becca says at the same time.

There's a beat and we both laugh. 'There's going to be a lot of that in here,' I say. I've watched enough seasons of this show to know how awful the Does can be to each other—and that's from the footage that makes the edits. God only knows what goes on when the cameras aren't rolling or what's edited out—all the squabbles, derogatory comments, and bouts of bullying that don't make the cut. It's likely we only see the tip of the iceberg on television.

But this is a reality television show, a competition, and with all of us living together, I have no doubt Stag Manor will become a human pressure cooker over the coming weeks. Something else to be wary of and worry about.

Becca shrugs off my comment, adding, 'Tall-poppy syndrome. When people think you're better than them—even if *you* don't think it—some of them want to tear you down.' She seems quite resilient, though I suppose that makes sense when you're smart and you look like a supermodel; you must get used to people targeting you out of jealousy.

Becca had not been joking about her love of Vegemite—she's about to slather her fourth piece of toast with a thick layer of the sticky black spread.

'Are you campaigning to be a brand ambassador?' I tease. With my squidgy tum, I'd scoured the fully stocked pantry and fridge for something soothing and I've opted for a tub of yoghurt, hoping that will settle it. Elizabeth, who looks a lot better than she did when we saw her upstairs, has made herself a mug of tea, and we are sitting at the breakfast bar with one of the other Does, Kaz, an Australian from Perth.

Becca laughs at herself. 'I know, I'm like a teenaged boy.' She screws the lid onto the enormous jar. 'I blame studying,' she adds, 'It's good brain food. Sometimes, when I'm working on an assignment, I'll eat a whole loaf of Vegemite toast in a day.' Ewww. I don't even like Marmite. And how can she practically live on bread and still look like that? *Abby, do not cut down this lovely tall poppy!*

'I cannot *believe* I came all the way to the antipodes for *this*,' says Daphne, British ice queen, who is holding court in the adjacent lounge room. The four of us share a look of solidarity, a silent agreement to eavesdrop from the breakfast bar.

'How do you mean?' Tabitha, also British, asks Daphne.

'Yeah, are you talking about Sydney or the house?' asks Merrin, another of the Australians. ''Cause this place is *amazing*. I mean, the view alone—'

'Well, clearly I mean the house,' interrupts Daphne, her voice thick with condescension. 'It's not as if I'd show up to Heathrow without any idea of where I was going. Though I did *not* know I'd be flying *economy*. Had I known *that*, I would have made my own arrangements.'

I steal a glance over my shoulder and see Tabitha and Merrin exchange frowns. Is Daphne *really* Roberta's number one pick for Bride? That's not exactly good news. She seems as *en*titled as she is *actually* titled (she's Lady Such-and-Such) and being a favourite, it's likely she'll be in the Manor the entire time I am. I suppose it was naïve of me to think I'd befriend *all* the other Does, especially having encountered those utter cows upstairs.

Daphne continues her tirade. '*Surely*, they could have found us someplace more suitable? It's bad enough having to share a room, but to not even have an en suite!' Becca and I may not have the view, but at least we don't have to share the main bathroom.

Kaz starts guffawing loudly, and spins on her stool to face the lounge room. 'Hey, Daph, you sure you're gonna survive all this hardship?' she asks, the ring of laughter in her voice. Daphne starts at the sound of her name—well, half of it—places her hand on her chest, and stares open-mouthed at Kaz.

'Are you addressing *me*?' says Daphne.

'Uh, *yeah*. No one else here called "Daph".'

'It's Daph*ne*,' she spits, her eyes narrowing to glary slits.

'Right. Sorry, Daph*ne*. So, Daph*ne*, are you gonna be right, love? We could ask if they can move you to a hotel or something.' There are a few titters of laughter from the others, but that may be the nervous variety—this is quite a tense moment.

'Good god,' says Daphne, waving a hand about loftily.

'Can no one take a joke anymore? Obviously, I'm not going to ask to move off site. How would that look to the Stag? I was just saying that compared with some of the more *classic* homes I've stayed in around the world, this is rather gauche—I mean, it's as though a back issue of *Architectural Digest* vomited—and it's a tad too small for twelve people, that's all.'

The line about *Architectural Digest* is actually rather funny—like something Anastasia would say. Though I can't use it, of course.

'Oh, totally,' says Kaz. 'It's a real bitch when your twenty-million-dollar waterfront home doesn't sleep twelve comfortably.' It's a great retort, and though Daphne's only response is to send her eyes skyward, it does seem to diffuse the situation. It's also likely Kaz's estimate about the value of this house is close, if not accurate—she works in commercial real estate as an engineer.

I'm about to swivel back around to finish my yoghurt, when two Does cross the near-invisible line from outside to inside, both in swimsuits and dripping wet. 'Did you go for a swim?' asks Merrin, even though it is obvious.

'Yeah,' says Justine. 'The water's beautiful—so refreshing.' If she keeps parading around here in that bikini once the cameras start rolling, she's bound to be a crowd favourite. And she may just catch the eye of a casting agent or two. It's a decent plan for landing that role on *Neighbours*.

'It's warm in the water, but a bit brisk out of it,' says British Doe, Ellie, whose teeth are starting to chatter. I also notice how her pale skin has pinked across the shoulders and remind myself of the importance of sunscreen.

Laura, another Australian, enters carrying an armful of beach towels. 'Found 'em,' she says, handing one to Justine, then Ellie, who wraps herself up like a burrito. While they dry themselves, I do a quick head count. Ten. 'Oi, you lot,' says Tara as she descends the stairs with Kylie. 'Whaddya say we get this party started prop'ly?' With the addition of our two (wonder) Villains, we are now twelve.

'Ooh, yes, please,' says Kaz, jumping off her stool and opening an overhead kitchen cupboard. 'Fully stocked bar, anyone?' More squealing, which reverberates off the litany of hard surfaces. Who knew that a group of twenty- and thirty-somethings could make so much noise?

I look along the breakfast bar, then over at the lounge room. Merrin, a reserved woman from Tasmania, looks slightly petrified by the ensuing ruckus, but Becca shoots me looks that say, *'Why not?'* and Elizabeth shrugs noncommittally.

'So, who do you think the Stag will be?' asks Tara. 'One of those snooty toffs, ya reckon?' she adds, throwing a not-so-sly look at Daphne. Daphne, to her credit, meets Tara's gaze and raises her eyebrows. Too bad the cameras don't start rolling until tomorrow, as this exchange would be perfect for the season premier.

'I've heard rumours it's an Aussie billionaire,' says Justine. Well, *that* would get you noticed by the casting agents, love, rocking the arm of a billionaire. She's wrong, though. The little I do know about Daniel the Stag is that he's British. Jack let it slip that they'd cast him around the time we met in Prue's office.

The conjecture about whose heart we are all (ostensibly)

here to win gets rowdier as the night goes on. Kylie, apparently, '… will be turning down the pin outright if the guy's showing any sign of receding—no lie.' Those are her words, not mine, and as soon as she says it, I start cataloguing attractive bald men, rounding off the list with Taye Diggs and Jason Statham. Though I do love Jack's longish, floppy hair. And his green eyes and those lips.

'Abby!' says Becca, poking me.

'Oh, sorry, what's that?' I've been daydreaming (at night-time) about Jack which, along with pinching myself, I should also stop doing.

'Want to head up?' she asks. 'It's looking like it's only going to get sloppier.' I heard someone saying something about skinny dipping earlier and in the absence of cameras—our last hurrah, so to speak—most Does are in various stages of inebriation, except Merrin and Elizabeth who are noticeably absent.

I look at the digital clock on the oven—9:58pm—then survey the group one more time. 'Yes, brilliant idea. Though, I'm not sure how much sleep we'll get with all this going on.' But not long after Becca and I head upstairs—cries of 'lightweights' at our backs—I feel myself slipping into sleep, my final thought, a gorgeous Australian man.

Chapter Eight

The Stag In Sydney Recap:
Throw Another Shrimp on the Barbie
by Anastasia Blabbergasted

G'day! It's hunting season again—and this time it's
particularly special! For those of you who like your
reality television with a side of Bondi Beach and a
shrimp or two on the barbie, then this season is for
you! That's right. This season, *The Stag* comes to you
from the stunning city of Sydney.

We open the episode with sweeping shots of rugged
shorelines and coves of white sandy beaches, and
glorious vistas of Sydney Harbour—look, there's the
Opera House and the Sydney Harbor Bridge! And
for those of you back in the UK, curled up by the
heater and snuggling under the duvet, that glorious
ball of bright fire in the sky is called 'the sun'. Some

of you may remember it from that day back in July 2011.

And for Stag Manor this season, gone are the remnants of aristocracy—no marble staircases, no velvet furniture or heavy drapery, not a smidgeon of Downton Abbey-esque décor here. No! Stag Manor is all about sharp angles, polished cement floors, glass for days, and a spectacular water feature straight out of *Grand Designs*—all evoking the glitz and glamour of one of the world's most expensive waterfront locations. (Psst. It's rumoured that Nicole Kidman lives next door!) No doubt we'll get lots of shots of the Does looking longingly out the window—*at that view!* This is real estate porn at its finest.

Though, I'm sure the Does could have done without traipsing through that crunchy gravel between the limousine and the front steps of Stag Manor. I imagine there will be more than a few tears shed over ruined Manolos.

A ctually, I don't have to imagine anything, as there were tears shed. Wannabe Justine threw an enormous tantrum and tossed her 'ruined' sky-high silver heels into the rubbish. One of the production crew fished them out and, apparently, they've been sent to the shoe doctor (whatever that is).

And that was the least ridiculous thing that happened on day one of filming.

I know I'm here to peak behind the curtain, so to speak, but I could never have imagined the absurdity of filming the first episode—our so-called 'arrival' at Stag Manor. We started filming early evening, each of us dressed in our finest and primped just so, after spending the better part of the day getting ready. The preceding night's hangovers (for those who didn't go to bed at a reasonable hour) had worn off by lunchtime when the whole Manor erupted into semi-organised chaos: twelve women; five bathrooms; hairdryers blasting continuously for at least two hours; (more) squeals; (more) tears—stuck zippers are such a tragedy; oodles of false compliments—'Oh, you look *gorgeous*'; Carlie run off her feet; and in the midst of it all, *me*.

Well, Doe Abby, the hopeless pretender.

As soon as I cracked open my eye shadow palette, everything that makeup artist extraordinaire, Nadia, had taught me flew out of my head. I'm so grateful for Becca, who is not only generous with her time, but a bit of a whizz in the makeup department. I was just as surprised (and pleased) when I looked in the mirror after she finished as I'd been on makeover day—me, but prettier.

Once we were all deemed camera ready, we took turns filming our arrival at Stag Manor, one by one stepping out of a lone limousine that had simply conducted a circuit of the circular driveway to deposit us at our very own front door (like we hadn't already moved in). 'Ooh, ahh, what a beautiful home,' we mugged for our close-ups. Aside: I *knew* there was only one limousine.

And I swear this is the absolute truth, we finished filming all the 'arrivals' before Daniel even showed up!

Of course, there was a lot of excitement when he did arrive—Does on tiptoes, clambering over each other to get a glimpse while we waited around the side of the house for our turn to meet him. At least that part was authentic—the first time we actually met Daniel was on camera as he welcomed us to Stag Manor.

'Oh hello, welcome to the home that you're already living in. It makes perfect sense for me to do this, even though I don't live here.' And, of course, it made even *more* sense that we arrived at our new home carrying our belongings in tiny clutch purses—itty-bitty versions of Mary Poppins' bottomless carpet bag, obviously. Ooh—another angle for my exposé!

I was eighth in line to meet Daniel and watched as Becca (number seven) disappeared around the side of the Manor. It was likely only minutes, but seemed much longer as I struggled to keep my nerves in check by counting out my breaths—in-two-three-four, out-two-three-four. *Finally*, Carlie, who was overseeing proceedings, double-checked her iPad-clipboard and waved me forward.

I rounded the corner of Stag Manor, plastered what I hoped was a winsome smile on my face, and repeated *'do not trip'* to myself a dozen times as I made my way to the front steps and carefully climbed them. I almost sighed with relief when I made it to the top unscathed—huzzah! I can walk in heels—but I remembered that a camera was watching my every move, every expression, every *breath*.

Daniel waited on the front doorstep, smiling benevolently like he was Prince William in the receiving line for a

Royal Command Performance. We introduced ourselves, he kissed my cheek, we made small talk—none of which I remember—and then I went inside where I was met with seven whispering wild-eyed women.

It wasn't until the Soirée—filmed outside on the patio under the 'moonlight' (carefully placed lighting) that I started to get a real sense of who Daniel is. Speaking of which …

And let's talk about our Stag, Daniel the investment banker! Fifty shades of yay, I'd say! What an absolute dish—those steely blue eyes, that swoop of flaxen hair. When they make the film based on this season—and why wouldn't they?—Dan Stevens will absolutely *have* to play our scrumptious Stag. In that suit, with that perfectly knotted tie and that flash of flare in a pocket square, he looks as though he's auditioning to be the next James Bond. Cue Shirley Bassey! Cue Adele! Cue a Shirley-Adele collaboration. Oh, Danny Boy indeed!

Oh, smarmy, priggish prat indeed! Hah. If only I could write that.

Now, let's just have a quick chat about our Does. Only twelve this season, narrowing the field from the usual sixteen, but who can blame the producers? Six flights from the UK—seven if you count our Danny Boy—and that massive Airbnb bill—no wonder they've cut the Doe-age down by 25% (Thank you to

Mrs Walters, my fourth form Mathematics teacher. You always said I would use percentages one day—and look!). So, we have six British Does and six Australian Does (who for some reason think its charming to refer to themselves as 'the Aussie Chicks') all vying for our Staggy, Danny Boy.

As I usually do, I have categorised our Does as follows:

- (potential) Brides
- Villains
- Dark Horses
- Miscellaneous
- Filler

And as always, let's begin with the **Filler**.

This is harder than I thought. I know these women now, as we've been in the Point Piper house—sorry, Stag Manor—nearly a week.

I absolutely adore Becca. She reminds me a little of Lisa and I'm so thankful she's the person I share a room with. But the 'tall poppy' comments have ramped up—sometimes deliberately within her earshot—with the (wonder) Villains now eliciting support from Justine, who (disappointingly) plays along. Becca continues to shrug it off good-naturedly, but I suspect she's not as resilient as I'd originally thought.

And it's definitely jealousy. When it takes you more than an hour to put on your makeup and do your hair just so you look like 'you', that must erode your self-esteem. That's me being generous, though, because Tara and Kylie are outright nasty women.

Becca's also one of the women here to find love. As far as I can see, only about half of us are. But this just makes me more protective of her and I truly hope she steers clear of banker wanker Daniel. Good god, he's a twat. I don't think I have ever met a man as up himself. Maybe Becca will fall in love with someone from the crew—perhaps even Harry, Jack's brother.

I adore Harry—and I'm just realising now that he and Becca would be perfect for each other. He's so lovely—a little more 'blokey' than Jack, as the Australians say, but like his brother, he's gregarious and clever and he looks you in the eye when he's speaking to you. Unlike Daniel. Daniel is one of those people who's always looking over your shoulder to see if someone more interesting is coming along, something I discovered at the Soirée. And I suppose that when it comes to me (being the most normal-looking woman in Stag Manor), 'someone more interesting' could be just about anyone.

The first time I saw myself onscreen—last night I was secreted away to the Control Room to watch a rough cut of episode one, as well as some outtakes—I was aghast, recoiling so violently and emitting such an awful guttural sound, that Jack had laughed. When I realised he wasn't laughing at me, just my reaction, I joined in, as did Harry. I hope it gets easier to watch myself, but let's just say it's unlikely I'll ever be cast as a television presenter.

It's also getting tricker to be around Jack and we're

barely a week in. He's just so annoyingly attractive with those quirky logo T-shirts and sexy, worn-in jeans he wears. Even the way he rubs his jaw when he's thinking, his face settled into that adorable little frown of concentration, is attractive.

When we're with the other Does and the crew, it's a little easier to maintain my distance, my professionalism—I'm just another contestant—but last night when it was the three of us, he was so friendly, so lovely, so *Jack*, I almost forgot why we're both here. But as much as I want us to be friends (and yes all right, more than that), I have a job to do and so does he. This may not be his dream job, but he and Harry need this season to go well, and I need to keep my (emotional) distance lest I give the game away.

I'm also trying to forget that humiliating conversation we had on the flight about Daniel. How did I ever think that Jack might be interested in me romantically? With all this whirling through my mind on a loop, it's a minor miracle I've been able to get any words onto the page at all.

I sigh, resigned. I have to finish this recap. Surely, this will be the hardest one, simply because it's the first and this is where I set the scene and categorise all the Does—including *me*. Perhaps the rest of this season's recaps will flow from my mind practically fully formed as I type, like they usually do.

And perhaps the Spanish Armada will sail into Sydney Harbour.

Filler

And as always, let's begin with the **Filler**. With a

pared-back cast of Does this season, only a couple fit into the Filler category—these are the women who are merely here…

Oops, I need to write like I'm *outside* the Manor.

… merely there to make up the numbers. You needn't learn their names—Daniel certainly won't, as was evidenced by his behaviour at the Soirée. 'What's that one called again?' he asked, probably not as surreptitiously as he hoped. The Doe in question was **Tabitha**, one of the British women, but you don't need to remember that. Poor Tabitha will likely be on a plane back to the UK before her jet lag wears off. The other Filler Doe is **Laura** from Tamworth (also known as the woman who doesn't stop talking). No one likes country music *that* much, Laura. Calm the he-haw down!

That's not a particularly kind thing to say about Laura but less than a week in, I've already had my fill of 'all thangs country music'. And besides, Anastasia said it, not me.

Villains
These are the women who have obviously been cast for their (innate) ability to stir up trouble and pepper the pot, to put others down behind their back (shall I leave out a bowl of cream for you, ladies?), and to fawn all over our Danny Boy without any desire whatsoever to win his heart. They'll be here just long

enough to cause some reasonable damage to the other Does' self-esteem, and to throw a few red herrings into that peppered pot.

Just two this season, as far as I can tell——but they are both punching above their weight class. **Tara** hails from London——the East End, her accent tells me——and when she inevitably gets the boot and returns to the UK, she will undoubtedly have a lengthy career as a gangster's moll. And **Kylie**——I'd wager she aced her (Australian equivalent of) A-levels in 'How to Act Like a Mean Girl'. With her dogged sarkiness, she could give *me* a run for my money.

Well, that much is true. More and more, I've become a self-appointed Doe Wrangler, steering Becca, Elizabeth, and a couple of the others clear of the firing line whenever possible. As someone privy to the machinations of this bizarre little ecosystem, and as the oldest woman in the Manor (Doe Abby may be twenty-eight but *I* am thirty-three), I feel it is my duty.

Aside: Thank you to my long-gone nan. Nan, I don't remember much about you——just glimpses and feelings, really——but I thank you for passing along your English Rose complexion, allowing me to convincingly play a twenty-something.

Miscellaneous
Ah, yes, the Does who are tricky to categorise, so get

their own category—that's me cheating a little, I'm afraid. Do forgive me!

I'll come back to this section. I haven't decided if Doe Abby is Miscellaneous or a Dark Horse.

(potential) Brides

It's safe to say that there are actually *three* Does in contention for the role of Bride this season. **Becca**, the beauty from down under, is the total pack-age—beautiful, smart, and kind. She does have a penchant for Vegemite that borders on the unnat-ural, but perhaps if she wins Daniel's heart, we can convert her to Marmite.

Justine, another of the Australians, is definitely in with a chance! Did you *see* Daniel's eyes light up when she climbed out of the limousine? And didn't she do that with all the practised ease of … well, someone who has been in many a limo. Destined for stardom is actress and model Justine and, just maybe, she'll swap walking the red carpet for walking down the aisle!

This is unlikely, as Justine has been rather vocal about wanting a regular role on *Neighbours* after she departs the Manor. Or *Home and Away*. She's not picky, apparently.

Last in (serious) contention for our Danny Boy's heart, is the lovely British Doe, **Daphne**. If one were to prick her finger, no doubt she'd bleed blue, such is the long pedigree of royal blood coursing through her veins. She's poised, elegant, and regal, and with her career in philanthropy, can't you just *imagine* Daniel and Daphne as the power couple about London Town? I'd bet that Daphne can, if that tight grip on Daniel's arm at the Soirée was anything to go by.

I'm almost choking on these words as I type—total lies! That said, it's been almost fascinating watching Daphne. She's an utter snob and *such* a cow, but in an instant, she can turn on the charm. And that's not just with Daniel, but also with Jack and Harry. If there is a man within 'cooee'—an Australian idiom I've learnt from Kaz—Daphne is exactly as described in this recap. But as soon as the men disappear, so do her manners. She's horrid. No wonder Roberta likes Daphne so much—it's pure narcissism, plain and simple.

Dark Horses
Ellie, one of the British women, *must* be considered a Dark Horse. For a start, she's a natural beauty, all doe eyes (perfect for *The Stag*) and alabaster skin. She also has a kooky sense of humour, the first Doe ever to show up with a ventriloquist's dummy of herself—imagine *that* going through the airport scanner! Daniel may have been surprised when they emerged from the limousine (shocked, really), but that dummy has some cracking jokes. Keep an eye on this one!

Ellie is lovely, but even I've been somewhat disturbed by how often she's accompanied by Little Ellie. And *I* currently have *two* alter egos.

Another Dark Horse is **Abby**, also British. What is it she does for a living again? She dodges those questions with the acumen of someone who works in a windowless building on the banks of the Thames. Speaking of James Bond … perhaps we have a *Jane* Bond in our midst. She also has a wicked sense of humour and Danny Boy is going to have to keep his wits about him with Abby. But what might just win our Danny Boy's heart—despite Abby being, shall we say, the most *ordinary* looking woman in the Manor—is her tendency to look after the other Does. Though 'big sister' status may not be sexy enough for our Staggy.

Also a Dark Horse is Australian, **Karen**—or rather ***Kaz***. (Isn't it, er, *charming* how the Australians shorten their names and add a zed?) Kaz is a structural engineer from Perth. She is brash, sassy, and has a bawdy sense of humour. Perhaps she and her hard hat are the perfect foil for banker boy, Danny—opposites attract and all that. Kaz likely wouldn't let Daniel take life—or himself—too seriously. She certainly caught his eye a few times at the Soirée when she tossed back her fiery red tresses and laughed long and hard.

Now I've decided that Doe Abby is a Dark Horse, back to the odd bods—or rather, 'oddest bods', as all the Does are a little odd, simply for being here—me included.

Miscellaneous

Ah, yes, the Does who are tricky to categorise, so get their own category—that's me cheating a little, I'm afraid. Do forgive me!

Let's begin with **Merrin**, who harkens from Tasmania, a land of natural beauty, wonderful wine (though, isn't that half of Australia?), and *cats*, apparently. Merrin has *five* cats, something she happily expounds upon whenever another person is in earshot; I've already (unwittingly) learnt their names. Ordinarily, I'd categorise Merrin as Filler, but she's such a quirky one. And though Daniel violently sneezes any time she's near—that dastardly dander—surely popping an antihistamine is a small price to pay for true love. But I do wonder if Merrin *would* move to London for Daniel, forsaking Sassy, Fluff, Tiger, Scabs (I wouldn't dare ask), and One-eye (must be self-explanatory).

The toughest Doe for me to categorise this season, and hence the reason she's sitting firmly in Miscellaneous, is **Elizabeth**. Bookish, earnest, softly spoken Elizabeth, who is very pretty in that frail, pale, and unobvious way, hails from a small town in Devon where she is a Reception teacher. Although she's the

most introverted woman in Stag Manor, Elizabeth
seems like the sort of woman who would tell a
stranger that their skirt was caught in the back of
their knickers. *I* like her, but I wonder if Daniel will.

Like Becca, I adore Elizabeth—she is such a darling and
I cannot understand what has impelled her to be a contestant on this television show. After discovering her sobbing in
her bedroom after only an hour in the Manor, she's one of
the Does who I am keeping an eye on—particularly as
someone like Daniel—*or any of the horrid women, for that
matter*—could eat her alive if allowed to. Metaphorically
speaking, of course. Doubtful we have any cannibals in our
midst. Dementors, perhaps.

Oh, god, I suppose I should say something about the
host. He's, er … well, he's terrible. *And* he's sleazy, his eyes
always trailing after the Does—even me. Still, I came here
to do a job and I needn't be kind. I'll be restrained, however.
The people of Britain do not need to know that Roberta
(and perhaps Jack) hired an utter sleaze to host their show.
Besides, I haven't seen any evidence of his inappropriate
behaviour in the footage, so how would Anastasia (who is
believed to be in London right now) even know about it?

There is so much I have to keep straight in my head!

And last, and possibly least (the jury is still out), is this
season's host. I'm not sure how Johnny Toffs
managed to miss out on filming in Sydney (sack your
agent, Johnny!), but this season we are graced (?) by
the man who hosts *The Buck* (the Australian version

of the show), Gordo (short for Gordon, apparently) Watts.

Gordo comes to us from a long line of hosting jobs in the Australian reality television realm and has about as much personality as a dry washing-up cloth. Someone needs to tell Gordo that he's hosting a show about finding love, set in one of the most beautiful cities in the world, rather than a funeral. Lighten up, *Gordo*.

So, there you are. It's too early to say this season – so many strong contenders for Daniel's heart – but if I had to say right this moment who he will choose …

There's a soft knock on the door and I look up as Jack peers into the room. 'Hey,' he whispers.

Hey,' I whisper back, reverting from Anastasia to Abby in an instant. I wish I could just be Anastasia with Jack. *She* doesn't have this intense and distracting crush on him.

Jack slips inside the tiny room and closes the door quietly behind him, then leans against the wall. Today's T-shirt says, 'Stop Reading My Shirt'. Bollocks—now I've read it again. That makes at least a dozen times since I laid eyes on him this morning. But I am not entirely to blame—the words just sit so nicely across his chest. Still, I feel caught out and raise my eyes to meet his, hoping he doesn't catch my embarrassment. 'So, how's it going? You nearly done?'

'Er, yes, actually, just the last line to write.'

He nods. 'Becca was asking after you.'

'Oh, right. What did you say?'

'That I thought I saw you down at the beach.'

'I should probably go down there after this—get some sand on my feet, really sell that lie.' I hear the edge in my voice and soften my reply with a smile.

'Sorry, I wasn't sure what else to tell her,' he says.

'No, no, it's …'

'Tricky,' he says, completing my thought.

'It is.'

'How's this room? Is it okay?'

'Oh, yes, absolutely. It's perfect.' I'm seated at a card table, sitting on a folding chair, and I'm surrounded by shelves stacked with enormous packages of toilet roll and kitchen towel, and industrial-sized cleaning products. Everyone's empty luggage is piled up in one corner, and as it is a storeroom, there is no air circulation, so it's also rather stuffy.

He grins at me and my stomach flips. 'It's shit and I'm sorry.'

'No, really, it's perfectly serviceable—I only need to be in here when I'm writing.'

'We just wanted to make sure you'd be hidden away, somewhere none of the other Does would dream of entering.'

'Is that why the sign on the door says "Danger! High Voltage"?'

'Sneaky, huh?'

'Indeed, though "Cleaning Products" would have

worked too,' I retort, my wit working hard to keep my heart from taking over the conversation. Although he looks drained after the first week of filming, he is still achingly attractive in that effortless, tousled way. I want to get up from my chair, wrap my arms around his waist, and tip my chin up for a kiss.

I don't though.

'Some of the women are a little …' he says, trailing off.

'Messy? Precious? Incapable of looking after themselves?' I ask.

He throws up both hands. 'Hey, you said it, not me.'

'Let's call this a safe space when it comes to the show. Open slather. No holds barred. Complete honesty. How does that sound?'

He eyes me, a slight smile on his face. 'Maybe.' Oh, I see. He doesn't trust me. Not wholly, in any case—*and* he thinks I might fall madly in love with Daniel. Hardly. I'm more likely to run off with Gordo.

He rubs the back of his neck with one hand, then closes his eyes momentarily and winces a little. 'Are you all right?' I ask.

This smile doesn't reach his eyes. 'Yeah, just tired. I'm going to head out soon.'

'Do you want to read the recap before you go?' I ask. He'll read it eventually, of course, once I submit it for feedback. But what matters to me right now is that Jack knows he can trust me, that I won't do anything to jeopardise the success of the show. And even though he looks like he needs a decent night's sleep, I also don't want him to go just yet.

'Sure, yeah. That'd be good.'

He comes to stand behind me and leans over, placing one palm flat on the table next to mine. He's not touching me, but I can feel the warmth of him radiating against my back and I realise how easy it would be to lean back …

'I just need to …' he reaches around me to the touchpad of the laptop and scrolls to the top of the page. God, I didn't even have the presence of mind to do that simple thing. It's like he can scramble my mind just with his proximity.

Jack's fingers glide across the touchpad from time to time as he scrolls the recap and reads over my shoulder. His face is inches from mine and despite the late hour and a full day of filming us lounging on the private beach and talking about Daniel, he still has that 'fresh cotton sheets' smell. I should ask him what laundry soap he uses.

'This is really good,' he says. The vacuum he leaves when he steps back and resumes his position against the wall, is palpable. *Compose yourself, Abigail!* chides my inner voice.

'Thank you,' I say, simply. When it comes to my writing, no need to be unnecessarily modest.

'Your description of Daniel works—really sets him up as an aspirational love interest.' I hope Jack doesn't think that *this* version of Daniel reflects how I really feel about him. But how would he know otherwise unless I tell him?

'What's the point of telling him, Abby? You already know he's not interested in you,' I tell myself. I suppose it's best to steer clear of discussing Daniel—for now, at least. 'The part about Gordo … not too much?' I ask.

He laughs and the sound fills the small space. 'Oops,

sorry,' he says in an almost whisper, 'forgot where I was. No, the part about Gordo is bang on. The guy's a dick.'

Now it's my turn to laugh, though mindful of our covert status, it's more of a snigger. 'I was wondering how you felt about him. You certainly haven't given anything away.'

'See? You're not the only one who has to pretend. And you've done a good job of categorising the Does. That will really set up the storylines Roberta and I have been working on.'

I'd love to have more insight into this part of the process, especially what they have in mind for Doe Abby. Or perhaps not. *What if (poor, pathetic) Abby falls for the Stag!* I still feel ill when I think about them scheming behind my back, Prue ack-ack-ack-ing at how clever she'd been.

I'm also mindful that the 'storylines' on these shows, particularly *The Stag*, are contrived, manipulative, and some-times plain awful. I can only imagine the pleasure that Vile Demon Woman Roberta derives from conjuring uncon-scionable plot points.

'Oh, good,' I reply to Jack's comment about the Does.

'I like that you're a "Dark Horse" too.'

'I went back and forth between that and "Miscellaneous".'

'Nah, she's—sorry, *you're*—definitely one to watch,' he says, looking right into my eyes.

Three parts of me—my mind, my heart, and my stom-ach—are all in agreement at last. I, Abigail Jones, am falling hard for this lovely, clever, rumpledly handsome Australian. He's so gorgeous, I'm even making up new words.

'Hey, when you finish up …'

'I know, I'll pack up the table and chair, and put the laptop back where I found it.' It was hidden in an empty box on the top shelf next to the kitchen towel.

'Cool—thanks. Have a good night.'

'You too.'

He slips out of the door throwing me a smile before he closes it behind him.

'You're definitely one to watch,' he'd said. Is that because he's invested in me winning Daniel's heart, or because *he's* watching me? Oh, please let it be the latter. I look down at the laptop screen, then tap out the final line of my recap.

So, there you are. It's too early to say this season – so many strong contenders for Daniel's heart – but if I had to say right this moment who he will choose, it's Daphne!

Chapter Nine

We're standing on the pier about to embark on a group date aboard a luxury yacht. There are only six of us, 'three of each' as we now say about the not-so-friendly rivalry between the 'Brits' and the 'Aussie Chicks'.

I'm with Becca, Kylie, Daphne, Kaz, and Elizabeth. There was a lot of pouting and stomping about Stag Manor when Gordo announced who would be going on the date. Tara, East End super villainess, was certainly not shy. 'This is fucked,' she'd growled as she left the lounge room. A door slammed moments later.

Now, *there's* something they never show on television—how disappointed the Does are when they're left out. It's all faux smiles and golf claps. 'Oh, that's amazing, darling! You'll have *so* much fun.' Definitely fodder for my exposé—how much acting there is in this supposed reality television show.

On the pier, Daphne—British blue blood—is scowling at the yacht. Perhaps it's smaller than what she's accustomed to—so many yachts, so little time. And she does 'summer in Monte Carlo, you know' (you must have a certain level of wealth to use the word 'summer' as a verb). Any moment now, I expect she'll whine something like, *'But, Gordo, where's the helicopter pad?'*

(Annoyingly) Jack and Harry aren't editing in any of her sour-faced snobbishness. As mandated by Roberta, Daphne is still the top contender for Bride and she'll come across to viewers as someone they can champion, an appropriate choice for Daniel.

Ah, Danny Boy, you utter …

'Ahoy, ladies,' he calls to us from the deck of the yacht. I outwardly grin as I see a camera swing in my direction. Inwardly, of course, I am cringing. Ahoy, ladies? Did he come up with that all on his own, or did schmaltzy Gordo write that line?

'Ready for a day of fun out on Sydney Harbour?' he asks. Six heads nod like puppets from *Thunderbirds*. Apt really, as Daphne *is* the Lady Penelope type. In complete contrast, Kaz shouts up to him, 'Yeah! Now let's stop hanging around here like shags on rocks.'

Daniel's smile falters for a second and I wonder if the camera will pick it up. Kaz is a breath of fresh air in the Manor and I've found myself gravitating towards her more and more. If Daniel actually did deign to consider her a potential love interest—unlikely, as I've seen footage of him describing her as a 'the blue-collar girl' despite her advanced degree in engineering—she could teach him a thing or two about not being such a pretentious arse.

'Well then, come aboard, me mateys!' Daniel accompa-

116

nies this absurd line with a beckoning arm gesture, and I can't help the giggle that erupts from my mouth. Becca throws me a sideways glance and I try to disguise the laugh as a cough. Oldest trick in the book, but I suspect she isn't buying it when her eyes narrow. We fall into a loose line and cross the gangplank onto the yacht. Daniel is there to 'help' us with the last step, taking each of our hands in turn and kissing us on the cheek.

I'm last and when he leans down to plant his kiss, I'm consumed by a cloud of his cologne. It's heady and spicy and a bit much for 10am. 'Can I steal you for a moment, Abby?' he says in my ear.

'Cut!' calls Harry. 'Sorry, everyone, audio didn't pick that up properly, Daniel. Becca, you and Abby go back down the gangplank—just halfway—then come up again. A little louder this time, please Daniel.'

Becca and I shuffle down the gangplank and wait for Harry's cue. She turns to me quickly. 'Hey, do I have lipstick on my teeth?' she asks quietly, baring her teeth at me.

'No, all good,' I reply.

'Thanks. I keep forgetting not to bite my lip—nervous habit,' she says.

'Aaand cue the Does,' calls Harry. 'Action!'

Becca and I repeat our yacht boarding and this time when Daniel asks if he can steal me away, it's like he's shouting across a crowded square. I manage not to flinch, however, as I do not want to film our scene for a third time.

'Cut! Got it,' says Harry. 'Thanks, everyone. Next set-up is on the rear deck—all Does except Abby. Abby, Daniel, follow me to the upper deck, please.'

Getting 'alone time' with Daniel—a mini date within a group date—puts a target on my back—especially as I'm first. No doubt, snarky Kylie will have something nasty to say. It may irk Becca too. Disappointingly, she's rather keen on Daniel, though I am not sure why. Every conversation I've witnessed between them—both in person and onscreen—has him condescending to her, as though she is *not* one of the cleverest people here. It's her looks, I'm sure of it. She could forgo the qualifications in data analytics and step right onto a catwalk in Milan, no question. Likely Daniel doesn't have the correct chip in his brain to reconcile her beauty with her intelligence.

I follow Harry and Daniel up a narrow set of steep stairs to the upper deck and when we arrive, Jack is there talking to someone who I presume is the captain—a safe assumption as she's wearing head-to-toe white, all crisply ironed, with epaulets on her shoulders, her outfit capped off with a captain's cap. She smiles as she passes, then descends the stairs, presumably to launch us into the azure blue waters of Sydney Harbour.

'We're just setting up over here,' says Jack, indicating the seating area where the set dresser is putting on finishing touches. She punches a throw pillow into shape before placing it alongside the others, casts a scrutinising eye over the scene, then nods at Jack and Harry before leaving the deck.

Harry steps up, but my gaze is fixed on Jack who stands off to the side and leans against the railing—all rumpledly handsome, damn him. Today's T-shirt is sans slogan but has a particularly deep V. I'm admiring that V when a horn blares and the boat starts to move.

'Right,' says Harry, commanding my attention, 'so this is your first date, just the two of you …' My tum gets squidgy.

I was briefed last night about having alone time with Daniel, so I've been swotting up on Doe Abby's biography. Though, when Jack mentioned it, he'd said 'conversation', not 'date'. Most dates on this show end with an obligatory kiss and I absolutely do *not* want to kiss Daniel—especially not in front of Jack. Maybe I'll be fortunate enough to suffocate on Daniel's cologne before he can kiss me. A quick trip to A&E, or the Australian equivalent, is preferable to locking lips with the Stag.

Harry continues. 'So, you know, "get to know you" type questions—upbringing, aspirations, favourite things—that kinda stuff. And try to remember to mention the view, 'kay?'

'As you wish, Mr Director,' says Daniel, ruining *The Princess Bride* for me forever.

We settle into the seating area and, under the guise of smoothing out my shorts, I ease away from Daniel who has sat so close, he's practically on top of me. Harry calls, 'Action,' then waves at a steward who enters the shot and pours two glasses of fizz. Again, it's 10am. I've barely digested my Weetbix—Australia's take on Weetabix—and now I'm expected to sip fizz and make nice with the banker wanker. I'm not sure which of those thoughts is responsible for my intensifying queasiness—or it could be the gentle rise and fall of the yacht on the harbour.

'So, Abby,' says Daniel, locking his eyes onto mine and appearing to take an intense interest in me. 'What's your story, then?' Good god. If I didn't know any better, I'd swear this was a scene from a soap opera—one of those American ones where they stare at each other during long moments of silence.

'My story?' Good question, Daniel. Panicked, I realise that all of Doe Abby's backstory has flown out of my head, like in those anxiety dreams about sitting your exams and forgetting everything you've learnt.

'Yes,' he says, moving closer. There's no way he's attracted to me—I'm far too plain for the likes of Daniel. What on earth is he playing at? 'Tell me all about yourself. What makes you *you*?'

My synapses finally start firing and a wave of calm washes over me—Doe Abby is here. 'Oh, not much to tell, really. The usual upbringing—same nanny throughout my childhood—Nanny Ward. Prep school, college, gap year' —I ensure I say this as 'gap yah' to really sell it— 'university to study foreign policy, then a proper job. That's it, really.'

Doe Abby's potted history reveals that her social standing will be at least on par with Daniel's and he nods at me encouragingly. 'But your accent,' he says (Uh oh!), 'I'm trying so hard to place it.' Time to play my trump card—deflection, something I have become increasingly skilled at since I've been in the Manor.

'Oh, you needn't waste your time. Let's just say that it's been cultivated to be borderless—*region*-less, even.' I'm not sure how I'm coming up with this nonsense, but I smile enigmatically and take a sip of fizz to punctuate the point.

'But what do you m—'

'My job,' I say quickly to cut him off. 'I can't say much more, so you'll just have to take my word for it.' I've embellished my backstory a little—on paper, Doe Abby is a nondescript 'public servant'. Suddenly, Lisa's voice echoes in my mind. *'I'll be your de Bergerac,'* she'd said, referring to coaching me on all things 'growing up privileged'. What I hadn't counted on was that, in the moment, my mind would steal from her verbatim. Doe Abby is essentially Lisa, and as soon as I have the realisation, I know that I can successfully play this role for the next seven weeks. I'll just have to channel my bestie.

Daniel is looking at me with what seems like appreciation. 'You're an interesting one,' he says cryptically.

'How so?'

'Well, for one thing, you don't primp and preen like most of the other Does.' It's an accurate observation. I've seen a lot of primping and preening since we congregated in the Manor, especially as Harry is right about to call 'Action'—women arranging themselves 'just so', posing to look as alluring as possible. Whereas, I have no idea what my 'best side' is. Even the lovely Becca is a bit of a preener, but I can't agree with Daniel without coming across as catty.

'Oh, I think that's just extenuating circumstances, don't you? Everyone wanting to put their best foot forward?' There, that was diplomatic.

'Perhaps, but you don't seem to care about your appearance.' Ouch. That's a bit much, Daniel. My thoughts must sour my expression because his back-pedalling is almost comic. 'Oh no, sorry, not to say that you aren't attractive. You *are—very*.' Now he's laying it on a bit thick. 'I just meant that you're more of a *natural* beauty.' Hmm, definitely full of it.

'Like Kaz,' I say, taking another sip of fizz.

'I'm sorry.' A crease forms between his brows.

'*Kaz* is a natural beauty. That glorious red hair, that smile. She's quite winsome, don't you agree?' He squirms slightly and I must say, Doe Abby is finding this change in dynamic highly entertaining.

'Er, yes, quite,' he says, though it is obvious he thinks the polar opposite—his loss. Kaz is a darling. Regardless, I smile at Daniel benignly, inwardly chalking up the win.

This is the part of the conversation where I'm supposed to ask about him. 'So, did you always want to be a banker?' I ask, widening my eyes to appear especially interested. I take another tiny sip of fizz, peering at him over the rim of my glass.

He shrugs and, just for a moment, I get a glimpse of an *actual person*. Then he plasters on a smile and that person disappears. 'Family business, you know how it goes—almost a legacy. From about age seven I was telling everyone I was going to be a banker like my father. Of course, investment banking is far more complex than it was in my father's day. But I don't want to bore you with all that.'

'*I don't think you could possibly understand "all that",*' more like. Still, there is a melancholic thread just below Daniel's well-practised charm, and I can't help the stirrings of empathy. But right as I realise that he leans across to kiss me. I turn my head just in time and his lips land on my cheek.

'Don't look so shocked,' he says, a lilt of laughter in his

voice. 'As I've said, you're attractive and I find you interesting. Why wouldn't I want to kiss you?' he asks.

I must have a face like thunder because he laughs—full throated and blatantly at my expense, the sod—and just like that, any empathy I'd felt for him vanishes. 'You know, I've watched every season of *The Stag* …' I say, getting dangerously close to the truth.

'Is that so?' He leans back and crosses one ankle over his knee, his foot dangling. Classic power move—I must have him on the back foot (so to speak).

'It is, and the one thing that's always bothered me' —it's not the *one* thing, as Anastasia can attest to, but I am Doe Abby right now and she opted to come on this show— 'is how quick the Stag is to kiss all the Does. If you're throwing kisses about like a beauty queen at a parade, how are any of us supposed to take you—or this—seriously?' He frowns, but I can't tell if it's because he's considering what I'm saying or because he's not used to being told off.

'A first kiss is supposed to *mean* something, Daniel. It's supposed to be fraught with excitement, a delicious tension that builds and is only released when the lips come together. And then, there's a sort of melding of the two people, a sense of rightness.' His frown has morphed into something else—intrigue, perhaps.

'It certainly shouldn't be rushed, or ill-considered, or thrown away as though it's nothing,' I conclude. I realise when I stop talking—or would we call that a rant?—that this is Abby speaking. *Me*—not a fabrication that a producer conjured, then put down on a page.

Daniel's drops his foot to the ground and leans forward,

locking his eyes onto mine again. 'You're a romantic,' he says.

'I suppose I am.' I sip more fizz, just for something to do.

'Fascinating,' he adds, his eyes roaming my face like it holds the secrets to the universe.

Just as I am patting myself on the back for wangling my way out of kissing him—for now, anyway —Kylie appears at the top of the stairs, plants her hands on her hips and calls out, 'Is it my turn yet?' It's unclear whether she's been sent up here, but if she hasn't, then well played, Kylie!

Harry silently signals to her to move into shot. She catches on and looms over us, glaring down at me. 'Well? Can I talk to Daniel now?' she asks me. '*Alone*?' she adds, as if that wasn't already implied.

An out! Thank you, Kylie, you horrid woman. 'Absolutely! He's all yours,' I say. I leap up, realising I may have been a tad too willing to depart and, just to stir the pot, I lean down and kiss Daniel's cheek, lingering much longer than my lungs can stand. It really is awful cologne.

'Until next time,' I say to him pseudo-quietly, but purposefully loud enough for everyone else to hear. He looks up at me wide-eyed, a smile playing on his lips, and I hear a harrumph from Kylie. Oh, bollocks, I've forgotten to mention the view like Harry asked. 'And isn't that a gorgeous view!' I cry, my arms outstretched. I glance at Harry and he shakes his head at me—hmm, they may not be able to use that footage.

I cross to the stairs and just before I head down, I cast a glance at Jack, who's looking right at me and frowning. Not sure what to make of that, I raise a hand 'hello'. He mirrors the gesture but the frown stays firmly in place—perhaps he didn't like my line about the view either. He folds his arms and goes back to watching the Kylie–Daniel scene play out, and her throaty laugh bellows from behind me as I make my way downstairs.

'*You're a romantic,*' Daniel had said.

I suppose I am. Though a fat lot of good it's done me so far.

Before joining the others on the rear deck, I pause at the railing on the side of the boat and tilt my head to the sun, inhaling deep gulps of the fresh air. It's redolent with the brine of the water and, faintly, the lemony notes of eucalyptus trees. The yacht is cruising not far offshore and quite slowly it seems—though this is my first time on board a yacht, so I don't really have a point of comparison.

My eyes drink in the view as we pass some of the most beautiful homes I've ever seen—in person or in photos. Some are mostly glass and severe angles, like the one we're staying in, others are boxy and rendered in cement, an array of colours from stark white to a rainbow of pastels, some are more traditional. There's a mock Tudor and even a few faux Tuscan villas. Actually, that style seems to be quite popular along this stretch of coastline.

'She's a beauty, isn't she?'

Jack.

If I'm honest with myself, I'd hoped he'd come find me and a smile alights on my face as I turn towards him. 'The yacht?' I ask.

'Sydney,' he replies. 'The yacht's beautiful too, but I meant the city.'

I look back at the passing view. 'It is. But it's not *all* like this, is it?'

He chuckles softly. 'No, in some parts, it's like anywhere else, but still … You know, every time I fly in—especially from overseas—there's this real sense of homecoming, like it's awaiting my return so it can welcome me home.'

I look at him again and he seems wistful. 'Is London like that for you?' he asks, meeting my gaze.

'The city itself, you mean?' He nods. 'A little. I've been nostalgic for it at times since I've been here, but not in the way you describe. I mean, there's my mum's house—that's home to me—but London is just … it's just a city where I happen to live. But I haven't really been away that many times—just holidays, really, during the summer. It must be different when you travel a lot for work, then get to come home.'

'Yeah, maybe that's the difference. Hotel rooms lose their lustre when you're staying in them for long stints. You just want to be home.'

'Where *is* home for you?'

'Where do I live?'

I nod.

'Not far—Bronte. It's about five Ks that way,' he says, his arm extending over the rise of the hill in front of us.

'And you like it there?'

'Yeah, for sure. Me and Harry share a flat. It's in an older building—early last century—but it's been renovated so the kitchen and the bathroom are decent. High ceilings. Lotsa light. It's nice. And if you stand on your tiptoes, you can see the water from our balcony. "Water glimpses" they call it.' We share a smile.

'It sounds lovely.'

'Yeah, it's all right,' he says, his mouth spreading to a grin. 'Harry's super messy, though. He leaves his shit everywhere and sometimes I have to pull rank as big brother. You know, "clean up your room, baby bro," that kinda thing.'

Now I'm grinning. 'Do you fight over who does the washing-up?' I ask.

'Constantly. Nah, just kidding. I cook, he cleans up. He cooks, I clean up. Trade off, you know.'

'Sounds fair. Are you any good? At cooking?'

'Dunno. You'd have to ask Harry.'

'Did I hear my name?' When I turn around, Harry is coming downstairs from the upper deck. 'I hope he's not talking shit about me.' He pretends to eye his brother suspiciously.

'Quite the opposite,' I say. 'Jack says that of the two of you, you're the best cook.'

'Too right,' Harry says.

'And the most modest,' I quip, and Jack laughs loudly at his brother's expense.

'Hey! How can I be expected to be modest when I'm smarter *and* better looking than him?' Jack's laugh gets louder and I can tell this is a well-practised brotherly routine. 'Right, we need to get back at it. Abby, you should probably go join the others at the back of the boat. Jack, let's go talk to the captain about where to drop anchor.'

We disperse and, though I'm disappointed that my time with Jack has come to an end, I've had a little glimpse into his life here in Sydney. I had liked Jack almost instantly when we met in London——he's kind, he's intelligent and thoughtful——but seeing him here in his hometown, in his element, there's this easy-going side of him that's emerging. And, unfortunately, it makes him even more appealing.

But I need to keep my wits about me. Almost every move I make is on camera, I have two additional personas to keep straight, and I'm here to work. *Nothing* about this situation is conducive to falling in love. Ironic, right?

'*There* you are,' says Becca as I round the corner and emerge onto the rear deck. I catch a slight edge in her voice, hinting at those nerves she mentioned earlier. She probably thought I was up there with Daniel the whole time, trying to win his heart. 'I saved you a spot,' she adds, softening her tone and indicating the sun lounger next to her.

'Thank you,' I say, placing my beach bag next to it. We were told to bring a swimsuit, toiletries, and makeup so they can film us swimming off the boat after lunch, then we can freshen up for the afternoon. Jack said the plan is to film us on the deck at sunset, just before six. It's a long day——most of them are——and the expectation to be 'camera ready' for such extended periods is already testing my patience.

'You're looking very *nautical* today, Abby,' says Daphne from the lounger next to Becca's. I look over at her, then down at my outfit of navy linen shorts, a Breton top, and navy espadrilles. I can't tell if she's being genuine or having a laugh.

'Er, thank you,' I say before settling onto my lounger.

Just as I stretch out my legs and wriggle into a comfortable position, she adds, 'You've taken today's outing so *liter-*

ally. How very sweet.' Her voice drips with condescension and I cannot believe I thought—even for a moment—that she was being complimentary.

I retrieve my sunglasses from my beach bag and put them on. When I turn in Daphne's direction, I lower them and peer at her over the top. 'How very kind of you to say so, Daphne. Though, I'd give anything to master that OTT High Street look like you have.' I slide the glasses back into place and watch her just long enough to see her mouth drop open before I turn away. I lean back against my sun lounger and seconds later, a hand clasps mine, squeezing it quickly before letting go—solidarity from Becca.

'Daphne, we're setting up for your alone time with Daniel,' calls a member of the film crew from the upper deck. Daphne pops up like a Jack-in-the-box and stalks off, her heels clacking on the deck.

'Oh, you gave her a serve, you did,' says Kaz who's lounging across from us, chuckling. I shrug. 'Nah, really. Even *I* could tell and I have no idea why "High Street" is so insulting.'

Elizabeth, also across from us, sits up and moves to the end of her lounger, then scans the deck for cameras. None about at the moment—a reprieve. We're all wearing microphones but even though they're switched on throughout filming—the frequent battery changes being a tiresome ritual I'm still not accustomed to—we've been assured they'll only use the audio if there's accompanying footage.

'"High Street" is only really an insult to someone like Daphne,' Elizabeth says to Kaz in hushed tones. 'It's saying that she shops in chain stores.'

'Ahhh, right. Yeah, that makes sense,' says Kaz. 'Totally up herself, that one. We get it, love, you're like, super rich and fancy. The way she tells it, you'd reckon she has eligible men lining up round the block.'

'Because of her title you mean?' asks Elizabeth.

'Yeah. Her family must be loaded, right?' asks Kaz. 'Makes you wonder why she even came on this show.'

'It does make you think,' says Elizabeth. 'She doesn't *seem* to be here for love.'

'Definitely not,' says Becca. 'You can tell the ones who are.' She looks at the three of us. 'Like us.'

Elizabeth nods solemnly. 'Although, I'm not sure Daniel would want to be with someone like me.'

'Why do you say that, Lizzie?' asks Kaz.

I have two thoughts at once——Elizabeth is definitely not a 'Lizzie' and, as I've previously contemplated, I agree with her about Daniel. Elizabeth is kind-hearted——a truly lovely person——but I can't imagine Daniel valuing that trait above status, or beauty, or wit.

'It's just … well, you have so much personality, Kaz. You're vivacious and full of life …'

'Aww, thanks,' Kaz replies, beaming.

'And, Becca, you're beautiful and brilliant …' I glance at Becca who presses her lips together rather than graciously accepting the compliment. 'And you're so bold, Abby. You always say what the rest of us are thinking.'

I hadn't realised I've been doing that——or rather, that Doe Abby has. It's no doubt a by-product of not caring one iota if Daniel wants me or not. I'm here to do a job, and that's it. 'And, you're looking out for us,' adds Elizabeth. 'Well, those of us who are less … uh …'

'Less bitchy? That the word you're looking for, Lizzie?' asks Kaz.

That brings a small smile to Elizabeth's face and she shrugs. 'I suppose so. I wouldn't want to put that label on anyone, though.'

'And that right there is exactly why you have as much a chance with Daniel as anyone,' I say, matter-of-factly. 'You are genuine and kind and lovely. He'd be lucky to have you,' I say. 'Very,' I mutter to myself.

She seems to accept that and, nodding shyly, returns to her reclined position and goes back to her book. From the title and the cover, it's a gruesome crime thriller and it's a hint that there is more to this sweet, softly spoken woman than meets the eye.

Kaz throws an arm over her eyes. 'I'm gonna have a snooze, girls. Wake me if I start to go pink,' she says.

'That was nice of you,' says Becca quietly. I look over at her.

'Just telling the truth. Elizabeth *is* lovely.'

'Yeah, but these girls are our competition. *We're* in competition too.'

'You really like him, don't you?' I ask.

'Yes, I do. He's so charming, you know. There's this confidence about him that's …' I resist the urge to complete her thought with 'incredibly arrogant'. 'Aussie guys, they're different. Most of the guys I've dated, they're super laidback, not a care in the world, the "loveable larrikin" type—which is nice for a laugh, but it wears thin when you realise that they expect you to do all the work in the relationship.'

'Right. That sounds——'

'It's exhausting, is what it is,' she says, cutting me off.

'I can only imagine,' I reply, having little frame of reference. But if I ever end up in a proper relation-ship—sorry, *when* I do—I want it to be a partnership. I want to be with someone I can lean on *and* support, someone who thinks about me and my needs as much as they let me look after them and theirs. I'd hate being the one 'doing all the work'.

'You know, my girlfriends think I'm stupid for coming on the show. They're all on dating apps. "Come on, Becca, it's that not hard; just swipe right." But besides my best friend, Julie—her partner is one of the very few good ones out there—most of my friends end up dating dickheads and losers. And, yeah, there are some guys at uni that seem nice, but they're, like, super shy, and if I try to talk to them or hang out, they run a mile in the other direction, like they're afraid of me or something.'

'They probably are,' I interject, 'intimidated, I mean.'

'Or maybe they just want to keep to themselves and I'm bothering them,' she concludes glumly.

'I'm sure that's not it, Becca.' How is she so insecure? I'd love to delve into this further but there's a camera pointed at us now and I'm not sure she's realised. She takes a deep breath and sighs it out, then starts a little as she notices the camera. When her eyes meet mine, they ask, 'How much have I revealed?'

'So,' I say, feeding her the next line, 'you're looking for

someone who is confident, someone who can hold their own with you, a true partner.'

'That's right,' she says, composing herself, 'and Daniel, he's so confident in who he is. I find that really attractive.'

I nod, pretending to agree and in my periphery, the camera operator give us a thumbs up—he's got what he needs. He then swings the camera onto Elizabeth and Kaz, who's snoring softly. God, I hope Harry and Jack don't feel the need to put *that* in the show.

'Thank you—again,' says Becca reaching for my hand again and giving it a squeeze.

'Really, it's nothing.'

'It's not nothing to me. I know we're in competition, but I'd like to think of us as friends. Is that weird?'

'No, not at all. Friends,' I say, and we share a smile.

'It's weird, don't you think?'

'What is?' I roll on my side and face Becca who's propped up in her bed, an abandoned book in her lap.

'This. All of it. Sometimes it hits me that I'm in this house, on this show, like I'm really *in* it now, and I get this weird sense of claustrophobia. Do you get that?'

YES. All the bloody time! And this is Stag Manor and not a steamy jungle teeming with creepy crawlies and deadly animals like in *I'm Super Famous, I Want Out*. Aside: Why would anyone sign up for that show?

'It *is* odd,' I say, schooling my tone so this sounds like a normal conversation. Becca doesn't need to know that I'm constantly on the brink of blowing this ruse to kingdom come. Although, every day it gets a little easier not to obliterate my career with a carelessly chosen word. Perhaps, by the time I leave the Manor, I may actually be ready for this assignment.

'I keep thinking about my girlfriends,' she says her face fixed in a frown.

'What about them?' I prod.

'Do *you* think I was stupid to sign up for this? I mean, I know you did too and we all have our reasons for being here but …' She trails off and I'm again struck by how little esteem Becca seems to have for herself—and I should know. It's like gazing into a mirror. But I'm not *me* right now.

'You came here with the hope of finding someone who's a good match, someone who sees you as you are, right?' I don't mention the absurdity of pinning her hopes on Daniel, as he seems fixated on her appearance, nor that she doesn't seem to understand her own value.

'Glass houses, Abby. Lisa would say the same about you,' I remind myself. Shoving aside my own (dire) need for introspection, I say, 'Then that's as good a reason as any. Look, these days there are a million ways to meet someone.' Such as being rescued from a murderous lift. 'And think of the success stories that have come out of this show—several couples are still together in the UK—*and* here in Australia.' *'And even more couples haven't lasted,'* I think but don't say.

'Mmm, true,' she says. 'So, why did you decide to come on the show, Abby? You've never said.'

I remember the conversations I had with Lisa leading up to this assignment, her convincing me to focus on the positives—an entirely new wardrobe, a free trip to Sydney, keeping my job at Feed Your Mind, and most importantly, writing my exposé—my breakout piece—and kickstarting my (hugely successful) career as an investigative journalist.

And of course, there's Jack and the chance to get to know the gorgeous, quick-witted, affable Australian—as a friend, yes, but perhaps as something more …

I may be here on assignment, but I still have an answer to Becca's question. 'Hope,' I say simply.

Chapter Ten

'Abby, will you wear this pin?' says Daniel. He's far too close and wearing more cologne than usual, but I smile up at him and say, 'Of course,' as though it's perfectly natural to be standing on a beach in a cocktail dress and heels. Speaking of, I shift my weight onto my toes to keep from sinking into the sand as Daniel takes a small metallic pin shaped like antlers and slides it onto the neckline of my dress. I give myself a mental brownie point for not flinching as the pin pricks my chest, then smile at Daniel and take my place in the row of Does who have all been 'pinned'.

Gordo steps forward and with the solemnity of a funeral director, says his line. 'Merrin, I'm very sorry to say that you haven't received a pin and, therefore, it's time for you to leave Stag Manor.'

Merrin looks more relieved than a dumped Doe should, and I imagine she's looking forward to getting back to Tasmania and her five 'fur babies' as she calls her cats. She gives the remaining Does hugs goodbye—something barely tolerated by Daphne, Tara, and Kylie—and waves cheerily as she tromps up the beach, her gown bunched in one hand to make the going easier.

'And that's a wrap, everyone,' calls Harry.

'Oh, thank bleedin' 'ell for that!' says Wonder Villain Tara as she whips off her heels, digs her microphone and battery pack out of her dress, shoving them into Carlie's hands, and without so much as a 'goodnight', departs the waterside scene.

'Goodnight, ladies,' says Daniel. He smiles and waves—I'm now convinced he thinks he's Prince William—then crosses the sand and strides up the path to the Manor. His town car will be waiting out front to take him to the Stag's apartment, not far from here in Rose Bay.

I slip off my shoes and pick them up to tip out the sand, then scrunch my toes into the tiny granules. Heaven. Post-filming duties have now become routine and we adeptly 'de-Doe' while the crew packs up cables, lights, cameras, and sound equipment. Once free from wires and battery packs, we assemble in a loose knot of four.

'We doing the usual?' asks Kaz, who also has her shoes in hand.

'I am,' I say. For us, 'the usual' is our post-Pin Ritual gathering on the patio overlooking the water. As the other Does scurry back inside, likely to get out of their uncomfortable attire and get ready for bed, Kaz, Elizabeth, Becca, and I take our time meandering up to 'our spot'.

'I'll grab us some bubbly,' says Kaz, disappearing inside.

'Looks like someone's trying to get your attention, Abby,' Becca whispers to me.

'Sorry?' I follow her line of sight to Jack, who's standing half in the shadows and looking our way. We're not supposed to be meeting up tonight, so I wait for some sort of signal that something urgent has come up. A moment passes. No signal—just rumpled handsomeness and a friendly wave.

'Goodnight,' he calls in our direction.

'Goodnight,' we say in unison as he disappears around the side of the Manor towards the annex.

'He was just being friendly—to all of us,' I say to Becca quietly, hoping that I'm right *and* wrong. Right because Jack absolutely *cannot* show me any favouritism or undue attention—it would be highly inappropriate and might blow our cover. And wrong because I *want* him to show me undue attention. In fact, I want him to show me all kinds of attention that would be deemed 'undue' and 'inappropriate'.

'Uh, huh,' she says, casting me another side-eye. She's been doing that a lot lately; perhaps she suspects that Jack and I have more than a producer–Doe relationship.

Now that we are well into the season—week four of filming—Jack and I have established our working routine and several times a week, we meet in the Control Room to view 'the dailies', raw footage of the show. It was my idea—*solely* to enhance my recaps, mind you. Sometimes Harry joins us, but he's usually off doing production preparation, so it's just me and Jack.

But although he's friendly, Jack always maintains a professional distance—both in proximity and behaviour. Since we started filming, there's never been even the *slightest* hint of flirtation. I sometimes wonder if I imagined our flirtatious banter in the lounge at Heathrow and on our flight. Even if it did happen, that feels like a century ago and coupled with Jack's belief that I might fall for Daniel—snort! As if!—I'm certain I've been 'friend-zoned'.

Still, there's no harm in fantasising, right?

But on reflection, perhaps there is. Becca is smart and more than once, I *may* have returned to the room after 'meditating'—my terribly wanting alibi—grinning from ear to ear and feeling all swoony. I'll need to be more careful lest I give the game away. And, apparently, so will Jack.

I say nothing more, hoping the matter will be forgotten and stretch out on one of the sun loungers, though the sun is long gone and above us are a myriad of stars dotting the inky sky. It's beautiful out here, a fragrant breeze carrying the tang of citronella candles, lit to keep the mosquitoes at bay for night shoots. As the others settle in to the left of me, I tear my gaze away from the overhead vista and stare down at my poor feet, which are rubbed raw from wearing heels in the sand.

But despite my sore feet and dating a man I cannot stand, I have a lot to be grateful for, particularly that amongst the cows and the cats, I've made three lovely girl-friends—something hoped for but also surprising. I'm also grateful that after a lengthy evening of filming, the others don't feel the need to fill the silence. Even when Kaz arrives with the fizz, she pours in silence, handing around the glasses and, unspoken, we agree to sip quietly and just *be*. How lovely is that?

As I sip, I do a mental roll call. Merrin was the fourth Doe to depart Stag Manor. As I predicted (or rather, as

Anastasia did), Filler Does, Tabitha and Laura, were the first two to depart. Dark Horse Ellie—she with the ventriloquist's dummy—is also gone. Not surprising, really. She was sweet but she also brought that dummy out at every opportunity and Jack and Harry had a quiet word in Daniel's ear about sending her home. Daniel had been reticent at first, with Ellie being one of the most attractive women in the Manor, but he relented after she took Little Ellie on a group date to Taronga Zoo, upsetting the (poor) squirrel monkeys.

So that leaves eight. The four of us, Tara and Kylie (the British and Australian Villains), Justine (wannabe actress and potential Bride), and Queen Cow Daphne, who according to Jack, is still Roberta's number one pick for Bride.

The 'Us and Them' dichotomy that started out as the UK versus Australia, has now become 'Naughty versus Nice', like Father Christmas is in the Manor and has assigned each of us to a list. But only in my mind—I'd never mention it to the others.

'I'll miss Merrin,' says Elizabeth quietly.

'She was lovely,' I reply. 'But I sensed she was incredibly homesick.'

'Sensed? Come on, Abs,' says Kaz, 'She was dying to get out of here. All us girls crammed in here together? She hated it—definitely the most introverted of the lot of us.'

'More so than me?' asks Elizabeth.

'For sure, Liz. You're really coming out of your shell.' I glance across at Elizabeth—or Lizzie or Liz, depending on Kaz's mood—and she's biting her lip, a smile threatening to break free.

'Kaz is right,' says Becca. 'Think about the date on the

yacht. You didn't even get alone time with Daniel' —Ouch, that's a little harsh, Becca— 'but then he picked you for the one-on-one cooking date! And you said it went well.' Becca is being magnanimous. She was desperate for that cooking date, yet here she is plastering on a smile in support of Elizabeth.

Maybe she doesn't think of Elizabeth as a threat. I wonder if she thinks that *I* am.

Elizabeth beams. 'It did go really well. He's a bit hopeless in the kitchen, to be honest, and I'm not saying I'm the best cook in the world, but the chef did compliment my knife skills. And Daniel … well, he …' She trails off but as I've already seen it play out onscreen, I know what she's about to say. I cringe inwardly, anticipating the epic fallout from her next words.

'He kissed me,' she says, plainly pleased with herself. She sips her fizz, perhaps to hide the blush that's stealing up her cheeks.

Becca and Kaz's reactions are polar opposites. 'Good for you,' says Kaz, good-naturedly backhanding Elizabeth on the shoulder. It's become clearer over the past couple of weeks that Kaz is here more for the camaraderie and 'a break from it all' than she's here for Daniel—and this solidifies my opinion.

Becca, on the other hand, is silent. When I glance down the line of loungers at her, her jaw is set and I can't tell if she's angry or hurt or some awful mix of both. 'You didn't say anything about him kissing you,' she says quietly.

'Oh, um, I …' Elizabeth's voice trails off into vapour. Because what is there to say? There were twelve of us—all seemingly vying for the same man—and now there are eight. The situation is, at best, bizarre and, at worst, *The Hunger Games*. This is a Doe-eat-Doe world they've created here on the banks of the most beautiful waterway in the world.

And for some of the Does, the feelings are real. It matters to Elizabeth—probably more than it should—that Daniel has shown her even a morsel of attention, let alone *kissed* her. It matters to Becca—again, more than it should—that he falls in love with her, because she has it in her head that there is no one in this entire country who can give her what (she thinks) she wants.

And here I sit, in this privileged position, where I know that Daniel didn't want a one-on-one date with Elizabeth ('the quiet one', as he calls her), but that Roberta had insisted as a mid-season red herring. I can only imagine why he kissed her—he's monstrously vain, so maybe he just felt like it, having no regard whatsoever for her feelings.

I stare up at the sky, awash with an overwhelming helplessness. I cannot think of a thing to say that will re-establish the fragile bubble of friendship that we've been building. 'I'm going to bed,' says Becca suddenly. She leaves so quickly, there's a slight breeze in her wake.

'Me too,' says Elizabeth, slipping away with a frown on her face.

'Goodnight,' I call benignly at their backs.

'Night, girls,' says Kaz.

My mind ticks over and I realise that I have my story—the *real* story for my exposé—about how damaging this show is, how fragile friendships form in a matter of days, even hours, then shatter in a moment. How the very premise of the show is designed to manipulate women's self-esteem.

Kaz gets up and moves to the lounger next to mine. 'Well, this part sucks,' she says. Her words break the tension and the snigger that rises from my chest and escapes is a relief. My idea dissipates but I'll come back to it later. 'You okay?' she asks as I expel a long sigh. I turn to look at her, my new what-you-see-is-what-you-get friend, and her concern is evident.

I shrug. 'Not really.'

'Yeah, when I signed up for this, I thought, "What the hell? I might find love and if I don't, I might make a friend." And now I've made three. Look, you might've guessed that I reckon Daniel is a prize dick …' I snigger again and she nods '… and that's probably because he is.' At that, I bark out a laugh, then clap my hand over my mouth. It's rather late and I don't want to disturb the others.

'And I really have no idea why he's kept me around as long as he has,' Kaz continues. *I* do—she's extremely entertaining and the viewers will adore her—but I keep quiet. 'I mean, we're chalk 'n' cheese, but I plan on staying as long as possible, just to hang out with you girls.'

'And, no offense, if *you* like him,' she adds.

'Oh, none taken,' I reply.

'*Do* you?'

'Do I what?'

'Like Daniel. Have feelings for him?'

'Oh, er, I'm still testing the waters, I suppose. I mean, love is … it's a big thing, isn't it?' I sound like a blithering idiot; I'm glad this exchange isn't being filmed.

I glance at her and she is peering at me, a curious smile on her lips. 'And you're not just sticking around because of that producer guy, right? Jack?'

Oh, bollocks. 'What do you mean?' Bollocks, bollocks, bollocks. I *knew* I'd be terrible at the deception part. I've obviously let my guard down and first Becca and now Kaz are onto me.

'Look, if you *don't* like Daniel and you wanted to leave, you could just say no to the pin, right?' she asks.

'Yes, I suppose.'

'I mean *I* say yes because this has already been one of the best holidays of my life. But I get the feeling that you've got other reasons.' I bite my lip. God, I will never, ever play poker; I'd lose the shirt off my back. 'It's okay,' she says reassuringly. 'I promise I won't say anything, but I've seen the way you look at him—Jack. And, hey, you've come all this way to find love. So what if it's not with the Stag? Who cares? This is all just bullshit anyway.'

Sod it, she's right—about *everything*. This conversation confirms it—I need to be much more careful around Jack. And I'm going to have to tell him to do the same around me. His friendly waves and our little chats may be innocuous to him, but they could jeopardise this whole charade.

'All right, Abby love, I'll let you go,' says Mum.

'Have a lovely afternoon, Mum.' I can just picture her sitting in her tiny conservatory, cup of tea getting cold on the table by her chair, a Georgette Heyer book, open and inverted, placed next to it. The sting of missing her is acute.

'Oh, and one more thing …' There's always 'one more thing' she wants to tell me as we wrap up our weekly calls. 'Your Aunty Lo says to send a photograph of you cuddling a koala.'

I laugh quietly. I can just imagine what Aunty Lo *actually* said, especially as she thinks I'm here on an extended holiday. Probably something like, *'And tell her that a cuddle from a koala is almost as good as a cuddle from a man.'* She's a character, my aunty, and she's been fixated on my (mostly non-existent) love life since I was seventeen. But I'm so grateful Mum has her close by——particularly with me being across the world.

'You tell Aunty Lo that I'll do my best,' I say quietly.

'All right, will do. Keep well, Abby. I love you.'

'I love you too, Mum.' It's one of the few truths I've been able to share in weeks.

'Bye now.'

'Bye.' I blow a kiss down the line and end the call. My ear is hot from where I've had the phone pressed against it for the last twenty minutes, but I can't chance the sound of a tinny voice echoing around the room and alerting the others to my clandestine labours. I may be tucked away at the back of the property in my little hidey hole, but I'm not sure how soundproof it is.

I lean back against the uncomfortable folding chair and assess my current situation. I'm miles from home and anyone who loves me, I've barely made a dent in my exposé, and I have a massive, completely inappropriate crush on

Jack who, even if he did feel the same way, couldn't act on it or he'd probably lose his job.

But that's just me fooling myself, or rather *torturing* myself. There's no way Jack feels the same way. We're friends and nothing more. I am one of three people on this entire show who knows his true motivations for producing it. He simply sees me as an ally, someone who understands that ambition can drive you to sell a piece of your soul to make your dreams come true.

There should be a word for that—like one of those compound German words. Aside: I've always loved those words—so precise and clever. Let's see …

roleplaybetrayexposépayday

Perfect. It even rhymes. So that's my word, but what about Jack's? He just wants to finish this project, bank the money, and start his and Harry's production company.

soulsellingnottellingsavingupforstorytelling

Hmm, not bad.

There's an unexpected tap on the door. It eases open and there he is as if I've conjured him—Jack. My poor friend-zoned heart starts galloping, but I school my face into a welcoming, *platonic* expression.

'Run out of kitchen roll at home?' I hear myself say. *I* may sometimes forget that I'm witty, but at least my mind doesn't.

He grins—a response that's incommensurate with my meagre joke. 'Mind if I come in?' I shake my head and he slips into the room and closes the door softly behind him. Today's T-shirt says, 'Same shirt, different day'—clever.

'Talking to someone at home?' he asks, indicating the phone on the card table.

'My mum.'

'And how is she?' It's nice that he's asking, but it is extremely late and there's no reason for him to still be at the Manor—that I can think of, anyway. So, he's either stayed around long enough to have this conversation, or he's gone home and come back again. Either way, I can tell he has something important to say and he seems to be hedging.

'Mum's fine. She's been spending a lot of time with her closest friend lately, Lois—my Aunty Lo.'

He smiles. 'That's good. She must be missing you.' I nod, my eyes locked onto his. God, he has lovely, lovely eyes. They match his lovely, lovely mouth and everything else that's lovely about him. I need a new word. Writers always have words they overuse and mine has recently become 'lovely'.

'Look, there's something I want to talk to you about,' he says. Finally, we're getting to the crux of why he's here.

'Yes, I know.'

He blinks at me, confusion stamped on his face. 'You …?'

'Jack, it's' —I glance at the phone to see the time— '12:13am, which is late even by your standards and it's only by chance that I'm in here, but you must have thought it important enough to check. *And* we've worked in close proximity for a while now. You have your tells.'

He grins mischievously. 'Is that so, *Abigail*?'

Now it's my turn to blink at him. Well, game on! 'That is so, *Jack*. I can tell when you've had enough of Daphne's rudeness, or Tara's swearing, or how frustrated you are when Gordo messes up his line for the fiftieth time. I know when you just want to get the shot so you can eat, that you find it near-impossible to make any decisions first thing in the morning until you've downed three back-to-back coffees, and that sometimes you think we're funny when we're not supposed to be and you struggle to keep a straight face.'

Oh, god. It really is late. I should never have said all of that. I sound like a stalker. One with a massive crush. At least I didn't mention that I know how he likes said coffee. Though I do——black, two sugars.

'I sometimes forget that you're also Anastasia and have that amazing eye for detail,' he says, amusement creasing the corners of his eyes. Thank god he didn't say, *'I sometimes forget you're an investigative journalist ...'* He may suspect that I am writing my own piece, but I hope he doesn't——and if he *does* ... Oh, god, I hate all of this.

Deflect! 'So, what is it?' I ask.

'Oh, right.' He shakes his head and stands up straighter. 'So, I had a call with Roberta today.' This is not news; he speaks to her most days. 'And she's *loving* your scenes with Daniel, especially the chemistry between the two of you ...' The *what?!* I must be a better actress than I thought. '... so, she's reconsidered your ranking...' Oh, god——*please*, let him not finish this sentence. 'And she's decided that you're now top two.'

Ugh, he finished it——exactly how I knew he would. Where is Cadmus the God of Writing now and why isn't he looking after *this* writer on this stupid, *stupid* assignment?

This is *not* how I wanted things to go—top two was *not* the agreement.

'Wait …' A sudden thought sickens me. 'What about Becca?' Becca is falling hard for Daniel and if I'm moving into a top-two slot, then where does that leave *her*?

'She'll stay in the top four along with Justine.' He says this matter-of-factly and until I came on this show, I would never have believed it was possible to manipulate someone the way that Roberta intends to manipulate Daniel—sorry, has *already* manipulated Daniel.

'Daphne's still Roberta's top pick for Bride,' Jack continues. So, not only will this hurt Becca, but they're pitting me against Daphne? Er, *no*. I'd prefer to avoid her wrath, thank you very much. '*Unless …*'

'Unless what?' As my mind scrambles to latch onto a shred of clarity in this appalling turn of events, there's another horror just out of grasp.

'Unless *you*—' He stops speaking abruptly and I'd bet a million pounds it's because of the expression on my face.

'Unless I want Daniel for myself? Is that what you're saying?'

'I just thought …'

'You just thought that *I*, a professional journalist,' —that's laying it on a bit thick, as I am only here as a staff writer— 'someone who is here simply to do a job that I didn't even want, was *forced* to take, in fact' —he visibly flinches at that, but I am on a roll and I am not backing down— 'would actually fall for a pompous, vacuous idiot like Daniel, because what? Because he's not bad looking and has a lot of money? Because I should be *flattered* that someone like that would even look twice at me?'

'No, I … that's not—'

'I'm not *Elizabeth*, Jack.' It's cruel to say that about my friend, even if it is true, and I hate myself for it. This assignment is turning me into a version of myself that I don't particularly care for.

Jack's eyes narrow and a vein pulses in his neck. 'Okay, thanks for clarifying that,' he says tersely. 'Stupid of me to even consider your happiness.' He goes to leave. But I can't let him—not yet. What about Becca?

'Jack!' His hand drops from the door handle and he turns around. 'Do you think we can get Roberta to change her mind? Becca … well, she really likes Daniel and … can we talk Roberta out of it?'

He shrugs. 'Look, it's not like it's a done deal. You know how it works—we can guide Daniel but, ultimately, it's his choice.' I notice how he says 'guide' instead of 'manipulate' but let that go. 'You don't want to end up top two, don't give him any reason to keep you around,' he adds.

'Right. You mean while simultaneously pretending that I really like him and hope he'll choose me?' I retort.

'Yeah, something like that,' he says, his eyes cold.

He goes to leave again, but while he's here I may as well raise the other thing. 'Also …' The muscles in his shoulders tense and he faces me again, his expression devoid of friendliness. Ironically, that's exactly what I'm about to mention. 'I know that we've been working closely and that a …' I want to say 'friendship' but that may not be the right word, especially now. '… a familiarity has formed between us …' He nods curtly and it takes all my will to say the next words. '… but some of the Does have started to notice and—'

He cuts me off by raising his hand. 'Yep, I got it. No worries.'

He turns to leave. This time I don't stop him and he doesn't even say goodbye.

After the door closes, I stare down at the phone on the card table. I did the right thing. If Jack genuinely thought that I might be interested in Daniel, then he doesn't know me and we aren't really friends. And with this new turn of events … God, I'm hating Roberta from afar right now. Maybe a tornado will whip up and deposit a Kansas farmhouse on top of her.

And Jack … he'd looked so … crestfallen, hurt, angry … all of the above.

I did the right thing, didn't I?

Chapter Eleven

'So, Abby,' says Carlie, the production assistant, 'describe what you like most about Daniel.'

She had to start with the hardest question. I'm on camera, filming a confessional and I'm supposed to reveal my innermost thoughts (well, Doe Abby's) to be shared with millions of viewers around the world. Of all the pretending I've had to do, including with Daniel, I find confessionals the hardest. The camera is *so close* and I know from watching the dailies and rough edits that they zoom *right in*.

This means that every twitch and eyelash flutter, every nuance of what I say and how I say it is captured for all the (viewing) world to see. I don't even like photographs of me——I'm constantly telling Lisa to delete the ones she takes——and it's been no fun at all to discover that what I've been telling myself all this time is modesty, is actually vanity.

Abigail Jones, just as vain as the next woman, at your service.

And it's not like we're sequestered away in private for these confessionals; we're set up in a corner of the garden where the crew has erected a trellis draped in fake greenery. It's a little cringeworthy—how garish it is, yes, but also how exposed we are. I know from experience that anyone who wants to listen—*as in the other Does*—can, and easily.

It also doesn't help one bit that Jack is *right there*, leaning against the garden wall with his arms crossed, watching me and scowling. I hate that we've gone from friends to colleagues—make that *hostile* colleagues—and I've yet to find the right time to apologise for jumping down his throat the other night. I may have been a tad over sensitive. Carlie's also watching me, her growing impatience evident.

'Well, Daniel's so charming,' I say, Doe Abby speak for 'smarmy'. Carlie circles her finger in the air, a signal to continue. 'And, he has a great sense of adventure,' I add with what I hope is a convincing smile. That translates to Daniel doing any bizarre, awkward thing that he's asked to do for the sake of the show. Like a couple of days ago when he and three of the Does finger-painted each other, then rolled around on a canvas to make 'art'. I'm not joking.

It was like something you'd see at the Playboy Mansion, not Stag Manor. Still, those catty cows, Tara and Kylie, and wannabe Justine had seemed into it—especially Justine. It's like she's gone from dreaming of a role on *Neighbours* to starring in something a little more … er … *adult*.

Carlie's finger loops faster. 'And, I mean, Daniel's so …' I drop the façade, my smile fading and my shoulders slumping.

'Cut,' says Carlie.

'Sorry,' I say. 'I'm just a little self-conscious talking like this.' Well, that's not a lie, even if my reasons differ from Doe Abby's. I glance in Jack's direction and his scowl has intensified. *'Go away, Jack,'* I will him with my mind. Sadly, I have no mind control ability whatsoever; otherwise, he would have fallen madly in love with me by now and swept me away from all this madness.

Jack remains rooted to the spot, his jaw tense and his eyes hard. He's like a solar eclipse—compelling, yet dangerous. *'Look away, Abby, look away!'* I tell myself. Too late, my emotional retinas are burnt to a crisp.

Carlie's expression is hardly any better with her lips pressed into a frustrated smile. 'How about this?' she says. 'Just say a few words about how Daniel makes you feel.'

Hah, if only! Incensed. Annoyed. Bored. Mildly disgusted. *Very* annoyed. *'Come on, Abby, you can do this. You spin words out of thin air for a living.'* The internal pep talk works. 'All right,' I say, sitting up straight. Carlie smiles, genuinely this time, though it's likely just relief. Mine is the last Doe confessional for the day and I'm sure she's desperate to wrap up proceedings and get home.

'And we're rolling. Any time you're ready, Abby,' she says.

'When I'm with Daniel, he makes me feel special,' I say as convincingly as possible, adding a shy half-shrug to really sell it.

'Cut. That's perfect, Abby, thank you.' She starts packing up as I disentangle myself from my microphone. In my periphery, I notice Jack slinking off to the annex.

'Abby! Come on!' calls Kaz. She, Becca, and Justine are waiting for me on the patio so we can play gin rummy, which has somehow (under Kaz's governance) turned into a drinking game.

'Coming!' I call. 'I just need a quick wee.'

'Gross, Abs,' says Becca. Since learning Lisa's nickname for me, Becca has adopted it, which I *love*; it makes me miss my bestie a teeny bit less.

'Sorry,' I call over my shoulder. When I enter the Manor, Elizabeth is on one of the ridiculously long sofas (definitely a Stag Manor staple, no matter which continent it's filmed on), her feet tucked under her and reading a book. I make a detour and perch on the end of the sofa. 'Hello,' I say. Her eyes scan to the end of a line and then lift to meet mine.

'Hello.' Her tone lacks its usual sweetness but I forge ahead.

'We're playing gin rummy out on the patio if you'd like to join us,' I say hopefully.

She looks outside, scans the group, then frowns, her eyes dropping back to the book. 'I'd rather read.'

I suspected she'd say as much. Since the night of the last Pin Ritual, when she told us about kissing Daniel, Elizabeth has actively avoided Becca and, to some extent, me and Kaz. Last night, she walked into the living room and the second she saw Becca, did an about-face.

'I don't know how to make things right,' Becca said to me later in our room. 'I like Elizabeth, I do, but … god, that was so hard hearing her talk about Daniel like that. Argh, this sucks! Should I even try to fix things, Abs?'

It was an excellent question and I could tell Becca felt

awful but I didn't have an answer for her then and even now, as I try to cajole Elizabeth into joining us, I'm not sure it's the right thing to do. I hate that there's a rift between them, and so does Becca, but this is a *competition*. What did I expect? That we'd all become best friends and, as each of us are picked off and packed up, we'd simply carry on merrily?

'Are you sure?' I ask Elizabeth.

She puts down her book and gives me a look that is one hundred per cent schoolmarm, a side of her I haven't seen before. 'I'm sure, Abby.'

Just then, Gordo arrives through the front door, trailed by Harry and Tim, who's carrying a camera on his shoulder. '*Layyy-deees!* Gather round please,' Gordo sings out.

This is unexpected, as we thought we'd finished filming for the day. My fellow card players come in from the patio and the other Does drift into the lounge room from the kitchen and upstairs. Some pairs of eyes are wild with excitement, some weary, others (like mine) wary. When Gordo shows up unannounced, it's to announce something, like a date.

The camera pans across the gathered Does, and the not-so-subtle adjustments are almost comical—shoulders back, stomach in, chin lifted, 'best side' towards the camera. I don't bother to disguise my annoyance—I really was looking forward to playing cards. I wonder if Harry and Jack will include the footage of me frowning at Gordo when they edit together the next episode.

'So, ladies, you're probably wondering why I am here.' Out of the corner of my eye, I catch Daphne tuck her razor-sharp blonde bob behind her ears. '*Preener*,' I think unkindly.

Gordo pulls a glossy envelope out of his inside coat pocket and holds it aloft. 'Inside this envelope are the names of three *incredibly lucky ladies*.' He lingers on the last three words—perhaps he gets paid by the second. And I'm not sure how he's done it but from his mouth, the word 'ladies' is steeped in innuendo. Lll-ayyy-deees. Ewww.

'Tomorrow, these three Does will be going on a special date with Daniel tooo …' More upbeat than usual, Gordo is dragging this out as if he's announcing the BAFTA for Best Actress in a television series. Come to think of it, I could be in the running for that this year. '… the Hunter Valley for a day of wine tasting!' Ooh, that sounds *wonderful*. For the first time since we started filming, I hope my name is in Gordo's envelope.

'Now, who will the lucky ladies be?' He waves it around like a magician at a children's birthday party. *Someone*—likely Harry, or perhaps even Jack—has had a word in Gordo's ear. His line delivery has vastly improved. Gordo the Magnificent is much better than Gordo the funeral director and I mentally file that away for Anastasia's next recap.

Gordo breaks the seal of the envelope and pulls out a stiff card, reads it, then looks about the room. 'Daphneee …' The Ice Queen's shoulders do a smug little shimmy. 'Beccaaa …' Becca's behind me, leaning against one of the floor-to-ceiling glass doors and when I catch her eye, she winks at me, a broad grin on her face. I turn back around, hoping that the final name is mine. 'Aaand, Abbyyy!' says Gordo. Yes!

I feel Becca's hand squeeze mine. 'Abs, this is gonna be

amazing,' she says in my ear and I grin. I am in *Australia* and tomorrow I'm going to wine country with my friend. It's lovely to pretend—even for just a moment—that that's all there is to it.

'Oh, bugger right off,' says Tara, skulking back upstairs. Gordo's mugging for the camera, but he's soon forgotten when Kylie speaks up and Tim swings it in her direction.

'Oh, who cares? I've been to the Hunter a million times,' she drawls. 'It's no big deal.'

'Then why have you been there a million times?' asks Becca, her voice low. I stifle a giggle.

'The Barossa's *way* better,' Kylie adds, although it's unclear who she's taking to—no one seems to be listening.

Tim gives Harry the nod, indicating he got all that on camera, and I wonder if Kylie's aware that she's playing right into the villainous role they've assigned her. Or perhaps she's as horrid in real life as she is in the Manor.

'That's a wrap everyone,' says Harry.

'For real this time?' I ask. 'No other surprises planned, Harry? Kylie Minogue's not going to come and make us pancakes in the morning, is she?'

'Hah!' Becca laughs.

'Nah, nothing like that,' Harry says, chuckling. 'Have a good one, everyone. Hey, Gordo, let's go, mate.'

Before being called away, Gordo was trying in vain to chat up Daphne. What does he think will happen? That if Daphne's not chosen by Daniel, she'll fall straight into his arms? As he leaves, he cocks his finger at her and winks. Daphne looks like she's bitten into something sour and even I feel sorry for her. When she glances around the room seeking solidarity, her eyes meet mine and I crinkle my nose and make a face——*no one* deserves to have that letch fawning all over them. Daphne looks away, horrified, then leaps off the sofa and heads upstairs.

'My apologies, Daphne!' I want to shout after her. *'Sorry for being empathetic!'* Evidently, by showing her a modicum of kindness, I've deeply offended her. Lesson learnt!

The other Does have also dissipated to various parts of the Manor, including Becca and the rest of my gin rummy gang who've gone back to the patio. The only one left in the lounge room is Elizabeth and she resumes reading and starts working her lip as though she's about to chew through it.

'Abs, come on! Kaz has dealt,' calls Becca. Hopefully, cards will be a good distraction. I need to steer clear of all this drama.

'Coming!' I call. 'After I go for a wee!'

———————

Well, this is not what I expected.

I'm not sure how I saw this foursome panning out——particularly as I know that we three Does are the top contenders for Bride——but whoever planned this date is just plain sadistic. I hope it was Roberta, or even Harry. I'd hate to think that Jack had anything to do with it.

The day started out perfectly fine. We drove here in a convoy of two minivans, Tim squeezed in with us so he could film us 'ooh-ing' and 'ahh-ing' as we crossed the Sydney Harbour Bridge (that part was actually very exciting) and the rest of the crew, including Harry and Jack, followed closely, lugging the film equipment.

Leaving the metropolis of Sydney in our wake and heading north-west towards the Hunter Valley, the scenery induced even more exclamations. Not surprising, really—gently undulating green hills dotted with stands of eucalyptus trees and neat rows of vines. We even saw a group of kangaroos in a field. A 'mob' they're called, according to our driver. They'd seemed non-plussed as we flew past, lifting their heads to watch us and continuing to chew on their lunch the ways cows do.

And despite being stuck in a vehicle with both Daniel and Daphne (who still won't deign to look at me, let alone speak to me), I considered it a lovely start to the day. Not long ago, we arrived at our destination, a boutique winery, and were shepherded into the tasting room (closed to visitors for filming), presumably to taste wine.

How silly of me! While the crew are scurrying about setting up, Harry and Jack have pulled us aside to explain the day's filming. First, we'll each film our alone time with Daniel, something I had (stupidly) not foreseen and (it probably goes without saying) am dreading. Only *then* will we get to taste the wine. What this means is that I am about to spend (what will feel like) a millennium alone with Daphne and, as I've mentioned, *there isn't any wine!* Torture, pure and simple.

'So, what kinda dates?' asks Becca. Excellent question, Becca. I hadn't even thought of that. Presumably, they'll want shots of us wandering amongst the vines, gazing at each other longingly. Ugh. Despite what Roberta seems to think about our 'chemistry', gazing at Daniel longingly is going to take far more acting ability than *I* possess. I doubt Kate Winslet could pull it off.

Harry's eyes are ablaze with excitement. 'So, guys, get this. You're going on adventure dates.'

'Hah!' exclaims Daniel, rubbing his hands together. Well, he seems delighted, but when I look at Daphne, I see a reflection of my own horror. *Sacré bleu*, Daphne and I agree! Were we not practically sworn enemies, I would high-five her or cry, *'I'm with you, sister,'* or something like that.

'Sorry, what do you mean by "adventure dates"?' she asks, eyeing Harry warily. Another brilliant question and my mind reels with possibilities. At least this explains why they haven't given us any wine yet.

I glance at Jack just as he runs his hand along his jaw and I know from this simple gesture that this twist was Harry's doing. Actually, from the way he's looking at his brother, Jack may have tried to talk Harry out of it. 'Yeah, we're not exactly dressed for "adventure",' says Becca, who's wearing a floor-length floral maxi dress.

'Well, except maybe Abby,' says Daphne snidely. I glance at her linen palazzo trousers and smart chevron tank top, then down at my own outfit. I look perfectly nice, thank you very much, *Daphne*. I'm wearing the jeans that make my bum look good and a flowy silk blouse.

'Hey, guys, remember who you're talking to here,' says Harry, a broad grin on his face. 'We've taken care of all that.' He signals to a crewmember who dashes about depositing bags at our feet.

'So, Becca, you'll be going abseiling …' She grins,

sharing an excited look with Daniel. While Becca clearly thinks abseiling will be fun, I can't think of anything worse than plummeting to your death because you've (stupidly) decided to dangle from the side of a cliff by a half-inch thick rope.

'Daphne, you and Daniel will be going four-wheel-driving …' Now *that* would be fun. 'And Abby, you and Daniel are going horse riding.' Harry looks well pleased with himself, but I am (of course) horrified. This is far worse than discovering I have to spend time alone with both Daniel and Daphne.

'Excellent!' says Daniel. Yes, all very well for you, Daniel. You get to spend the day having fun and *I* … I have to do the ONE THING that terrifies me more than anything else, *including* abseiling!

Or do I? '*Think, Abby!*' my mind shouts.

I stand rooted to the spot with fear, watching as activity buzzes around me. Daphne, Daniel, and Becca start rummaging around in their respective bags. 'Harry, which date is first?' asks Daphne. 'Should I get changed now, or …'

'Oh, right. Actually, Becca and Daniel will be going abseiling first.'

Daphne shrugs, looking terribly bored (she probably is). She makes her way to one of the tables and sits down, inspecting her cuticles, and Becca and Daniel go into the bathrooms to change.

'*Abby, do something!*'

'Er, Harry, may I have a word?' I say, signalling for him to join me away from the others. I head over to some wooden shelves that display everything from artisan crackers

to quince paste to sets of coasters with different grape vari-
etals on them.

'Hey, Abby, what's up?' he asks.

'I'm just wondering if I could possibly do something else.
Anything else,' I add. 'Even the abseiling,' I hear myself say,
though I immediately regret it.

'Oh … ah … you can't do the abseiling, I'm sorry. The
insurance won't cover it.'

'Oh, but Becca …?'

'Yeah, she's Australian, so …' I'd rather not go into the
ins and outs of why an Australian can do the more
dangerous activity, so I drop it.

'What about the driving then?'

'Sorry, Abby, I mean, I can ask Daphne if she'll swap,
but your bio … You're supposed to be good at horse riding.'

'That's not *me*,' I say, my voice raspy and desperate. This
isn't me either; I hate being this Abby, all panicky and rude.

Jack approaches, turning our conversation into a huddle.
'What's going on?'

'Doe Abby can ride a horse, and *real* Abby is terrified of
the bloody things,' I whisper.

'Ohhh,' says Harry, 'gotchya.'

'Sorry, Abby, I didn't know,' says Jack.

'How could you? Hang on,' I say, narrowing my eyes at
Jack, '*Did* you know?'

'I swear, Abby, I had no idea.'

'But didn't *you* write Doe Abby's backstory?'

'No, that wasn't me. That was Roberta.'

'Will we be leaving soon?' asks Daniel from across the
tasting room. He's returned, wearing a pair of tan chinos

and a slim-cut navy T-shirt, as well as some sturdy hiking shoes. He may be a massive wanker, but he does look rather good when he's dressed more casually. He catches me looking at him and lifts his chin arrogantly like Joey from *FRIENDS*. *'How you doin'?'* I hear in my head and I smile as though I am utterly smitten with this twat.

'Uh, yeah, mate, just give us a sec,' calls Harry before turning his attention back to me. 'Hey, how 'bout I go ask Daphne if she'll swap dates with you?'

'Oh, would you?' I ask, awash with relief.

Harry jogs over to Daphne and I watch the scene play out with my bottom lip between my teeth. Lisa said that they probably wouldn't ask me to go horse riding and if they did, I just needed to tell Jack I was too scared. It turns out to be Harry who is getting me out of this, but no matter, a hero is a hero is a hero.

'Absolutely not! I'd much rather drive around the countryside than climb on a horse.' She won't swap dates with me. Harry's murmuring something to her. 'Well, too bad, she should have told you so on her application form.' Right. So, now Daphne knows it's because I'm scared to ride a horse and she still won't swap dates. How did I ever think she'd do anything for someone other than herself?

I'm now awash with the opposite of relief—gut wrenching, squidgy tum and bum fear.

'Sorry, Abby,' says a voice low in my ear. 'We'll just get some quick shots of you on the horse and call it good, okay?' When I look at Jack, his concern is evident.

I nod. 'Thank you,' I say, my voice strangled.

He squeezes the top of my arm and leaves me standing beside the quince paste and coasters.

As steeped in terror as I am, it occurs to me that these are the first civil words Jack and I have exchanged since our argument the other night.

Now all I have to do is survive the day so I can make things right with him.

Chapter Twelve

'Abs!' Even though I am ensconced in my hidey hole—not exactly my favourite place—there's nothing like hearing my bestie's voice. God, how I've missed her—even with phone privileges this is only the second time I've spoken to her since I arrived well over a month ago.

'Hi, Lise. I miss you so much.' It also feels like forever since I've been able to say exactly how I feel and my eyes prickle with tears as my throat tightens.

'Oh, babes, I miss you too. So sorry it's been ages; work has been manic.' I conjure an image of her skulking about wearing a trench coat, peering around corners, and tapping her nose to signal her contact. It makes me giggle, my tears momentarily forgotten. 'So, tell me everything. How is it? How are you?'

I exhale heavily. Those are huge questions to answer and I'm not sure where to begin. 'And spare no details,' she adds, 'this is my first proper lunch break in ages and I'm taking the full thirty minutes.' Right, so spare no details but be fast because the clock is ticking. But isn't this what I'm good at, composing digests? 'You don't mind if I eat while we talk, do you?' she asks. 'I've managed to nip out to Pret and I snagged the last egg salad sandwich—practically stole it from out of some banker wanker's hands.'

She's got me laughing now and, of course, I'm picturing her and Daniel—King Banker Wanker—wrestling over a squished egg sandwich. 'You eat, I'll talk.'

She replies with her mouth full and I have no idea what she's said, so I proceed. 'Right. So, there are only eight of us left, and I've made some friends now' —muffled mouth-full, 'Mmm, good,' from Lisa— 'and Daniel's still as smarmy and full of himself as ever, and we had this date—this awful, *awful* date. Oh Lise, they put me on a horse! And I nearly fell off!'

She coughs and I suspect it's because she's choked on her sandwich. 'Wait, what? Didn't you tell Jack that you don't know how to ride?'

'Yes, I did that. But it was too late to change activities, and it was terrifying, but I didn't die—'

'Obvs …'

'Well, yes, *obvs*, but there was this horrible moment with Daniel afterwards …' I rest my forehead on my palm, the mere memory making my head feel heavy. 'Lise, he kissed me.'

'Oh, no! Really?'

'Uh-huh. And it caught me way off guard and … oh god, Lise, *Jack* was there.'

'Ohhh, of course.'

'Yes, exactly.' We're both quiet for a moment.

'So, speaking of …?' she probes.

'Nothing. Nothing is happening, and I'm fairly certain I've ruined any chance of rectifying that.'

'Because you kissed Daniel?'

'I didn't … *Daniel* kissed *me*.'

'But surely that was obvious to Jack?'

'I have no idea, because we don't talk much anymore unless it's about the show.'

'But last time we spoke, you said you two were chummy.'

'We were, yes, but then I shouted at him.'

'Oh, Abs.'

'And I told him he was being far too friendly with me around the other Does—because he was—and that if he wasn't careful they might twig to something. Since then, he's kept his distance.' She doesn't reply and I think we've been cut off. 'Lisa?'

'Just thinking. How much longer is the filming supposed to last?' she asks.

'Oh, and that's the other thing. Rather than top four, Vile Demon Woman wants me in the top two.'

'What? Why?'

'Because of Daniel.'

'Because he kissed you?'

'No, that happened before the date from hell. Oh, *god*, I wish I could forget this whole thing. I just want to come home!' She sniggers and, though she may very well be laughing at me, I join in at my own expense.

'But Abs, *this*, this is what you have to write—all this

nonsense. You're still going to write that piece, right, the exposé?'

'I hope so. Yes. No, I absolutely will. If I'm forced to be here then something good must come out of it. And there's so much to write about. Vile Demon Woman. Cow-ish, bitch-faced Does in the Manor. Watching my friends get picked off like this is *The Hunger Games*. The *acting*—and that's not my acting I'm talking about, that's the other Does. It's all going in there!' I rant.

'And what about Jack?' she asks, just as I start to run out of steam.

'I told you, I don't think he's interested in me like that.'

'Right, but you've thought about how you can protect him in the piece, right? If you're not careful, it could be a blow to his career—and his brother's. Henry, was it?'

'Harry,' I reply numbly. She's right. I don't want to hurt Jack—or Harry. I'll need to find a way to write the piece, either positioning them as pawns to garner reader sympathy or omitting them altogether, which would be disingenuous in a 'tell-all'.

'Harry, right. Geez, Abs, you are in a pickle.'

It helps—and it doesn't—to hear that. There's no one else I can talk to about all this and I hadn't realised how much I've been bottling it up. But to have it confirmed that I am, indeed, 'in a pickle' is less comforting than I'd hoped.

'So sorry to do this, babes, but I've got to head back.'

'No, no, of course. Thank you for listening.'

'I wasn't much help, was I?' she asks.

I'm so practised at lying now that this one flies from my

mouth before I even form the thought. 'You absolutely were. Just talking about it has helped immensely.'

'Oh good,' she replies, and it doesn't make me feel any better that I have fooled the super spy. 'You'll figure it out, Abs. It'll be all right.' It's essentially 'pep talk for beginners' speak, but I hope she's right.

'Thanks, lovely. Speak soon,' I say, even though I have no idea when that will be.

'Bye-ee.' She ends the call and I'm struck with a wave of nostalgia for London in the autumn, bundled up in boots and a mac, munching on an egg salad sandwich while sitting riverside and watching the boat traffic on the Thames.

Instead, I am in stunning Sydney, in a million-pound mansion, getting paid to experience something unique, and I am absolutely miserable.

I've never been more mortified in my life.

And once, Mum and I watched *Basic Instinct* together because she loves Michael Douglas films. Not only was it quite the education for a fifteen-year-old, but my mother had 'ahem-ed' her way through every sex scene. By the end of the film, her throat must have been red raw. But I would trade places with teenaged Abby in a heartbeat rather than sit here with Harry and Jack watching the latest episode of *The Stag*. Because most of this episode will feature the winery date.

I have my notebook perched on my lap, pen at the ready and as I watch the opening, I scribble something about 'scenery porn' just to keep my fingers from worrying the corner of the pages into pulp. I suppose a comment about the scenery is apt, really, as embossed on the cover of my notebook is 'Travel Journal'—a ruse just in case any of the other Does see me writing in it.

Onscreen, there's a close-up of Daniel and if I didn't know him at all, I'd describe him as handsome, especially as he is sunlit and his blonde hair is luminescent. 'I'm so excited for today, getting to spend more time with Daphne, Becca, and Abby,' he says, his eyeline slightly left of the camera.

'What makes each of them special?' asks Carlie from offscreen.

Daniel grins and I foresee thousands of heartstrings across the world being tugged. 'Well, Daphne is … she's so refined, very sophisticated. We run in similar circles and I can certainly imagine a future with her.' Of course, you can, Daniel; she's the only Doe who's as pretentious as you are. God, Roberta will lap this up when she sees it.

'And Becca! She's such a beauty, just stunning, so *lithe*.' Is he describing a woman or a racehorse? 'She takes my breath away, quite frankly.' I roll my eyes. No mention of her kindness, her warmth, her intelligence.

'And what about Abby?' prompts Carlie. I swallow hard, intrigue and dread coursing through my veins in equal measure.

Daniel's eyes narrow sightly and he tilts his head in contemplation as a smile curls his lips. 'Abby is … she's intriguing. She's attractive, quick-witted, and a bit of a romantic. But I also sense that she's playing things close to her chest, which is a bit of a contradiction with how she wears her heart on her sleeve. It's rather beguiling, actually … her being so mysterious; she's like a puzzle to unlock …' he adds wistfully, his smile getting wider.

Good god! Is Daniel falling for Doe Abby? Jack tosses me an indecipherable look over his shoulder. Harry's watching the screen, but he's nodding slightly as though answering my unasked question.

The first date is Becca and Daniel abseiling. Despite the unflattering harnesses and bulbous helmets, neither would look out of place in an advertisement for an outdoor adventure company. I write that down. As the technicians check their gear and give them a briefing, Daniel appears to be getting more and more nervous.

'You okay?' asks Becca.

'Oh, yes, absolutely.' He smiles, but it comes across as more of a grimace.

Becca reaches over and gives his hand a squeeze, the way she does with me sometimes. 'You'll be great,' she says.

He nods quickly but his mouth turns down at the corners and he starts chewing on the inside of his lip. It's odd seeing him out of his comfort zone like this—vulnerable, even—and I remember the glimpse of Daniel the person I saw on the yacht when he talked about going into the family business.

Becca abseils first and having done it many times before, she's (of course) brilliant at it, making it look easy. Cameras film her from the top of the cliff face and the bottom, and one of Harry's crew abseils down with Becca capturing her broad grin and cries of, 'This is amazing!'

At the bottom of the cliff, she's unclipped from the ropes and looks up at Daniel. 'You ready?' she calls. Her voice echoes against the rockface.

'Er, no, but here goes,' says Daniel.

'Is Daniel afraid of heights?' I ask.

'No, I reckon he just got nervous about going over the edge,' replies Jack.

'Right.'

There's a clunky edit that Harry and the editor will smooth out where the camera operator had to unclip, run around to the 'back' of the cliff where they'd ascended, and repeat his descent to capture Daniel on film. I can't imagine how nerve wracking that would have been for Daniel—psyching himself up to go, but then having to wait. That's one thing about filming this show—lots of 'hurry up and wait' moments.

Daniel eventually eases over the edge, his fear palpable. 'I still can't believe we got him to do this,' says Harry. 'When we told him about it, he seemed fine, but he was totally packing it the whole time.' Australian speak for 'terrified', I imagine. 'Still, gonna make for good TV, especially the next bit.'

Jack nods slightly, but I stay silent.

Daniel duck walks awkwardly down the rock wall, Becca spurring him on with encouraging words. When he reaches the ground, he is obviously relieved and as he's unclipped from the ropes by one of the technicians, he starts an almost endless loop of, 'Did you see that? I did it. I did it. Did you see?' Again, more glimpses of Daniel the *person*.

Daniel removes his helmet and he and Becca come

together in the perfect onscreen clinch—so perfect, it's like Harry scripted it and had them rehearse. Becca's arms wind up around Daniel's neck, his around her waist. Then she lifts a hand to wipe his damp fringe from his face. 'You were amazing,' she says.

He grins at her. '*You* were. It was your voice that got me down that cliff.' Calm down, love, it's not like you went off to war. Ooh, a line for Anastasia. I scribble it down.

'I'm proud of you,' she says, her voice catching. Their lips come together in perfect synchrony, and they kiss—at length. As in, an exceedingly long kiss that seems to go on forever and a day.

There are a multitude of reasons I'm squirming in my seat, my unease growing with each second. First, Becca is my friend and I don't typically watch my friends passionately kiss someone. She's also falling hard for this twat, and if this were Lisa, I'd be warning her off him.

It's also impossible not to think of kissing Jack like that—especially as he is right there and he's wearing his 'I aim to misbehave' T-shirt (my favourite), and I love how it clings to his well-defined shoulders. *'Stop it, Abby! The slim possibility of you ever kissing Jack ended when you screeched at him like a banshee,'* I think, admonishing myself.

I blow out a frustrated sigh, which Harry misinterprets. 'Yeah, it's a bit much, eh? We can just fast-forward a bit.' He presses a button on the console in front of him, then Becca's face fills the screen—it's her confessional.

'I've just never felt this way before,' she says, full lips taut across perfect teeth. She shakes her head as if in disbelief, her glorious mane of dark curls cascading down her back. She looks like she's in a shampoo commercial.

I'd known that they'd kissed, of course. Despite us (ostensibly) competing for Daniel's heart, she couldn't help but gush to me when they returned from their date and he and Daphne left on theirs. It was two hours of 'And then he said …' and 'Oh, my god, Abby, I can't believe this …' and the worst one, 'I think he feels the same way.'

I'm certain she mistook my concern for jealousy because she'd followed that up with, 'Sorry, Abs. He definitely has feelings for you too.' Though, now having seen his confessional, she might be right. Bollocks.

All this is flying through my mind and we haven't even got to my date yet. I look at the nearly blank page in my lap and scribble 'shampoo commercial'——not particularly mean and hopefully funny enough for Anastasia's readers.

Daniel and Daphne's date is a snooze fest. They have zero chemistry. She *looks* perfect, of course, having refused to wear the adventure outfit chosen for her——why should she change if they were just going to sit inside a vehicle the whole time? But as the four-wheel-drive bounces along a rutted gravel track, Daphne's white knuckles and grimaces reveal that she's less than impressed by Daniel's propensity to aim for potholes. She's also making mincemeat of her 'squeals of delight' and sounds like a wounded seal.

I write it all down.

When Daniel parks the vehicle outside the tasting room, there are several shots of the vehicle itself, including the badge on the front grill——product placement at its finest—and then we're back inside it where Daphne and Daniel chat benignly about 'their adventure'.

Seemingly out of nowhere, he leans across and kisses Daphne in a way that can only be described as 'brotherly'. She allows it and I flash on an image of the two of them in bed together. *'May I kiss you before intercourse, Daphne?' 'If you must, Daniel.'*

I bark out a laugh at their expense and write it in my notebook. Jack throws me another look over his shoulder, this one accompanied by a wry smile which I return—an echo of our former camaraderie.

'Ready, Abby?' asks Harry. 'Your date's next.'

'Right, er, yes.' I sit up straighter, though how that will help me watch myself on this date is a mystery.

The first shot is me and Daniel walking towards the horses, both holding riding helmets. My bum really does look good in those jeans, I note, but that's definitely not going in a recap. Each horse has a handler and one of the horses is skittishly pulling at its reins.

'God, I hope that's not mine,' I say.

Daniel reaches down and grasps my hand. I'd forgotten he'd done that. 'I'll take that one,' he says, which is actually quite sweet. I'd forgotten that too. When we reach the horses, the handlers ask us to don our helmets, which we do, and when I struggle with the strap, Daniel reaches under my chin to help. I smile at him and say, 'Thank you.'

'You'll be *fine*,' he says, his eyes boring into mine. 'I'm right here.' In the Control Room, I roll my eyes. Maybe it's Daniel who will get offered a role on *Neighbours* instead of

Justine. He's certainly mastered that unique brand of soap opera intensity.

'Have you both ridden before?' asks one of the handlers.

'*I* have,' says Daniel, 'I ride all the time, actually. My father owns a horse stud—thoroughbreds, of course …' He casts an eye over the two horses and his expression sours. Ahhh, there he is! The Daniel we all know and love to hate. I scribble down the words, then read them back and cross them out. As snarky as Anastasia is, there's an impermeable line she cannot cross when it comes to the Stag himself.

Onscreen, I'm helped onto my horse—Womble, she's called—and Daniel expertly hoists himself onto Pudding—a silly name for a horse—and then we're off.

And by 'off' I mean we commence a slow and gentle ride amongst the fruit-heavy grapevines—just as Jack had promised. When the horses clear the end of the row, Daniel suggests that we head away from the vines towards a gently sloping hill. 'I can teach you to trot,' he says.

'Er, no, that's all right,' says Doe Abby. Real Abby wanted to say, *Are you out of your bleedin' mind?* like Tara would.

'Come on, it'll be fun,' cajoles Daniel.

Doe Abby looks off camera at Harry, where he was standing next to Tim and bites her lip. Daniel circles his horse back to mine, then proceeds to tell me the ins and outs—or rather, the ups and downs—of trotting. I took none of this in at the time, panicked as I was. Doe Abby's eyes are pleading now, and real Abby—me, right here in this room—is suddenly quite annoyed with Harry. He could have (and should have) shouted 'cut' by this point.

Onscreen, Womble starts getting antsy—probably because horses can intuit when their rider is uncomfortable (or so I'm told) and this rider is definitely uncomfortable. 'I don't know how to trot,' says Doe Abby. 'Let's just go back now. *Please.*'

'Come on, I've taught you how,' says Daniel, ignoring my plea. Er, *no*, Daniel, barking instructions at a terrified person is not 'teaching' them. My fear is obvious, but so is my annoyance at Daniel and watching the scene play out on the monitor conjures everything I felt at the time.

'Why didn't you stop it?' I ask.

Harry taps a button on the console and freezes the image—it's of me scowling. He turns around in his chair. 'Sorry?'

'Why didn't you say "cut"? You knew I was terrified. And Jack said you'd just get a few shots of me on the horse, and that would be that. You could have stopped it before it even happened.' Now, both Abbys are scowling.

Harry bites his lip and I note that Jack doesn't come to his defence. 'You're right. And I'm sorry. It's just that you were safe—'

'You didn't know that,' I retort.

'Again, you're right. But I thought you were, so I let the cameras roll.'

I look at frozen Doe Abby. 'Play,' I command.

'We can skip ahead,' he says.

'No, I need to write this up,' I reply tartly.

He taps the button on the console and the equine horror show begins. Onscreen, Daniel goes from cajoling to bullying in three-point-two seconds. 'Come on, Abby, you're being absurd. Here, let me show you.' When Daniel reaches over and slaps Womble on the arse, shouting, 'Yah!', Doe Abby's eyes widen in horror, as mine do watching the replay.

Womble, bless her, takes off across the paddock, me bouncing on top of her like a rodeo cowboy on a bronco. Daniel cries, 'Bugger,' and takes off after us on Pudding. By the time man and horse cross the paddock, Womble has run out of steam and stops to nibble on a tuft of grass.

Although the cameras couldn't keep up, our microphones were working perfectly and way off in the distance, Doe Abby swings a leg over Womble and jumps to the ground, a tirade spewing from her mouth—well, my mouth.

'That will be enough to keep the censors busy,' I think. Unfiltered, Doe Abby sounds like a longshoreman on leave and I hear a snort from Jack's direction, which he tries to disguise as a cough. That's my trick, so I am onto him immediately. 'It's not funny,' I snap.

He responds by shifting in his chair and muttering, 'Sorry.'

Doe Abby plants her hands on her hips, giving Daniel a full serve of 'What the bloody hell did you think you are doing?' and other (even more colourful) rhetorical questions.

Daniel dismounts Pudding like the experienced rider he is—elegantly—and clasping Pudding's reins, he walks over, trying to placate me. 'Hey, hey, you're all right,' he says. *'Was he talking to me or the horse?'* I wonder. I write that down. And although Daniel's back is to the camera, I remember the exact look of condescension that he'd plastered on that smug mug of his. 'See? You did it. There was nothing to worry about.'

Like Womble, *I* had run out of steam by then and Doe Abby gathers up Womble's reins and starts walking her towards the tasting room. 'Abby, don't be like that,' says Daniel. He catches up, Pudding in tow, and places a hand on Does Abby's arm. 'Wait, please?' Doe Abby stops and huffs, looking at him expectantly.

'Was I very badly behaved?' asks the smug twat. By then, Tim and his Steadicam had caught up to us, so Daniel's twatishness is captured perfectly in a glaring closeup.

'Yes!' replies Doe Abby. I feel her pain acutely and even now I want to slap Daniel.

'I'm sorry,' he says, though he couldn't sound less sincere. 'Forgive me.' He was rubbing my arm so vigorously I thought he'd wear a hole in my sleeve. I write that down.

'Fine, I forgive you,' Doe Abby says curtly, walking away from him.

This is it and I hold my breath.

'Abby, *wait.*' Daniel catches up and turns Doe Abby around to face him. 'I really am deeply sorry.'

By this point, all I'd wanted was to hear 'cut' so I could head to the tasting room and request an enormous glass of wine—even if we weren't up to that part yet. 'Fine, I accept your apology,' says Doe Abby.

'I *am* proud of you, you know,' Daniel says. 'You did *wonderfully.*' It was such a ridiculous thing for him to say, that I had burst out laughing.

On the monitor, Daniel—possibly mistaking my laughter for falling madly in love with him—stops my mouth with a kiss. It's not terribly long—not as long as it had felt at the time and certainly long as long as the tongues-

and-all kiss he'd shared with Becca earlier that afternoon—but it had caught me entirely by surprise.

Which is why I hadn't pushed him away, but I can see immediately that it will appear to everyone who watches that I wanted Daniel to kiss me.

Everyone. Including Jack.

Chapter Thirteen

'We put you there for a reason, Abigail, but your latest piece is banal, dull, boring, and *insipid*. I practically fell asleep.'

It's perhaps the harshest review I've ever had (not to mention the distracting synonym overload) and believe me, Anastasia attracts plenty of trolls. My mouth is midway through forming a syllable when Roberta interrupts. 'You're there to *enhance* the recaps, not *dilute* them. Quite frankly, if I don't have a vastly improved revision by tomorrow, we're taking you off the show.'

Well, there's nothing I can say to that. The sting of humiliation warms my cheeks and without checking, I know I've achieved beetroot status. I can handle criticism, I can handle a dressing down— I've certainly tested Prue's patience on more than one occasion—but this is the first time I have been called incompetent.

And it's in front of Jack.

Humiliation Level: One hundred million kajillion + one

And humming along beneath my professional humiliation is the knowledge that Jack's potential as a love interest has just become nil. He (inconceivably) thinks I have feelings for Daniel; I've (literally) asked him to stay away; and rounding out the 'steer clear of Abby' trifecta, he's now witnessed me receive a bollocking from Vile Demon Woman—a.k.a. his boss!

Prue's sycophantic voice trills from the phone's speaker. 'I'm sure there's no need for that, Roberta. Abigail is an excellent writer, but even those are prone to a hiccup now and then. No doubt she can bring this back around, just as you've asked.'

How considerate of her to speak on my behalf.

'See that she does. Jack, are you still there?'

'Uh, yeah, I'm here.'

'Can I have a word? In *private*?' she asks.

He glances over, sending a sympathetic smile my way, which makes me feel even worse. I study some remnants of tape on the table in front of me and pick at it the residue with a fingernail. 'Uh, yeah, sure. I'll call you back in five.'

'See that you do.' He leans over to end the call when Prue's voice echoes around the Control Room.

'Abigail, I'd like to speak to you privately, too. Call *me* in five minutes.'

Oh, this cannot be good. I lift my eyes to Jack's and he's making the 'eek' face. He presses the red button on his mobile phone and the silence is both welcome and deafening. I abandon the tape removal and stand. I have four minutes and fifty seconds to figure out what to say to Prue so I don't get 'fy-ahed'.

'Abby, wait just a sec. Are you okay?'

I appreciate that he's asked, but I have no idea how to answer. *Let's see, my job at Feed Your Mind was only ever a stopgap until I established myself as a proper writer, but it's all I have right now and I'd like to keep it if I can. And I never wanted—nor even asked—to come on this show and it has been (at best) a bizarre experience, and (at worst) a parade of awkward incidents, a mounting pile of lies, and trials of fragile friendships. And I've just been dressed down for doing poorly at something I usually excel at. But, yes, I am perfectly fine, thank you.'*

What I actually say is, 'I'm all right.' I add an *insipid* smile—my new least favourite word thanks to Roberta—and leave before Jack can ask me anything else or *worse*, try to cheer me up. I slip out of the Control Room, listen for any movement from the main part of the house, and head to my hidey hole—a fitting place to lick my wounds and grovel to my editor.

In the storeroom-cum-office, I retrieve the loaned phone and laptop from the box on the top shelf, plugging in both to charge, then set up the card table and unfold the folding chair. There's something calming about the now familiar ritual and I settle into the chair and pick up the phone. It's programmed with three numbers—Mum's, Lisa's, and Prue's—and after I speak with the latter, I am going to attempt to get hold of my best friend—secret missions be damned.

Prue picks up on the second ring. 'Abigail,' she says simply, though her tone of voice is softer than usual. 'How are you?' I have worked with Prue for seven years and never once has she asked me this.

'Er, I'm all right.'

'How are you *really*?'

Is this a trap? Am I going to confess my true feelings only to have Prue pulverise me into oblivion? But what (else) have I got to lose? If this all goes pear-made-of-a-pile-of-poo-shaped, I'll pack up my flat, move back in with Mum, and write my exposé—better yet, I'll write a whole book about the crime against society that is *The Stag*. I'll get a publisher, crack bestseller lists across the globe, and become famous—*proper* famous, not anonymous famous.

Abigail Jones: bestselling author, talk show guest supreme (Hello, Graham Norton!), and 'It Girl' about London (If I'm aiming high, I may as well go the whole hog).

Prue is waiting patiently for me to reply, which for her is a minor miracle. 'I'm terrible,' I confess. Just saying those two simple words makes the spasms in my squidgy tum lessen.

'Tell me.'

'I really want to do a good job, Prue. You know me—my standards for my work are exceptionally high, perhaps even higher than yours.'

'Mmm.' Her way of agreeing with me. Or disagreeing—I can never tell.

'But I hadn't anticipated how hard it would be to maintain a professional distance. I have no idea how undercover operatives do it—I can't even imagine. You see, I've made friends here. And not just amongst the other Does—there's the crew too.' I will not tell her about my crush on Jack, of

185

course, nor about our friendship-in-stasis. I'm not even sure if he and I *are* still friends.

'And I see how hard Jack and Harry are working to make this a good, solid season of the show——entertaining, just what the fans want——but I'm also seeing behind the scenes and I *loathe* the machinations of it, how the situations are manufactured and manipulated. And I hate that the Stag kissed me. *Hate* it. I didn't sign up for that. I mean, I did, but I didn't.

'Daniel's a horrible person, the worst type of man——the type who tries to make you feel like he's doing you a favour by liking you. And then there's Becca——she's my closest friend here in the Manor and for some reason, she really likes him. I have absolutely no idea why she can't see through his bullshit, but that's what this show does to a person, makes them blind to the things they wouldn't put up with in real life.

'I don't know, it's just so *intense* all the time. Once I knew I had no choice in the matter, I decided to make the most of coming here and I thought I would cope better. And I certainly didn't think it would impact my writing. I'm really sorry, Prue. I know I've put you and Feed Your Mind in an awful spot with Roberta.' Exhausted from my admission, I slump back in my folded chair.

After a moment, Prue replies. 'It's me who owes you an apology, Abigail.'

'Sorry?' I ask. I can't possibly have heard her correctly.

'It's true. I put you in this terrible position. I was blinded by the possibilities——what this could mean for Feed Your Mind——and I didn't properly consider the effect the experience might have on you.' I'm having trouble reconciling the image of Prue I have in my head with the woman whose voice I'm hearing. I say nothing because nothing comes to mind.

'Do you know, when you came to interview for the staff writer role all those years ago, you actually reminded me of myself.'

'No effing way.' The words are out of my mouth before I can stop them, and I clap a hand over my mouth. 'Er, sorry Prue,' I say, a rather feeble apology when I've just insulted my boss. I realise with a start that she's ack-ack-ack-ing at me down the line. Prue's laughing.

'Oh, Abigail, I so wish this were a video call—to see your face right now.' She dissolves into more ack-acks, then sighs. 'Oh, I haven't had a good laugh in eons. But back to you. You *did* remind me of myself—that's absolutely true. I, too, graduated with honours and hold a bachelor's in journalism. Like you, I worked in a bookstore to make ends meet before securing a staff writer position. And like you, I wanted to be a "serious journalist"—I even had a piece published in *The New Yorker* once.'

I'm gobsmacked.

Prue and I started our careers in practically identical ways. Does this mean I'm destined to *become* Prue, wreaking havoc on young staff writers, ruling my online empire from a windowless room? Oh, Cadmus, I hope not. I'd look terrible with a chin-length bob!

'You've gone silent,' she says.

'I … er, yes. Sorry. That's …'

'Surprising?'

'Er, yes.'

'Well, I'm not telling you this to shock you, Abigail, though I should have suspected it might. I'm telling you this because you are an exceptionally talented writer and I want you to succeed. And not just at Feed Your Mind—I have no doubt that you're destined for bigger things than our little online magazine.'

'You really think I'm talented?'

'Of course! That piece you did for *The Guardian* last year on the importance of public libraries to small communities was outstanding.'

'You read my piece?'

'I read all the pieces you write under your own name.'

Hearing that Prue not only reads my work—my proper work—but *likes* it, has opened up a whole new level of 'chuffed'. 'Er … wow. And thank you.'

'No need to thank me. What sort of editor would I be if I didn't keep professional tabs on my writers?'

'Oh, yes, quite.'

'But I'm realising now that I've done you a disservice, Abigail.'

'How so?'

'I've watched you become comfortable at Feed Your Mind as Anastasia, and I haven't really pushed you.'

Confronted with this notion, I realise it's true. Prue typically receives my pieces with what I had presumed was indifference—I'd met her requirements, so no need for edits. But hearing her now, perhaps she *has* been allowing me to hum along unchallenged.

'And that will no longer do,' she says.

'How do you mean?' I ask, the knot in my tum tightening again. I really hope Prue isn't going to choose now—when I'm thousands of miles from home and in emotional turmoil—to push this little bird out of the nest. I send a quick plea to Cadmus.

'Here's what I'm thinking. Turn this around—as I know you can do—and re-submit the latest recap. Then get to work on your tell-all—*properly*.'

What? How can she possibly know about that? 'My, er, tell-all?'

Ack-ack-ack. 'Abigail, I am a highly intelligent woman and, as I've said, I *know* you—having once been you. If you're not writing an exposé in parallel to your Anastasia pieces, I will shave off my left eyebrow.' The image of Prue sans an eyebrow is too much to bear and I burst into giggles. 'There's my girl,' she says.

'Sorry, Prue. I didn't mean to——'

'And stop apologising. I need your mind in the game, Abigail—your sharp wit, your unique turn of phrase—and it won't do if you're wallowing in self-pity or grovelling for forgiveness. Understood?'

'Er, yes, understood.'

'Excellent. Have the recap on my desk by close of business today.'

I check the time on the laptop screen. It's just after 10pm here, which means I have a late night ahead of me.

'All right, will do, Prue. And thank you. I really apprec——'

'Enough of all that. Speak soon.' She ends the call and I take the phone from my ear and stare it.

Oh, Cadmus. As if this situation weren't surreal enough already, I may have just fallen down the rabbit hole.

The Stag in Sydney Recap: Only Fools and Horses
by Anastasia Blabbergasted

We're nearly at the halfway mark of *The Stag in Sydney* and there have been more twists and turns than the Monaco Grand Prix!

This week's episode begins in Australia's stunning Hunter Valley, home to some of the world's best Chardonnay and Cabernet Sauvignon—*apparently*, that is. The antipodeans have heard of a little place called *France*, have they not? Regardless, this is the sort of scenery porn typically reserved for British Airways advertisements—stands of eucalyptus trees, neat rows of vibrant green vines, heavy with plump bunches of grapes, and rolling green hills. Breathtaking.

And doesn't today's threesome have our Danny Boy grinning like … well, like a man on a date with three women?!

And why wouldn't he be? First up, there's the beautiful Becca, who he calls 'lithe'. I'm fairly certain that word is more often used to describe racehorses,

Daniel, but I'll give you a pass—no doubt her OTT beauty has got you tongue-tied—especially as you've set the tone perfectly for a rather 'horse-themed' episode.

Date number two is sophisticated thoroughbred Daphne. Viewers, perhaps we should have a competition—first person to catch Daphne with a hair out of place wins a year's subscription to *Horse and Hound*!

Rounding out this equine episode as date number three is Dark Horse, Abby. The poor love will *literally* find herself astride a horse before she can say, 'Oh, no, I'd really rather not,' and whatever her mystery job turns out to be, it certainly isn't 'cowgirl'. But I'll come back to that.

With Becca up first, *abseiling* of all things—is this *The Stag* or *I'm Super Famous, I Want Out*?—there is a glimmer of hope that the world's most beautiful woman will at least look frightful in a helmet and a crotch-hugging harness. Alas, no, and we mere mortals are left to love-hate her from afar.

And Danny Boy surprisingly shows that while he may be a master of many things—expertly pouring a flute of champagne, wearing designer sunglasses just so, crunching big numbers and making international trades—Bear Grylls' job is absolutely safe. Are those *tears* in his eyes?

Ever-amiable Becca—another reason for us to love-hate her—is there at the bottom of the cliff to champion Daniel and receive him with open ~~mouth~~ arms. I'm certain that even the camera operator looked away during that clinch. 'Whoa, you two, this is a family show!' (It isn't, but I had to take a cold shower after that kiss.)

Just when we thought Becca may be the front runner for Daniel's heart, in comes (unsuitably attired) Daphne! (**Aside:** They *did* tell her she was going off-roading and not to a garden party, right?) Their date, exploring the Australian bush in a four-wheel-drive, is quite the adventure with Daphne squealing delightedly (or is that screaming in terror?) at the appropriate times—Daniel driving into a muddy hole, Daniel sliding the vehicle sideways around a bend, Daniel nearly crashing the vehicle into an enormous eucalyptus tree. I hope Range Rover felt it got its money's worth with that not-so-subtle product placement. 'Even the least experienced drivers can't crash one of our vehicles!'

Their date is wrapped up with a kiss so chaste, it reminds me of the 'balcony kiss' from every royal wedding since the dawn of time (without the cheering crowds, of course).

At this point in the episode, we discover that there *is* something outdoorsy Daniel is good at and, with my heavy-handed foreshadowing, surely you've guessed that it must be horse riding! Now, if you can count—and I'm assuming you can, at *least* to three—then you'll realise it's Abby the Enigma up next. And if we thought Daniel looked terrified as he descended that cliff face (and he did), that pales in comparison to Abby as she approaches Womble the horse.

Another aside: I absolutely loved the Wombles in my childhood—*and* horses. I would (very much) have liked a horse called 'Womble', or a Womble called 'Horse', for that matter.

Poor Abby awkwardly sits astride Womble nervously worrying the reins as though she can make a genie appear and wish to be whisked to safety. Meanwhile, (man about vineyard) Daniel seems to be in his element! Cut to the obligatory shot of them riding between the rows of grapevines and then THE INCIDENT.

For those of you who get squeamish, or those who don't care for profanity (even if it's bleeped out), look away or skip ahead now.

THE INCIDENT unfolds thus: Daniel encouraging Abby to trot. Abby valuing her life and opting not to. Daniel determining that the best way for Abby to learn is to slap her horse on the arse. Womble taking off across a field far faster than any Womble has ever moved before. Daniel catching up to them on his horse (whose name I have forgotten). Daniel getting a (verbal) walloping from Abby (you go, girl!). Both dismounting and Abby sensibly walking Womble back home (wherever that is). Daniel apologising profusely and making Abby laugh (self-deprecating laughter really *is* the best medicine). Daniel kissing Abby!

So, there you have it. Three mini-dates and three kisses. Excellent batting average, Daniel. Even Donald Bradman's was only 99.99.
But wait! There's more!

I'd like to remind you that the foursome is at a *winery*. And if that's not enough of a reminder, some (awfully close) drone shots of (probably terrified) grapes on the vine will definitely do the trick.

Yet another aside: I *really* hope that doesn't affect this year's vintage.

Meanwhile, back in the tasting room …

The lovely, lovely vintner (anyone who pours wine that generously is lovely in my book) takes the four-some through his entire tasting menu. I had not pipped Daphne as a 'spitter', but as she takes those micro sips, then delicately spits them into the bucket,

I can't help but admire A) her restraint (after that drive with Daniel, *I'd* need some decent glugs of wine) and B) her ability not to dribble down her front (I tried the sip-n-spit technique while on a mini-break in Bordeaux once. It was not pretty).

Becca, on the other hand, seems well practised at this wine tasting business—she is an Australian, after all and I've heard it's a national pastime. Her effusive 'ooh-ing' and 'mmm-ing', coupled with her ability to describe each wine like she's writing a wine catalogue, certainly catches Daniel's ~~eye~~ ear.

And where is Abby during all of this? At one end of the bar, getting absolutely sloshed. Was it THE INCIDENT that drove her to drink, or sharing her date with two strong contenders for Bride? Whichever, there's a slight wobble in her stride as the foursome thank the lovely, lovely vintner and climb aboard the Stag Express back to Stag Manor.

Speaking of …

What *do* five Does get up to when the others are away for a day of fun and adventure?

This is not a riddle—this is a montage scene! What an absolute treat! For the first time in *The Stag* history, it's time to break out the scrunchies and leg warmers and get yourself ready for an 80s-style movie montage, replete with the backing of 80s pop anthem, 'Girls Just Wanna Have Fun' by *the* Cyndi Lauper. (Credit to the producers for this spark of genius.)

- Does splashing about in the water at the private beach
- DIY mani-pedis
- Bitching about other Does behind their backs
- Sunning themselves on sun loungers
- Reading
- DIY bikini waxes (off-screen, behind closed doors—thank goodness)
- More bitching about other Does behind their backs
- Day drinking

And is that Kaz *braiding* Elizabeth's hair? Is this Stag Manor or *The Saddle Club*?

By the time the foursome arrive back at the Manor and Daniel wishes each of his dates a rather awkward goodbye ('Goodbye now—I've kissed all of you today, so I am not quite sure how this is done'), the stay-at-home Does are in various stages of inebriation, sun stroke, and ~~boredom~~ satisfaction after a day well spent in one of the world's most beautiful cities.

(Did I mention there was a montage?)

Cut to the Pin Ritual!

Gordo, having shown more zeal than usual earlier in this episode (perhaps he's had some coaching), reverts to his prior sombre tones and I'm not sure if we're going to learn who's staying and who's going home, or who will be fed to the sharks at dawn. (*Are* there sharks in Sydney Harbour? Goodness, I hope not. That would really put a dampener on those harbourside frolicking scenes.)

Daniel plays his part in the Pin Ritual as usual—almost comically pausing between each name as though trying to remember where he is and perhaps even his *own* name—and then there's a shot of the last two Does awaiting a pin, Elizabeth and Kaz.

I am torn. Call this 'Anastasia's Choice'. Kaz is a self-professed 'cack' (one of the many Australian expressions I've picked up this season) and is terrific fun to watch, yet I adore Elizabeth—she's a darling and if she's the one to go, I'll miss her sweet, bookish presence in the Manor.

Daniel takes a deep breath. 'Kaz, will you wear this pin?' Kaz steps up, her ubiquitous ear-to-ear grin splitting her face. 'For sure. Yeah, mate, totes.' See? I only understand half of what she says, but I love her to bits, the cack.

Cut to a close-up of Elizabeth. Oh, how I want to climb through the television screen, give her a massive hug and make that trembling lower lip and those welling tears disappear. Thank goodness that as soon as Gordo says, 'It's time to leave the Manor,' the other Does rally around and hug her while I sob into a handful of tissues.

Well, *most* of the Does do. There's now an even bigger divide between Villains, Tara and Kylie, and the others. I'm also not sure where the (increasingly) aloof Daphne fits into the Doe dynamics, perhaps somewhere in the middle in no-woman's land, or is that 'no-Doe's land'?

Regardless, so ends another topsy-turvy episode of what is turning out to be my favourite season of *The Stag* to date. Not sure about you but after that, I need a lie down and a giant glass of Australian Shiraz. Actually, that could be rather messy. I'll just take the wine.

Til next time …

I really don't want to go home just yet, and I hope this is enough to let me stay.

Chapter Fourteen

I magine this: You are across the world, far from your loved ones, with a camera shoved in your face 24/7. You came seeking love, yet you have just been rejected in front of twenty people and your rejection will soon be gossip fodder for twenty million more.

AND YOU CANNOT LEAVE.

Poor Elizabeth. She was denied a pin *five days ago* and she's still in the Manor. The story everyone else has been told is that there was a mix-up with the flights. But like Elizabeth, I know the truth. Her passport is missing. Jack has taken ultimate responsibility—this happened 'on his watch' as he says, and he's personally driven Elizabeth to the consulate to fast-track a new one, but even that could take a couple of weeks. Until then, she's stuck here.

That's fine when she's with the 'Nice' Does—or even Daphne. Daphne may be a snooty cow, but she's reasonably harmless and never openly harasses anyone. But if Elizabeth's left on her own, even for a moment, the wolves—a.k.a. Tara and Kylie—descend.

She's supposedly back in England, so she's never on camera and they're taking full advantage. They've gone from the occasional barb to full-on 'mean-girl' bullying, saying the nastiest things right to her face.

'You're so plain and boring; how did they even cast you on this show in the first place?' Kylie said to her last night.

Without hesitation, I'd leapt to Elizabeth's defence. 'You shut up, right now.'

Kylie just laughed at me and Tara followed up with, 'Yeah. As if Daniel would want a mouse like you. I'm surprised you lasted as long as you did.'

Becca stood, advancing on them threateningly. 'Get out,' she growled, and they scarpered out to the patio, giggling like naughty schoolgirls.

'Thank you,' Elizabeth said to Becca. 'And you, Abby.'

'Hey, you don't deserve that. They're just bitches,' said Becca.

Elizabeth, still visibly shaken, nodded but I could tell she was unconvinced. 'You've got us, all right?' I said.

Becca followed up quickly with, 'Definitely. We've got your back.' Elizabeth seemed a little brighter after that, and even agreed to join us for a few rounds of gin rummy with Kaz.

If there's a silver lining to this horrible situation, it's that Elizabeth and Becca have finally mended their fractured friendship. Still, I'd wager that Elizabeth wishes she'd taken up Jack's offer of a hotel. She'd declined, citing that she'd rather be in the Manor with the rest of us than in a lonely hotel room.

Ironic really—as someone who has gone from living alone to living with eleven others, there are times when I'd kill for a lonely hotel room. Even for a night.

And in the midst of all this schoolyard bulling, I keep reminding myself that Tara and Kylie are grown women—they hold down jobs, they have family and friends who presumably love them (or on reflection, perhaps not and that's where their bad behaviour stems from), and they are (otherwise) functioning adults.

It wouldn't surprise me if they're behind Elizabeth's missing passport.

Actually …

I tap softly on the Control Room door. I'm not sched-uled to be viewing anything this evening, but I want to share my theory with Jack and Harry and see what they think.

The door opens a crack and a sliver of Jack's (lovely) face appears. 'Oh, hey, want to come in?' he asks, opening the door wider. It's the most welcoming he's been towards me in some time and I entertain a morsel of hope that *our* frac-tured friendship will also mend soon.

'Er, yes, I just wanted to have a word with you and Harry about something.'

'Yeah, sure.' I follow him inside, seeing that Tim and the editor, Silvia, are also there. On the monitor is a still of Tara and Kylie—conspiring, no doubt, and apt, as they're who I'm here to talk about. Only, I don't want to say anything in front of the others. Jack must twig.

'Hey guys, can you take a break? Say, ten minutes?' he

says, leaning against one of the desks. Tim leaps out of his chair. 'Hey, Abby,' he says as he rushes past me. Silvia makes a notation on a tablet and smiles as she leaves. Then it's just the three of us, the brothers looking at me expectantly.

'Right, so I'll be quick as I know you have work to do. It's about Elizabeth's passport.'

Harry nods, his eyes narrowing in interest and Jack expels a frustrated sigh. 'Oh, wait,' he says, perking up, 'has it been found?'

'Er, no.' His shoulders slump and he indicates that I should continue. 'But I've been thinking. It doesn't make sense that it just magically disappeared. We've all got those safes in our rooms and that's where Elizabeth said she put hers when she first arrived, right?' They both nod. 'And when Tabitha left the Manor, she had to retrieve *her* passport from the same safe.' Harry's eyes narrow even further and Jack presses his lips together.

'So, what if she forgot to relock the safe and Elizabeth's passport was just there for the taking?'

'We thought of that,' says Harry, 'and as much as we hated doing it, we asked every member of the crew if they'd "seen" it.'

'We're confident that none of them had anything to do with it and at this point, we're thinking that either Elizabeth moved it—you know, the way people do sometimes—put it in a "safe place" then forget about it. Or …' He throws Harry a look and Harry nods at him. 'Maybe one of the cleaners took it.'

'We're hoping it's the former, of course,' Harry rushes to add.

'But that's just it. I have a different theory.'

Jack's chin lifts slightly, showing his interest, then he licks his lips. It's an innocuous gesture—his lips must have been dry—but all I can think of is how incredibly attractive he is. And how much I want to shoo Harry away and launch myself at Jack so I can kiss those newly wetted, perfect, perfect lips.

'So, what's your theory?' prompts Harry.

I look at him, horrified that he's somehow read my mind, though I try to disguise it. But having been caught out fanaticising about Jack, I've lost my train of thought. 'Oh, yes, right, sorry. What if one of the other Does took the passport? Or even *two* other Does?'

They both look perplexed. 'Hear me out. I know that there are police checks and character references and all that, and I'm not suggesting you let someone in the Manor who's running a fake passport ring out of their bedroom, or anything like that. But there are a couple of nasty sorts in the Manor. Bullies. And I know you know who I am talking about, and they've been *awful* to Elizabeth, especially since she was eliminated from the show.

'What if they took the passport? To keep her around a little longer so they can torment her—their little "plaything". Even if we do nothing, I suspect they'll soon get bored and that Elizabeth's passport will magically reappear in her underwear drawer, or something. Then they'll probably make fun of her for that—a last hurrah, so to speak. The bitches.'

Harry grins. 'Tell us what you *really* think, Abby.' It's the first time I've said anything nasty about the Villains in the

Manor without the buffer of Anastasia and it feels rather good to let it out.

'That does make sense,' Jack says.

'So, now what?'

'Now, Harry and I figure out a way to talk to Tara and Kylie about it, *diplomatically*.'

'Why diplomatically?' I ask. I'm now convinced I'm right, even without a shred of evidence.

'*Because*,' says Jack, as though he's explaining something simple to a child, 'we can't very well march into the lounge room and shout, "Hey, did you two steal Elizabeth's passport as a joke?"'

'Well, obvs,' I reply, miffed.

'Well, that's why. If they did take it, it's serious. It may even be a police matter. You can't just go about taking people's passports, you know.'

'I do know that, thank you, Jack. That's why I'm here.' We eye each other across the room, adversaries again. Bollocks.

'Okay, you two, we're getting a little off track,' interjects Harry. To Jack, he says, 'We could just search their room. Fabricate some kind of date, get them out of the Manor …' Ooh, I like this idea!

Jack rubs his chin, a frown nestled firmly in place. 'Can't do that. It's a violation of the privacy clause in their contracts. It's also wrong, *very* wrong.' I hate to admit it, but he's right, and I also hate admitting to myself that his strong moral compass is highly appealing, immediately negating his misdemeanour of patronising me.

'Yeah, yeah, you're right,' says Harry.

'Right, well, I've done all I can—'

'You mean, come in here and open a giant can of worms?' teases Harry.

'I mean, help you solve an enormous problem. It could be another week or two before Elizabeth gets her replacement passport and we can't just have her stuck here—miserable—for all that time.'

'And if you're right, we can't let it slide,' says Jack. 'And not just for Elizabeth's sake. If this got out, it could do serious damage to the show.'

I point at him. 'What you said.' Jack smiles at me and we're allies again. And I won't lie. That smile does wonders to my insides, but right now there are more pressing matters than my annoyingly steadfast crush on Jack. 'Right, I shall leave you to it. Let me know if there's anything more I can do.'

Just as I get to the door, Jack calls out, 'Hey, Abby?'

I turn. 'Mmm?'

'Thanks. Really. I reckon you might be right, and we do need to get this figured out.'

I grin. It feels good to be helpful. 'Bye,' I say, slipping out the door. I head back to the main house and poke my head in Elizabeth's open door. 'Hello,' I say. She starts at the sound of my voice. 'Oh, sorry, I just came to see how you are and to say goodnight.'

She lays her book beside her—another of the grisly crime thrillers she loves—and swings her legs over the side of her bed. 'Oh, that's all right,' she says. 'Just me being jittery. Did you want to come in?' She indicates the empty bed opposite and I cross the room and perch on its edge.

'So, how are you?'

'Oh, you know, busy, busy, busy. These books won't read themselves.' She nods her head in the direction of a stack on her bedside table.

'Wouldn't it be the best job ever to get paid to read?' I ask.

She laughs. 'I'd love that. Though I'd miss the children. That's one thing I'm looking forward to, seeing my pupils.'

'What age again?'

'Four and five.' I have no experience with children that age, so I just smile. 'Abby, I wanted to thank you again.'

'For what?'

'For being so nice to me …'

'Elizabeth, we're friends. You don't need to thank me for that.'

'Well, yes, all right, but I am grateful to you for standing up for me. I've never … I grew up in a small village and went to school in a slightly larger village—we were all quite close and everybody got along, so I've never been around this type of behaviour … I'm not sure I even know what to call it.'

'Bullying.'

'I suppose that's right.'

'It is, trust me. There were girls like that at my school and if it weren't for my best friend, Lisa, they would have been on at me constantly. She was my buffer, she and our little gang of friends.'

'You're *my* buffer, you and the others—Kaz, Becca.'

'We are.' I reach across the space between us and grab her hand, giving it a squeeze, Becca style. 'And it's probably got nothing to do with you—they're just messed up people. They clearly didn't have a Reception teacher who loved them the way you love your pupils.' She smiles at that. 'They're just basic bitches being bullies.' At my alliteration, she starts giggling.

'Anyway, this won't be forever. As soon as your passport gets sorted, you'll be on the next flight home.'

She nods, her giggles diminishing. 'I'm just really embarrassed,' she says.

'About what?'

'About Daniel not wanting me, then being stuck here, humiliated.'

'Hey, it's Daniel's loss. You're a catch, you really are. And, think of it this way, all of us, bar one, are going to feel rejected. Who knows, *I* could be the next to go. Ooh, maybe we'll get to fly back to the UK together.' I receive a half-smile for that, but then she shakes her head.

'No, Daniel likes you. I can tell. Maybe you're his bride-to-be, Abby.' Perish the thought, but I will not make gagging sounds in front of Elizabeth. I leap up.

'Right, I'll see you in the morning,' I say, making my way to the door.

'Goodnight,' she calls after me.

I pause at the doorway. 'Goodnight, and remember, we're just down the hallway if you need us.' I close the door behind me and head to my room.

Becca is seated on her bed cross-legged, slathering on an enormous blob of hand cream. Her hands look like they're covered in yoghurt. 'Good session?' she asks.

For a moment, I forget that I was supposedly meditating.

'Er, yes. I feel … er … refreshed.' I cross to my bed and start getting changed into my nightgown. We had a few days of modesty in the beginning, where we'd each disappear into the bathroom to get dressed, but that wore thin rather quickly and now we just change in front of the other. Sometimes, I sneak a peek at Becca out of curiosity. I've never seen a body that perfect up close before.

'I never saw the appeal myself,' she says, still on meditation. 'I mean, I've tried it—you know, at the end of yoga class—but I can never really concentrate. My mind always wanders off.' It's not lost on me that she says this right as *mine* has wandered off.

'But that's an important part of it, letting the mind wander,' I say. I had to read up on meditation as soon as I adopted it as my alibi for sneaking away to the Control Room or my hidey hole. 'You allow the thoughts to come, then let them go, and return to the one thing you're focused on. Practicing mindfulness, it's called,' I add. Come to think of it, maybe I *should* be meditating. It would certainly be a nice break for my overly active monkey mind.

'Well, it seems to work for you.'

'How do you mean?' I ask.

'Well, sometimes you're gone for an hour or two at a time. So, you must be good at it, the focusing part.'

It's been a while now since one of my lies slapped me in the face with a dead fish. 'Er, yes, I suppose so. Oh, I just saw Elizabeth.' Deflection—another tool in my arsenal of deceit.

In an instant, Becca's face radiates empathy. 'How is she?'

208

'I imagine she's been better, but I reaffirmed everything we talked about—you, me, and Kaz—that she has us, none of this is her fault, and that Daniel just wasn't the right man for her …' Becca nods solemnly at this and I'd bet a first date with Jack she's agreeing because she thinks he's the right man for *her*. 'And that the Cruella Sisters are just bullies.'

It was Becca's (absolutely genius) idea to call them the 'Cruella Sisters'. It's the perfect nickname—not only because of their matching hairstyles in platinum blonde and inky black, but that either one could out-evil Cruella herself—though the original one who made a coat from Dalmatians, not Emma Stone's version, the poor love.

Anastasia would have loved using the nickname in a recap, but it's gone on the list of 'things I cannot speak of lest I give myself away'.

'*Yeah*, they are. Any word on her passport?'

'Er … no, nothing.'

'She must be desperate to get home, poor thing.'

'Yes,' I agree.

'Still, it's probably … actually, never mind …' Becca trails off, still rubbing her yoghurt lotion into her cuticles.

'What?' I'm on my way into the bathroom, but something about Becca's tone stops me.

She looks at me like she's deciding whether to reveal something. 'Look, I hope you don't think I'm a bitch or anything, but with fewer Does here, it means more time with Daniel, right? And the more Does that get sent home it's … I guess I'm just impatient for the serious part to start.'

She has my full attention now. 'I'm not sure I know what you mean.'

'You're going to think I'm a bitch.'

'Don't say that. You're not a bitch.'

She sighs. 'Look, it's highly unlikely that Daniel's going to pick one of the Cruella Sisters. They *are* bitches, for one thing, but they're just so … you know … meh.' She's right about that—they're two completely unremarkable women, save for the remarkable way they've elevated 'bitchiness' to a whole new level. 'And I love Kaz—I can totally see us being friends in the real world.' It's not the first time a Doe has alluded to life in the Manor as being detached from 'the real world'—most of us think that way, especially me.

'But Kaz doesn't give a shit about Daniel—or even like him. I see the faces she makes when she thinks no one's looking. And Justine—she'll leave the Manor, get an agent, and be happy as Larry. So, that just leaves you, me, and Daphne. And god knows what Daphne's motivations are. I can't tell if she's really interested in Daniel or just wants to win. Though, he seems to like her, I guess,' she says, lowering her eyes and frowning.

I'm silent, as I sense a big revelation coming and after a moment, Becca lifts her eyes to mine. 'And I know Daniel has feelings for you.' I shake my head—it's an impulse, but real Abby was quick to protest when Doe Abby should have agreed with Becca. 'No, it's true, even if you don't believe it.' At least she didn't think it was out of character for me to disagree with her.

'But …' Oh, god, there's more. This may be the most uncomfortable conversation I've had since I got here—including asking Jack to tone down his friendliness towards me. And as necessary as that was, I frequently berate myself for it.

'I get the feeling that you're torn,' says Becca. This is dangerously close to the truth and my stomach sours. I'm only halfway through this assignment and my position here is already tenuous—I *still* haven't heard whether Roberta was happy with my revised recap. 'I can see you have feelings for Daniel ...' She can? This will never stop surprising me—that I am a better actress than I thought possible. '... but there's also Jack, isn't there?'

Oh, so she's *not* talking about me being torn between Doe Abby and real Abby. I send a silent thank-you to Cadmus, but now I need to decide how much to let on. I'm friends with Becca, but the foundation of our friendship is a lie. Who knows what she'll think of me if she ever discovers the truth? And my feelings for Jack are a big part of the truth.

What can I say that will protect my true identity but explain my poorly disguised feelings for the gorgeous Australian? 'You've got me,' I say with a shrug. I may as well play the hand I've been dealt and keep as close to the truth as possible.

She rewards me with a grin. 'I *thought* so.'

'Oh, really?'

'Well, yeah. I mean, whenever he's around you stare at him and you get this kind of starstruck look on your face.'

Oh, bollocks. Deflect, deflect, deflect. 'But how do you know I haven't got a crush on Harry? Or Tim? Or even Carlie?'

She tilts her head to the side. 'Abs, come on, it's *Jack*.'

'He is rather gorgeous.' God, it feels good to say that out loud. 'But it's just a crush. He's nice to look at, but I barely even know him,' I lie. If she can believe I have feelings for Daniel, hopefully she can believe my feeling for Jack are, at most, a schoolgirl crush.

'Sure, I guess, but if you decide that you do like Jack more than Daniel, and I completely understand if you don't, but if you do … maybe don't accept the pin next time,' she pleads, her eyes filled with hope.

If only it were that simple.

But if Roberta decides to keep me here, I will have to accept every pin I'm offered. Except the final pin, that is. No matter what, this assignment finishes here in Sydney. I am not living 'happily ever after' with the Stag for the sake of an online column—especially *that* twat. But I can't say any of this to Becca.

'I won't, I promise,' I reply, adding a promise I can't keep to my stinking pile of lies.

Chapter Fifteen

'You're done with that, right?' Kylie reaches across the counter and takes Elizabeth's bowl just as she's dipped her spoon into it. No, she wasn't done with it and now there's milk and cereal all over the counter.

There's a stunned silence from the four of us—me, Becca, Kaz, and Elizabeth—as the blonde Cruella Sister makes a big to do of tossing the bowl into the sink.

As three voices explode in anger, all demanding that Kylie apologise, there's a low growl from the other end of breakfast bar. 'Clean it up.' That sounded like it came from Elizabeth. I hold up a hand to quieten the others as Kylie turns around and leans against the sink, arms folded and smiling smugly at Elizabeth. 'I said, "Clean it up",' Elizabeth snarls, her voice low and menacing. Becca's eyes widen as she glances my way. Kaz sits back against her stool and matches Kylie's folded arms, her gaze riveted to Elizabeth. She looks both proud and amused.

'Are you talking to *me*, you piss-weak little shit?' I'm

about to protest again——how *dare* Kylie speak to her like that, or anyone for that matter——but Elizabeth's voice cuts through my thoughts.

'*Clean* it up,' she repeats, louder this time.

'How about, "No fucking way"?' Kylie laughs, then pushes herself off her perch and makes to leave.

Elizabeth (literally) stands her ground, leaping off her chair and blocking Kylie's exit. 'Clean it up!' she shouts. 'You made this mess, so *you* clean it up!'

'Get out of my way, you nutter.' Kylie goes to step past her, but Elizabeth slams a palm into her shoulder. I'm off my stool immediately, certain that a cat fight is about to erupt.

'You clean it up now, or I'll——'

'You'll *what*?'

I pull up just as I reach Elizabeth, Kaz close behind me, and turn at the sound of the additional voice. Tara has descended the stairs and in several long strides, she traverses the distance to the kitchen. She glares down at Elizabeth who, to her credit, lifts her chin in defiance. 'You'll what?' Tara taunts, clearly not expecting an answer. I'm ready to reach for Elizabeth and pull her from the fray but there's something in the shift of her stance that makes me hold off.

'I'll wait until you're both asleep,' she says, her voice gravelly, 'then I'll sneak into your room and cut off that ugly, frazzled Morticia hair of yours,' she says to Tara. '*And* your disgusting platinum mop,' she directs at Kylie.

Kaz barks out a laugh and I have to clap a hand over my mouth so I don't do the same. I hear Becca's familiar giggle behind me, then I can't control it anymore and I burst out laughing. It must be infectious, because Elizabeth starts laughing too.

Kylie and Tara share an incredulous look, then all hell breaks loose. 'How dare you!' 'You're just jealous!' 'You fucking mole, you come anywhere near me—'

Just as I'm thinking it's a shame this isn't being filmed—Elizabeth standing up to these bullies would make for great television—Jack's voice booms across the room.

'That's enough!'

Silence, as six Does freeze like actual deer frozen in headlights.

'What's going on?' Justine wanders in from outside, her skin glistening with saltwater—like every other morning, she's just been for a swim.

Jack doesn't reply, but instead makes a beeline for the fracas. 'Kylie, Tara, I'd like to speak to you privately, please.'

They both start speaking at once. 'That's not fair.' 'It was *her*.' 'She threatened to cut my bleedin' hair awf!'

'Stop!' God, he really can command a room when he wants to. *Rawr*. 'I mean it. Upstairs to your room, right now.' My mind flashes forward to an image of me and Jack at home, one of our teens playing up and him taking charge. I won't lie, it's a very sexy flash-forward.

Daphne is coming downstairs right as Jack marches the Cruella Sisters up to the second storey. The evil twins push past her roughly, and I swear I hear, 'Well, I never,' from Daphne. When she joins us in the kitchen, she's clutching at her string of pearls. 'What in god's name is going on?' she asks, looking between us.

'Kylie was being a prize bitch,' says Kaz, 'then Lizzie stood up to her and then Tara, in full-on, supremo bitch mode, joined in and—I swear to god—I was a millisecond from decking her, but then Jack broke it all up. You missed the whole thing.'

I catch Harry jogging up the stairs out of the corner of my eye, walkie talkie in one hand, a suitcase in the other. Something is about to go down.

'Are you all right?' Daphne asks Elizabeth.

'Uh, yes, thanks.' Elizabeth exhales a long sigh and collapses onto the nearest stool.

'Well, then well done you,' says Daphne. As if the morning hasn't been bizarre enough, Daphne chooses now to start being a *person* and Elizabeth perks up considerably at the praise.

Becca gets her a glass of water and we're sharing excited recounts when we hear loud crashes from upstairs. We exchange looks, American soap opera-style, then watch as Tim appears, camera on his shoulder, and sprints up the stairs. This is followed by a stream profanity that echoes through the cavernous house.

Tara.

She's being kicked out of the Manor and if they air any of this footage, they'll need more bleeps than when Daniel smacked Womble's arse and sent her racing across a field with me on top. There's more crashing about and without discussing it, we've crept en masse towards the bottom of the stairs to get closer to the action.

'I will fucking *sue* you!' shouts Tara. She appears at the railing at the top of the stairs, dragging her suitcase. 'What the bleedin' 'ell are you lot staring at?'

We scatter like ants in a rainstorm and I head for the lounge room and plop onto one of the sofas, where I've got a direct view of the unfolding scene. Tara makes her way downstairs, her heavy suitcase hitting each stair with a thud. The profanities keep flying, and Tim follows hot on her heels, capturing the whole incident on camera. It's even got a microphone attached, which is a good thing, as Tara rips the battery pack from her waistband and throws it down the stairs, then claws at her microphone cord, violently tossing it aside as soon as it's free.

When she gets to the bottom of the stairs, her eyes scan the enormous room, pinning each of us with a vicious glare. 'And fuck all you slags, especially you, you fucking cow,' she says to Elizabeth. 'Lying about me stealing your passport. You just watch your fucking back.'

'Oh, do shut up, you foul-mouthed harpy.'

'Hah! Bravo, Lizzie,' says Kaz, clapping and bellowing out a hearty laugh. The rest of us join in, clapping and cheering Tara's departure and I've never seen a person's head explode before, but there's a first time for everything and it looks like that may just happen.

'Fuck all of you!' she screams. She swings open the front door so hard, it smashes into the wall, then drags her suit-case down the front steps of the Manor and along the gravel driveway, no doubt a difficult feat when *not* in a lather. Tim follows her and the rest of us congregate on the front porch to watch the departure of the worst Villain in *The Stag*'s history.

In a final hurrah, Tara turns and gives us, the Manor,

and the 'entire fucking world' the finger—her words, not mine.

'I'm not sure where she thinks she's going,' says Jack, who I hadn't realised was standing right behind me. 'We haven't even booked her flight yet.'

'And it's not like she can walk all the way to the airport,' says Harry, who's also joined us.

'So, what are you going to do?' I ask.

Jack rubs his chin and looks at his brother. 'What do you reckon? Send Carlie after her in one of the vans?'

'Yeah, I guess so.'

'Believe me, if it wasn't in her contract that we'll fly her home, I'd let her fend for herself,' says Jack.

'Did she really take my passport?' asks Elizabeth.

'Uh, yeah. Actually, here.' Jacks retrieves her passport from his back pocket and Elizabeth is so overjoyed, tears spring to her eyes.

'Oh, my goodness, thank you.'

'Actually, you can thank Abby. She's the one who figured it out. How 'bout we all go back inside and I'll catch you up,' he says.

Kaz slings an arm around Elizabeth's shoulder as we make our way inside. 'I'm so proud of you, Lizzie. You were amazing standing up to those cows.'

Elizabeth is suddenly her shy self again and ducks her head, the colour in her cheeks rising. 'Thanks.' When we're all seated in the lounge room—all the remaining Does except Kylie, who is glaringly absent—Jack addresses us while Harry goes off to find Carlie so she can collect Tara from the side of the road. Roadside Villain taxi for one?

'Right, so without going into too much detail, it turned out that Tara took your passport, Elizabeth, and Kylie knew about it. So, I spoke with the executive producer this morning and she agreed that Tara would be removed from the show immediately and that Kylie will not receive a pin at the next Pin Ritual.'

'Wait, so you're making Kylie go through with the Pin Ritual?' asks Justine.

'Uh, yeah. The stolen passport wasn't her doing, but she kept quiet about it when she could have—*should* have—come forward, so she's off the show too.'

'So, that means we're all safe,' says Kaz. 'The six of us,' she adds, looking around the group.

'Uh, that's right. You'll all be here for at least another week.'

'Yes!' says Kaz and knowing her little secret—that she doesn't like Daniel and is having her first proper holiday in years—I'm happy for her. I am also happy for Elizabeth, who can finally go home. And even though we all have different reasons for being here, or wanting to stay, the others seem pleased with the news.

'Elizabeth, can I talk to you outside for a sec?' asks Jack, indicating the backyard.

'Yes, all right.' She joins Jack on the threshold where the glass bifold doors have been opened, and they go out the patio and start talking in low murmurs.

Just then, Tim re-enters the Manor. 'How far did she get?' asks Kaz.

'Right to the end of the road. You know where that giant pink house is at the T-junction?' There are various affirmative responses——we've driven past that house every time we've left the Manor. And I don't mind pink, but who paints their fancy mansion the colour of an Easter egg?

'Yeah, she stopped there, but I got tired of being shouted at, so I came back.'

'Yeah, no need to stick around and get abused,' says Justine.

I yawn, then glance at the clock. Is it really only 9:50am? It feels like it's already been a full day, but we'd better get moving. Daniel's due at 11am and we need to be camera ready. Today, we're playing some weird version of 'Truth or Dare'. Ooh, I wonder if Kylie is supposed to join in. We haven't heard a peep from her since she went upstairs at Jack's command. I doubt she'll want to show her face but if we're going through the pretence of her being eliminated this week, then surely she needs to be in the footage leading up to the Pin Ritual?

I'd call this feeling 'schadenfreude' if there had been even a *second* when Kylie and I were friends. So, I guess that makes it 'justice'.

'Er, lovelies,' I say, even though Daphne's here too, 'our Stag is arriving in just over an hour and we need to get ready.' With the way they reluctantly peel themselves off the sofas, it's as though I've said it's time to spring clean the Manor. I guess I'm not the only one who's already shattered.

I'm about to follow the others upstairs when Jack calls, 'Hey, Abby, have you got a sec?'

'Of course,' I say, turning back. *'For you, Jack, I have all the seconds,'* I think. I join him and Elizabeth on the patio. 'Everything sorted?' I ask her.

She nods. 'They've booked me on a flight in the morning.'

'In the morning? But that's so soon.'

She grins at me. 'I've been in the Manor an extra *week*, Abby. I just want to go home now.'

'I know, of course you do. It's just … I'll miss you.'

'I'll miss you and the girls, too, but we'll stay in touch and I visit London sometimes. We can catch up.' Reality is rudely intruding on my Stag Manor bubble and I don't care for it one bit. I don't want to think about being back in London—more accurately, I don't want to think about being back in London having said goodbye to Jack, my (former) potential love interest and (now) sort of friend.

'Can we at least give her a proper send off?' I ask Jack.

'What do you mean?'

'Like a dinner, or something—tonight. Just us Does.'

He rubs his chin, the gesture I've come to know as him thinking something through. 'I guess that would be okay. We're only filming today, so … Is that what you want, Elizabeth? Or would you prefer a quiet night?' Oh, of course—I should have asked her what she wants.

'Sorry, I shouldn't have assumed,' I say.

'No, no, it's a lovely idea. I'd like that. But maybe it can be all of us, not just the Does.' She looks up at Jack. 'So, you and Harry, and how about Carlie and Tim as well? They're the crewmembers we spend the most time with and I've actually become quite friendly with Carlie.'

Jack smiles at her. 'I'll talk to Harry and we'll arrange something. Oh, not *Daniel*, though, right?' Elizabeth makes a face like she's sucked on a lemon and I stifle a giggle. 'Thought not. Anyway, I'll take care of it.'

She grins again. 'That's brilliant! Right, I'm off to pack and tell the others about tonight. And, Abby, they're flying me home business class!' she adds.

'It was the least we could do,' says Jack.

Elizabeth practically skips off, then runs up the stairs. 'Oh man, I feel like I need a stiff drink.' Jack makes his way over to the wicker patio furniture (think every film you've ever seen set on a tropical island) and falls into one of the chairs.

'Are you all right?' I ask, sitting opposite him.

He puts his head in his hands. 'That really could have gone another way. I was totally packing myself.'

'Really? You seemed fairly sure of yourself to me.' I recall the way he ordered Tara and Kylie upstairs and squirm in my seat when my body warms at the memory.

Jack lifts his head. 'Fuck me …' I suppose that responding, *'Yes, please,'* isn't appropriate, so I stay silent. 'In all the time I've worked in reality TV, that's the worst situation I've ever been in.'

'So, how did you know that they took the passport—or did you decide to confront them and see if they caved?'

'Nah, we knew for sure. We couldn't search their room, 'cause that would have, you know …'

'… Breached the privacy clause,' I say, finishing his thought.

'Exactly, but I realised that we *do* have the rights to all the audio we record even when you're not on camera.'

'Oh, yes, of course. You're not allowed to use those

recordings on the show …'

'… But we own them, so they were fair game.'

'That's brilliant!'

'Well, thank you.' He looks well chuffed. 'It was a shit of a job, of course, but Harry and I took turns, working through most of the night, and we hit the jackpot this morning, right before we confronted them. Tara saying how she wished she could brag about it to everyone. And Kylie egging her on—that's how we knew she was also culpable.'

'God, Jack, you must be exhausted.' It's only now that I notice the stubble and the dark shadows under his eyes—*and* that he's wearing the same T-shirt as yesterday. This one is Kermit coloured and says, 'It's not easy being green'. It's clearly not easy producing a reality television show either.

'Yeah, I am—mostly relieved, though. Hopefully, we can get Tara on a flight today.'

'*Or*—and hear me out—there are no seats on any flights for at least the next few days and she has to sit in a hotel and stew. No! Even better—a *motel*—a rubbish one.'

'You're something of an evil mastermind, you are,' he says, the corners of his eyes creasing mischievously.

'I'm just overly attached to justice,' I retort.

'Hmm. I'd feel better knowing she's on her way back to the UK and not our problem anymore.'

'Well, there's that too, I suppose.' We share a smile and my breath catches a little.

'Hey,' he says, serious again, 'really, thank you, Abby.'

'For what?'

'For everything—for figuring it all out, for being such a good friend to Elizabeth,' he replies, his eyes filled with appreciation. 'This could have dragged on for weeks, but now we're good. *And* we're on the home stretch.'

The home stretch—another allusion to all this ending soon—possibly even sooner if Roberta wants me gone. But with Jack's eyes locked on mine and us talking properly for the first time in ages, my little Manor bubble has got even smaller and for this one perfect moment, it's just us. I don't want to ruin it by asking whether my rewrite was enough to keep me here.

'Right,' he says, slapping his palms on his thighs and making me start. Moment lost, bubble popped. 'Oh, sorry, I didn't mean to startle you.' I shake my head at him, smiling. 'I've just got a million things to do.'

'Go! See if Carlie found Tara and let her know where she's taking her.' It's either the airport or a hotel, or if Jack reconsiders my suggestion, a rubbish motel.

'Yes, first on my list.' He stands. 'Then I'll organise something for tonight and get set up for filming in' —he checks his watch— 'shit, an hour.'

'I've thrown you in it, haven't I? Sorry, I hadn't realised you and Harry were up all night.'

'Nah, it's all good. We can grab a kip after we wrap up filming this arvo. It'll be cool. We'll probably just order something in, have a few drinks, hang out—and no cameras.'

'Sounds perfect,' I say. And if it weren't for the other eight people who'd be there, it also sounds like the perfect *date*. Though, in front of the others, I will have to be Doe Abby—the version of me who likes Daniel, not the gorgeous Australian.

Chapter Sixteen

The Stag in Sydney Recap:
One Big Happy Family (sort of)
by Anastasia Blabbergasted

Well, there was no way that we could have seen this coming! The latest season of *The Stag* is keeping this girl on her proverbial toes!

Remember last week when lovely Elizabeth was eliminated by not-so-lovely Daniel and had to say goodbye to her friends in the Manor? Of course, you do! It was only a week ago. So, imagine our collective surprise when we discovered that she's been in the Manor ever since, because the Cruella Sisters conspired to steal her passport and she was left stranded far from home and out of love!

And what about the Cruella Sisters, the yin and yang

of dreadfulness? It's hard to pinpoint which of them is worse. Could it be Tara with her potty mouth and tendencies towards bullying, or Kylie with her potty mouth and tendencies towards bullying? You see the dilemma!

But with Tara the mastermind behind snatching said passport, she may just pip Kylie at the post.

The good news is … (drumroll please) … Tara has been booted out of the Manor! In a departure reminiscent of … well, we've never seen this type of behaviour on *The Stag* before but one of those meltdowns from *Actual Homemakers* comes to mind. Bleep this, bleep that, and a skyward middle finger to boot as she departed in the most ungracious manner. I suppose she walked all the way to Sydney airport, luggage—and emotional baggage—in tow!

But what of Kylie? Well, I don't think even *I* could have decided a more fitting punishment for being in cahoots with Tara! Kylie will be made to see out the rest of the week in the Manor then wend her way through what will be an agonising Pin Ritual. Huzzah! The producers have done it again. Cruel? Yes. But just? A *resounding* yes.

But before we get to shots of Kylie skulking—and sulking—about the Manor, keeping the lowest (lowlife) profile ever, what about that dinner party to celebrate the return of the passport and Elizabeth finally being able to fly home to England?

Daniel's invitation must have been lost in the mail, because he was a no-show; though, that could have been because Elizabeth, now rejected by him, has realised what a massive twat he is. She's deserving of someone far kinder, far less egotistical, and with a shred of human decency.

But not to worry—plenty of eye candy in his place, with Manly Man About the Manor, Harry, the series director, Tim, the adorable camera operator, and, of course, the extremely gorgeous Jack—Harry's brother and the show's producer. Jack is like a hipster crossed with a tech geek played by a Hollywood mega star. Yum, yum.

And hasn't he caught the eye of our Abby? It's unclear at this stage if the feelings are reciprocated, but he *does* seem to, at minimum, consider her a friend. So, jury remains out on this one, but if Abby makes goo-goo eyes at him just once more (all that staring at his lips is *so* obvious, Abby), Staggy Daniel will twig, and we may just see a (tom)cat fight for Abby's heart.

But that's not the only extra-curricular crush, fling, or flirtation amongst the cast and crew!

No, no, no! As it turns out, the reason Australian Justine spends so much time looking longingly at the camera has less to do with her ambitions of stardom than originally thought. While it's been clear for some time that she has absolutely no interest in Staggy Daniel, the true object of her desire has only just come to light. It seems that Justine and Tim *know* each other, as in before *The Stag* and *biblically*. Having dated a few years ago, this convergence of reality television and reality has meant not just a reunion, but a rekindling!

Let's raise a glass to the happy couple!

Rounding out this dinner party are Daphne (glimpses of the *woman* this week, not the Ice Queen, so one to watch), Kaz (can they *please* give this woman her own show? Or perhaps just drop her into all other reality television shows and let her do her thing), the beautiful (inside and out) Becca (I am hugely concerned with how much she wants to win Daniel's heart, as he is more obsessed with her looks than any other attribute. I wonder if Harry is single——Hmm), Carlie (the one crewmember who seems to have no specific job title but is across practically everything – also a complete darling, having endeared herself to most of the Does), and of course, the guest of honour, Elizabeth.

Didn't you nearly fall off your sofa when Elizabeth confronted her bullies, the Cruella Sisters?

She seems like she wouldn't say boo to a goose and perhaps this is her first ever 'boo', but inside that sweet, shy woman is a LIONESS! Roarrr! I actually snorted tea out of my nose when she said that line about cutting off their hair (all right, it was wine). And 'Oh, do shut up, you foul-mouthed harpy!' shall go down as one of the best lines in *The Stag's* history. Honestly, next time I'm having a bad day and need cheering up, I will conjure the memory of that scene, especially the looks on the Cruella Sisters' faces.

So, this pseudo family gathered for a casual dinner of takeaway Thai, merrily passing containers around the table, along with (what seemed like) some rather delicious Australian Riesling, chatting and sharing stories from home. Rivalry between the Does was temporarily forgotten, or at least put on hold, and my favourite part of the dinner was Kaz's story about, er, ball sports …

So far, it's a brilliant recap—possibly one of Anastasia's best. I can't submit it, of course, but it could make excellent fodder for my exposé. I'll ask Jack for a memory stick so I can save it and take it with me. A little fib should do—something about capturing my recaps for future reference.

It *was* an enjoyable dinner, and a proper send off for

Elizabeth. She's flown home now, as has Tara the Terrible—different flights so Elizabeth didn't have to worry about running into her at either end. Jack and Harry also made Tara sweat it out for an extra day, letting her think there might be criminal charges. There won't be—Elizabeth didn't want to go down that route—but Tara didn't know that until the morning she flew back to the UK. Brownie points for Harry and Jack, awarded by my sense of justice.

Good riddance to bad rubbish.

And Kylie has barely shown her face. She sneaks down for food when she thinks no one will be about like an oversized mouse. No doubt she's desperate to get out of the Manor, especially as she only lives a state away.

And that story that Kaz told at dinner. Oh, my—*hilarious*. Such a shame it won't be on the show.

'So, you know 'cause of my job, I'm on construction sites all the time, right? So, I'm on this site—massive high-rise, in the heart of downtown Perth—and I've been on the project for *months*, right, so I've gotten to know a lot of the guys and that's not sexist, by the way—just no women on this project. Anyway, this one day… hang on, let me set the scene. So, it's lunchtime and it's a sea of orange high-vis vests—'cause that's what we all wear, right?—and a bunch of guys are kicking a footy around, like twenty guys, and I know a lot of 'em, familiar faces, you know. And I'm walking past—super professional, right? I'm in my dungarees, my high-vis vest, hard hat, work boots, the lot. And I'm not *actually* their boss—but I'm also *kinda* their boss, because I'm the lead structural engineer, right? Anyway, so they're kicking the footy around and one of them calls out, "Hey, Kaz, come play footy with us." Now, I am *terrible* at team sports—always picked last in Phys Ed at school, right? So, without thinking—even for a *second*—I reply, "Sorry, boys, I suck at anything that involves balls."'

There was a beat at the table, a collective intake of breath, then she added, 'And even after *that*, I still don't catch on to what I've said 'til one of the blokes—and I have no idea who it was—says, "Well, then you should *definitely* come play with us."'

At that point, we all burst into raucous laughter—even Daphne. 'And wait!' said Kaz.

'Oh, god, there's more?' asked Justine, who was almost doubled over with laughter.

'Yeah, so, I'm frigging *mortified*, of course, and I just get the hell out of there and go get some lunch, calm myself down. And when I get back to the onsite office, the frigging football is sitting on my frigging desk! No lie!'

By then, I was laughing so hard I couldn't breathe. 'And to this very day,' said Kaz, wrapping up her long but compelling story, 'I *still* haven't lived it down, 'cause once in a while, I'll meet up with one of those blokes on a new project and they'll be all, "Hey, Kaz, wanna play footie?"' Kaz shook her head at herself and when I caught Jack's eye across the table, he winked at me.

I don't know if it was a 'between friends' type of wink, or something more. It was likely the former, as all our conversations of late have been about the show and he hasn't been to my hidey hole since I suggested he keep his distance. Why, oh why, did he have to do as I asked? I have wasted many an hour imagining (in excruciating detail) what

I'd like to do to him if he ever does show up. Again, there's no harm in fantasising, right? *Right?*

And I still haven't learnt if I'll be writing the next recap from here or from home. It's not due for a few days, though—we haven't even filmed this week's Pin Ritual yet, the one with the foregone conclusion of Kylie's departure. I wonder how Daniel has taken the news about the Cruella Sisters. He's barely shown any interest in them beyond that strange 'painting' activity, so perhaps he won't care.

With my monkey mind swinging between wondering, worrying, hoping, and imagining, I'm suddenly shattered and let out a long, loud yawn. I should take up meditation (for real), but the few times I've tried have been excruciating. Honestly, how do people quieten their thoughts enough to focus on just one thing? I'm not sure my mind is wired that way.

I return to hoping, namely that Roberta has forgotten all about pulling me off the show. Surely, she must have more pressing things on her mind with all that's happened. And if not, I hope she realises there's been enough disruption to the season already and that she should keep me—no matter what she thought of my rewrite.

Top two. With Daphne …

That doesn't factor in what Daniel wants, of course, and if I had to guess he's far more into Becca than Daphne—as superficial as his interest might be. Roberta, channelled by Jack, can nudge him along all she wants, but that doesn't mean Daniel will do as she suggests.

What if he decides to get rid of Doe Abby next? Then the whole Roberta situation will be moot. Gah! I'm in limbo—professional and emotional limbo. And I am sitting in a storage room writing something that will never see the light of day, just because it's (marginally) better than letting these thoughts run rampant through my mind.

There's a tap at the door. It's either Jack, or our resident human-cum-mouse, Kylie, has found my hidey hole and wants to borrow it. The door opens a crack and a (gorgeous) pair of green eyes appears and those 'Jack and Abby' fantasies start playing out across the cinema screen in my mind. It's suddenly stiflingly hot in here.

'Hey, you *are* in here,' he says, opening the door wider and stepping inside my 'office'.

'You've been looking for me?'

'Uh, yeah. Becca said you were meditating, but this isn't one of your usual times for writing. So, stupidly, I checked the gardens—front *and* back—*and* the beach before heading here.'

'You know I only do my nocturnal gardening on Tuesdays,' I reply.

'I'll keep that in mind,' he says, grinning. 'So, what are you working on?'

I glance at the screen and see the paragraph about Abby crushing on Jack, then slam the lid of the laptop. 'Er, just playing around with some ideas.'

'Oh, okay.' There's a flicker of something unpleasant across his face; perhaps I was too curt.

'So, you were looking for me?' I ask cheerily.

'Yeah, actually, I have news.'

'Oh?' I ask this as casually as I can but inside I'm

squirming. Almost every time Jacks has news my life gets more complicated.

'I just spoke to Roberta—caught her up on the exits from the Manor, talked about upcoming storylines and date ideas, and do you want the good news first, or the even better news?'

I perk up. Good news? Please, Cadmus, let me be staying!

'Either. Both. Yes, both.'

He laughs. 'Well, can't give you both at the same time, so I'll start with the good news. Roberta loved the rewrite you did on the last recap and she wants you to stay on.'

'Really?'

'Yeah, really!'

'Oh, that is such a relief! I'd really hate to leave the show now, especially considering the relationships I've formed.' Uh-oh, Icarus, flying too close to the sun again. 'I mean, I want to do a good job, the best job I possibly can, and being here with yo—er … everyone … that just makes the recapping all the easier, what with the insight I've gained and the relationships—with the other Does, I mean. And *Prue* will be really pleased—ecstatic even. And I am, too—pleased, that is. *Really* pleased. Er … really.'

And I *really* must stop talking now as I'm spouting nonsensical rubbish and have used my 'really' quota for the week—actually, make that the month.

'Great. I thought you would be. And it definitely helps—you staying. We've already lost two Does this week—'

'Oh, right. Of course, how silly of me. I hadn't thought

of that. You *need* to keep Doe Abby, at least for the time being.'

'No, wait, sorry, that came out wrong. I just meant that it's a relief all round—you get to stay and we can hold off on bringing in the Interloper for a couple more days.'

'The Interloper?' I ask.

'Yeah. Haven't I …?' I have no idea what he's talking about and he must sense my confusion. 'Oh, right, I haven't told you yet. And I forgot, you don't have them on the British version of the show.'

'No, definitely not familiar,' I say.

'Well, an Interloper is a Doe who comes into the Manor part-way through the season. It's usually because something hasn't gone to plan and we need to ramp up the drama. Or it's just to ramp up the drama,' he adds, wryly. 'And with Kylie and Tara both leaving this week, we need to play the Interloper card a little earlier than planned. She'll be joining us the day after tomorrow, after the next Pin Ritual. I'm sorry, I must've had a complete brain fart and forgot to tell you.'

'So, is this the "better news" you said you had?' I am not a hundred per cent sure this *is* good news. If the Interloper is coming into the Manor to 'ramp up the drama', then she's most likely another Villain.

'Sorry?'

'You said you had good news and better news. Is this the better news?'

'What? Oh, no … I'd completely forgotten about Stevie—that's the Interloper.' He snaps his fingers. 'That reminds me, I must get her dossier to you. I should probably just upload it to your laptop——that way there's no chance of it being discovered.' I haven't seen Jack this disorganised or frazzled before, but I suppose it's understandable. He still has the dark circles he acquired during that sleepless night ferreting out the passport thieves.

'So, maybe just leave it in the usual spot and I'll upload the file first thing tomorrow?'

Wait. What? It twigs that Jack wants to upload something onto this laptop——the one on which I have just written about making goo-goo eyes at him. 'Er, how about you pop it onto a memory stick for me? I was going to ask you for one anyway, so I can save all my recaps——you know, for … er …'

'Oh, yeah, that's fine. I'll do that.' Phew.

'So, what *is* the better news, then?' Not only deflecting——now one of my superpowers——but it's getting comical how often this conversation has gone off piste.

Jack runs a hand over his forehead, pushing his floppy hair from his face, then starts laughing. 'Can you tell I've hardly slept for the past few days?' he asks, releasing his fringe to flop down onto his forehead. 'My mind is so chaotic right now. I can barely string two sentences together and I keep forgetting what I'm talking about.'

'Welcome to my world,' I say, laying on the sarcasm as thick as Becca's Vegemite.

He laughs properly now. 'Is that what it's like inside your mind too? Spinning plates, I call it.'

'Exactly like that.'

'Only mine keep crashing to the floor,' I say right as he says, 'Only I'm dropping more than I'm spinning.'

We grin at each other. 'Jinx. You owe me a Coke,' he says.

'A Coke?'

'Come on, you must have heard that one?'

'Jinx, yes. Though, I'd prefer a decent Chardonnay to a Coke.'

'Actually, so would I,' he says. Now all I want to do is drink Chardonnay with Jack. Actually, I'd like to do a lot more than that and it's starting to feel hot in here again. It's clear his mind has wandered off too, as he's currently staring at a box of toilet roll. 'Er, Jack?'

'Mmm, yeah?'

'The better news …'

'I'm so sorry. Right, so the *better* news is that next week, you've got one of the one-on-one dates with Daniel. And not only that, but I've snagged the best date for you. You're gonna *love*—'

'Hang on, I have a one-on-one date with Daniel next week?'

'Yeah, and you're going to love—'

'So, is that really what you think "better" news is?' Oops, already over my quota and I've used another 'really'——but this time it's *really* warranted.

'I don't understand.'

'Why would I want a one-on-one date with Daniel? Can you get me out of it?'

'Abby, I … I'm at a loss here. Why do you want out of the date?'

'Because!' *'Because the only man I want to date is you … you daft, moronic nitwit!'*

'Are you worried about doing something you're scared of? Because I haven't even told you what the date is.'

'No, it's not that. Wait, what *is* the date?' Sometimes curiosity is a distracting cow of a thing.

'It's a visit to a wildlife park. You know, cuddling koalas, hand-feeding kangaroos, that kinda thing.'

His voice lacks warmth—my doing, I know—but now I'm torn. I'd love to go to a wildlife park and cuddle a koala—*and* I'd get that photograph for Mum and Aunty Lo. But it would mean spending alone time with Daniel and why (oh, *why?*) does Jack think I want that?

'That does sound nice …' I say.

'So why the hesitation? Why that look on your face, Abby?'

'What look?' My hands fly to my cheeks, which are warm.

'Well, I'd describe it as "horrified". I mention a one-on-one date and you look like I'm sending you to the gallows—*naked*. What the hell's going on?'

'I don't see why you're so suspicious of me all of the sudden.'

'It's not suspicion, Abby, I'm just baffled. Do you want to go on a one-on-one date with Daniel or not?'

'No!'

'Well then why the hell did you kiss him?'

'What?' I ask, incredulous.

'You heard me. On the winery date—you kissed him.'

We exchange Paddington Bear hard stares. 'I *didn't* kiss him,' I say, my voice low and pointed.

'*Well, it sure looked like it to me!*'

'Lower your voice. Someone will hear you.'

He expels out a frustrated, angry sigh. '*It looked like it to me.*'

Something else twigs. 'And why do *you* care if I did kiss Daniel?'

'Oh, so now you *did*?'

'Why does it even matter? Doesn't it play perfectly into the twisted little plan that you and Roberta have concocted? Top two Does!' I shout.

'Hey, that's all Roberta—I had nothing to do with it. Come on, Abby, you know that.'

'Do I? Isn't that why you've been so distant, why things are so off between us?'

'Seriously? *You're* the one who told me to stay away!'

'But I didn't mean it!'

'What? I …'

'And now I have to go on a one-on-one date with Daniel, that priggish twat, and *that's* your "better news"?'

'Wait, sorry, I'm confused. You just said you kissed him.'

'I did not. I said, "so what if I did?".'

'Well, did you?'

'No! I didn't! Daniel kissed me. And he caught me by surprise and before I even knew what was happening, it was over. I'd nearly been thrown off a *horse*, I'll have you know, so forgive me for being *so* out of sorts that I wasn't quick enough to fend him off like I did last time!' I glare at him, but inside I can feel the fight leaving my body—sheer emotional exhaustion, is my guess.

How have Jack and I got ourselves into this stupid, tangled mess?

His eyes scrutinise mine, then crease at the corners as an amused smile takes hold. 'I'll have you know …?' he asks. 'Who are you? *Daphne*?'

'What? No, I …'

In the aftermath of raging at Jack, finally saying all the things I've wanted to say for weeks now, the relief makes me vulnerable to his charm. It's impossible to tame the corners of my mouth but I'm still cross and I drop my chin to hide my traitorous mouth.

'You're smiling,' he teases.

I look up at him through my lashes. 'I'm not. I'm very annoyed. At *you*. I'm very annoyed at you.'

'And why's that?' He crosses his arms and tilts his head to the side. It's adorable, especially as a lock of hair has flopped over one eye.

'Because you're daft, that's why.'

'How? Why, what do you mean?' he asks with a slight edge of defensiveness.

I lift my chin. 'I *mean* that even after I told you I don't want to be with Daniel, that I don't fancy him in the slightest, you still thought I had kissed him willingly.'

He shrugs. 'I figured you'd changed your mind.'

'Oh, you did? Is that one of the chapters in your book, *Everything I Know About Women*, by Jack Freeman?'

'It's more of a pamphlet, really.'

I shake my head, the laughter that's bubbling up inside me impossible to resist, and then I snigger. 'You utter …' I say through the laughter.

'I think the word you're looking for is "genius",' he counters.

My laughter subsides, turning into a sigh—part relief, part contentment, perhaps slightly tinged with resignation. Jack is a worthy opponent in word play, and I chalk up another point on the plus side of the 'Abby crushing on Jack' balance sheet. No one wants to be with someone they can walk all over. Well, I don't, anyway.

But that still leaves us at an impasse. I haven't told Jack the truth. And he hasn't asked.

His expression softens and he takes a small step towards me. 'So, why didn't you want Daniel to kiss you?' he asks, his voice barely above a whisper. All right, so *now* he's asked.

I take a steadying breath and look him in the eye. 'Because … I fancy *you*, actually.' I hadn't envisioned telling him surrounded by toilet roll and kitchen towel but there you have it.

His eyes don't leave mine, and I see the myriad of thoughts crossing his mind; eventually, it settles on just one. 'Right, I see,' he says quietly.

'Yes.' I bite my lip—not something I typically do, but it seems apt. Perhaps it will stop me from saying other humiliating things.

'Well, actually, that's the *best* news.'

'It is?' My mind starts screaming a dozen different things at once, and the loudest and most commanding is, *'Jack fancies you back, Abby!'*

'You have no idea …'

I'm rooted to the spot in shock as Jack crosses the short distance between us faster than Usain Bolt. Then his hand is on the back of my neck, pulling me towards him and those perfect, perfect lips, the ones I have fantasised about for

241

months now, touch mine. They're softer than I imagined, yet also firmer, insistent and I feel the tip of his tongue against mine and I sink into him, our bodies together, my arms winding their way around him, my palms pressed against his back. His fingers work their way into my hair and we kiss deeper and deeper until time means nothing and all I know is the feel of him against me, his smell, his taste—

There's another tap at the door and we jump apart, eyes wide and wild and breath ragged. When Harry's face appears in the doorway, I'm mortified as it must be completely obvious what we've been doing, and what we were (very possibly) about to do if not interrupted.

'Oh, shit, sorry guys. I just … it was getting a little loud. I could hear you arguing from the Control Room, so I just wanted to, uh … I'm gonna go.' It's hard to say who is more embarrassed of the three of us and we watch in silence as Harry closes the door.

So,' I say brightly, 'We have an Interloper coming …'

Chapter Seventeen

'Now, Becca, how do you feel about an Interloper coming into the Manor?' asks Carlie.

It's confessional time, but as there are so few of us left, we're all standing off to the side watching while we wait our turn. It's like school photographs, only more painful.

Becca, ever gracious, answers, 'Look, we're all here to find love, and if this new Doe turns out to be the love of Daniel's life, then that's what's meant to be. I hope he chooses me, of course, but in the end, I just want him to be happy.' Is this a confessional or the interview segment of a beauty pageant? I'm surprised she doesn't add, 'I also want world peace.'

I make a mental note of the 'beauty pageant' quip for Anastasia, but as for the rest? I simply cannot see Daniel making Becca happy, especially once the lustre of the show wears off and they are left with each other exactly as they really are. Becca will be her lovely self and Daniel will treat her like a pretty plaything, eventually revealing what a massive twat he is, and she will be miserable.

As her friend, I can't say any of this. As her fellow Doe, I definitely can't. So, I have promised myself to keep my mouth shut and be there for her when the other shoe (inevitably) drops and she needs a friendly ear. Of course, if he doesn't choose her, she's also going to need a friend.

'Cut. That's great, Becca, thank you. Kaz, you're up!' Kaz walks onto the confessional set and plops herself down on the garden bench.

'Rolling,' says Tim.

'Same question, Kaz, when you're ready,' says Carlie.

'Yeah, I'm not gonna lie, it's a bit of a blow, but we'll see what happens, eh?'

Short, sweet, and to the point. Kaz leaps up without waiting for 'cut' and stands next to me. 'I figured that was better than, "I can't believe I'm still here, so who bloody cares?"' she whispers and I burst out laughing. Carlie throws a silencing look over her shoulder and I clap a hand over my mouth.

'Justine!' calls Carlie. 'We're still rolling, so just answer when you're ready.' Justine sits, looks into the camera, and says, 'Well, I mean, we're getting to the pointy end of the competition and that's when the Interloper shows up, so I guess it's to be expected, really …' She adds a shrug. To me, her confessional shouts, *I don't care one iota about winning the Stag's heart,* but Carlie seems fine with it and scans our little herd of Does.

'Daphne, you're up,' she says, waving her over.

Daphne takes her time getting situated, smoothing out

first her dress, then her (already perfect) hair. She sits slightly angled away from the camera (highlighting what I know she thinks is her good side) and lifts her chin. 'And when you're ready …'

Daphne plasters on a smile. She's so good at it, the fakery, that for the umpteenth time I hope Daniel chooses her. They'll be marvellous together—Barbie and Ken brought to life, donning their plastic smiles for the paparazzi as they attend charity events and fancy dinners and island hop about the Mediterranean. That's what incredibly wealthy people do, right?

'Well, I can't say it makes me particularly happy.' With her accent, it sounds like 'heppy' and I wonder why, if she's so 'unheppy', she's smiling like that. 'But I suppose one just gets on with it, don't they? This is a television show, after all.'

Tim's head drops. This is not good footage and Carlie is going to have to coax something better out of her. 'Right, so, how do you feel about Daniel, Daphne?'

'What? Oh, I have feelings for him, of course.' Liar—I don't believe for one second that she's falling for Daniel.

'So how do you feel about another Doe entering the running for his heart?' prods Carlie.

'Disappointed,' Daphne answers. From her tone, this is (finally) the truth, and I watch her closely as Carlie gives her the 'continue' signal. 'And unfair, really. We've all been here since the start, we've—*I've* formed a relationship with Daniel. It's hard enough that there are still four other women in his life, and now we're adding a fifth to the mix.' Oh, now *this* is brilliant footage. 'And that's quite crushing, really.'

There's no fake smile now and, surprisingly, I feel for her. Whatever Daphne's motives are, she hopes to leave the Manor betrothed and she's having a harder time of it than she's ever let on before.

'Awesome. Thanks Daphne, we've got what we need.'

She looks a little startled, as though she was mid-thought. 'Right, I see,' she says, standing and moving off to the side. It's my turn and I'm on the move even before Carlie calls for me.

I sit down, look right into the camera—the red light is on, so no point in delaying—and say, 'It's completely unexpected and it's thrown me for a loop. I mean, here we are, top five and we're suddenly told that it's top six! It's a bit of a slap in the face, to be honest.'

'To be honest!' Oh, Abby, *you're* the enormous liar.

'Cut, and that's a wrap. Thanks everyone.' Tim and Carlie start packing up the confessional set and I join the rest of the Does who have formed a loose circle. When I glance at their faces, there's an array of expressions.

'Now what?' asks Justine. 'Do we just wait for them to show up?' She means Daniel and the Interloper, Stevie, who are currently on a date at an undisclosed Sydney location. Though, Doe Abby doesn't know Stevie's name yet, so I stay silent.

'Good morning, ladies!' Ugh, Gordo. He saunters through the Manor and joins us on the patio, trailed by a camera operator and a sound technician.

'Good morning, Gordo,' we sing-song, like we're in nursery.

He claps his hands together and bounces on the balls of

his feet. I can't decide which Gordo I find more annoying——this one, all pent-up energy like a puppy on speed, or the sombre one. Couldn't they have got a Hemsworth brother to host? Aren't there, like, fifteen of them kicking about Australia?

'How are we this morning?' Gordo asks, dragging this out far longer than necessary. Even with the camera pointing in my direction, I don't curtail my frown. There are various murmurs in reply and he continues like we've all said our lines with the perfect amount of enthusiasm. 'I have a wonderful surprise for you.'

'Is it about the Interloper?' asks Kaz. I do love how she gets to the point.

'Actually, it's about you. You're all going on a group date today!'

Now this I did not know, and I am immensely pleased. Group dates are safe——very little chance of being ambushed by a kiss——and I cross my fingers behind my back that it is something quintessentially 'Sydney'.

'You are *all* … wait for it …' Good grief, if we *must* you imbecile——oops, I may have muttered that out loud. Kaz elbows me confirming that I did. '… having lunch at the Opera House, then you're climbing the Sydney Harbour Bridge!'

'Hooray!' I cry.

'But what about the Interloper?' asks Daphne. Oh, yes, quite right; I'd forgotten about her.

'She and Daniel will be joining you!' says Gordo. He really needs to read the room. Group date? Fine. Group date with the Interloper who's just had one-on-one time with *our*

Staggy? Not so fine. At least for Daphne and Becca. Becca's beside me and I reach for her hand; she returns the squeeze.

Gordo talks at us for a few more minutes and I hear none of it because my mind is chewing on something else entirely. I'm having one of those 'this is real' moments, a potent realisation that has arrived like a bolt from the blue. These are *real people*—in a contrived situation, yes, but that doesn't make this any less real for my fellow Does.

Justine's eyes are (inappropriately) locked onto Tim, her recently (re)acquired boyfriend. And her goal of a career in television must now seem within reach.

Kaz, with her high-pressure job, basking in the 'holiday' she's foregone for years now and generally having a wonderful time.

Daphne, cool and distant, but with an undercurrent of desperation. It's clear she wants to win this, even if her motives aren't.

Lovely Becca, who's in this wholeheartedly. I so want her to find the type of relationship she's yearning for. And while I cannot stand Daniel, I know it's patronising for me to discount them being happy. No one knows what truly happens between two people. Maybe their relationship has depth I cannot see—a romantic iceberg.

And when did I, Abigail Jones, perpetually single and rather a novice at love, decide I was the world authority on it? Anastasia may have her take on love—her cynical, acerbic take—but what about me?

What do *I* know of love?

As if on cue, Jack appears on the patio, his damp mop of hair signposting that not too long ago, he was naked under a stream of water. Oh, I am in serious trouble and with a camera pointing in my direction, I school my face into a neutral expression while inside I am lit up like a pinball machine. Bing, bing, bing.

Thirty-six hours ago, I was kissing that man! That gorgeous Australian right over there! The one in the 'I'm kind of a big deal' T-shirt. *'Oh, yes, you are, Jack—indeed you are.'*

After our kiss—kissus interruptus—Jack leant his fore-head against mine and said, 'I have wanted to do that since the day I saved you from the lift.'

'Really?' I whispered. Even after being ravished amongst the loo roll, I was still uncertain of Jack's feelings—perhaps because of his obsession with the Abby–Daniel storyline.

He pulled back, looking down at me with a smile. 'Come on, Abby, you must have known?'

I shook my head. 'How could I? You were all busi-ness—friendly, yes, but from my recollection, we only spoke about the show.'

'Then we have *very* different takes on that day,' he replied, his eyes roving the features of my face.

'What was your take?' I asked quietly, obviously fishing but I didn't care. I wanted to hear lovely things about myself.

'First impression?'

'All of it.' He grinned at me.

'Well, after we got off the lift, you were … you were …' He trailed off, seemingly lost for words.

'I was …?' I prompted.

'Well, for one, you were wearing the hell out of that dress and with your cheeks all flushed … and, you know, you were out of breath …' I blinked at him, unsure of where he was going. 'Well, my mind went somewhere … rather … inappropriate for work, if you get what I'm saying.' Oh, so *that's* where.

I half laughed, half hiccupped and he grinned at me as I clapped a hand over my mouth.

'See?' I nodded. 'And *then* in the meeting, you stood up to Roberta … I still can't believe you did that.'

'She was being horrid.'

'She was. But no one ever stands up to her. You were so … *impressive* in that meeting—this beautiful, smart, audacious woman.' His smile dropped away and he peered at me intently and, although I'd fished for them, the lovely things he'd said had me reeling a little. 'Did you really have no idea that I liked you? 'Cause I thought I was being too obvious.'

It was time to come clean. 'I did think … at first … maybe … When you and I were talking at the bar in the airport—'

'When we were *flirting* at the bar in the airport,' he interjected.

'Yes,' I conceded with a shy smile. 'And then on the flight … that conversation about our families, our aspirations … but then you told me about your plan with Roberta—to give me a chance with Daniel. And that's when I knew.' I shrugged.

'Knew what?' he asked, frowning.

'That what I felt was one-sided.'

'Oh, Abby, no. I just … I couldn't act on it so I kept telling myself that it was all in my head and then you and Daniel—'

'There is no me and Daniel,' I huffed.

'I *know*. I know that now, believe me.' He sighed. 'I really messed this up, didn't I?'

'Well, yes.'

He chuckled. 'You're very honest,' he said.

At that, *I* chuckled. 'Says he to the woman who is currently playing *two* roles.'

'No, I mean it. I should have worked it out. I mean, I produce this show where I'm watching people's interactions all the time, gauging their feelings, yet I was completely blind to what was going on with you.'

'I'm just as much to blame,' I said.

'I agree.'

'What?' I swatted him playfully.

'Sorry, go ahead. How are *you* culpable in all this?'

'When I got it in my head that you didn't fancy me—'

'Oh, I fancy you ...'

'Well, yes, I know that now. But *before*, I tried to dismiss all my feelings. And every time we talked and it was easy and *fun*—so fun, Jack—well ... I just kept telling myself that I was firmly in the "friend zone" and to stop wishing I weren't.'

'I'm really sorry, Abs.' He pressed his lips together, seemingly milliseconds from some serious self-flagellation.

'Apology accepted,' I countered brightly. His eyes softened, his face settling into a sad(ish) smile. 'I love you calling me that, by the way,' I added.

'Abs?' I nodded and he dipped his head for another kiss. This one was less urgent, less like two people starved of affection going at it in a storeroom, and just the loveliest kiss I've ever had in my entire life.

'So, now what?' I asked when we pulled apart.

'Yeah.' He sighed. 'It's going to be tricky. We can't let on to anyone else. I mean, Harry knows now, but he won't say anything. It's just …'

'You could lose your job.'

'Yep. And you yours.'

'Yes.'

We were quiet for a moment.

'It's only a few more weeks,' I said.

He nodded, that sad(ish) smile back in place. 'If he kisses you again, I may not be able to restrain myself.'

My brows rocketed to my hairline. 'Oh, is that so?' Another nod. 'And what exactly would you do if you were unrestrained?' I could imagine a multitude of things he could do to *me* unrestrained.

He shrugged. 'You know, write him a strongly worded email, something like that.' We shared another chuckle. 'Let's just be really careful, okay, especially with some of the others already thinking we're overly friendly.' It was my turn to nod. 'It's bad enough that one of my crew is screwing a Doe. God, if Roberta gets wind of Tim and Justine, she'll have my guts for garters.'

'Wait, what? They're *sleeping* together?'

'I don't know that there's much sleeping going on,' he said dryly, 'but we've had to reprimand him.'

'But *here*?'

'Well, she's got her own room, don't forget.'

'Oh, right, of course.'

'Anyway, when it all came out at dinner the other night, a lot of things started making sense—you know when you just *feel* like something's not quite right, but maybe you're imagining it?' I nodded. I was extremely familiar with that feeling. 'Yeah, well after that, Harry and I had a word with him.'

'Eek. I bet that was no fun.'

'It was the opposite of fun.' He sighed again and rubbed his chin. 'So, are you going to be okay with us laying low?'

'Absolutely,' I said.

'Really? 'Cause I'm kinda thinking we shouldn't even be in here alone.'

I looked about at the shelving units and luggage piled up in the corner. 'Because of how romantic it is? Because there's no way we'll be able to control ourselves in such a perfect setting?'

'Something like that.' He smiled. 'But I … you're … oh, hell, just out with it, Jack. I *like* you, Abby, and it doesn't matter if we're amongst the toilet paper or on a boat or a long-haul flight, or even if I'm saving you from a lift—'

'The giant jaws of death,' I interjected. It earned me a grin.

'Right. The giant jaws of death. The setting doesn't matter. *You* matter. I've been going nuts watching you with Daniel. Just …' Another sigh. 'We need to be careful.' I nodded again and squeezed my arms tight around his waist to let him know I understood. 'It's only a few weeks, like you said,' he added.

'A few weeks and then …'

'And then I'm taking you out.'

'Ooh! Do you mean on a one-on-one date?'

'Yes.' He smacked his lips against mine.

'Before you ask, I *will* wear this pin,' I said solemnly. I got another kiss, then he left me to my writing.

My writing … of the piece I would shop around as soon as I got home, the piece that would expose the underbelly of this 'reality'. And then another thought had struck me. When all this ended and Jack and I *could* be together, I was supposed to get on a flight home …

'Abs!' Kaz is poking me.

'What?' I've been so lost in replaying the Jack and Abby love scene that I've missed Gordo telling us about the rest of the day.

'We have to get ready.'

'Right, so …?'

'Wow. You were *really* off with the fairies. We get dressed for lunch—all dolled up—then pack something caz to change into for the bridge climb.'

'Oh, right, yes.' I look about and realise that everyone else is in a flurry of activity and the other Does have already headed upstairs to get ready.

'It's gonna be awesome,' says Kaz as I follow her inside. I sneak a peek at Jack as I walk past and we lock eyes—just for a second—and the look says everything that we can't.

———

Up close, the Sydney Opera House is wondrous—even more so than seeing it from the window of a high-rise hotel.

The minivan pulls up just past the gatehouse where we'll

decant to the forecourt, and we wait inside as Tim, Carlie, Harry, and Jack pile out to set up the shot of us arriving. 'And, getting ready …' Harry calls to us. 'Action.'

Jack opens the van door then steps out of the shot and we climb out as elegantly as possible, experienced now in not looking at the camera unless asked. We talk excitedly amongst ourselves and exclaim over the beauty of one of the most recognisable structures in the world, and none of this is staged. Even the Australians gawp in amazement.

'You know, I must have been down here a couple dozen times,' says Justine, 'and it never gets old. It's just stunning.' There's general agreement.

Facing us are the 'mouths' of three of the sails—that's what those enormous white sections are called, although they look more like the petals of a lotus flower to me. And with the dark glass contrasting with the stark white of the tiled sails, the structure seems both geometric and organic, a remarkable combination of the two.

Following Carlie, who's not on camera, we ascend the dozens of wide steps spanning the breadth of the Opera House and I watch tourists milling about taking photographs. Most of them, like us, seem awe-struck.

But *nothing* could have prepared me for the inside.

Where the lines of the external structure seem almost organised, inside is a beautiful chaos. This is where cement, wood, steel, and glass meet at odd angles or seamless curves, where red carpet and brass hand railings are the perfect embellishments, where staircases are illuminated by sunlight spilling in from above, and where the architecture of the concert halls protrudes into the foyer as inverted opera boxes.

My mouth remains open as my eyes flick to the hundreds of details in this magnificent structure.

'Cool, huh?' says Kaz. 'I've only been here once before, but somehow you forget how amazing it is 'til you're standing in it.'

'Indeed,' I whisper reverently.

Carlie not-so-subtly gestures for us to follow her to Bennelong, where we're having lunch. We congregate at the top of an impressive staircase to wait for the maître d' while Tim, Harry, and Jack pass us to set up another arrival shot. The restaurant is empty, which seems odd.

'Carlie, what day is it?' Days of the week stopped having meaning a long time ago; in the Manor, the passage of time is marked by events instead of days, such as my weekly deadline or filming the Pin Ritual.

'Of the week?' Carlie asks. I nod. 'Tuesday,' she replies. Right, so Bennelong must not be open on Tuesdays. I crane my neck, taking in the opulent architecture and décor when I hear the tinkling of polite laughter. My eyes land on Daniel who's standing at the far end of the restaurant near one of the enormous windows with a blonde woman. This must be Stevie.

But before we meet her, we must 'arrive'. The maître d' steps into place ready to welcome us and Harry calls, 'Action.' We trail down the stairs into the restaurant in an untidy line. 'Cut! Sorry, can we have a bit more "ooh-ing" and "aah-ing" please? I mean, look where we are, people!' Harry scolds good-naturedly. He shoos us back up the stairs and when we're all in position, including the maître d', he shouts, 'Action.'

This time, we make sure Harry gets his 'money shot'—though it's possible that we've gone too far in the other direction—that was some effusive 'ooh-ing' and this is reality television, not CBeebies.

We're obediently following the maître d' to our table, the camera capturing every moment, when Daniel's voice booms out across the cavernous space. 'Oh, look, they're here!' he says, as though he hasn't just watched us arrive—*twice*. I then watch, perplexed, as he holds out his hand to Stevie who reluctantly takes it, then walks her over to the rest of us. 'Hello, everyone. I'd like you to meet Stevie.'

Good god, if Becca looks like a Victoria's Secret model, then Stevie looks like Victoria herself. In fact, her likeness to Karlie Kloss is so uncanny, I peer at her suspiciously. Daniel graciously plays host as though it is perfectly normal to introduce his new girlfriend to his five other girlfriends. As he says each of our names, Karlie—I mean, *Stevie*—shakes our hands, looking us of each in the eye and smiling warmly.

All I can wonder is how on earth Harry and Jack are going to turn this charming, polite woman into the new Villain.

Chapter Eighteen

'You right there, Daph?' asks Kaz, turning to look behind her. 'Daph' is far from 'right'. Her knuckles are so white from fervently grasping the handrail, that if the wind changes, they'll stay that way.

'Uh, yes, quite. Thank you,' she says. Liar. It's the second time I've thought this about her today——the first was regarding her (questionable) feelings for Daniel, but this? This is serious. She's terrified and we're not even halfway up the bridge yet.

'Just watch my feet and take it one step at a time, 'kay,' says Kaz. 'You can't fall——we're literally attached to this thing——but that will help stop the vertigo.' Kaz is being especially kind to Daphne and I feel for her too. I recall the day at the winery when she wouldn't swap places with me——horse riding for off-roading driving——and I'm realising now that it was probably due to her crippling fear of heights. I wish she'd said.

'And I'm right behind you, Daphne,' I say. Her blonde

head bobs with a sharp nod. Why on earth didn't she have a word with Jack and Harry? She could have whined about the unflattering blue and grey jumpsuits we're wearing and begged off for fashion reasons. No doubt they would've accepted such a feeble excuse, if only for the big fat 'B for bride' metaphorically stamped on her forehead. It's baffling why she's gone through with it, another reason I'm finding her more intriguing as we lumber towards the end of the season.

The 'climb' is exactly that—climbing hundreds of stairs towards the apex of the enormous steel arches, a network of crossbeams surrounding us, as intricate a pattern as a cobweb. An image of a giant mechanical spider pops into my head, spurting steel from its spinnerets and I shudder. Why would my mind conjure something so hideous? Especially with this view!

I peer over my shoulder at the city, my gaze panning down to Circular Quay. I'm certain I could never tire of this view—the ferry traffic, the Botanic Gardens, the high-rise buildings, dense and gleaming, and the wide expanse of the harbour. And, of course, that glorious Opera House, dazzling in the late afternoon sun, almost glowing with the amber light. Its silhouette, the lines of that unique, curvaceous structure will be indelibly etched on my mind.

As will that lunch.

The food was sublime and an enormous step up from what we cook for ourselves in the Manor, which tends to be sub-par pasta dishes and pot noodles. All local produce, imaginatively combined and served to look 'just so'. I couldn't tell you which was my favourite. The beetroot and radish salad was not only delicious, it arrived looking like a garden on a plate. I almost didn't want to eat it, but when Kaz started moaning in ecstasy beside me after her first bite, I tucked in. The next course was roasted lamb with olives—*Olives*! Who would have thought?—and for dessert, a scrumptious play on a white peach Bellini.

What was less than sublime was the awkward conversation. Daniel seemed to forget he was on a date with six Does and spent much of lunch focused on Stevie, while she attempted to engage the rest of us in conversation. It was like watching a table tennis match where only one person knows they're playing.

The worst part was witnessing the dual train wrecks of Becca and Daphne—though, in retrospect, Daphne's eventual retreat to the loo, pale-faced and clammy, likely had more to do with her dreading the bridge climb than the arrival of Stevie.

Becca, however, was on fine form—if 'fine form' means 'being her worst self'. Her jealousy was so evident, she could have played Elphaba in *Wicked* without donning a scrap of makeup. 'So, Stevie, you're from Adelaide?' she asked, even though we all knew full well.

'That's right.'

'So, do you support the Crows or Port?' These are football teams, apparently—though Australian football, not real football.

'Uh, neither. I'm not really into footie.'

'Really? I thought it was a requirement in South Australia—you're assigned a team at birth and spend the rest of your life barracking for them.'

Kaz leant over and whispered, 'What's up with her?'

'Oh,' replied Stevie, laughter in her voice, 'I haven't heard that one. My family is mad about wine, though. My brother and his wife have a winery in the Adelaide Hills.'

'So, a family of drinkers, then?' Becca replied tersely. At that, I poked her under the table and she shot me a sharp look. It was not her finest hour.

Now, as we trek ever upwards, I'm questioning whose wisdom it was to ply us with a sizeable meal—*and* paired wines—then have us climb the Sydney Harbour Bridge! Had I been in charge, I would have swapped the order of events.

I look to the left; this view, intersected by the crossbeams of the bridge, is where the harbour narrows into a series of irregular coves, with greenery and buildings competing for pride of place by the water. And as we get closer to sunset, the sky starts looking like it's on fire.

'Don't ya reckon, Abs?' calls Kaz from up ahead. As is happening more often lately, I've been 'off with the fairies'.

'What's that?'

'Best view eva!' she calls out.

'Oh, yes, absolutely,' I reply. Daphne murmurs something unintelligible. 'Not long now, Daphne,' I say. Justine and Becca are chatting animatedly behind me, also about the view, and it occurs to me (and not for the first time) what an odd bunch we are. Had we not been thrust into this bizarre situation, literally cast in our various roles, I would never have met these women, two of whom are becoming close friends.

I suppose, if nothing else comes of this experience—specifically, my career as an award-winning journalist, which is currently doomed as I have been focusing on far more pressing matters, such as avoiding kisses from one man while seeking them out from another—I will have accomplished that.

That and, hopefully, something more tangible of the romantic nature with Jack. Though, I am not sure what that could be. Any time I ponder the Jack and Abby love story, particularly what might happen beyond our time in the Manor, I'm stumped. He lives here. I live in the UK. I'm not sure what I was thinking getting entangled with him, other than finally placating my libido. Those are very sexy T-shirts.

I trip up the next step and recover, gripping the railing tightly. Strains of Daniel's laughter waft from up ahead where he and Stevie are at the front of the group. Not only beautiful, charming, and polite, but apparently hilarious, is our Stevie. Tim, who's tethered to the opposite handrail, passes us, camera on his shoulder and I smile brightly as though I'm having the best fun! It's only half a lie. The view is spectacular.

We're nearing the top of the climb when Daphne, whose fear has been so intense, she hasn't made a peep this whole time, starts shouting, 'No, I can't. I can't. Please stop. Please can we stop.'

Our party comes to a halt—well, all except Daniel, who Stevie has to call back. Daphne sits awkwardly on a step, her face now ashen and her eyes wild. Kaz and I bob down either side of her. 'Is she okay?' asks Justine over my shoulder.

'Er, not really,' I reply—*surely*, it's obvious.

'Be right there, Daphne,' calls Jack. When you're tethered to a bridge, 'being right there' is not as simple as jogging down the stairs. One of the guides must hook Jack onto the other handrail—the one Tim is tethered to—then unhook him from the first handrail so he can make his way down to us. As soon as he can, he joins our crouched little huddle. 'Hey,' he says to Daphne, 'I know you're scared. We'll help you get down, okay?'

'No, no, I can't … I can't move.'

Jack, Kaz, and I share a concerned look over her downturned head. 'I'll be with you every step of the way. Literally,' he adds, though the mild humour is lost on Daphne.

Daniel and Stevie appear on the steps above us, Harry just behind them, and now we're all bunched up like giant purple-grey grapes.

'Come on now, you're just being silly. Up you get.'

Daniel. Daniel being a massive twat. Every other person stares at him with either 'shut your mouth' or '*what* did you just say?' looks, including Stevie. Though, I don't check behind me to see what Becca thought of his unhelpful and callous directive.

'She's having a panic attack, Daniel,' says Stevie, her tone even, but he just shrugs and rolls his eyes. Good god, if Daphne gives permission to use this footage—I'm sure Jack and Harry wouldn't screen it otherwise—they'll have to do some creative editing to avoid showing Daniel exactly as he is. A massive twatface.

Stevie murmurs something to Harry who's just behind her and he nods. 'Ah, can we clear some room, please?'

Harry asks us. 'As much as we can.' I rise, my knees protesting at having climbed most of an enormous bridge, then squatting down for too long, and we systematically shuffle out of the way—Becca, Justine, Jack, and I down the stairs, and the others up. The same guide helps Stevie navigate around Kaz and soon she's able to sit next to Daphne on the step.

I'm fascinated, unable to tear my eyes away, yet also aware that this is an extremely private moment for Daphne. I've had panic attacks—I was certainly close to having one when I was atop Womble the horse and I will never forget the giant jaws of death that nearly took my arm off at the Feed Your Mind offices. But this seems far worse than anything I've experienced. How on earth are we going to get her down if she is unable to budge?

Stevie talks to Daphne in low tones for what feels like an eon but is likely only minutes. 'I really feel for her,' Jack says to me quietly.

I sneak a glance at him, hyper aware of his arm brushing against mine, and our eyes meet. How I wish it were just us up here and that we were already on our one-on-one date. His eyes crinkle ever so slightly at the corners—smising, I think it's called, smiling with your eyes. Whatever it is, it's lovely and for a second, I forget where we are and the current situation.

'This must be why she didn't want to swap with you at the winery,' he says, dragging my thoughts away from kissing those perfect, perfect lips.

'I was thinking the same thing earlier.'

'She's not as tough as she makes out,' he says.

'I'm realising that.'

'Thank god we had a psychologist up here, eh?' he says. I'd forgotten that about Stevie, and I add 'clever' and 'compassionate' to her Doe scorecard. She may just be the perfect woman, and now I'm convinced she's a terrible replacement for the Cruella Sisters.

'Anyone else you'd like with you?' Stevie asks Daphne. She's made incredible progress—Daphne no longer looks as green as she did before.

'Just you,' says Daphne, her voice barely audible.

Stevie lifts her head and searches out the guide who's been helping and signals for their assistance. Our tethers will all need to be reordered so Daphne and Stevie can descend, and we're joined by the second guide to sort out the tangle of harnesses and tethers. Even Tim needs to be moved.

Still, the guides are practised and it's not long before the two blonde heads of Stevie and Daphne start getting smaller and smaller, and a third guide comes up to meet them from below.

'Well, that was all a bit dramatic,' says Daniel. 'Shall we head to the top now? I've got a wonderful surprise planned.' He claps his hands then rubs them together, creepily waggling his eyebrows at us. And when he says he has a surprise for us: A) He hasn't organised a thing, the production crew has and B) It had better be one of the Hemsworths.

There are modest affirmative responses—mine sounds remarkably like 'bollocks'—and after some more disentangling we're off again. When we reach the apex of the bridge a short time later, 'Daniel's' surprise is revealed, and (no surprise) it's not a Hemsworth.

Instead, it's two waiters (also in jumpsuits, only fancy black ones), one with a tray of canapes and another with a tray of fizz. Better than a slap in the face with a dead fish, I suppose——or a live one, for that matter.

We gather in a loose knot and help ourselves to drinks. It's the first time I've drunk fizz from a sippy cup with a wrist band——novel, yes, but also an essential safety feature, as there are people below us——driving, cycling, some mad idiots even running. I eye the canapes warily and resist the urge to scoff down a mediocre-looking vol-au-vent, despite being (more than) a little peckish after climbing for an hour.

'Shall we get some photographs?' asks Daniel like it's just occurred to him. 'How about one on one?' Wonderful——not only will I have to smile, I'll need to be in close proximity to Daniel and his cologne (which, as usual, I can smell from ten feet away).

One by one we move into position next to Daniel——another feat of manoeuvring because (of course) we're all still attached to the bridge! Daniel puts his arm around each of our shoulders as we stand where we're told and say, 'cheese'. It's all rather cheese-*y* and when it's my turn I take a deep breath as surreptitiously as possible, hold it, then step into position.

The guide who is taking the photographs suddenly thinks he's Lord Snowdon or something and starts giving us a series of directions. 'Turn slightly, head up, smile,' that sort of thing. There's only so long I can hold my breath and I gasp for air just as Lord Snowdon's camera shutter clicks.

'Oops, let's take another one.' I sigh, crank out another faux smile and I'm about to step away into clean, non-fragranced air when Daniel catches my hand in his and pulls me closer.

'I'm really looking forward to our date, Abby,' he says.

Our date? What date? Oh god, I'd forgotten we've got a one-on-one date coming up. 'Oh, yes, of course.'

'So, are you a koala or a kangaroo type of a girl?'

'Sorry?' What on earth is he talking about? Is this one of those silly 'if you were an animal, what type would you be?' questions? Oh, right. The wildlife park. I'd forgotten that too.

'No, you're more of a Tasmanian devil, aren't you?' he says, as if he's already made up his mind. And if that leering grin means what I think it does, Tasmanian devils must be lascivious little bastards. Though he may be right. I read somewhere that many of them have chlamydia. Actually, sorry, that's koalas.

Daniel's still leering at me, perhaps imagining me whirling about him kicking up a dust storm like in that Warner Brothers cartoon. I managed to extricate myself by waggling *my* eyebrows right back at him and walking slowly backwards—not exactly clever when standing on top of a bridge and Jack catches me just as lose my footing.

'You right there?' he asks, his hands firm around my waist. Not only am I 'right', but I may just swoon so he can catch me again.

'Er, yes thanks.' I compose myself and flash him a grateful—and I hope *innocent*—smile before carefully making my way over to the others. I arrive just in time to hear Justine whinging about Daniel. 'What a dick. Can you believe how he treated Daphne? I mean, she's not exactly my favourite person, but still.'

And Becca defending him. 'Some people just aren't good in a crisis. That doesn't make him a bad person.' *'That may not, but everything else about him does,'* I think.

Justine seems to be at the end of her tether, so to speak. 'For real? You know what, Becca, you can just *have* him.'

'He's not exactly yours to give,' retorts Becca. I'm not loving this side of her. It's completely at odds with the Becca I know and, surely, the person you fall in love with should bring out your best self, rather than your bratty, catty self?

'*Whatever*,' says Justine, sark cranked up to eleven. If we were in the Manor right now, one or both would storm off and there'd be slamming doors.

I flick a glance at Daniel and from the look on his face, he's overheard (at least some of) the fracas. No need to hedge my bets on who's being sent home tonight. Justine has just put herself in the firing line.

WORST. PARTY. EVER.

Until now, the Soirées have been mildly enjoyable, but this one is rather … er … *dull*. Even a deluge of Roberta's synonyms couldn't do it justice.

Almost as soon as Daniel arrived, Becca sidled up and asked if she could 'borrow him for a second'. That was a lot more than a second ago and they're standing on the beach, heads together and talking (what appears to be) earnestly.

Daphne is moping on a sofa *reading* (a first for a Soirée). Justine is stretched out on a sun lounger doing her nails, micro filings of dead cells littering the skirt of her cocktail dress; though she does brush them away from time to time (oh, the excitement). And, by the sounds of slamming cupboard doors, Kaz is still scouring the kitchen for some 'decent nibblies'.

To round out this action-packed evening, Stevie and I are on the patio sitting in wicker armchairs and sipping tepid, watered-down fizz from overly ornate crystal champagne flutes. These are only used for filming ever since Justine dropped one on the kitchen floor and it shattered into a bazillion pieces. Not only was the clean up a heinous chore—shards everywhere—Carlie let on that they cost around twenty quid each. For a *glass*.

And the fizz is watered down with sparkling water because of the Soirée where the Cruella Sisters got horribly drunk and decided to go for a midnight swim in the harbour. Harry had to go out and rescue them, which they thought was terrific fun—'Oh, Harry, save me, save me'—and (poor) Harry did not.

We're accumulating rules because of previous Does' transgressions, I conclude glumly. Though I'm likely not as glum as Harry and Jack—it's going to take a lot of imagination to excavate anything of interest from *this* Soirée.

'Uh, Abby, can I ask you something?' says Stevie, her voice soft and curious.

I lean closer, mindful that there's a camera around here somewhere and our microphones are on. 'Of course.'

'So, it's only Becca who actually likes him, right?' Well,

the microphones may as well be off, because there's no way *that* will make the edit.

Within the safety of 'unusable footage' I look at the twosome talking on our private beach, then back at Stevie. 'Well, there's Daphne too,' I reply.

Her dubious look says it all but she adds, 'Even after today?'

'Mmm, good point. Then, yes, only Becca likes him.'

'So, what are you all doing here?' She laughs and I join in, the maniacal laughter of the slightly mad.

'Same thing as you, I suppose. We came here looking for love.' It's an easy lie to tell after all this time, though my thoughts flit to Jack.

'And not finding it …' Stevie muses.

'Something like that.'

'I cannot *believe* how he reacted today. Panic attacks are nothing to be dismissive about.'

'You were amazing with her,' I say.

'I did what anyone else would have done.'

'No, you did what no one else *could* have done and many wouldn't have.' She shrugs off the compliment.

'Are you disappointed?' I ask.

'About Daniel?' she asks, her eyes questioning.

I nod, adding, 'Mmm-hmm'.

'Well … *yeah*, actually,' she says. 'I mean, they sent me this video package of him, and he seemed like a really interesting guy—the travelling, his career—and *decent*, you know, saying how close he is to his family.' I bark out a laugh. 'So, not close to his family, then?'

'Look, I have no idea which Daniel is going to appear on

270

televisions across the world.' I absolutely do. 'But I doubt he'll resemble the real Daniel.' He absolutely will not.

'Mmm, yeah. It won't be the version from the bridge today, that's for sure.' She scrunches up her beautiful face, endearing her to me even more. 'I took leave to come here,' she groans. 'Like, proper holiday leave and this is … ugh … I should have gone to Thailand with my girlfriends.'

'Look, I'm so sorry it's rubbish.' I really do commiserate with her. I'm here because I have a job to do, but her motives were pure. 'You *could* just leave.'

She shakes her head. 'I'm like you. Contract—at least top four, possibly even top two or three.' Oh, so Roberta is still tugging on those puppet strings. 'That's why *you're* still here, right,' Stevie asks, 'you're contractually obligated? Sorry, I just assumed.'

'Oh, yes, absolutely!' I fib. God, these bloody contracts! All these promises to the Does regardless of what the Stag wants. It's an aspect of the show I (naively) hadn't anticipated—even though *I* was guaranteed top four.

I look back at Becca and Daniel on the beach. If the way he's stroking her arm is any indication (and, ewww), then it's clear what he wants and (Roberta willing) he may just get it. I'm suddenly overcome with shivers; seriously, what does Becca see in him?

'Well,' I say cheerfully, turning my attention back to Stevie, 'you could do what Kaz has been doing—pretend you *are* on holiday—enjoy the accommodation, the excursions—'

'You mean the dates? The ones with Daniel?'

'Minor inconvenience.' Stevie laughs again and I can't

help comparing this laugh—full and genuine—with the false titters she shared with Daniel at Bennelong. Poor Stevie. She probably *should* have gone to Thailand.

———

Well, no surprises here. Gordo steps forward, 'I'm sorry, Justine, but you did not receive a pin. It's time to pack your bags and leave the Manor.'

We've had half-a-dozen departures from the Manor in the past month-and-a-half—indifferent shoulder shrugs, tears (from Elizabeth), lightning-fast retreats (by Kylie, the villain and Merrin, the cat-loving Tasmanian) but this one will go down as my favourite.

Justine throws her arms up in the air and shouts, 'Yasss!' She breathes out an enormous sigh as though she's dodged the biggest bullet ever (and let's face it, she has), then starts dancing and skipping around the backyard, making her way back to the Manor. 'Ciao!' she calls, waving vigorously and disappearing inside.

Harry yells, 'Cut,' and the rest of us visibly slump. If nothing else, I will get a strong core out of all standing about with perfect (camera-ready) posture. As we turn off our battery packs and hand our microphones over to Carlie, Daphne slips into the Manor, her face like a thundercloud. It's clear that she hasn't forgiven Daniel for his twatishness and I wonder what that means for her potential Bride status. God knows what *her* contract says—perhaps she can't leave early, even if she wants to.

Gordo and Daniel are getting de-microphoned (much

harder for men wearing suits than for us in our slinky cock-tail dresses) when Kaz hooks her arm through mine. 'The usual?' she asks. It both delights and baffles me that she's still here, and I wholeheartedly agree to a late happy hour.

'Whaddya say, Stevie, join us for a drink or three?' Kaz asks.

'Uh, yeah, sure, that sounds good. What's going?'

'Hah, what's *not* going is more like. The food here sucks, but the booze is top shelf and there's plenty of it.'

Stevie chuckles at that. 'She's right about the food,' I add. 'Lots of packet stuff, and mostly we fend for ourselves or someone makes a large pot of pasta.'

'Well, you're in luck. I'm an excellent cook,' says Stevie. Of course, she is. She'll probably cure cancer while she's in the Manor. And after watching how amazing she was with Daphne today and with how lovely she's been to the rest of us, she's impossible not to like. Again—definitely not a Villain.

We're nearly at the Manor when Daniel calls out after us, 'Goodnight, my lovely Does.'

We share an amused look, then turn and wave, saying, 'Goodnight, Daniel,' in unison. Daniel is in a huddle with Jack and Harry, and Becca lingers off to the side looking like a groupie hanging out at a stage door. 'Becs! You comin'?' asks Kaz.

'In a moment. I just …' her voice trails off.

'Okay, but I'm making you a margarita! And you're gonna drink this one!' Kaz laughs at her own joke and disappears inside.

Stevie pauses. 'I really don't get it,' she says, casting her eyes back to the beach where Becca is now talking to Daniel again.

'No, me neither.'

'At least you girls are here,' says Stevie. 'And Kaz is a crack-up,' she adds quietly.

'She's brilliant—good value, as you Australians say.'

'Oi, you lot, get in here and give me a hand.'

'Speaking of …' Stevie and I grin and head inside. 'By the way,' I say out of the side of my mouth, 'her cocktails may very well knock you on your arse.'

'What are you saying about me?' Kaz asks when we get to the kitchen. I'm not sure how she's done it in the short time she's been alone in here, but it looks like a bomb has gone off.

'Just telling Stevie what a disaster you are,' I say, gesturing at the mess. 'Like a whirling dervish of destruction.'

Kaz pauses her cocktail making and points a swizzle stick at me. 'Watch it, Abs, or I'll make you one of my kitchen sink cocktails.'

Stevie laughs. 'What the hell is that?' she asks, sliding onto a stool at the breakfast bar.

'What the hell *isn't* it, is the better question,' I retort, sitting next to her.

'Eh, it's a little bit of this and a *lot* of that,' says Kaz, chuckling. She puts the lid on a cocktail shaker and starts shaking it so energetically I duck. There was an incident last week where the top flew off mid flourish and we were all covered in sticky pink liquid. And the walls. And the cupboards. And the floor. We were finding tacky drips of pink goo on various surfaces for days.

'Calm down, drama queen. I've put the lid on tightly this time.' I shake my head at her, smiling.

'So, how is it?' asks Stevie, 'Living here all together, I mean.'

'It's all right—yeah, pretty good, actually,' says Kaz, right as I say, 'Exhausting.'

'Oh yeah?' says Stevie, looking between us. 'You first,' she says to me.

I'd love to spout off about living a lie—well, it's a conglomerate of lies now—while missing Mum and Lisa but not wanting to leave in a few weeks with things still fresh between me and Jack.

'It's just …' I decide to lean into the one truth I can share. 'I get homesick. There's my mum—we're very close—and my bestie, Lisa …'

'That's understandable,' says Stevie. 'They're the people who know the real you, the people you can be yourself with,' she adds, getting dangerously close to the truth. It's like a salve for my heart to feel understood, but I need to steer us in another direction.

'I mean, I've got the girls, of course …' I smile at Kaz who winks. 'But it's …'

'It's not the same thing,' says Stevie, finishing my thought.

'No, it really isn't. Oh,' I say, catching my faux pas, 'that doesn't mean I don't adore you, Kaz.'

'Ahh, darls, don't worry about it. We're good.' To Stevie,

she says, 'Thing is, I'm not in competition with any of the girls, see, so I can just be myself and chill. So yeah, I mostly love it here. But it does get a little … you know, intense sometimes.'

'Like a pressure cooker,' I say.

'Not surprising, really,' says Stevie. She leans in and lowers her voice. 'The professional part of me is fascinated—the dynamics, the relationships …' She raises her eyebrows and I *so* wish she and I could have a good natter about all things Stag Manor. It would be great to have a psychologist's perspective for my piece.

'Here you go girls.' Kaz expertly decants our drinks into cocktail glasses and slides them across to us. 'Don't wait on me, start drinking. Go!' she commands, pouring measures into the shaker for her own drink.

Stevie raises her glass towards me and we both say 'Cheers' and take a sip. 'Hoo,' says Stevie, 'That's, uh … potent.'

'I told you,' I say with a smile. It's delicious, though, and after today, it's going down a treat.

'And you, Kaz? Are you missing home?'

Kaz pauses and looks at Stevie thoughtfully. Eventually, her face breaks into her signature smile and she belches, 'Nah!' Stevie and I chuckle. 'But for reals,' she says, resuming her cocktail making, 'I have a high-pressure job, which I love, but needed time away from. I have an awesome family—Mum, Dad, and my brother, Daz' —Daz is short for Darren, and I'm not proud of how much I laughed when I first learnt about the Karen–Darren/Kaz–Daz name thing— 'but *I'm* the timid one in my family and time away was much needed. Just like in here, family life can get a little intense, especially because my brother's just gotten engaged and now it's all wedding, wedding, wedding. *And* then there's my ex …'

My ears prick because Kaz has never once mentioned her 'ex'. Most people have them, of course, but when someone refers to an ex as '*my* ex', then *that's* the one that matters, the one that moulded them, or broke them, or possibly both. Let's just say, I have never once referred to Angus the cheating Scot as 'my ex'.

'Partner or spouse?' prompts Stevie, her tone schooled in gentle inquisition.

'Spouse—husband, now ex-husband,' says Kaz. I'm shocked to discover that Kaz has been married—and that this is the first we've heard of it—but Stevie nods serenely like the pro that she is and I do the same. 'Seven years, no kids, one dog—Lola,' Kaz continues. 'I just love her little face so much,' she adds, her voice switching to baby talk. She lifts her eyes to us, 'I miss Lola like mad, but I'm kinda used to it now, being apart from her. I only get her on weekends.' I'd not heard of shared pet custody before.

'And you get along okay?' asks Stevie. 'With your ex?' I sense that Kaz wants to call 'cut' on this conversation and I'm proven right when she smiles brightly and says, 'Yep. Anyway, that's me.' She decants her cocktail and, surprisingly, starts wiping down the bench. Usually, it's one of us who cleans up after her, so this conversation must have unnerved her more than she's letting on.

'Do you think I could have one, please?'

Daphne has slipped into the kitchen undetected and climbs onto a stool on the other side of Stevie. Kaz doesn't skip a beat and behaves like it's the most natural thing in the world for Daphne to join us for post-Pin Ritual drinks. It isn't—another first to add to tonight's tally.

'How *are* you, Daphne?' asks Stevie.

'Much better—thanks to you.'

Stevie (again) waves off the thanks. 'Happy to help.'

'Actually, a big thank you to all of you—Kaz, Abby. You were so lovely to me today, and I …' Daphne's voice catches and she blinks back tears. Stevie reaches out and pats her arm. 'Anyway, enough of all that.' Daphne shakes out her blonde bob, sniffs, wipes under her eyes with the pads of her ring fingers and composes herself in three-point-two seconds. If it were me, I'd have been a blubbering mess just as quickly. 'So, Kaz, what concoction are you plying us with this evening?' she asks.

'Well, this has vodka and Aperol, but for you, Daph, I'm thinking of something with *te-qui-laaa*. Oh yeah, margarita, baby!' She waggles her eyebrows.

Daphne smiles but shakes her head. 'Oh, no, I don't—'

'Hey, bartender's choice—that's my rule, your ladyship,' Kaz insists. Uh-oh, that 'ladyship' comment is going to earn Kaz a right dressing down.

I'm gobsmacked when Daphne flaps a hand in the air and says, 'Oh, all right, then. A margarita it is.'

Kaz grins at her. 'Look at you! Go, Daph!' Daphne flashes a chuffed smile, and their little exchange is one of the most surprisingly lovely moments I've experienced in the Manor.

'Hey.' Becca.

'Hey, Becs, it's margarita time!' says Kaz with cheeky grin.

'Uh, no thanks. I'm just gonna crash. It's been a long day.'

The clock on the oven says it's just gone 8pm. 'You sure?' I ask. 'Top five, all together …' I add, hoping to cajole her into staying.

'Nah, I'm good. Thanks anyway.' She practically sprints to the stairs, then takes them two at a time.

'What's up with her?' asks Kaz.

'I think she might be falling in love,' I say.

'For reals? With *Daniel*?' says Kaz, incredulous. 'Ah, sorry, Daph.'

'No, no. Not to worry.' Hmm. I get the sense that Daphne is starting to cool on Staggy, or perhaps she's cooled entirely. Any moment now, she could start singing, 'Let It Go'.

'Well, I guess that makes one of us, then,' says Kaz, who dissolves into proper 'bahahaha' laughter. It's infectious and in moments, we're all chuckling with her.

Oh dear. Five Does left and only one wants the Stag.

Chapter Nineteen

And cue the idiot! Sorry, I mean Gordo.

We're all seated on the (ridiculously long) sofas awaiting news of our fates—or rather, *dates*—while Gordo the Magnificent (for he is in full flourish mode this morning) flits about waving envelopes in our faces. Two one-on-one dates and a group date are (literally) on the cards and though I already know I'll be cuddling a koala by day's end (just like Aunty Lo hoped for), I cannot help but notice the grimaces besetting the faces of Daphne and Stevie. As always, Kaz is 'just chilled' (her words not mine), and Becca appears to have ants in her pants.

'And the first one-on-one date *is* … Abby!' I squeal in faux delight while the others faux clap. 'You and Daniel are off to a wildlife park this afternoon, where you will consort with the local fauna, then have a picnic lunch.' Yes to the koala cuddling, but I'm happy to skip the soggy sandwiches and lukewarm fizz, thank you very much.

Becca turns to me, 'That'll be so fun, Abby,' she says

with a tight smile, yet it's clear she wishes it were her. She's also stopped calling me 'Abs', another indication that the shifting sands beneath our friendship are … well … shifting. Nevertheless, she was my first friend in the Manor and I adore her, so I am desperately trying to keep up my end of the friendship. That includes supporting her (misguided) want of Daniel and staying in our room despite there being six bedrooms and only five Does remaining.

I'm (almost) certain she still believes I want to be with Daniel, so she must be trying to reconcile our friendship and our status as roommates, with us being in direct competition. And if last night is anything to go by, she's even pulling away from Kaz. Perhaps she's considering moving into a room on her own. I wouldn't blame her, but I'd be sad to see her go.

'Aaand, the next one-on-one date is for …' Gordo pulls a card out of the second envelope. 'Becca!' Oh, thank god! Becca squeals in delight and laughs, clapping her hands softly under her chin. Across the room, Daphne and Stevie visibly relax and Kaz bites off a cuticle and spits it on the floor. 'Becca, you and Daniel will take a helicopter ride over Sydney Harbour.' Her eyes widen with delight.

'And for you lucky ladies on the group date,' says Gordo, retrieving the card from the final envelope, 'you'll be off to the theatre to see Cate Blanchett in *Medea*!' At that, Daphne perks right up.

'Sorry, did you say we're going to the theatre? To see Cate Blanchett in *Medea*?'

'That's right! With drinks beforehand at Bar One overlooking Sydney Harbour. Oh, won't that be nice!' Gordo adds, laying it on extra thick. But really, other than having drinks with Daniel, which should be easy enough to pretend their way through, it's a terrific date for three women who don't give a rat's arse about the Stag—even if it is an odd choice for the show. It's not like Tim and his camera will be allowed into the theatre, and even if he were, it's hardly compelling to watch four people sit side by side in the dark. No doubt, footage from the cocktail bar will be the real star of the show—so to speak.

'What's Madaya?' asks Kaz.

'*Medea* is an ancient Greek play by Euripides,' says Daphne. I studied it at university—not my favourite Greek play, but I'm a little green about missing Cate Blanchett on stage. '*Koalas!*' I remind myself.

'Hmm. But it's not in Greek, is it?'

'No, no, it will be in English. You'll like it, I'm sure. It's about love and revenge, and at its core is an extremely strong woman.' It's the first time I've seen Daphne's eyes lit up like this and even Stevie and Kaz seem to be gaining interest.

'Right,' says Gordo. 'I'll leave you to it. Have a spectacular day, ladies, and I will see you soon.' Daphne doesn't even seem to realise he's left, launching into a detailed description of the play.

'I'm going to get ready,' says Becca, excusing herself.

Harry circles his finger in the air, signifying that Tim should keep rolling on Daphne, then catches my eye. With a surreptitious cock of his head, he signals for me to go to the Control Room, and I slip out while Daphne has a captivated audience. 'Oh, cool,' says Kaz as I leave the room.

I make my way out to the annex and knock on the Control Room door. Jack opens it, takes my hand, and pulls me inside. His lips are warm when they press against mine and I snake my arms around his neck. His arms wrap around my waist and a thousand million sparkles of light bounce around inside me as I inhale his cotton-sheets-drying-in-the-sunshine scent. I want to kiss him like this forever.

Eventually, though, the kiss ends and we regard each other from the confines of our hug. 'Hello,' I say quietly.

'Hi,' he replies and we share a smile.

'I'm *so* glad we decided to keep our distance, and that we haven't snuck in *any* alone time or kissed or anything,' I tease.

'Yeah, I should have known that was a terrible plan. It's been harder than I thought …'

'But we still need to be careful.'

'I know.' Jack drops his hands from my waist and I reluctantly let go of him. He crosses to his desk and starts tidying, something I do when I'm worried or stressed.

'What's wrong?' I ask.

He stops tidying. 'Look, I know how you feel about Daniel, but …'

'Our date later?'

'Yep.'

'I won't let anything happen,' I say, though I'm not sure if I'm reassuring myself or Jack.

'I know you don't *want* anything to happen, Abby, but it's a one-on-one date with only five Does left in the Manor. He's going to expect—'

'Right. Of course. A kiss.'

'Yeah. I mean, won't it seem weird otherwise?' He fidgets

with three pencils, lining up the tips, then the ends, and then the tips again.

My mind and my heart are at odds. *'It's just a kiss,'* says my mind, *'for your job—for research.'*

'But I only want to kiss Jack from now until the end of time,' says my heart—the drama queen.

'Look, do what feels right in the moment, okay?' says Jack. His lips flatten into a line and he needn't say anything more.

We're in a pickle, as Lisa would say. 'What feels right' is to flee from this ridiculous situation—taking Jack with me, of course—and avoiding the decision of whether to kiss Daniel altogether. Oh Cadmus, if only.

'I will. Was there anything else? I should get back.'

'Just … I … is it weird to say that I miss you? I mean, I see you every day, but I …'

'No, not at all, but we're nearly there.'

'I know. But top *two*, Abby. I don't know how much longer I can watch him get closer to you.'

'Top two? But … surely not now, not with Stevie, Becca *and* Daphne.' Jack is chewing on his lower lip. 'What? Jack, just tell me.'

'Look, nothing's set in stone, but at this stage of the season, you've got to understand that I'm on the phone to Roberta at least once a day, sometimes twice, or even three times. What may seem like little occurrences out there in the Manor, they can have seismic impacts on the storylines.'

'What "storylines", Jack? You and Harry and Roberta can plan as much as you want, but those are *people* out there. They will feel how they feel and behave how they want to behave. Roberta doesn't have the power of mind control, you know.'

'Unless we're talking about her controlling your mind, Jack,' I think harshly.

'I know, I do, believe me. But with Daphne cooling on Daniel, she's no longer Roberta's top pick for Bride. In fact—'

I interrupt. '*Oh!* Stevie said she might be top three but now that's with me and Becca, right?'

'Right. And in Roberta's mind, you're still top two.'

'But that's just what she wants. I mean, I could completely screw up this date on purpose and then Daniel will send me home. This could all be over at the next Pin Ritual. It's obvious he's going to choose Becca, anyway.' I have mixed feelings about this, of course.

There's something else Jack's not telling me; he also seems to be debating with himself whether he should. He forces a smile that drives a stake of unease into the pit of my stomach. 'It'll all work out, Abs,' he says.

He comes back over to me and gazes down. His eyes are darker today, stormier—olive-coloured instead of the vibrant green they usually are. I know he's carrying a huge weight of responsibility for the success of this season and I don't want our feelings for each other to impact his ability to do his job.

'All right,' I say, conceding. I'll allow him to placate me because, right now, it seems easiest for us both. 'I'll go on the date and do my best to simultaneously keep him interested and at arm's length.'

He smiles—genuinely this time—and pecks my lips. 'Not long to go, now.'

'No, not long to go, now,' I parrot.

I crack open the door and peer out. There's no one about, so I slip out and head upstairs to get ready for my date with a koala.

'When were you planning on telling me?' I ask curtly.

Harry swivels in his seat. 'It had to be someone, Abby, you know that.'

We're watching the episode in which Justine was eliminated and I've just made a sickening discovery.

'Yes, I understand that, Harry, but why *Becca*? She's possibly the furthest thing there is from a Villain.' Not entirely true with some of her recent behaviour, but I am proper cross now. They've brazenly thrown Becca under the proverbial bus and in this episode, she's portrayed as surly and competitive—and she completely monopolises Daniel's time. Well, I suppose she *has* monopolised Daniel, but only because the rest of us want nothing to do with him.

Jack's expression is undecipherable. 'It sucks, I know, but when I suggested Daphne for the Villain—and, let's face it, she would have provided a *lot* more usable footage—Roberta balked. The way she sees it, Daphne's probably out at the next Pin Ritual. And it's not just her cooling on Daniel. He's barely looked her way in a couple of weeks.'

'Right,' I say, 'and Stevie turned out to be lovely and

286

Kaz is too much of a darling,' I add, throwing gasoline on the 'Becca as Villain' fire.

'Exactly,' confirms Jack.

'And that left you and Becca,' says Harry.

Of course, a solution! 'So why not me then? Doe Abby isn't me—not really. Why can't I be the Villain?' Harry and Jack share a loaded look.

'Uh, I'm gonna give you two a minute,' says Harry, leaping up and exiting before I can comprehend why.

'Jack?'

He sighs heavily. 'Roberta did mention you …' He seems unwilling to finish his point.

'And?' I prompt.

'And I talked her out of it, Abby. I didn't want to put you in that position—*literally*. It's bad enough you were strong-armed into this, but to make you the Villain? I wasn't going to do that, though' —he laughs tartly— 'if we *had* gone that route, you've certainly given us enough ammo. Do you know how many times we've caught you frowning or rolling your eyes on camera?'

'You could make a montage?' I quip, attempting to lighten the mood.

'Exactly.'

'Are you sure you didn't let your feelings get in the way of this decision?'

'Of course I bloody did!' he retorts.

'Ouch, Jack.'

'Sorry. I'm sorry, Abby. I just … I couldn't stand the idea of sitting in this room and watching them edit you into something you're not.'

'But you're already doing that with Doe Abby.'

'No—'

'Yes—'

'Newsflash, Abby. Doe Abby, the person who stands up for herself and for her friends, who's clever and funny and caring—that's *you*.'

It is? But Doe Abby is worldly and mysterious and put together—all things I'm not. Jack's wrong.

'And I can *see* what you're thinking,' he says, 'and I'm *not* wrong. You and Doe Abby are the same person, the only difference being how *she* feels about Daniel and how *you* do. That's it. So, yes, too bloody right I kiboshed the idea.'

'All right then.' I am not quite sure if I've been put in my place or on a pedestal. Perhaps both, but either way it's clear that Jack sees me very differently to how I see myself. And I quite like it.

'When do you need to get this episode across?' I ask.

'Day after tomorrow.'

'Can you give me 'til the morning?' I'm glad the tension between us has lessened, but I really want to find another solution.

'For what, Abby?' he asks, his weariness evident.

'I want to talk to Prue.'

'But …' Confusion flits across his face. 'Why?'

'There has to be another way, Jack. Becca has a kind heart. She doesn't deserve to be portrayed as a harpy. And if she's the Villain *and* she ends up with Daniel, then the media, all the show's followers on Twitter, Instagram, they'll *vilify* her. *I* will have to vilify her as Anastasia. Did you think about that?' He sighs again. 'I know it's extra work to make the switch, and I'm sorry, but … please just give me 'til tomorrow morning?'

'Okay, fine.' Brilliant—I've worn him down! He crosses to the door and pokes his head out. 'You can come back in now,' he says to Harry.

Harry returns, looking between us. 'We all good?' he asks.

'Depends what you mean by that, baby brother. Abby, want to fill him in?'

'I suppose that's fair.' I launch into my tentative plan, and Harry visibly deflates at the thought of all the additional work. 'I promise I'll help as much as I can. I'll even do extra confessionals if I need to—in different outfits!' I am grasping now. And Prue may very well say no and this will all be moot.

'Yeah, yeah, okay,' says Harry, 'but we need to know asap, okay? Not tomorrow morning, but, like, *now*-ish. Can you go call your editor?'

'Right now?'

'Yeah. And if it's a go, I can get Silvia back in and we can work through the night.'

I look at Jack and he shrugs. 'You two are the best. I'll be right back.' I leave before they can change their minds.

In my hidey hole, I pace as Prue's personal mobile rings and rings without an answer. It's early in the UK—and a Sunday—but having been on the receiving end of Prue's inappropriately timed phone calls, I'm somewhat surprised when her recorded voice message starts. 'Gah!' I hang up and call again, hoping she'll realise it's important and pick up.

'Abigail, my goodness. Do you know what the time is or have you forgotten there's a nine-hour difference?'

'Hello Prue,' I say cheerily. 'I need to speak with you.'

'Mmm.' Prue's judgey sound.

'It's important.'

'Well, hurry up, Abigail, I'm about to fall back asleep.' There's a male voice in the background murmuring something unintelligible. 'Oh, yes, darling, thank you—would *love* a cuppa.'

In the entire time I've known Prue, it has never once occurred to me that she has a 'darling' in her life (or that she'd use the word 'cuppa') and I'm a little perplexed. 'Abigail?' No time for perplexity, it seems.

'Er, yes, well, we've hit a bit of a snag on *The Stag*,' I say. I'm nothing if not able to rhyme at inappropriate times. She's silent so I continue. 'We lost our Villains, as you know. And the Interloper, Stevie, was a potential replacement, but she's turned out to be heroic and kind and a little too perfect to be a Villain. I mean, not a perfect Villain, but a perfect *person*. And Daphne's probably off the show soon—all sorts going on there. So, Jack and Roberta decided it should be Becca, but she's also not villainous—a little misguided in her affections for Daniel, the tosser, but she definitely doesn't deserve to be the Villain, and now that it's likely she'll be chosen by Daniel—'

'You want to be the Villain,' she interjects.

'Oh … yes.'

'Why didn't you just say that rather than rabbiting on for five minutes?'

'Er, sorry.'

'So, we need to consider if you being the Villain will impact the Anastasia recaps in any way.'

'Yes, exactly.'

'Mmm.' This is her 'I'm percolating' sound—quite distinct from her 'I'm judging you' sound. 'Actually, this might benefit us.'

'Oh? How so?' I ask.

'Well, just think. When Daphne leaves, you'll be the only British Doe and if there are *any* suspicions that Anastasia has insider knowledge, that she is in *any way* associated with *The Stag*, then making you the Villain will quash them, don't you think? Why would anyone malign themselves, even via a pseudonym? Actually, Abigail, I think this is rather clever of you.'

'You do?'

'Don't you?'

'I, er …'

'We really need to work on your ability to give yourself credit when it's due, Abigail.'

'Right. Though, there is just one more thing.'

'Yes?'

'My mum.'

'What about her?'

'I'll need to tell her, you see—about why I'm really here. I can't have her watching *The Stag* thinking I'm a legitimate contestant and see me being all nasty and selfish. It would devastate her.'

'Mmm.' Uh-oh—it's the thinking sound combined with the judgey sound. 'And there isn't any other way?' she asks after a few moments of thinking-judging.

'No,' I say, resolute. I need her to agree. This is my line in the sand. I will not hurt my mother for the sake of my job. Well, any more than I have. She's not going to like hearing that I've lied to her—for *years*.

Prue's end of the line is silent again and I worry that she's hung up or gone back to sleep. 'All right,' she finally says, 'but sworn to secrecy, mind you.'

'Absolutely. I promise.' I grimace, knowing Mum will find it extremely difficult not to tell her friends I'm only *playing* an uncaring and competitive cow on *The Stag*—especially Aunty Lo. Oh, god, Aunty Lo. What will *she* think of me? But there's no way I can extend the bubble of trust to her. She means well, but she's about as watertight as a sieve.

'Right, now if that's all, Abigail, I'd like to start my morning properly. Oh, thank you, darling,' she says to her … ahem … gentleman friend. I can only imagine what a 'proper start' to a Sunday is for Prue when she has a man in her bed. Actually, I'd rather not.

'Jolly good, Prue. Cheerio!' I end the call before she can question why I've added nineteenth century vernacular to my vocabulary. Because I panicked, that's why. I've only considered Prue to be an actual person for a short time and I'm not entirely comfortable with it just yet.

I have one more call to make before I head back to the Control Room to tell Jack and Harry that Operation 'Abby the Villain' is a go.

She answers on the third ring. 'Hello, Mum, I need to tell you something.'

Nearly an hour on the phone with Mum, the whole time knowing that Harry and Jack are waiting (impatiently) to hear the verdict, and I have finally assuaged her concerns. At least, I hope I have.

'Yes, Mum, I am completely serious.'

'Yes, I know it's a far cry from what I wanted to be doing.'

'No, I'm not in any danger.'

'No, you can't tell Aunty Lo about my real job.'

'Yes, I know it's a big ask.'

'I'm sorry, Mum, really. I never wanted to disappoint you.'

'I love you too.'

I press the red button and sit back heavily against the folding chair. Of this entire experience, that has been the hardest part, that conversation. She's my most cherished person in the world and I hadn't realised what a burden it was lying to her all this time. There's a weight that's been lifted, sure, but in its place is an almost crippling guilt.

I glance at the phone in my hands. What's the chance that Lisa will answer this early on a Sunday? Zero. I'll try to catch her another time; I really need my bestie right now.

Chapter Twenty

Onscreen, my face lights up, a study in pure joy as the keeper hands over a koala called Thor. In stark contrast to his name, the sleepy, docile animal curls his arms around me and settles onto my hip like a baby. He looks about slowly, taking in his many admirers with aplomb like the mini celeb he is.

'His claws were poking into my arm, but I never wanted to let him go,' I say to Jack and Harry as we watch Doe Abby—well, *me*—coo at the koala and stroke his back.

'Yeah, he was really cute,' says Harry.

We're watching the re-cut of the most recent episode and I'm both dreading and dying to see what Harry has accomplished. 'Dying' because it's been a rather hairy day-and-a-half since I spoke to Prue about making me the Villain—our most clandestine operation since I landed in Australia—and I want to see if we've pulled it off.

I had to reshoot my original confessional and we filmed

a couple more to intersperse throughout the episode, wardrobe changes included. However, we couldn't film in the backyard like we usually do, as that would give the game away, so Harry dressed a corner of the Control Room to make it 'confessional worthy'. He even did all the filming, making slight adjustments to the backdrop while I snuck into my hidey hole to change outfits.

Meanwhile, Jack called a 'special meeting' of the other Does to talk them through the final weeks of filming—and what better place to hold such a meeting than the Manor's private beach (as in, well away from the annex). Doe Abby was suffering a terrible headache, so was excused, and I was able to sneak away for filming.

It was extremely exciting and to strike the right chord, I *really* let Anastasia come out to play. Oh, those viewers are going to *despise* me—which is why I'm also dreading seeing this version of the episode. I've finally got used to seeing myself onscreen, but this will be altogether different. I'm not sure how easy it will be to watch myself be villainous.

Daniel steps into frame to pet Thor the koala, and Doe Abby grins up at him. Poor Jack shifts noticeably in his seat. I feel awful about it and I hadn't meant to share a moment like that with Daniel … It's just … well, *I was holding a koala!* I would have grinned at anyone, even Vile Demon Woman!

Onscreen, the keeper talks about the plight of koalas and the park's breeding program and Doe Abby and Daniel nod solemnly. In the Control Room, Anastasia's voice starts playing in my head, fully formed sentences pouring from my frontal cortex shrouded in that snarky, acerbic tone. This has been happening more and more lately and I start writing in my notebook.

It's the moment we've all been waiting for——an excursion to meet some of Australia's much-loved (and much-feared) fauna at a wildlife park! Abby looks utterly enchanted by Thor the (adorable) koala, who's propped on her hip like a giant fuzzy babe. Though someone's having a laugh——God of Thunder? With those sleepy eyes at half-mast, more like God of *Slumber*.
And I don't know about you all, but if I were Abby, I'd be hard pressed to choose between Thor and our Stag, Danny, who looks particularly fetching in that casual ensemble of form-fitting jeans and (do I spy product placement?) Calvin Klein T-shirt. And no man on the planet has rocked a pair of aviator sunglasses this well since Tom Cruise felt the need for speed! Delish!

I scribble furiously to keep up with Anastasia.

Next up on our wildlife adventure, cue the kangaroos! Or should that be, cue the *curious* kangaroos, as that buck seems doggedly determined to discover the content of Abby's pocket. And are those squeals of delight or horror, Abby? Either way, Daniel does a gentlemanly job of intervening and by 'gentlemanly', I mean gesticulating (comically) and shouting 'Shoo!' The kangaroo seems unfazed, however. Perhaps he only speaks Australian.

And isn't Pickles the wombat quite the revelation? Weighing in at a svelte 35kg, she may be the tiniest wombat in the whole park, but she's with packed with personality. And how amusing that wombats say 'hello' by nibbling on your toes! I'd wager that Abby is rethinking those (fetching) sandals. More squeals of delight/horror and then the oddest photo op this season, Daniel and Abby seated side by side and holding a squirming Pickles across their laps. As soon as it's over, Pickles scurries into her burrow without even a backwards glance, the marsupial equivalent of 'I'll be in my trailer'. I'm guessing she's not used to working with amateurs.

A spectacular montage scene follows, showcasing a remarkable selection of Australian native fauna including echidnas, emus, seventy-four varieties of parrots (that's me exaggerating a tad, but seen one cockatoo/parakeet/lorikeet, seen them all, right?), Tasmanian devils (**Aside:** Weren't you just the *teeniest* bit disappointed that they weren't spinning about like mini tornados?), and possibly the oddest animal on the planet, the platypus.

These creatures look like an otter mated with a duck! Though, as adorable as they may seem, did you hear the keeper say that they're vicious and that their claws are *venomous*? Unfortunately, Daniel's poorly conceived retort went down like the Hindenburg. 'But aren't *most* creatures in Australia just out to kill you?' Not only does it earn him a tut and a shake of a head from the wildlife keeper, you must have caught the roll of Abby's eyes.

And can we just have a quiet word about Abby? What is *with* her today? She's hot then cold then scorching then tepid. Does she have a case of the guilts because her bestie-in-the-Manor-cum-roommate, Becca, is *also* falling hard for Staggy, or perhaps she's adopting that age-old strategy 'treat 'em mean to keep 'em keen'. That was Shakespeare, right? Henry IV Part II, if I recollect correctly. But back to Abby – smiling serenely at Daniel while cuddling the koala, then mocking him with eye rolls. Abby, Abby, Abby … Don't play this game for too much longer or Daniel may not prick you with his pin – ahem – so to speak.

Time for lunch!

No sooner has Daniel's arse hit the picnic blanket, does he turn the conversation back to one of his favourite topics, himself. 'I don't know why my comment about Australian animals being poisonous landed so flat. Australia has seven of the ten most deadly snakes in the world!' he huffs.

'It's venomous,' says Abby.

'What's that?'

'Those creatures are *venomous*—their venom is *poisonous* to us.'

Uh-oh. Abby is playing a (dare I say it) venomous game here – from Daniel's expression, he does *not* like being corrected. What follows is a rather amusing scene in which Daniel hints at Abby making him up a plate and Abby hints right back that she'll just have 'a little of everything, thank you,' putting him on the spot. Come on Daniel, I have every faith in you—surely you can toss a few olives and a piece of cheese onto a plate?

Actually, that last line was more me than Anastasia. I cross it out and watch the screen.

'Have you enjoyed the wildlife park?' asks Daniel—a banal question from a banal man.

'Absolutely. It's been amazing. You?' asks Doe Abby.

'Oh definitely, though I have to say I'm more partial to the wildlife in Africa.' Doe Abby's eyes widen—onscreen, it plays as interest but what I was really thinking was, *'You are a pretentious twat.'* Of course, Daniel interpreted my reaction as carte blanche to spout off about 'the big five of Africa' as though I hadn't learnt about them in school like everyone else in the world.

Ooh, Anastasia will love that. I jot it down in my notebook.

Doe Abby keeps munching on the picnic assortment, nodding occasionally and making noises that could either be construed as 'oh, how interesting' or 'this cheese is unbelievable'.

'I'm boring you,' says Daniel suddenly. He puts down his plate and stares glumly off into the distance. Doe Abby finally stops shoving food in her mouth and also puts down her plate.

'No, not at all. Very interesting stuff.' Daniel looks at Doe Abby and tilts his head to the side, then raises his eyebrows, and Doe Abby laughs. 'All right, perhaps just a little.'

'I don't *mean* to get all didactic like that.'

'I know.' I didn't, but it's what you say when someone's self-flagellating, isn't it?

'I just … I want to impress you, but I come off sounding like a pompous arse.' Doe Abby bursts out laughing—and I promise I wasn't being deliberately cruel—and Daniel joins in. 'I'm glad you find my shortcomings so amusing,' he says.

I knew I needed to keep him on the hook, so replied, 'It's not that. It's just … it's good to see *you*, Daniel, and not the pompous arse you sometimes come across as.' Saying 'sometimes' instead of 'always' was me being generous.

'I'm not particularly good with women,' he says.

'What?' I'd been properly stunned by that and it shows on my face.

'It's true. That's why I came on this show. I mean, I see

people—well, *saw*. But it never went anywhere. Two or three dates, maximum, and they either wouldn't take my calls or they'd give some feeble excuse for not seeing me. I swear, the women of London must have the cleanest hair in all the world. Anyway, after dozens of such experiences, it suddenly occurred to me that *I* might be the problem.'

'I see.'

'And I've come all this way and I fear I may be messing things up.'

'How so?' asks Doe Abby.

Daniel stares off into the distance again. 'Well, I sense I've put Daphne off—that palaver on the bridge—'

'I'd hardly call her panic attack a palaver.'

'No, no, that's what I mean. My *reaction* was the palaver, only I didn't know how to make amends and now she despises me.'

'I doubt she despises you, Daniel.'

'*You* do.'

'I do not.'

'But I always catch you frowning at me and any time I try to amuse you or engage you in conversation, you get a certain look on your face. Actually, it's not dissimilar to how you're looking at me now.'

'Oh,' says Doe Abby, raising her hands to her face.

'Do you even like me, at all?' he asks. At that, I'd been caught completely off guard. I mean, what is there to say to that? I'd had less than a second to react—any longer would have been a dead giveaway—but it was one of those moments that seemed to stretch out for an eon as I weighed up whether or not to be truthful. In the end, I landed on the side of kindness (also known as lying).

'Of course I do.'

'Well, then why do you always keep me at arm's length or constantly frown at me?'

And here comes the biggest lie wrapped up in the biggest truth I've told since I got to Australia. 'Because I'm insecure. I'm not the prettiest woman in the Manor, nor the cleverest. I'm not particularly interesting and I still have a bucket list as long as my arm, not having accomplished much for a woman of my age.'

'You are hardly a plain Jane, Abby—you're very attractive. You hold up your end of an argument, without question, and you certainly don't let *me* get away with anything. That's one of the reasons I find you so intriguing.'

It was exactly where I'd wanted him to be—*needed* him to be—if I was going to end up in the top two, as mandated by Roberta. All I had to do was drive it home, so he'd be properly ensnared.

'Well, then, thank you. That's … thank you, Daniel.'

'You're welcome, Abby.'

'And I suppose I owe you an apology,' says Doe Abby.

'How so?'

'For making you feel that way, like I don't have feelings for you.'

Daniel's eyes lock with Doe Abby's. 'May I … may I kiss you?'

Jack is squirming in his seat again and clears his throat. 'We don't have to watch it. We all know what happens,' I say.

Harry spins in his chair. 'But I want you to see how I cut it together with the confessional.' Harry seems intent on showing off his editing skills at the expense of his brother's happiness—and mine, if I'm honest—and the rest of the scene unfolds. Doe Abby nodding softly, Daniel wriggling closer to her and then the kiss.

At the time I'd felt nothing. I feel all sorts of things now, however. Discomfort. Disgust. Disappointment. A myriad of other 'dis' words. I never want to kiss Daniel ever again and I certainly don't want to *watch* myself kiss Daniel. All I want to do right this minute is kiss Jack, so that *he's* the last man I've kissed.

'This bit, this bit …' says Harry, pointing at the screen.

'And that's how it's done,' says Doe Abby talking directly to camera. 'Play hard to get, then give him a little morsel of attention. Easy. There's no way I won't at *least* get to top two now. And if I keep playing my cards right, he'll choose me. Oh, I would absolutely *love* to reside in a big fancy house in London, jetting off on holidays, sailing about the Caribbean, and living in the lap of luxury. Yes, please, Daniel darling.' Doe Abby bats her eyelashes beguilingly. 'I mean, I'm from money, of course, but *Daniel*—being an investment banker, he's proper rich, if you know what I mean.'

'What about Becca? She seems keen on Daniel and aren't you two close friends?' says Harry off camera.

Doe Abby tilts her head and shrugs. 'I suppose we were when we first got here, but this is a competition, isn't it? Only one of us gets to be with the Stag and I want that Doe to be me. Besides, I have enough friends.'

'Will you let on to Becca and the others that your game has changed?'

'Why would I? Keep your friends close and your enemies closer, right?' A sneer tugs at the corners of Doe Abby's mouth and the screen goes black.

'Awesome, eh?' asks Harry.

I don't answer but fix my eyes on the back of Jack's head. 'Jack? What did you think?'

Jack turns towards me and I detect a tinge of sadness in his eyes, which tugs at my heartstrings. 'You did a good job, Abby. And these new confessionals … they'll make the next episodes easier to put together. We won't have to fudge it so much in the editing.'

I'm torn. The professional writer in me wants to have done a good job, but the 'just Abby' me, the me who has fallen for the gorgeous Australian, wants to leap out of my chair and give him a hug. Professional Abby wins, however. There's far more riding on all of this than the Abby and Jack storyline, like his career.

'Do you think Roberta will be pleased?' I ask. 'You said she wasn't particularly happy about swapping out Becca for me.'

'She'll be fine with it.' He flicks his eyes to his wrist. 'You'd better go get ready, Abby. The Soirée starts soon.' To Harry he says, 'You too, baby bro.'

'Shit, too right.' Harry leaps up. 'Catchya out there, Abby. Good job,' he says, giving my shoulder a pat as he passes.

I stand, reluctant to leave. 'Can I just ask you one thing?' asks Jack, now sounding slightly—no, let's make that *extremely*—miffed.

'Er, yes, of course.'

'So, *do* you like him now?'

'Daniel?' My response is part rhetorical, part incredulous—but for Jack, it's like red to a bull.

'Who else?' he replies caustically.

'Are we going to have a tiff now, Jack? *Are we?*' This question is purely rhetorical and while we exchange Paddington Bear hard stares again, I don't wait for a reply. 'Why is it that any time we discuss this show, this completely bizarre, messed-up show, we end up at odds with one another? No, for the last bloody time I don't bloody like bloody Daniel, *Jack*. I'm playing a role. A role that you and Roberta and Prue and Harry all want me to play—*need* me to play.

'And, yes, Daniel opened up to me and, *oh my god*, it turns out he's not quite the utter twat that I've always believed him to be. But "not being that much of a twat"' —I angrily do the air quotes— 'is hardly a glowing reference, now is it? Oh, lucky me, a man who's not-quite-a-twat thinks I'm attractive and interesting. Alert the media immediately! I'm about to get married!

'And in the meantime, while I'm throwing myself on my proverbial sword to keep Becca out of harm's way—something I can never tell her, mind you—you're in here sulking like a petty-minded schoolboy. It's bad enough having to prop up Daniel's ego, but having to do the same for you? It's ridiculous and, quite honestly, I've had enou—'

'You're right,' he interrupts.

'I know I am.'

'I'm sorry.'

'All right, fine—good.' I go to leave.

'Abby.'

I turn to face him. 'I only ever wanted you, Jack.'

'Wanted? As in past tense?'

'Perhaps this isn't a good idea.'

'No, it's … Look, it's only a couple of weeks 'til this is all over. We can work it out, okay? Please, just … let me make this right.' He takes a few steps towards me and when he's close enough for me to see just how olive-green his eyes are (a built-in mood ring, of sorts), he says, 'Please?'

I huff, a micro smile threatening at the left corner of my mouth. 'You're a complete idiot. You do know that, right?'

'I do and thank you for reminding me.'

'Well, somebody has to.' Before he can sweet talk me into a kiss, I need to get out of here. Part of me wants to make up with him, but he's just so infuriating! There's only one person I need right now, so when I close the Control Room door behind me, I turn right instead of left and slip into my hidey hole.

I'm both shocked and relieved when Lisa picks up on the second ring. 'Abs! You're lucky to have caught me, babes. I'm between meetings and have exactly' —she pauses— 'three minutes before I'm due back. And fair warning I'm dying for a wee—'

'Do *not* take me into the bathroom with you,' I warn—like it will have any effect whatsoever.

'Hah!' she barks, 'too late. So, what's going on?' I try to ignore the sound of my bestie on the loo, as the clock is ticking, and get straight to the point.

'There're five of us left, one going tonight but not me, and Vile Demon Woman now wants me in the top two—'

'Jesus! Top two!' The toilet flushes.

'Yes, exactly. So, of course, I had to make nice with Daniel and on our last date, he opened up to me *and* he kissed me again—'

'Ugh.'

'It was fine—I barely remember it—but Jack's being all possessive and strange and I just had to give him a serve—*again*—and I haven't even told you the hardest part yet.'

'Ninety seconds,' she says.

'Right. So, I'm the new Villain.'

'Sorry, *what*?' She's obviously in the corridor now as she's lowered her voice, but her incredulousness bounds its way from London to Sydney intact. 'Babes you are many things, but you are not a Villain by any measure.'

'That's the thing, see, I had to step in. And I've just seen the latest episode and, Lise, I'm *awful*!'

'Well, you gave it your best shot, Abs, but you just don't have it in you.'

'No, as in, I've done it. I'm going to be hated by people across the UK, possibly the *world*.'

'Wow, *really*?'

'Yes! Anyway, I was really calling because I'm not sure what to do about Jack. He's got all jealous and insecure. I—'

'So sorry, Abs, but I've got to trot.' She covers the handset with her hand and I hear a muffled, 'Two secs.' To me, she says, 'Love you to bits. Talk soon and don't take any of his shit.'

'Which one? Daniel or Jack?'

'Either! Take no shit from no man, babes. Ever. Bye-ee.'

The line goes quiet.

Hardly eloquent, but Lisa's words ring in my ear. *'Take no shit from no man.'* Maybe I should have *that* printed on a T-shirt.

Chapter Twenty-One

I t's one of those moments I expected, yet it still shocks me.

Daphne did not get a pin.

Gordo's sombre tone when he says, 'I'm sorry, Daphne, but it's time to say your goodbyes and leave the Manor,' is completely appropriate (for once), because in the past week or so, Daphne has become one of us. Her stricken eyes lock with mine and I step forward and give her a hug for the first time since we met, her spindly arms wrapping around me and clinging tightly.

'It will be all right,' I say as Kaz encircles us in a group hug.

'Aww, Daph, I'm gonna miss you,' she says.

Becca and Stevie stand close by, patting Daphne on the back and it seems like forever before we hear, 'Cut.' Even then Daphne doesn't let go.

'Shall we get you inside?' I ask. I feel her nod, then gently pull away from her.

'Uh, Daphne, may I have a word?' It's Daniel and for a second everyone seems stunned, especially Daphne. Harry waves frantically at Tim who swiftly lines up the shot and starts recording, activating the (now more than ever) intrusive red light on the camera.

'Why's that?' asks Daphne, curtness cutting through the tears. 'What can you possibly have to say to me?' *'This is going to make terrific television,'* I think, hating myself for it.

Daniel looks about at the rest of us and then off-camera at Harry who nods encouragingly. It's clear he's regretting this turn in the narrative—one of his own doing—but there's a flicker of something across his eyes and when they land back on Daphne, they've softened somewhat.

'I want to apologise,' he says.

I share a look with the other Does and we step back to give them some privacy. Tim does the opposite, bringing the camera close, something that Daphne and Daniel must be so used to by now, they don't even seem to notice.

Daniel reaches up to pat Daphne's arm and speaks in low tones while she stares at the sand beneath her feet and says nothing. When Daniel's head dips, trying to catch her eye, Daphne finally lifts her gaze. I cannot imagine how humiliated she must feel, even if she was cooling on him. Though, if he's apologising for his awful behaviour on the bridge that day, it may make this parting even worse. He's human, he made a forgivable mistake, but he *still* doesn't want her.

She nods once—likely accepting his apology—but as he reaches for another pat on the arm, Daphne has clearly had enough. She pulls away and strides past us towards the

Manor. Kaz catches up with her and slings an arm around her shoulders. That Daphne allows this says as much about how far we've all come as it does this situation.

Stevie and I wave goodbye to Daniel, maintaining the façade that we give two hoots about him, and Becca hangs back. She'd shown her usual kindness to Daphne but she must be relieved that the numbers are dwindling and she's still here.

I need to talk to her soon, and properly. Well, not *properly* properly, where I come clean about being Anastasia and reveal that none of us want Daniel (in the slightest) and that she has a clear path. But just to see how she is. We haven't talked much lately, even though we still share a room. I wonder again if she's hoping to move into her own room—it might be a bit odd after having had the opportunity for weeks now. Perhaps it's one of those things that you leave too long, so can't work out how to do it without hurting the person, like an apology left too late.

Stevie and I pass Jack, who's been watching the filming from the lawn, and he smiles warmly. 'Goodnight, Stevie, Abby,' he says. I give a terse smile as we pass, still not fully forgiving him for being a nitwit, and he grins back. Did he miss that my smile was *terse*?

A few seconds later, Stevie nudges me. 'He's hot, don't you think?'

'Sorry?'

'*Jack*. Don't tell me you haven't noticed. Though, I reckon Harry is hotter. Whaddya say we ditch Daniel altogether and take up with the Freeman brothers?'

I laugh like it's the most hilarious thing I've ever heard,

as though I'd never *once* thought of taking up with a Freeman brother, never kissed one, and never imagined long, languid nights of making love with one of them. 'Hahaha-ha,' my voice trills with faux hilarity.

I stop laughing the moment we cross the threshold from the patio into the lounge room. Daphne is proper sobbing now, sitting on one of the sofas, her head in her hands and wailing. Kaz pats her back while shooting us a 'help me' look.

'Daphne!' I rush over, followed closely by Stevie.

Kaz leaps up and heads towards the kitchen. 'I'm getting us something to drink.' If even the unflappable Kaz is 'flapped' then this situation is worse than I could have imagined.

I sit in the spot Kaz has vacated and Stevie retrieves a box of tissues from an end table, then sits on Daphne's other side. 'Daphne,' I say. 'What's wrong? Are you upset because Daniel didn't choose you?'

She lifts her face from her hands and accepts a wad of clean tissues from Stevie, dragging them under her nose, then shakes her head and hiccups a few more sobs. *'If not Daniel, then what?'* I wonder. 'Is it leaving the Manor after so long? Leaving Sydney?' Her eyes well up again, another head shake, and she stares ahead, her gaze unfocused. 'Is it us? You'll miss us?' I know it's a long shot, but I literally cannot think of another thing that could induce this many tears. And perhaps Daphne's become more attached to us than I thought.

But the answer to my (obviously foolish) question is a disbelieving look, then a burst of laughter, which dissolves almost immediately into more tears. I glance at Stevie and even she seems perplexed. 'Sorry, Daphne, but I'm out of ideas. You're just going to have to tell us,' I say.

Kaz returns from the kitchen carrying a tray that bears a bottle and four glasses. 'Really, fizz?' I ask.

'Hey, in my book, there's never a bad time for bubbles, and why not celebrate Daphne's escape from Daniel the Dick?'

There's a moment of dense silence—I'm dumbstruck and Stevie must be, too—but it ends abruptly when Daphne starts laughing heartily. 'Daniel the Dick,' she says breathily, then dissolves into more laughter. It's the first time I've seen her completely unencumbered from her posh upbringing and reserved nature, and the three of us exchange concerned looks.

'Oh,' says Daphne, as her laughter dies. She expels some deeps breaths and accepts more tissues from Stevie, this time dabbing under her eyes delicately. Finally, she shakes her blonde bob, sniffs, and puts her shoulders back. 'I'm sorry about that. I suppose I got a little emotional.' And just like that, old Daphne is back.

'A little emotional?' asks Kaz. 'Ah, sorry, love, but that was a full-on meltdown.' She tears the foil on the bottle and untwists the metal cage. 'So, what's really going on with you? Actually, hold that thought.' She twists the bottle and it emits a whispered 'peh' as the cork releases. She makes short work of pouring four glasses of fizz and passes them around, Daphne's first. When we each have a glass, Kaz holds hers aloft. 'To our mate, Daph, who's been a bloody hard nut to crack, but who's all class.'

'To Daphne,' I say along with Stevie.

Daphne blinks, perhaps surprised by the kind(ish) words, and takes a sip and we all follow suit. 'Right, now the formalities are outta the way, what gives?' asks Kaz, seating herself across from us and propping her feet up on the coffee table. Where I've failed in getting Daphne to open up, I'm hoping Kaz's direct approach will succeed.

Daphne looks at us in turn, clearly deciding whether she can trust us. I can't really blame her, especially as our bonds of friendship are in their infancy, and she's still … well … *Daphne*. She sighs and her shoulders fall a little as she cradles the flute in her delicate fingers. 'We are completely and utterly broke,' she says, her eyes boring a hole into the shaggy grey and white rug.

'Who is, darl?' asks Kaz.

'My family, the Pemberleys,' she replies quietly.

'And what does that mean, "broke"? How broke is broke?' Kaz probes.

Stevie, the only one of us trained in this type of conversation, jumps in. 'Daphne, you don't have to tell us if you don't want to. But we're here if you need to talk——no judgement.' She looks pointedly at me then Kaz, and we chime in with our assurances. 'No judgement, Daphne,' I say. 'No way, all good here,' says Kaz.

Daphne lifts her gaze and says, 'My family's estate is heavily in debt. It's mostly because of the upkeep——the house, the grounds, the *staff*——tens of thousands of pounds a month. You have no idea what it costs to "keep up appearances" and my father and brother have done nothing but run it into the ground, borrowing against it for years. It's *shameful*,' she spits, her fury evident.

'But it's none of my concern, it is? I'm just the daughter, the youngest child, and how could I with my *arts degree* have any way of understanding *fiscal matters*? Only I do. Despite what they think, I'm very clever. And tired of being kept in the dark, even though it was obvious the situation was dire, I took myself off to see the family accountant behind their backs. That's when I discovered I was right to be concerned. There's not only nothing left of a centuries-old fortune, but we're mortgaged to the hilt and it's getting bleaker by the day.'

This is the most Daphne's revealed about herself and there's so much to digest. I know that many of the older estates across Great Britain are money pits—it's the reason the producers of *The Stag* are able to get such impressive locations for their shoots, and probably at quite a reasonable price.

'So, is that why you came on *The Stag*? Is that why you're here?' I ask.

'Yes, in a way. There's the prize money, of course, though £50,000 pounds would barely make a dent in what we owe, but I figured it could be an escape plan of sorts—a chance to finally snag myself a husband,' she says wryly. 'With my brother, Colin, and my father seemingly intent on losing our family home—my only home—and with me being a "certified lady of leisure" with no discernible skills or prospects, as Colin too often says—'

'Your brother sounds like a prize dickhead, Daph,' says Kaz, perhaps trying to be helpful.

'Hah!' laughs Daphne drily. 'He is, but in a way he's right. Since I was very young, I've been taught how to behave like a lady—I *am* a lady in actual fact, though the title is worthless, of course—but it was drummed into me that I would run in certain circles, partake of the life I was entitled to—*accustomed* to—then marry well and one day have the run of my own estate—be the lady of the manor, so to speak.'

'Wow, that sounds like something out of *Downton Abbey*,' says Kaz. 'Maybe we should call you Lady Mary.' She chuckles at her own joke.

'Well, if we're talking *Downton*, I'm more of an Edith, the sister no one expects much from.'

'Other than to marry well,' adds Stevie.

'Exactly. Marry well and get out of Colin and Father's hair. But the thing is, even though no one really talks about the money, or lack of it, everyone in our ever-diminishing, incestuous circle knows, so there *are* no prospects for marriage. Everyone's too wise to what's going on, that my "dowry" is gone. It's just me,' she adds, her voice catching slightly on 'me'. I want to throw my arms around her and give her a tight squeeze. I don't, though. She may have revealed her vulnerable side to us today, but she's still Daphne.

'And so when you met Daniel …' Kaz prods.

'Exactly—a perfect solution. Absolutely rolling in it, but new money, you see, so none of the judgement about me and my family, just a way out—possibly the most perfect Stag I could have hoped for.'

'To rescue you,' says Stevie and I suspect she's crossing

that invisible line between friend and therapist.

'Yes, I suppose.'

'His loss, Daph,' says Kaz, perhaps because it's what you say to a woman who's just been dumped.

Daphne smiles weakly. 'I'm not sure that's entirely true. He's probably dodged a bullet more than anything.'

'That's being a bit hard on yourself,' says Kaz.

'You can do much better,' says Stevie.

Daphne's head swivels quickly in her direction. 'Really?'

'Come on,' says Stevie, 'I know you agree with me. You've been distancing yourself from him for a while now, ever since that day on the bridge.'

Daphne nods. 'True. I've hated myself for it, though. Kept telling myself "chin up", "you can do this", "he's not that bad"——'

'He *is* that bad,' says Stevie.

'Possibly, but it doesn't matter. I've made a right mess of everything and god only knows what I'll do now.'

'You'll figure something out,' I say. 'Perhaps one of those charities you volunteer for will hire you——a proper job. You must have a lot of expertise that they'd find valuable.'

'Hmm, perhaps,' she says with a small smile——possibly a spark of hope.

'He's still pretty hot, though,' says Kaz——a total non sequitur. While we're all musing over the level of Daniel's hotness——I suppose if I didn't know anything about him at all, I might find him *vaguely* attractive, though I prefer floppy-haired, green-eyed Australians——Kaz finishes her thought with, 'for a wanker.'

Four women——two English, two Australian——collectively still for a moment, then erupt into raucous laughter. Even Daphne throws back her head, her hand clutching her pearls as she shakes with laughter.

'What's so funny?' Becca has just entered the lounge room and looks at us, puzzled.

'Hey, how'd it go with Daniel?' Kaz deflects Becca's question with unforeseen skill and the rest of us swallow our laughter.

Becca glances between us, still seeming puzzled, and her gaze settles on Kaz. 'Yeah … um … good,' she says with a smile. When she looks at Daphne, her smile instantly disappears. I can't even imagine being in Becca's position right now—feeling elated but not wanting to gloat. 'Are you okay, Daphne?' she asks.

'Never better,' replies Daphne with false cheer. Of course, *we* know the truth, but Daphne has trusted us and no good can come of correcting her.

'Oh, that's good,' says Becca, but she doesn't seem convinced. God, I hate this. I'm stuck in 'no-woman's land' unable to express loyalty on either side. *'You have zero control over this, Abby,'* I remind myself.

'Can I pour you some?' asks Stevie, indicating the open bottle. Huzzah! Stevie (and fizz) to the rescue.

There's half a second where the machinations of Becca's thoughts play across her face, then she breaks into a broad smile and says, 'Thanks. That'd be great.'

'Let me get you a glass,' says Kaz, leaping up and heading to the kitchen. Becca nestles into the sofa opposite me, Daphne, and Stevie, and our wait for Kaz thrusts us into an awkward silence. Too bad this isn't being captured on camera. Harry could compile an impressive montage of Does blinking blankly at each other, our expressions belying our internal monologues.

Daphne: *'God, do I really have to sit here and make nice, having just humiliated myself by revealing that I'm poor and desperate?'*

Stevie: *'What have I got myself into and when can I get the hell out of here?'*

Becca: *'Do not gloat. Be supportive. Be friendly.'*

And me: *'I so wish I could come clean to you all—tell you absolutely everything that's going on.'*

This has never been truer. It's odd, the sense of kinship I feel with these women, this 'elite' group who have experienced the drama, the elation, the friendship and 'foeship' of being a Sydney season Doe. Just last week, Daphne wouldn't have given me the time of day and here I am learning her deepest fears and woes.

How quickly our world changes in the Manor.

Kaz returns, pours a generous glass of fizz, and hands it to Becca. 'So,' she says, plonking down next to her, 'isn't this awkward as shit?' Becca's mouth quirks as she glances sideways at Kaz. 'What? It is, but you know what? I never in a million years thought I'd be in the top four. I mean, come on! Oh, sorry, Daph, not rubbing it in, I promise.' Daphne flaps her hand, dismissing the apology.

'But the best part of this whole thing,' continues Kaz, 'is you lot. You are all top chicks and, yeah, this is weird, all us pitted against each other and Daph going home—especially 'cause at first, I thought Daniel would pick you for sure, Daph—sorry, Becs …' Becca shrugs. 'Anyway, all that aside, I want to propose a toast.' Like me, the others have perked up and we watch Kaz with interest. 'To the coolest fucking Does this show's ever seen,' she says, holding her glass aloft.

I glance about our little group and the emerging smiles are genuine, including mine. Daphne shakes her head, titters, and in her clipped accent says, 'To the coolest fucking Does this show's ever seen.' We clink glasses, rising half out of our seats to reach across the void between us, then sink back into those ridiculously long, but extremely comfortable sofas, and drink to how fucking cool we all are.

———————

Harry just gave me the nod, our signal to meet Jack in the annex, but the Control Room was empty so I head to my hidey hole. When I open the door, Jack is leaning against one of the tall shelving units, wearing his 'I aim to misbe-have' T-shirt. I adore this T-shirt. It makes me think of all the misbehaving we'll get to do when this is over.

He grins, doing spectacular things to my insides—par-ticularly the lower half—and as soon as I close the door, he opens his arms. I cross the small space and wrap mine around his waist. 'Hey, you,' he says before dropping a smack of a kiss onto my lips.

'Hello, you, too,' I reply, though I am not satisfied with a mere peck and I take my time when I kiss him back. I love kissing Jack—adore it—*long* for it. He is the best kisser in the entire universe. I am confident of this fact even though my sample size is relatively small, because we fit together so perfectly—our lips, our bodies—and his kisses transport me somewhere I've never been before. Somewhere magical.

Oh dear, I've become a parody of myself which, considering who my alter ego is, may be something of an achievement.

The kiss eventually ends—always too soon in my opinion—and Jack peers down at me as our arms encircle each other. 'Okay, so pleasure out of the way…' My face scrunches into a knot of distaste. 'That came out wrong but you know what I mean.' I purse my lips in faux annoyance. 'Anyway, I have news. Actually, it's for all of you but it affects you differently, so I wanted to give you a heads up. It's, ah … it's a bit tricky.' He has my full attention now, my intrigue mounting by the moment. I wriggle out of his embrace, flip open the folding chair, and sit.

'Go ahead.'

He resumes his place leaning against the shelves, and only now do I see the tension in his shoulders. 'So, I'm not sure how much of *The Buck* you've seen,' he begins, 'but we always have a "meet the family" episode towards the end of the season where we fly the Does' families in to meet the Buck. It's only for the top four Does, and it's always a popular episode, but when we originally planned this season of *The Stag*, Roberta and I … well, we decided to skip it. We could have ended up with four British Does and that's a lot of airfares all the way from the UK.'

'But she's changed her mind,' I interrupt.

'Kinda. We *are* gonna film the episode, but Daniel's going to meet the families via video conferencing.'

'But if you're worried about airfares, I'm the only British Doe left.'

'True, but …' He leaves the thought hanging in the air

and I suddenly realise why he's so tense. Because *my* mum is not Doe Abby's mum. Doe Abby grew up wealthy and has two parents.

'Oh,' I say quietly. 'I see.'

'Yeah. I wanted to talk to you first … you know …'

'To give me a "heads up".'

'Yeah.'

'But you'll still need someone for the video conference, right?' I'm having a hard time piecing together what they're planning.

'Yeah, exactly, so we're gonna cast an actress and an actor—'

'No,' I say, interrupting, '*please* … just my mum. Or Doe Abby's mum. I don't want anyone playing my father.'

'I know your mum and dad aren't together anymo—'

'I don't have a father. I mean, of course I have a father out there somewhere but I just … I've just never met him. Sorry, that's not right. He was around when I was a baby, but …' I trail off, wishing we were talking about *anything* else. It's also not lost on me that Jack has a 'dad', whereas I have an absent 'father'—two vastly different kinds of parents.

'Abby, we can totally do the shoot with just your mum—well, you know … someone playing your mum.'

'Thank you.' I say, my voice raspy. This isn't something I talk about very often. Lisa knows, of course, though she never brings it up. Aunty Lo was around when it happened and we've talked about it a few times over the years but discussing my father with Jack in these circumstances—it's like a punch in the stomach. I never thought I could feel *winded* just from a conversation.

'Hey.' Jack crosses to me and bobs down in front of my chair. 'So, it's been just you and your mum your whole life?' I nod. 'That's why you're so close then?' Another nod. He squeezes my knee reassuringly, his eyes full of kindness and understanding.

Well, as long as I'm being completely honest with him … 'I told her, Jack,' I whisper.

'What do you mean? Told her what?' he asks.

'I told my mum why I'm here, why I'm *really* here—right after I talked to Prue about becoming the Villain. I didn't want her thinking it was *me* who was behaving badly. I wanted her to know I'm playing a role. I know I shouldn't have …'

'It contravenes your NDA, Abby.' He doesn't seem cross, just concerned.

'I know. I cleared it with Prue, though, and mum is sworn to secrecy. She can't even tell Aunty Lo—and she won't, I made her promise.' My stomach churns under the weight of my revelation.

'It's okay, I understand.'

'You do?' I can't disguise my shock and Jack smiles.

'Of *course* I do. All that stuff we talked about—you writing as Anastasia, and Harry and I doing these gigs—it's a means to an end, not the end itself. You have no idea how fast I was round to Dad's when I landed my first reality TV gig. "It's just a job, Dad. Just 'til Harry and I save enough money to start our own outfit." I reassured him so much, he ended up telling me to shut it. I just didn't want him thinking this was my dream job and that I'd turn into some smarmy dickhead. My dad's opinion of me means everything—so I totally get why you needed to tell your mum, especially since we've turned you into the Villain.'

'You're not mad.'

'No. I am getting a leg cramp, though, so I'm standing up now.' He tries to land a kiss as he stands and we knock noses. 'Ow, shit, sorry.'

I rub my nose. 'It's okay. It doesn't hurt much.' It does.

'Real smooth, huh?' he says, grinning down at me.

'Just imagine how smooth it would have been if you'd pulled it off.' We chuckle at his expense.

'So, getting back to casting your mum, what do you think of—'

'Hang on,' I say, cutting him off again. 'I've just had a thought. Can I talk to my mum before you make any decisions?'

'Uh, yeah, sure. We haven't got a lot of time, though. Think you could talk to her before tomorrow?'

'Absolutely.'

'Great. Now come here.' He takes my hand and pulls me up, then wraps me up in his arms again. And even though being in Stag Manor means I rarely think even a day ahead, let alone a week or more, all I can dream of as we kiss is being out of the Manor, away from prying eyes and ears (and camera lenses and microphones), and somewhere lovely, just the two of us, so we can ratchet up our PG-rated romance into something closer to *Fifty Shades*—so we can *really* misbehave.

Chapter Twenty-Two

Harry spins in his chair and grins at me. 'Your mum's as cool as, Abby.'

I grin back at him and return my eyes to the giant screen, beaming with pride. We're watching Daniel meet Doe Abby's mum—as in, his potential mother-in-law—and my mum is smashing it. Once the idea came to me, I knew it would be the perfect solution. And when I called her with my suggestion, she'd giggled with delight.

You see, my mum is a bit of an actress. Once I was able to support myself, she'd been able to give up two of her three jobs, and with all that 'extra time on her hands' (her words, not mine—I'd just wanted her to relax after work like normal people), she decided to do something she'd been longing to do for years: join an amateur dramatics society. Within months, she'd been cast in *The Importance of Being Earnest*—as Lady Bracknell, thank you very much. Aunty Lo, Lisa, and I went on opening night, front row centre, and after only a minute of her being on stage, I completely forgot I was watching my mum.

She was *magnificent*.

So, here we are ten years and twice as many productions later, and my mum is channelling her inner Lady B for her 'informal chat' with Daniel. And hasn't she got him on the back foot! *'Well done, Mum,'* I think.

It was a huge leap of faith for Jack, of course. We'd only get one shot; it wasn't like we could say to Daniel, *'Oh, by the way, Abby's mum who you just met? She was the stand-in. Can we go again?'*

And, although it was all very last-minute, Jack arranged for Mum to have some pampering of her own, including a new outfit, before she was collected by a town car and driven to a small studio in downtown London. She said she loved 'being feted about like Lady Muck' and I adored Jack all the more for being so thoughtful.

'Now, Daniel, our Abby is a career woman, as you know. How does that fare with you?' Mum asks, staring right into the camera.

'Oh, well, it's marvellous that Abby has her career in … uh …'

'Public service, Daniel. Surely, you've learnt *that* much about my daughter.'

'Yes, of course. It's marvellous that she wants to work with the … uh … public.' Mum's lips disappear into a thin line of disapproval. 'I've always thought that women should work outside the home—if they want to,' he adds, digging himself into a larger hole.

'I see. And in your mind, how does that factor into who does the work *inside* the home?'

'Inside?'

'Domestic duties, Daniel. Do you contribute or will Abby be expected to manage the household on her own?'

'Oh, well, it's just me at the moment, in my flat, and I … uh … I do have a cleaning woman who comes once a fortnight, so Abby wouldn't need to worry about that.'

'So, you *do* think it's the woman's role to take care of domestic duties?' Mum asks and I giggle. How on earth is Daniel supposed to respond to that?

'No, no, not at all. In fact, if it would make her more comfortable—*and* we'd decided to make a home together, of course—I could hire a *man* to clean for us.'

'Bahaha.' I can't help it. Daniel is unwittingly hilarious. From the shaking of Jack and Harry's shoulders, they think so too and Jack shoots me a wink and a grin.

'Let's move on, shall we?' asks my Lady B mum, commandeering the conversation once again. 'Tell me what you love about our Abby?'

'Oh, uh … she's forthright. She'll say exactly what she means,' he says brightly. Not the most romantic response, but it's not like I *care*. 'And caring,' he adds with perfect, ironic timing. 'And she can be very funny.' *'If only he knew,'* I think.

'And, of course, my daughter is *beautiful*.' *'That's laying it on a bit thick, Mum.'*

'Undoubtedly,' replies Daniel convincingly and I nod in appreciation of his excellent acting.

'And what about her lifelong dream?' Mum asks. Lifelong dream? This is a tangent we didn't discuss and I'm curious where she's going.

'Her dream, you say?'

'Yes, to own an exotic animal sanctuary. Surely, she's mentioned it?' If I'd been sipping on anything, it would have been a spit-take moment and I clap my hand over my mouth, sniggering beneath it.

'That's my favourite line,' says Harry, 'but wait 'til you hear his reply.'

I focus on the screen as Daniel's eyes widen and he struggles to compose himself. 'Oh, yes, the sanctuary! A wonderful idea—*wonderful*. In fact, my uncle has a parcel of land just north of the Scottish border that would be perfect.'

'Bahahahahaha.' This time Harry and Jack join in and Harry taps a button on the console in front of him to stop the replay.

'Told ya! At least if Daniel *does* choose you, he'll build you an animal sanctuary as a consolation prize!' Harry eyes are alight with mirth, but Jack stops laughing.

'Don't even joke about that,' he says.

'Oh, chill out, it's not gonna happen.' Harry shakes his head and taps another button to resume the replay. I watch Jack frown at his brother, then look back at the screen. I'm not sure why, but this time it doesn't irk me to see Jack's jealousy flare up. In fact—and I hope this isn't too egotistical—I'm rather enjoying it. I, Abigail Jones, have induced jealousy!

'Well, you've obviously got it all thought out,' says Mum in response to the Scottish land set aside to rehabilitate wayward lions and bears. 'And children?'

'I haven't any, no.'

'Well, I should hope not, but I was asking if you *want* them.' Goodness, if they ever film a *Downton Abbey* reboot Mum could easily step in as the Dowager Duchess.

'Oh, quite … uh, yes?'

'This isn't a quiz where you try to guess the correct answer, Daniel. Do you or do you not want to have children?'

'I do.'

'How many?'

'Oh, one or two, I suppose.' I doubt it. Daniel hasn't mentioned having children to me—or any of the others, as far as I know. Mum's mouth presses into a line again. 'Or more. It would depend … on what my wife wanted … what Abby wanted, I mean … if I … or she … well …'

'Hmm,' responds my mother and Daniel's expression is only a hair away from panicked.

'Oh, poor man,' I say. Not only has he revealed the depths of his shallowness (so to speak) but he's been duped by a pensioner with a penchant for the dramatic.

'Daniel, I'm terribly sorry, but I'm needed elsewhere. It's been *interesting* speaking with you. At the very least, you've given me a lot to think about,' she continues, as though this is a regency romance and it's *her* decision whether Daniel and I end up together.

Like me, Daniel should never play poker, as his relief is unmistakable. 'Excellent. Well, thank you … for your time, I mean. It was lovely to meet you, Mrs … uh …'

'Jones,' Mum supplies.

'Yes, of course, I knew that. Just a silly forgetful moment. I hope you'll forgive me.'

'Goodbye, Daniel.' Mum's end of the video conference cuts out halfway through Daniel's goodbye and he stares blankly at the screen, then closes his eyes and sighs. He's clearly chastising himself and I feel a small tug of compassion. He's not a *terrible* person. If anyone is terrible in this scenario, it's the three of us sitting here like voyeuristic puppeteers, laughing heartily at a man who believed he was speaking to a prospective mother-in-law.

Laughing *at* him.

Of course, as Anastasia, I've done this for years—satire is steeped in cruel but funny conjecture. But just as it's been getting more difficult to write unkind things about my fellow Does, perhaps this is a turning point with regards to Daniel. I recall the conversation we had at the wildlife park about his romantic misses, how he'd rebuked himself for being so didactic all the time, and I come to a rather stark conclusion.

He's a *person*, Abby.

Before I can consider the repercussions of this thought, the episode moves onto Daniel's video conference with Kaz's mum, dad, and brother, Daz, in which Kaz's recent disclosure that she's the reserved member of her family, is proven true.

I jot down various notes and laugh-out-loud lines for my recap, but my mind is preoccupied, fretting even. Somehow, I'll need to reconcile my newfound empathy for Daniel with what's to come as we film the end of the season.

'It's been good getting to know your mum these past few days,' says Jack.

'I'm glad. I like that you've sort of met.'

'I'll have to send her some flowers or something, as a thank you. She was awesome—way beyond what I expected.'

'I miss her.'

'I bet you do,' he says, trailing his fingertips along the inside of my forearm. 'Not long now.'

'I suppose.' I've a myriad of thoughts and emotions pinging off each other—a chaotic maelstrom of confusion. I'm worried, elated, ashamed, turned on. Really, Jack must stop stroking me like that or we'll end up consummating our attraction in the Control Room—more irony! Lack-of-Control Room, more like.

'Abs?' Jack peers at me, concerned. 'I know that look. What's going on in there?' he asks, his eyes flicking to my forehead then landing back on mine.

'If it ever gets out who I am—I mean, *really*—Daniel is going to come off looking like a dupe.'

His head tilts to the side and he nods like he's considering what I've said. 'Or he comes across as the vacuous dick that he is.'

'Perhaps. But then there are the other Does. They'll hate me.'

'Then we need to make sure it never comes out.'

'It doesn't matter. They'll hate me anyway after they see the latest episodes. I'm the Villain, remember?'

'They'll realise it's all in the editing—'

'But that's just it. It isn't. There are the confessionals

too.'

'Mmm, right. Who are you closest to? Kaz? Becca?'

'Yes.'

'Anyone else?'

'Elizabeth and I got fairly close and I thought perhaps we'd be friends when I return to England … I haven't said anything about her in my confessionals, but Kaz … and Becca …' I drop my chin. 'You know, before I came here, I thought this would be exceedingly difficult.'

'And you were right.'

'No, it's far worse than I thought.'

'Oh,' he replies, his voice thick with disappointment.

My head snaps up. 'No, no, not you. You're one of the bright sparks in all this—you and the girls. But now we've dragged my mum into it. And anyone who knows Mum and sees her on *The Stag* playing Lady Bracknell—it will be so obvious something's up! I stupidly didn't think that part through,' I add, giving myself a serve.

'Hey, hey,' says Jack, 'you weren't stupid. It was a good idea, Abby. And let's say someone *does* see your mum on the show—she can just tell them that we coached her. They'll buy that—people know that reality TV isn't really real.'

'Actually, you're right, that does make sense. You gave her a makeover and you coached her.' I sigh, relieved. 'And the girls?' I ask, hopeful he has another brilliant idea.

'Let's just play that by ear, okay?'

'Does that translate to "I have no idea"?'

'Pretty much, but I'll think about it, okay? And I'll talk to Harry. Maybe it's another NDA thing.'

'What do you mean?'

'Maybe we draw up new ones for Kaz and Becca so you can tell them *you* were coached—that we needed a Villain and you stepped in—even that we scripted what you said in your confessionals.'

'So … "Here Kaz, we're about to tell you something extra confidential, but before we do, sign this"?'

'Why not? Look, I'll talk to Harry, see what he thinks. I may even be able to sneak it past Roberta—go straight to legal.'

'Do you know what I look forward to?'

'What?'

'That one day soon, I'll be able to live my life without making or breaking a non-disclosure agreement.'

'It feels a bit like that, huh?'

'It's just another layer of deception—which I hate. You know, I'm fairly certain Daniel thinks I'm a spy.'

Jack laughs. 'Oh, he totally does. I'm sure that's a big part of why he's into you.'

'That and my passion for saving exotic animals.'

He chuckles. 'Your mum … oh, man … yeah, the first time I saw that I laughed for a good solid minute.'

'She's quite witty, isn't she?'

'Must be where you get it from.'

How have I never thought of that before? Or that *I'm* witty. I mean, Anastasia is, of course. *'God, Abby, when will you get it through your thick head that Anastasia's witty because you* are?' Bleh. It's exhausting even contemplating all the mental and emotional untangling I'll need to do when I get home.

Home. Another thing to untangle.

'Wherever I lay my hat, that's my home.' Well, that's been true

enough for the past eight weeks or so. Stag Manor has become like home, this motley crew like a family. I'll miss them.

'*There's no place like home.*' Mostly true, Dorothy, but this girl's home is devoid of a gorgeous Australian and no magic ruby slippers will fix that.

'*Home is where the heart is.*' Now we're getting to the heart of it, so to speak, the reason for my constant undercurrent of unease. Where *is* home if Jack is in Australia and I'm back in the UK? And even that question is an enormous presumptuous leap. What if everything I'm feeling is one-sided?

'Is there something else on your mind?' asks Jack, watching me curiously. Oh god, I can only imagine which thoughts have manifested on my face.

'Abby?' Dare I tell him the truth?

'I just …' '*Oh, Abby, out with it,*' I think. 'Jack, what are we doing?'

'What do you mean?'

'I mean, this is all quite fun and exciting, the sneaking about, but it's also rather …'

'Confusing?' he says right as I say, 'PG.'

'Confusing?' I echo.

'Oh, I thought that's where you were going with … never mind.'

'So, *is* this just a flirtation?' I ask, my throat strangling the last word.

'No, what? No, Abby, definitely not. I just meant … I … oh, shit. I am totally messing this up, aren't I?'

'I honestly have no idea, Jack. I'm new to all this. I don't know what *my* lines are, let alone *yours*.'

He smiles, his eyes creasing at the corners. 'You're incredible, you know that right?' I shake my head. 'Well, take my word for it.'

He dips his head and his lips capture mine, possessive and hungry. I slide my arms up around his neck, and my fingers caress the soft skin at his nape. Jack moans at my touch, his breath mingling with mine and his thumbs and fingers imprint on my lower back as he pulls me closer. My body is on fire, my insides tingling in the loveliest way, but my mind won't let go of one niggling thought.

'What happens now?'

And not *now*, as in right this minute, but when the show wraps and I am supposed to get on a plane back to the UK. I still don't know what we even *are*.

'Hey, do you have a sec?' Becca is standing in the doorway of our room and I invert my book and rest it on my chest. It's good timing. I just got to a racy part and, as much as I usually enjoy those, it will no doubt add to my frustration. Storeroom kisses are somewhat wanting.

'Of course, what's up?'

Becca frowns and crosses to her bed where she sits facing me. 'I think I should move out.' I've been waiting for this, of course. Two of us will go home after the next Pin Ritual and it would be (very) odd if the top two Does were still sharing a room.

Even so, I feel rubbish about it because the figurative

walls that are forming between us will become tangible. I place the book on my bedside table and sit up. 'Want a better view?' I joke and she smiles weakly. 'I understand, Becca. I'll miss you, but I do understand.'

'I've been meaning to——' She cuts herself off. 'It's just … it's never felt like the right time and now, with only four of us left. It's a bit …'

'It is.'

'And I keep thinking … what if it's us, Abby——top two?'

'I was just thinking the same thing.'

'Is that what you're hoping for?' she asks.

'You mean, it being you and me?'

'Yeah.'

'It's not a simple question, is it?' I reply. It's cowardly, answering a question with a question, but I've been dreading this conversation and even anticipated, it's still difficult.

'No.'

'Look, Becca, no matter what happens, I am genuinely your friend, all right?'

'Even if Daniel chooses me?' Ah, yes, the conundrum of a 'genuine friendship' built on a web of lies. What can I possibly say that's sincere but won't give the game away? Especially as I wouldn't wish Daniel on someone as lovely as Becca.

I scour my mind for the perfect reply and land on, 'If Daniel chooses you, then he is a very lucky man.'

Her smile brightens her eyes and she reaches across the space between us to grab and squeeze my hand. 'Same, Abs. If he chooses you.'

'N-D-A!' my mind screeches, though with all the truths I

336

want to tell Becca, the sheaf of legal pages would fill a filing cabinet.

'Do you want to stay here and I'll move rooms?' I offer in lieu of a confession. I can at least save her the inconvenience of having to pack, then immediately unpack.

'Nah, it's okay. I'll move into the Cruella Sisters' old room. It's got the biggest en suite,' she says, adding a cheeky smile.

The Stag in Sydney Recap: Ready, steady, go!
by Anastasia Blabbergasted

Well, well, well, faster than you can say, 'Crikey, is that Nicole Kidman?' *The Stag in Sydney* has taken a turn for the … er … surprising! If this were an episode of *FRIENDS*, it would be called, 'The one with the lesson in humiliation'.

This mad-capped episode commences with a series of sports day-style games to determine who gets the last one-on-one date with our Staggy! Think *Ninja Warrior* but with less ninja and far less warrior.

Gordo seems to be revelling in his role as race officiant, taking a ridiculously long time between 'ready', 'steady', and 'go'. Come on, Gordo, our Does have places to go and a Stag to see and *surely*, you're not being paid by the second!

First up in this ~~carnival of horrors~~ fun-filled and friendly competition, is the three-legged race in which Stevie is paired with Kaz, and Abby with Becca—a height mismatch of four inches. Typically, I love a good sight gag, but to Becca this is obvs *no* laughing matter and she (literally) drags Abby to the finish line in victory. Two points Gryffindor! Apologies, that's two points each for Becca and Abby. (**Note to self:** do not mix a rather potent G&T before recapping).

The egg and spoon race sends this recapper scrambling (get it?) for the *perfect* egg idioms to sum up the hilarity of watching grown women carrying raw eggs on eating implements.

Abby most certainly has egg on her face, dropping hers after only five paces. Stevie appears to be walking on eggshells and will never win if she doesn't pick up the pace. And is that Kaz's tongue protruding from her mouth in concentration? *Mais oui*, it is! Not eggy in the slightest but utterly adorbs. All these efforts are in vain, however, as Becca feathers her nest (egg) with another win! Huzzah! That's two points Abby and four points Becca.

Next up is a (ridiculous) game that has the Does scooping water from a bucket with a cup and running with it to fill a bucket on the finish line—back and forth, trying not to spill their spoils. I must have missed this activity during sports day—too busy sneaking ciggies out the back of the bike shed, most likely.

With her steady hands and speed walking, Becca looks set to win this one too—or perhaps it's Daniel's encouraging words from the sidelines that will lead her to victory. 'Come on, keep your eye on your cup!' he shouts helpfully. Two more points for Becca as she crosses the finish line with a victorious grin!

And I may not be a statistician, but with two events remaining and just four more points up for grabs, there's only one Doe who can possibly catch up to Becca, who currently sits on six. Come on Abby! You've got this!

The penultimate event is a wheelbarrow race in which Abby is paired with Kaz, who assures Abby she'll make an excellent wheelbarrow, only (shock, stun, amaze) she *doesn't* and they end up in a tangled heap of limbs, both rubbing their sore arses and stifling giggles. Becca and Stevie earn two points each for the win, rocketing Becca to top of the rankings, now impossible to catch.

But why would the producers call an end to these escapades when the finale is a *sack race*, the pinnacle of humiliation? Even though none of the other Does can possibly pip Becca at the post, the foursome don their sacks and line up at the starting line.

Aside: Hasn't that expression, 'she's so beautiful, she'd look good in a potato sack' come to life in Sydney's Botanic Gardens? No doubt, when women across Britain see Becca and Stevie rocking those sacks, hessian will become the next big thing! Topshop, start stocking up now!

Gordo calls, 'Ready, steady, and go!' and as if it weren't a foregone conclusion, Daniel (again being helpful) shouts encouragement from the sidelines.

'Faster, *faster*!'

'You can do it!'

'Oh, no, you clumsy things! Up you get.' Ouch, Danny Boy—not sure how encouraging *that* is. Kaz takes it in stride, however.

And the surprising, 'Come on, Abby!'

As Becca leaps over the finish line and drops her sack to the ground, Daniel claps politely. Oh dear—hardly the reaction of a man who's madly in love and, therefore, thrilled with the outcome. What *are* you playing at, Staggy?

Like the rest of us, the Does pretend to wait on tenterhooks while Gordo tallies the points and, after making quite a show of counting (all the way) to ten, he declares Becca the winner. Becca bounces on her toes and claps excitedly. 'Well done, everyone,' she says magnanimously. Meanwhile, Daniel is staring longingly at Abby.

Hmm. Not sure I can leave in the part about Daniel being disappointed when Becca won. But he was. While Stevie, Kaz, and I congratulated Becca for her win, as though we *hadn't* collectively thrown the competition, Daniel was standing off to the side pouting.

The crew buzzed about setting up the next shot—Gordo explaining the date, a private lunch under a marquee in another part of the gardens—and the relief I'd felt at never having to be alone with Daniel again turned to dread the second he sidled up to me.

'May I have a word, Abby?' he said. I sent a panicked look to Kaz who shrugged at me.

'Er, yes, all right.'

Daniel grasped my elbow and led me out of earshot of the others. He stopped and turned towards me, his expression pinched. 'I *had* hoped that *you'd* win, Abby, but it seems your ineptness on a horse extends to other sporting endeavours.'

Perhaps he thought he was being charming, that I would ignore the jibe and be flattered that he'd hoped I would win. And what of that? Why, when he clearly had Becca at his beck and call (so to speak), would he want me?

My budding empathy for him withered and died right there in that moment.

'Sorry to disappoint you, Daniel,' I replied tartly, nowhere in the vicinity of 'sorry' but my performance must have been bang on as he didn't seem to detect my sarcasm.

'It *is* disappointing. I wanted to talk to you this afternoon—*properly*.' My stomach clenched.

'About?'

'The animal sanctuary,' he said earnestly. 'Why didn't you mention it before? Why did I have to hear about your lifelong dream from your mother?' he whined.

'Because it isn't my lifelong dream. It's a fabrication, just like this whole charade. I have no interest in you at all and, furthermore, we've had a sum total of one hour's conversation in the past two months, so when exactly did you expect me to tell you about my lifelong dream, even if it were real?'

In my head, it was the perfect response—ripe with disdain. In reality, or the approximation of it, I said, 'I'm sorry, Daniel. I thought you might think it was frivolous, a pipe dream.'

'Not at *all*. It's so vital to give back, Abby …' It was extremely difficult not to laugh while being lectured on the importance of altruism by such a self-serving a man, but I managed it—*just*. 'And I've been seeking a cause—an important one—to throw my weight behind. It's an expectation of my father's, you see, and this could be perfect. Imagine what you and I could achieve with my—'

He stopped himself short and I just *knew* he was about to say 'money' before realising how crass that would sound.

'My means and my connections, as well as your nous and experience in the public service.'

It was horrifying to realise how much thought he'd given it.

'And I *love*' —my stomach tied itself into a knot at the L-word— 'that you never let me get away with anything. You'd keep me in check, you would—hold me accountable.'

I was beyond relieved that he hadn't declared his love for me, but his point was ridiculous. If only he knew how much I've let slide since we started filming, how many horrid and patronising things he's said that I *haven't* called him up on—like referring to my sporting prowess as 'inept'. I mean it *is*, but that's beside the point.

'What are you saying, Daniel?' I asked, my insides churning.

'I'm saying …' He looked behind him at the others and my gaze followed, just in time to see Harry striding towards us. Daniel turned back to me. 'I think it should be *you*, Abby,' he said hurriedly. 'Being with you would make me a better man.'

My stomach churns again now as I recall Daniel's declaration.

The good news: Daniel wants to cease being a massive twat.

The horrendously bad (i.e. terrible, unthinkable, and heinous) news: He thinks *I'm* the key to making that happen.

'*Become a better man with someone else!*' my mind had shouted.

Harry approached then, clearly oblivious that Daniel had just dropped a massive bombshell. 'Hey, you ready,

Daniel?' he said. 'We need you and Becca over at the marquee.'

'Right, of course. Uh, just one more moment,' said Daniel.

My eyes pleaded with Harry to rescue me, but he was too busy glaring at Daniel to notice. He huffed in frustration. 'Okay, *one minute*,' he said, before jogging back to the others. Then *Becca* caught my eye and frowned. It was Sod's Law that this scene played out in front of her and I had to tear my eyes away from her to focus on Daniel.

'So, what do you think?' he asked, his expression hopeful.

'Er … I just … It's not really the place, is it? Here in front of everyone.'

He pursed his lips. 'Good point. Perhaps I can persuade Jack and Harry to allow us a brief *tête-à-tête* before the Pin Ritual tomorrow night. Against the rules, I know, but' —he smiled at me and an awful shiver crawled up my spine— 'worth asking, don't you think?'

'Oh, absolutely.' '*NOT. Absolutely not!*' I'd thought.

'Daniel!' bellowed Harry.

'Coming,' Daniel called back. To me he said, 'Until then, Abby,' with an intensity usually reserved for period dramas. Then he skittered off to fulfill his Staggerly duties.

Now in my hidey hole, sitting on an uncomfortable folding chair and staring at the words on the screen, their meaning finally sinks in. Daniel is going to choose me. Bollocks. I need to talk to Harry and Jack.

And, Cadmus, there had better be a Pulitzer at the other end of this!

Chapter Twenty-Three

'You have to do something,' I say, prowling around the Control Room.

'What do you suggest?' asks Harry.

'Are you being sarcastic?' I snarl. Harry and I have never really exchanged harsh words before and I'm hoping we won't now.

He holds up his palms in surrender. 'Nope, just wondering what ideas you've got.'

'All right, then. But I don't have any, which is why I've come to you. Daniel absolutely cannot choose me.'

'She's right,' Jack says to his brother.

'Yeah, for sure, but how? This isn't like earlier in the season when we could, you know, *suggest* he might want to oust someone …'

'Or keep them,' says Jack, almost to himself.

'Who did you have to convince him to keep?' I ask. They exchange a look, one that says, *Do we tell her?* 'Oh, so me then.' Jack nods. 'Ironic, really.'

'Mmm,' he replies.

'What if …' I say, attempting to kickstart my problem-solving abilities but they remain stubbornly dormant.

'Hey,' says Jack, 'what if we do give you and Daniel a chance to talk, like he's asked, and you use the opportunity to turn him against you?'

'How about no?'

'Why?'

'Well, for starters, I've already celebrated the end of Abby–Daniel alone time and I can't think of anything worse. And besides, it wouldn't work. The more I push him away, the more desirable I become to him. Indifferent Abby, intolerant Abby, annoyed Abby——like catnip to that masochistic twat.'

Harry laughs heartily. 'I love how you put things, Abby. Thank god you're not writing about us. Wait, you're not, are you?'

I envision my neglected exposé, which is little more than a handful of scribbles and some unusable recaps. The minis-cule amount of content there is about the brothers is favourable, so Harry's question is a reminder that I'm failing twice at the same task. My word count is paltry and my 'heavy-hitting tell-all' has about as much heft as a bowl of custard.

'Er, no,' I say.

Jack runs a hand over his forehead, lifting his floppy fringe then letting it fall back into place. 'I suppose I could get in his ear, talk up Becca again. Or even Stevie.'

'Not Stevie,' says Harry. 'She won't have a bar of him. He picks her, we're gonna get a "no, thanks" in the finale.'

My eyes light up. 'That's it! Simple. If Daniel chooses me, I just say no. It would be a massive twist. Viewers would go mad for that, don't you think.'

'Not really,' says Jack, 'most viewers want the "happily ever after". You've seen how we're editing the lead-up to the finale—it's all about signposting the fairy-tale ending.'

'Right, I see. So, if Daniel chooses me, I just have to say yes. That's fine. No doubt I'll grow to love him in time. And you can come visit us on our yacht.'

Harry laughs again and Jack frowns. 'That's not what I meant, Abby. I'll have a word with him, like I said—try to steer him back towards Becca.'

'Glad it's you, bro,' says Harry, punctuating his relief with a loud yawn. 'Righteo, I need to catch Tim before he leaves for the day. See ya, Abby, and don't sweat it. Jack'll sort it for you.' He sounds far more confident than Jack appears.

Harry closes the door behind him and I'm alone with Jack for the first time in nearly a week. I cross the room to where he's leaning against a desk and raise a hand to his furrowed brow, sweeping aside his fringe. If only it were that easy to sweep aside this predicament.

His lips disappear between his teeth in a sad smile. 'I bet you wish you'd said no to all this—the show, I mean.'

I shake my head. 'No. Well, sometimes. But I did say no, remember, only to be told it wasn't an option.'

'I don't like thinking about you with Daniel,' he says quietly.

'So you've said. And nor do I, so, let's not. Let's focus on the job to be done, and then ...' And then what? I go home to London and Jack stays here in his flat in Bronte. No, definitely don't want to think about that. *'Job at hand, job at hand, job at hand,'* I recite in my mind as I chew the inside of my cheek.

'Abs, hey.' He reaches for my hand and I let him take it. 'I'll figure something out before the Pin Ritual, okay?' I nod, unconvinced, but there's a more pressing thought demanding my attention. He looks at me curiously. 'Something else on your mind?'

'Yes! All the things. All the things are on my mind, Jack! You. Me. Us.' I feel trapped by circumstance, both hopeful and despondent, leaning towards the latter. This is simply a flirtation, right? Forged in the lobby of Feed Your Mind, then over a three-pound blueberry muffin at that little café. And in an airport lounge. And a business-class cabin on an international flight. And, finally, in an airless storeroom surrounded by paper products.

We've gone from an adorable film-worthy meet-cute to skulking about—hardly the stuff of a romance novel. And most of the time we're together, we're discussing the show.

'What are we?' I want to ask. *'What are we doing? What can possibly come of this? When can I see you naked? Is there any chance this is more than a fling? And, really, when can I see you naked?'*

My eyes trace the contours of his face.

In addition to all this romantic turmoil are the worries about my fragile friendships with the other Does. Jack's idea about new NDAs was immediately kiboshed by Harry, who told him (and probably rightly so) that Roberta would 'chuck a massive wobbly' if she ever found out. I divined from context that this would be bad, which Jack confirmed in the form of an apology. My villainous behaviour will remain unexplained to the others. Eventually, I respond to Jack's question about having something else on my mind with a simple, 'No.'

'You sure?'

'No.' Honesty! At last! Though, this is as far as I will go. If I reveal what's in my head, no doubt it will come out unintelligible and whiny.

He smiles, then closes the small space between us to land a soft kiss on my lips. His hands reach around me to the small of my back, pulling me closer to him as I nestle in between his legs. I drape my arms over his shoulders and all thoughts fall away as the soft kiss becomes hungrier, more fervent.

'Ah, shit, sorry guys.' I leap apart from Jack and pin Harry with a scowl.

Jack's head drops to his chest and swivels from side to side. 'Jesus, Harry.'

'*Really* sorry. Just … uh … forgot this,' he says, crossing the room to retrieve a tablet from the editing desk. 'You guys should get a room, you know,' he adds cheekily before slipping out of the room.

'Out!' Jack bellows after him. 'He's right, though,' Jack says, his voice softening and his hands pulling me close to him again. 'We do need to get a room.' A shiver washes over me, the good kind.

'We do?' I ask breathlessly.

His head tilts as the corner of his mouth quirks. 'You know we do, Abby,' he says, the gravelly tone of his voice doing wonders for my insides. I could get lost in that voice, those eyes, that perfect, perfect mouth, but just as I'm about to lean in for another kiss, the door opens again.

'Sorry, again! Not looking!' Gah!

Harry holds his hand up to his face, shielding his eyes from us, but between Jack shouting, 'Get the hell out,' and Harry replying, 'I'm going, I'm going,' while gathering a sheaf of papers, sexy time is OVER. I need to get back, anyway. With only four Does left, I can't be absent for much longer or it will be noticed. I wave 'goodbye' as I slip out of the Control Room leaving Jack to figure out how to save me from that dreadful man.

In the lounge room, Becca and Stevie sit on opposite sofas, Becca stretched out the length of hers, and both reading. Becca lowers her book, one of the romcoms I brought with me. 'Good session?' she asks.

Session? What? 'Er …'

'Mediation session,' she adds.

'Oh … yes. Sorry, was quite focused—just a little fuzzy-headed.'

'Mmm,' she says, holding my gaze a little longer than usual. Oh god, is she suspicious? I glance over at Stevie, who seems absorbed in a WWII drama. 'Actually,' says Becca, closing her book and swinging her legs over the edge of the sofa, 'have you got a sec? I want to ask you about something.'

This time when I look at Stevie, her eyes flick to meet mine then return to the page. 'Of course.' Becca stands and walks out to the patio and I follow. She pulls out a chair at the long table and sits, staring out at the water where Kaz is bobbing about on a blow-up flamingo. I take the chair next to Becca.

'It's becoming real,' she says quietly. 'Or, *more* real.' There's a dead leaf on the table that's fallen from the eucalyptus tree overhead and she picks it up and twirls it by the stem.

'Yes, agreed.'

'I'm going to be honest with you, Abby.' Oh, god. 'I thought I could compartmentalise our friendship and my feelings for Daniel, but I don't think I can anymore. When I saw the two of you talking this afternoon, before the lunch date … I felt sick, you know. And it suddenly hit me that he could choose you and then I'll lose both of you.' She captures the leaf between her fingers, folding, creasing, and snapping it until it becomes a pile of leafy shards on the table.

'You won't lose me, I promise.' She glances at me, a furrow between her brows. 'You *won't*.'

'You can't say that, Abby.'

'Of course I can.'

'Well, no, you can't—because I don't think I'll be able to stand it.'

'What if he chooses you?' Oh, please let that be what happens. 'We can still be friends then, right?'

'How? How do you see that happening? I mean, think about our situation. We essentially have the same boyfriend—I mean, we're both dating him, we've both kissed him and told him our secrets, our dreams' —only her secrets and dreams aren't fabrications— 'and if Daniel and I end up together, how do you envision being friends with your ex and his new girlfriend—or *wife* even? That's not normal, Abby.'

My concept of 'normal' is markedly different from what it was a few months ago, something else I can't share with her. And I will never, *ever* refer to Daniel as 'my ex', that phrase steeped in deep, raw emotions.

'Maybe this conversation is moot and he'll choose Kaz,' I say, trying to lighten the mood. It doesn't.

'Look, I adore Kaz, you know I do—she's a great chick—but she doesn't give a flying fuck about any of this. She's still here because … well, she'll be fun for the audience to watch and she's basically making up the numbers. She's …'

'Entertaining,' I offer, impressed by how accurate Becca is.

'Exactly. And I love her to bits but she's not my competition—or yours.'

'What about Stevie?'

'Come on, Abs, Stevie rolls her eyes every time Daniel opens his mouth. She hates him.'

'Hate is a strong word.'

'Loathes? Detests? She doesn't like him, Abby. It's obvious she was only brought in to shake things up—the Interloper always is.' I remain quiet—no sense in arguing a position I know is untrue. Then the irony smacks me in the face, because isn't that what I've been trying to do? Prove to Becca that we can still be friends after *The Stag* even though, deep down, I know it's impossible?

Oh, god, I'm going to lose Becca.

And, yes, we've only known each other a couple of

months, but we've lived together that whole time, sharing not only a room but this unique experience. We've confided in each other. We've been a dynamic duo, standing up to bullies, supporting our fellow Does. She's a 'great chick', like she just called Kaz. And when you can count your close friends one hand, a friendship like this is precious.

But she's right. When all this is over, no matter the outcome, it's unlikely we'll stay friends. Maybe it's Becca who'll become 'my ex'.

———————

'Don't worry about it, darl. It lasted way longer than I expected.' Kaz is packing while I watch from the other bed and she has no idea why I'm as glum as I am. As anticipated (and dreaded), neither she nor Stevie received a pin in last night's Pin Ritual. Stevie's flight to Adelaide left early this morning and Kaz will be on an aeroplane back to Perth in a few hours.

'I know, I just wish …' My voice trails off, unable to explain my churning emotions—me, the writer, unable to express myself.

'What?' She stops folding and eyes me curiously. 'Something's up with you. What is it?'

I exhale slowly. Just like with Becca, if I tell Kaz anything beyond how much I'll miss her, I'll be crossing a line. And that could land me—and Jack and Harry—in serious hot water. 'It's just … look, when you watch the show, particularly the later episodes, *please* don't hate me.'

She tosses the half-folded T-shirt into her case and sits on her bed facing me. 'What the hell are you talking about?'

I shake my head. 'Never mind. Don't wor——'

'Spill. You know you can trust me, Abs.' She's right. I can and do trust her. And as she gazes at me, her brown eyes lacking any guile or malice, I realise that our friendship may just survive beyond *The Stag*.

'*What can I tell her?*' I ask myself. '*Nothing, Abby——it's not worth the risk.*' 'I'm not really able to say, but——'

'Well, now I definitely wanna know!'

'Really, it's nothing.' Why did I open this can of worms? All things considered I would make a terrible spy. I'd be given a state secret and be busting with it before I left MI6, blurting it out to the security guards in the lobby.

'Oh, I know what it is!' she says. 'They've made *you* the baddie, haven't they? Hah, of course! They needed one after the Cruella Sisters left.' Well, I can't be blamed if she *guessed* the truth, right? But before I can answer she throws her head back and laughs. 'Oh, that's bloody hilarious.'

I shake my head. 'Hilarious? Why hilarious?'

'Because! You're like the most decent person in here. Well, *Stevie's* a sweetheart——Becca too. Hang on …' Her head tips to the side, the machinations of her thoughts playing behind her eyes. 'You took a bullet for one of us, didn't you?'

'How do you mean?' God, if she were any closer to the truth …

'So, who was it supposed to be? Me? Damn, I wish I'd known. I'd *love* to be the baddie.' She punctuates this with a cackle. 'No, for reals, who? And how did you find out? Actually, never mind,' she says, leaping up and answering her own question, 'it's hardly ASIO around here, is it? I mean, it's a minor miracle that Daniel doesn't know we all think he's a massive dickhead. Well, except for Becca.'

I'm wondering when she'll take a breath when she asks, 'Abby, *come on*, who was it supposed to be?'

'Becca.' I expel the name like I'm choking on a hairball. Perhaps that's what this is—one giant karmic hairball where I'm having to atone for sins I accumulated in a previous life. I must have been the person who invented pyramid selling.

'Holy shit! Does she know?' asks Kaz.

'No—and she can never know. *Ever.*'

'No worries. Your secret's safe with me.' She resumes packing. 'Oh, hey, is that why you went off with Daniel yesterday at the Botanic Gardens? You being a baddie?' She waggles her eyebrows at me.

'Oh, er, no. Actually, it was Daniel who pulled me aside.'

'And?'

'It's nothing, really.' Her eyes narrow; she's dubious. 'He just wanted to ask me about something my mum said,' I say, deflecting.

'Oh, yeah, meet the fricking family. I can't *wait* to talk to mine. I'll bet you a thousand bucks my brother gave Daniel shit. He deserves it though, don't you think?' What I think about Daniel seems to change daily, even *hourly*—Daniel is a massive twat; Daniel is less of a massive twat; Daniel is a massive twat again. Fortunately, Kaz's question seems rhetorical.

'Ooh, did you have to do those sneaky confessionals where you're, like, a total bitch?' I shrug. *'I neither confirm nor deny these allegations.'* 'Don't worry, Abs, I know it's all a load of shit.'

This makes me giggle, a welcome release. 'I really cannot understand why you came on this show, Kaz. I'm so glad you did—*truly*—but it continues to baffle me.'

'Like I said, best long-service leave ever.'

'Really?' Now *I'm* dubious. 'How so?'

She stops packing again and counts off on her fingers. 'One—for sure! I spend ninety-nine per cent of my working life surrounded by blokes and it's been *awesome* having you girls to hang out with. Two—this place! It's fricking gorgeous and I totally lucked out with Ellie leaving two weeks in—my own room, baby! *And* there's the eye candy! I mean, come on. Harry is *hot*! And Tim. And even Jack's kinda cute in a geeky way.

'Plus, there's all the cool shit we've done and the private beach and the booze on tap. It's even been nice having a reason to dress up and make an effort. When you spend your days wearing a high-vis vest that clashes with your hair, it feels good to look like a *girl* from time to time, you know? And it's so frigging cool that I'm gonna be on TV! I mean, how many people get to say that? Like, hardly any!'

'You have a wonderful way of looking at the world—you're a true optimist.'

She shrugs good-naturedly and tosses the rest of her clothes into the case, seeming not to care how wrinkled they'll be on the other end of her journey. 'There!' she says, zipping it up. She checks the clock on the bedside table. 'Another hour before the car comes. Whaddya reckon? Time for a quick drink?'

It's barely even noon but with Kaz, it's almost always 'time for a quick drink'.

'What did you have in mind?'

'One of those bottles of white in the fridge isn't too shabby—the Chardy from Margs.' I learnt some time ago that 'Chardy' is 'Chardonnay' and 'Margs' is 'Margaret River', a wine region in Western Australia. Along with dozens of other words and expressions, I've added them to my 'Glossary of Australianisms', something I'm thinking of sharing with Anastasia's readers.

'Or are you more of a Pimm's girl this time of day?' Kaz teases, yanking me back into the conversation.

I chuckle. Doe Abby likely is a Pimm's girl, but I'll be happy with the Chardonnay. 'The wine sounds good. And we should see if Becca wants to join us.'

'Yeah, for sure—get in my final moments of hanging out with you girls. I'm really gonna miss you.'

I leap up and throw my arms around her, overflowing with affection for my lovely friend. 'I'll miss you too.'

She returns the hug, squeezing tightly. 'When I get outta here, I'll track you down on social media or something, 'kay?'

'Sure.' It's another reminder that all my worlds and personas are about to collide.

The Stag in Sydney Recap:
Hunting season is coming to a close
by Anastasia Blabbergasted

Well, well, well, hasn't this been an eventful season thus far?

As we head towards the finale of *The Stag in Sydney*, we commence the penultimate episode with four Does, ending it with only two. But before we get to that dramatic conclusion, let's take a moment to remember (or is it 'lament'?) those who have departed the Manor.

Our Filler Does, **Tabitha** and **Laura** (oh Laura, we will never forget your rather *voracious* love of all things 'country', right down to your cowboy boots and faux western drawl), departed (as foretold) in episode one, followed closely in subsequent weeks by **Merrin**, our Tasmanian cat lover who was *desperate* to get home to her pussies, **Ellie** and her constant companion, Little Ellie (narcissistic much, love?), and dear **Elizabeth**.

Oh, Elizabeth. Adorable? Yes! But it was clear from the outset that our Lizzie was far too timid for Staggy Daniel. Remember that overly chaste kiss during the cooking class? Rather cringey. There's more sexual chemistry between Paul Hollywood and Prue Leith on *The Great British Bake Off* than these two. That said, the Manor's very own Lady Di seemed utterly crushed when Daniel (literally) sent her packing.

Next up saw the departure of not one, but *two* Villains—**Tara** leaving the Manor under less than auspicious circumstances, middle finger raised high and spouting enough foul language to make a surly seafarer blush. It does make one wonder what took place to drive the raven-haired vixen off the premises, but perhaps she decided that she was destined for greater things—like running a ring of pint-sized pickpockets out of inner London à la Fagan from *Oliver Twist*.

Close on Tara's heels, **Kylie** was denied a pin at the next Pin Ritual, though unlike the yin to her yang, she left without so much as a peep, quiet as a little mouse. This did baffle me somewhat considering her … ahem … exploits in body painting, but perhaps her time in the Manor curtailed her predilection for drama. No doubt she's off somewhere meditating or something (wink, wink).

Justine was the next to depart the Manor and let's just say, she *may* have seemed a tad keen to leave. Perhaps she realised Daniel was not the man for her, particularly as she is an 'Aussie girl' through and through and relocating to London never seemed to appeal to her. That and she's a bit more 'party circuit' than 'charity season'.

Surprisingly, the most recent Doe to depart was our original frontrunner for Bride, **Daphne**.

Though a shock to the rest of us, it seemed no one was more surprised than Daphne herself. Did you her see hugging *Abby* after the Pin Ritual, clinging to her like drowning woman clutching a life preserver?! Haven't those two been at odds since day one in the Manor?

And (*ouch*), not seemingly satisfied with breaking her heart on (inter)national television, Daniel wanted one last word with the Lady of Stag Manor. Lo and behold, knock me down with an ostrich feather, it was to apologise! Daniel must have seen the error of his none-too-kind ways, having touted the 'stiff upper lip' approach to overcoming her panic attack (poor Daphne will likely never want to climb so much as a ladder again, let alone a bridge). It was a *tad* insensitive, Danny Boy, but well done you for making things right. Well, attempting to, in any case. That apology may have made you feel better but (poor) Daphne couldn't escape fast enough.

That brings us to the top four Does.

The impossibly beautiful Interloper, **Stevie**, who not only looks like a Bond girl, she's an accomplished psychologist to boot! And didn't the producers get a bang for their buck when she stepped in to help Daphne descend Sydney Harbour Bridge? Typically, a woman like Stevie would induce some industrial strength envy, but she has certainly fit in well with the other Does.

Speaking of 'fitting in', surely this season's Miss Congeniality Award goes to the affable and much-loved, **Kaz**. Though I picked her as a Dark Horse in my first recap, I *really* didn't expect to see her in the top four. Daniel must have realised early on——just like we did——how much fun she was to have around. And haven't we acquired quite the vocabulary of Australian expressions thanks to our Kaz, the 'cack'?

Sadly, however, Stevie and Kaz did not receive pins in this week's Pin Ritual, with Kaz laughing off the rejection and Stevie seeming to accept it in her usual measured way.

And then there were two!

As I predicted, the lovely **Becca** is still in contention for Bride and if I had to put my money on a front runner——and let's face it, I absolutely *do*——it would be our Becca. Not only does Daniel's gaze follow her about with laser beam precision (perhaps he's imagining how she'll look on his arm as they boot about London town), Becca seems to have made the strongest connection with Daniel, their quiet conversations often straining the limits of what the microphones can pick up. (Have you, like me, found yourself leaning in to capture every last morsel of their romantic escapades?) And though she is both beautiful and intelligent, it would be nice if Daniel spent more time complimenting the latter than the former (hint, hint, Staggy Boy!).

Shockingly, the other contender for Bride is **Abby**. And yes, she was also pipped as a Dark Horse, but her transformation to Villain has been sudden and extreme. Once caring and big sisterly, Abby has taken to snarky villainy so adeptly, my spinning head resembles that pivotal scene from *The Exorcist*.

And who could have foreseen her OTT confessional?

'If only Becca were as savvy as she is academic. She has no *idea* that I'm edging closer to Daniel *or* that her "yes-Daniel-no-Daniel-three-bags-full-Daniel" approach is wearing thin. He wants a woman who can challenge him. And that's me.'

Careful, Abby. If Becca catches even the slightest whiff of your altered loyalties, we may just see a 'scrag fight' reminiscent of *Actual Homemakers* (with thanks to Kaz for this delightful term). It's one thing to be in competition with your fellow Doe-friend, it's another when she's outright out to get you! And perhaps Becca is cleverer than Abby thinks, as I did glimpse a side-eye or two this week.

Speaking of, now that our retrospective and final roll call are complete, let's dive into the recap!

I've read back over what I started writing a couple of nights ago and with a few tweaks, the recap of those (stupid) games will fit in nicely here. I was going to play down the Abby–Becca rivalry that peaked that afternoon, but Jack said I need to lean into it. Anastasia would and this is *her* recap after all.

> Becca's prize for trouncing the other Does is the final one-on-one date with our Staggy, a romantic picnic in Sydney's stunning Botanic Gardens. Those Morton Bay fig trees truly are magnificent, if one is happy to ignore the plethora of black splodges hanging from the branches. Bats, apparently, though the Australians call them 'flying foxes'——like that makes them more endearing (it doesn't).

This is all me, not Anastasia, as I spent half the time we were in the gardens casting a wary eye skyward. I couldn't help but wonder what would happen if all those inverted mammals decided to take off at once and swarm us? Would they black out the sun? Would they scratch our eyes out and then eat us? 'Bats are cute,' my arse——a vital part of the ecosystem, yes, but hardly cute.

> But wait! Before Daniel and Becca can be whisked away for their romantic luncheon, who should

syphon Daniel's attention, but newly appointed villainess, Abby. Now, is that Daniel leading Abby away from the group for an impromptu interlude, or the other way around? Hard to tell, as even though they are miked, the camera crew aren't fast enough to capture their exchange close up. And, with the paint on Becca's trophy barely even dry, that is a fairly hefty revelation from Daniel.

'I think it should be you, Abby.'

My guess is that Abby and Daniel are standing upwind of Becca, as her tart expression and watchful side-eye give every indication that she can tell something's up, if not hear every word they're saying.

Goodness, I wish I'd taken a Dramamine before watching this episode—it's lurching about like a tin boat on rough seas!

It still makes me queasy to think about what happened with Daniel. It's now clear that I was tasked with the impossible—keep him simultaneously interested *and* at bay. But if Jack can't convince him that Becca is his best choice—essentially throwing her in the path of an oncoming (romantic) train—I am utterly screwed. It will either be the first 'no' in *The Stag's* history or I'll be choosing china patterns before the year's end. Why is my indifference, nay *disdain*, so appealing to him?

And in light of my most recent conversation with Becca, this next part will be excruciating to write.

Proceedings finally seem to get back on track when a (rarely seen) crewmember manages to shepherd Becca and Daniel towards a darling little marquee replete with a dining table for two, crisp white linens, and a table setting suitable for a wedding registry (foreshadowing perhaps?).

With Becca seemingly worried that Daniel's affections have turned in another direction, she certainly lays on the charm rather thickly over lunch. It's like a scene from *Bridgerton*, all coy looks and flirtatious repartee.

'If you could go on holiday anywhere in the world, where would it be?' This is first date chatter at best and did you see Daniel eye her curiously before responding, 'The Caribbean is a lovely spot to escape to over the British winter. I assume you've not been.'

'Actually, I have—I was on a trip to America with my friends right before uni and we got these cheap flights from Miami to Aruba. It was awesome.'

Touché, Becca. And have you learnt nothing from this season's Does, Daniel? Never *assume* anything. It will make an 'ass' out of 'u' and … well, only you in this case. Still, it's more likely that when Daniel says

'Caribbean', he means lounging about in six-star resorts donned in top-to-toe linen rather than dancing the night away in sweaty beachside bars wearing nothing but a bikini and a smile.

These two really are worlds apart. But perhaps, as opposites often do attract, there's a slim possibility that their union has a chance. Daniel spends the rest of lunch gazing adoringly (or is that lustily?) at Becca while she attempts to find topics of shared interest.

Sorry, what? I dozed off there for a moment. Can we please go back to the Manor and see what Kaz is up to? Much more fun.

Not sure if that will make it past the censors (i.e. Prue and Roberta). Actually, having re-read it, it's an indictment of Harry and Jack. Delete!

~~Sorry, what? I dozed off there for a moment. Can we please go back to the Manor and see what Kaz is up to? Much more fun.~~

By the time it's a wrap on lunch, I am just as baffled as Daniel appears to be about which Doe he will choose. 'Becca is just so beautiful, and it's sweet how she hangs on my every word.' Excuse me. I just vomited a little into my mouth. Sycophants are best when confined to politics, Daniel, rather than matters of the heart. And Becca, please remember

that you are a clever, bright, capable woman who
could take the world by storm if only you'd see
Daniel for the massive twat he is.

Bollocks—obviously can't write any of that either. Gah!
I glance at the time—just after noon in London. Dare I take
a wee detour to procrastination station? I'm supposed to
have this recap on Prue's desk by the end of her workday.
Then again, I can't possibly send it if it's utter rubbish, and
perhaps a chat with my best friend will help. I unlock the
phone and call Lisa.

'That you Abs?' she answers—huzzah!

'Yes! Why are you panting?' Oh god, I haven't caught
her during a lunchtime shag, have I?

'I'm out for a run.'

I'm both relieved and bewildered—Lisa does not run.
'You're *what*?'

'Yeah, I've been running at lunchtime with my colleague,
Ian.'

'For how long?'

'A few weeks. I can now run the full route without feeling
sick,' she says, her voice emanating pride.

'Well done, you,' I say, deciding I can reconcile this Lisa
with my Lisa another time.

'Thank you, lovely. So,' she prompts, 'is it important? I
can stop.'

'Could you? I don't mean to be a bother—'

'You go on ahead, Ian. I'll see you back there,' Lisa calls
amid taking large gulping breaths. 'Right, I'm all yours.'

'Where abouts are you?'

'Blackfriars—just about to cross the Thames and turn back.' I imagine Lisa wearing Lululemon and jogging alongside someone called Ian. In my mind, he's tall, lanky, and ginger.

'So, Ian …?' I venture. It's not just the running; Lisa doesn't socialise with colleagues either—or she never used to.

She chuckles. 'You've got me. He's a recent transfer into my department. Dishy as, and when he mentioned running at lunchtimes, I thought, "What the hell?" and dusted off the trainers.' Ahh, so that explains the out-of-character foray into the world of jogging. 'Hang on, I'll send you a sneaky pic I took of him when we were standing in line at Pret.'

The phone alerts me to an incoming photograph and when it pops onto the screen, it reveals that I couldn't have been further off in imagining Ian. He's shortish with dark hair. He's also extremely handsome, if his profile is anything to go by, which is just Lisa's type.

'You're right, he's a dish,' I say, realising that this normal, girly conversation is exactly the panacea I need. The knots in my tummy unfurl and for the first time in ages, I feel like I can breathe properly.

'So, enough about me and my lusty pursuits, what's going on with you then?' she asks, ending my reprieve from fretting. I exhale heavily, trying to determine where best to begin. 'Start with the Stag—what's the go with him?' Lisa's ability to divine precisely what I need in a confidant is uncanny. It's probably why she's my dearest friend.

'Well, for starters, he's besotted.'

'Still with Rebecca?'

'It's Becca.' I've corrected her on this before; you'd think a spy would remember the name of my best Doe-friend. Perhaps this Ian fellow has her off her game. 'And no. He's besotted with *me*. Well, Doe Abby. Actually, no, that's not entirely true. I've been letting some of real Abby seep into my persona—you know, not buying into his narcissism or superiority—and apparently, that's precisely what he is looking for.'

'Oh, god.'

'Exactly. Meanwhile, Becca's moved out of our room and she's told me our friendship is doomed, which breaks my heart. And it's getting more difficult to write the recaps, with how close I am to everything. I've got one due today and so far, it's utter rubbish. Essentially, everything's gone to shit.'

'Everything?'

'Yes.'

'Including things with Jack?' she nudges.

'Oh, well, no. I mean, I think we're all right. We've not had a lot of time together lately, what with the show ramping up. And it's getting exhausting, us being a secret, and I'm not sure how this can possibly work with me living in an entirely different country, but I'm terrified of raising it with hi—'

'Abs,' she interrupts, saying my name like a sigh.

'Yes?' This is where she gives me sage advice and makes everything all right.

'You need to chill the fuck out.' So much for sage advice.

'And what precisely should I do with that?' I ask sourly.

It's hardly something I can embroider on a pillow or make into a meme. All right, perhaps a meme.

'Look, you've known since the very beginning this would be difficult, right?'

'I suppose so, yes.'

'And you had weeks, *months* even, to get your head around it, to prepare—mentally, I mean.'

'Are you saying I should have seen all this coming? Because that's not exactly fair. How was I to know that Daniel would like me, especially as I've been surrounded by far more attractive Does—and more interesting, more accomplished …'

'God, Abby, stop with the self-deprecation. We've been through this. You're just as worthy of Daniel's affections—wanted or not—as any of the other Does. So, yes, you absolutely should have foreseen that he might fall for you.'

'But—'

'Nope, there is no "but" because if you keep insisting that Daniel is misguided in his affections for you, then what does that say about Jack? Is *he* deluded because he likes you?'

'No,' I say defensively.

'And are you undeserving of Jack?'

'Well … no, I don't think so.'

'Precisely. So you see the irony, don't you?' I do *now*. But how have I not seen it before? Have I been so busy compartmentalising the various Abbys that I've missed the similarities between them? 'Abs, you still there?'

'Yes, sorry—still here. Just pondering how I've managed to be so dim.'

'Don't be too hard on yourself.'

'No, that's your job.' She chuckles.

'Look, it's understandable you're out of sorts, but you're not doing yourself any favours by getting in a tizz. Why don't you do what I do when a work problem seems insurmountable. Just start with the simplest task, one you know how to do, then tackle the next most challenging task.'

Her method does make sense, but she's probably talking about international espionage whereas my dilemma is frivolous in comparison. Still, it's helpful.

'I suppose I could start by finishing the recap.'

'There you go. Pop on Anastasia and write the recap,' she says, as if Anastasia is a hat.

Come to think of it, that's brilliant. 'Oh, my god, Lise. You're right. The recap is rubbish because I've been writing it as *me*. I just need to channel Anastasia. She doesn't know these people; she doesn't give two hoots about them! Her job is to be the Queen of Snark and my job is to be her. You're a genius. Thank you.'

She laughs down the line. 'A bit OTT, Abs, but I'll take it. Look, I should probably get back. You going to be all right?'

'I suppose so. Like you said, one thing at a time. And all this will be over soon.'

'Exactly. When do you film the finale?'

My stomach lurches at the question and, once again, I'm a captive of my digestive system. 'Tomorrow.'

'So just remember, start with the easiest thing and tick that off.'

'So, recap, then figure out what to say to Daniel if he *does* choose me—perish the thought. I don't think there's anything I can do to make Becca change her mind—besides, once she hears the horrid things I've said about her as the Villain, she won't want to be friends anyway. But I will try to find some time to talk to Jack—properly, I mean—as much as that terrifies me.'

'There's my girl.'

'Thank you. I do feel marginally better, even though I wish I could magically skip the next few days and be back in London already.'

'I wish I could arrange that for you,' she says. But why can't she? Surely, the engineers at MI6 have mastered time travel by now? 'Abs, I've really got to go. I'll have to sprint back at this rate.'

'Yes, sorry, go.'

'I love you. And I'll see you soon.'

'Absolutely. And I love you too.'

I end the call, then lay the phone on the card table and stare at it.

'Daniel, I cannot possibly wear this pin when the love of your life is waiting right over there, even though, for some reason, you're too blind to see it.' That could make excellent television.

'Becca, I adore you and hope you can forgive all the horrible things you'll hear me say about you onscreen, as I was playing a role—a double role. You see, I am undercover and, for me, the only real part of this experience is the friendships I've forged with you and the other Does.' That will get me fired, if not sued. It's also only partly true as it omits my feelings for Jack.

And on the subject of Jack …

Jack, you are a clever, funny, kind, and talented man. You're also gorgeous as, and your kisses do wondrous things to my insides. I know this has probably been little more than a flirtation for you, but what if we spent some proper time together and see what it can become?'

Hmm. *That* may just land me the man of my dreams. Now all I need is the courage to say it.

Chapter Twenty-Four

I have never been so nervous in my life.

That includes sitting the entrance exams for St Mary's, every job interview I've ever had, and each time I've been called into Prue's office for a 'discussion'.

I stare at my reflection, my horrified expression juxtaposing how pretty I look. For the finale, I have been coiffed, styled, painted, and adorned and externally, I am the most 'camera ready' I've ever been. I only wish my insides weren't squirming like nursery students.

Speaking of … I am just about to pop to the loo for the third time since the makeup artist left when Carlie's head appears around the doorframe. 'Five minutes, Abby. Then we need you to head down to the garden for your confessional.' When she gets a proper look at me, her body follows her head, and she stands in the doorway staring. 'Uh, are you okay?'

'Fine!' I trill, my voice three octaves higher than usual.

'You don't look it. You look sick. Are you sick?'

'No, just … er … a tad nervous.'

'Really? Nah, you'll be right.' She waves off my nerves like they're perfectly normal—they aren't; I may actually be dying—and disappears down the hallway to give Becca her twenty-minute call.

A couple minutes later, I emerge from the loo feeling slightly better and take one last look in the mirror. I've been dressed in a long red silk gown with a ruched bodice and sweetheart neckline that nips in at my waist and floats to the floor. My hair has been pulled up into a loose, sexy up-do that looks like it might tumble out at any moment but, with this number of hairpins, (definitely) won't. My pedicured feet are adorned by red strappy heeled sandals that I had to practise walking in, and my makeup is perfection, right down to the velvety red lipstick.

As I said, I look pretty, possibly the best I've ever looked. Pretty and utterly terrified. I take a deep breath, look myself in the eye, and say, 'Do not screw this up, Abby.' As far as pep talks go, it's wanting, but it's the best I can do.

I carefully make my way downstairs, so as not to trip in my heels, and take in the buzz of activity that spills from the lounge room onto the patio and down the length of the backyard. After two months, I'm used to filming days in the Manor, but the energy today is different, almost super charged, and the crew's excitement about finishing this season is palpable.

'You look amazing,' says a voice from behind me. I turn to see a smiling Jack who's come from the direction of the annex.

'Thank you,' I say. His eyes drink in my appearance and

linger on my red lips. It's too bad I'm camera ready as I would love to sneak away and let him smudge my lipstick.

'How are you feeling about everything?' he asks.

'All right, I guess.'

He leans in and lowers his voice. 'I had a quick chat with Daniel just before. Hopefully, well …' He lets the thought trail off and we share a quick smile.

'There you are!' calls Harry from the patio. 'Come on through, Abby. We'll get your confessional done, then Becca's, 'kay?'

I nod, allowing myself one last glance at Jack. 'Good luck,' he says.

'Thank you. I need it.'

Outside, the set dresser is putting finishing touches on the trellis behind the confessional bench and she smiles at me as I sit down. 'You look lovely,' she says. I've gone blank on her name but say, 'Thank you,' then try to remember it as she works behind me. The simple thought process calms me, keeping my mind from chewing on and regurgitating my multitude of worries.

'You right there, Abby?' asks Carlie, though it must be rhetorical as she doesn't wait for a reply. Instead, she reaches down to arrange the layers of my gown, ensuring they fall 'just so'. 'Whaddya reckon?' she says to the woman whose name I've forgotten. They both step back and survey me in situ.

'Perfect.' Nameless woman smiles at me. 'Good luck,' she says as she and Carlie clear the set. Then it's just me—well, me, the boom operator, Harry, Tim, and the rest of the crew who are gathered to watch my last confessional. Even Jack makes an appearance in my peripheral vision.

'Be Doe Abby. That's all you have to do. It's a role, just like writing as Anastasia. She wants to win Daniel's heart and she's the Villain. You can do this.' A *much* better pep talk this time.

Tim adjusts the camera lens, watching the monitor closely, then activates the camera. 'So, Abby,' says Harry, 'tell us how you're feeling.'

A wave of calm washes over me and I speak straight into the camera. 'Excited. It's been a wonderful journey, getting to know Daniel, and here we are at the final Pin Ritual. I can't wait.'

'You sound fairly confident that Daniel will choose you.'

'Of course! We have a strong connection, and I'm a far better match for him than Becca.'

'How so?'

I can say what I like here, as neither Daniel nor Becca will hear it until after the show has aired. I also need to set up Doe Abby for a momentous, villainous fall when Daniel (hopefully) chooses Becca.

'Well, I'm British for a start and while it's sort of *charming*, it's become obvious over the past couple of months that Becca simply doesn't understand the British way of life, our sensibilities. Daniel and I also see eye to eye on philanthropy, having already discussed opening a wildlife sanctuary in Scotland.

'I suppose what I mean to say is that Becca's *lovely*, but Daniel needs someone who won't let him walk all over them—someone like *me. I* will keep Daniel in check,' I say emphatically, 'and that makes me much better suited to him.'

Ironically, this is true, but despite what he's said of late, I'm betting that Daniel will choose the yes-woman over the no-woman. And once he does choose Becca, I hope she will immediately come to her senses and drop him. If not immediately, then before she does something foolish—like marry him.

'What specifically did Daniel say that makes you so confident he'll choose you?'

'That he will.'

'Cut!' Harry's voice snaps me out of my reverie in which I've just channelled the worst version of myself and when I catch his eye, he grins, then bellows, 'Okay, someone go get Becca.'

'No need.' All eyes snap to Becca who is standing on the threshold between the lounge room and the patio. From the look on her face, she has heard every word I've said. Oh, god.

If I were in her situation, I'd run upstairs, throw myself on my bed and sob, but Becca is not me. 'I'm ready, Harry,' she says, walking out to the confessional set and standing right in front of me. 'You're in my seat,' she says, her jaw clenched and her eyes cold.

I rise, my legs trembling, and walk off the set into the lounge room where I collapse onto a sofa. I absolutely do not want to hear Becca's confessional—essentially the nails in the coffin of our friendship. I cannot *believe* she heard me say those horrible, horrible things.

'Abby, are you okay?' Jack again.

'Everyone keeps asking me that and no, I'm not.'

'I'm *so* sorry,' he says crouching next to the sofa. 'That was a complete fuck up. Becca was not supposed to be anywhere near the set. That's why your call times were fifteen minutes apart.'

I throw my hands up in the air. 'Well, the cat is well and truly out of the bag now. Becca will never speak to me again—and rightly so.'

'Maybe there's something I can do,' he says feebly.

I meet his eye. 'There isn't,' I say. 'It's done. I painted myself into a corner and that's it, that's all there is.'

'You weren't alone. Harry and I had paint rollers too.' It's lovely that he wants to make me smile, but I may only have one smile left in me today and I need that for the cameras. 'Let's just get this over with,' I say, hoisting myself inelegantly off the sofa. 'Would you mind …' I signal to where (presumably) Becca is reciprocating with a vile confessional of her own, and Jack jogs over to the bifold glass doors.

He watches for a few moments, then turns to me. 'She's done, but why don't you wait it out in here? We still need to get Daniel set up on the beach so we can film you walking down to him.'

Something occurs to me. 'Wait. I know I'm supposed to go first, but can we change the order, have Becca go first?'

'Uh, I can have a quick chat with Harry. Any particular reason?'

'Well, perhaps Daniel will clap eyes on Becca, looking as gorgeous as she does, and that will solidify his choice—of Becca, I mean. It's worth a try, don't you think?'

He shrugs, so I can tell he's unconvinced, but he says, 'Sure,' and disappears outside.

I sink back into the sofa and start chewing on my bottom lip before I remember the velvety red lipstick and stop. The more I think about it, the more I'm sure that Daniel just needs to *see* Becca and he'll make the right choice.

'Right choice'——hah! Right choice for whom?

Jack seems to be gone for eternity before he reappears. 'Okay, so Harry and the crew are setting up on the beach with Gordo, and Becca will go first. You should probably stay in here though——they're about to bring Daniel around from the Control Room.'

'All right.'

'Hey, at least we'll know pretty soon, right? And fingers crossed it will be Becca and all this goes away. Well, you know what I mean.' I do and I give him a smile for his efforts——a small one, but a smile all the same.

I listen from my spot on the sofa as the crew works seamlessly to finalise the camera positions, get Daniel and Becca miked and into place, and make final tweaks before I hear Harry's booming voice call, 'Action.'

But I cannot sit here doing nothing while my fate is decided——well, Doe Abby's fate——and I stand and creep over to a vantage point where I can watch and listen without being in the shot. Becca makes her way down to Gordo and Daniel, stepping carefully on the stone path that cuts through the lawn. Her dress is champagne-coloured, and with Daniel in his tuxedo and Gordo looking like he's offici-ating, it's like watching a wedding. Becca's hair is pinned up, loose curls captured by the light breeze, and even without seeing her face, I know she looks absolutely stunning.

Daniel's face is unreadable from here, but in moments, Becca stands facing him. Daniel leans down and kisses her cheek, which I hope is a good sign. The breeze has picked up now, pressing Becca's dress against her legs, revealing their shapely lines. It's also carrying away snatches of the conversation and I can only hear snippets—'beautiful woman', 'lovely time', 'difficult decision', then 'sorry, Becca'.

'Oh, god,' I say aloud. The daft bugger has gone and chosen me.

Becca's head drops into her hands and she shakes it so vigorously, hair starts spilling from her up-do. Gordo tries to soothe her, but she ignores him. It's when the breeze carries a sob in my direction, that my heart wrenches and I can stand it no longer. An idiotic twat has hurt my friend and I can't watch it unfold without doing *something*.

I stride out of the Manor and down the stone path with no regard for my safety (stone paths and spiky heeled sandals being a dangerous mix). Ignoring all the warning bells clanging loudly in my head, I step onto the beach and call out, 'Stop! Stop everything.'

It's hard to say who looks more surprised—Daniel, whose mouth hangs open, Gordo who looks to Harry horrified, like he's missed a cue, or Becca, who blinks her teary eyes at me, a furrow between her brows. Unfortunately, I didn't think beyond 'stop the proceedings' and when I reach them, we stand gawping at each other like some bizarre four-person surprise party.

Eventually, Daniel breaks the spell with my name. 'Abby? What's going on?'

'You're making an enormous mistake, that's what's going on.'

'No, I'm not,' he insists.

'Yes, yes, you are. You don't want to be with me.'

'I do. I *do* want to be with you.' Becca yelps, as if he's physically wounded her.

'No! You only think you do because you're a fickle, confused idiot.'

'I beg your pardon?'

'See? That, that right there. You say you want someone who'll challenge you but, really, it irks you. And here you have this *goddess* of a woman, who's bright and beautiful and kind, and you choose *me?* Idiot!'

'What are you on about, Abby? I heard your confessional, remember? I'm simple and unsophisticated and a bad match for Daniel,' says Becca, practically spitting the words at me.

'Wait, you said that?' Daniel asks me.

'Well, yes, but—'

'But what? Were you lying then or are you lying now?' Becca asks. 'Because either way, you're a *liar*.'

'I …' Oh, bugger all this to hell. I cannot tell the truth—the ripple effects of a few words could be career ending—and not just for me. 'Gah!' I cry in frustration.

'Oh, so *you* get to be upset, Abby? *You* do? You pretended to be my friend for *weeks*—only yesterday you were spouting all sorts of crap about wanting to be friends when this is all over. But it's a lie. It's *all* been a lie. You're no better than Tara or Kylie.'

All the things she's saying hurt—they're punches to my heart—but being equated with the Cruella Sisters is the worst. Still, I can say nothing.

'I trusted you, Abby. And you're nothing but a lying, manipulative *bitch*.'

'That's enough, Becca!' For a moment, I think it's Daniel—or even Gordo. But, as Gordo has stalked off the beach, throwing up his hands and mumbling about his agent, and Daniel is now perched on the edge of a sun lounger in an open-mouthed stupor, neither are my rescuer. 'Harry can we cut, please?' asks Jack curtly as he makes his way over to our grisly tableau.

'Oh, yeah, sorry. Cut!' I glance at Harry who's standing on the lawn and scratching his head. The rest of the crew look just as baffled and when I turn back to our little gathering on the beach, Jack looks livid.

'Becca, look, I'm really shooting myself in the foot here but Abby ...' He shakes his head and spits out a 'fuck', then expels a frustrated sigh.

I try to catch his eye, but there's obviously an intense internal discussion happening. '*Jack*,' I say, hoping I can stop him before this whole thing comes crashing down.

'No, Abby,' he says, finally looking at me, 'I can't ... I can't let this go on any longer. Becca, Abby took your place as the new Villain.'

'What?' gasps Becca.

'What does that mean?' asks Daniel from the sun

lounger, his synapses finally firing again. 'What is god's name is a "Villain"?'

Jack throws him a contemptuous look, then turns back to Becca. 'It's true. Harry and I … we messed up and Abby overheard us saying that with Tara and Kylie gone, we wanted to edit your footage to make you the new Villain.'

Becca looks at me, her confusion apparent. 'Is that true, Abby?'

'Yes.' Well, except how I found out, but I'll have to let that part go.

'It's true,' continues Jack. 'She confronted us and said that you were too good a person to be made into a Villain, that the viewers would end up hating you, and she didn't want that.'

'Wait …' Becca turns to me. 'So, that was all pretend, what you said in the confessional?' I nod and her eyes slick with tears again. 'Oh, my god, Abby.' I nibble on my lower lip, not caring one iota about velvety red lipstick. 'You made that sacrifice for me? That's so unselfish. And I … Oh, my god, I'm *so* sorry.'

'You have nothing to apologise for. If our positions were reversed, I would have thought the same of you.' I'm not sure how true this is, but the last thing I want is for Becca to feel worse.

'Oh, Abs,' she says, flinging her arms around me. I wrap mine around her waist and we hug tightly.

'I still don't understand what a "Villain" is,' calls out Daniel.

Becca and I pull apart and share a look. 'What don't you

understand about it?' I ask Daniel. 'There's always at least one Villain in every season of the show.'

'That's true,' confirms Jack.

'Well, how the bloody hell would I know that?' asks Daniel, his voice getting loud and pitchy.

'Hang on,' I say, 'have you never watched *The Stag*?'

'No, why would I?' he responds, his face sour. It's like I've asked if he trawls for his clothes in rubbish tips.

Becca flicks her head in my direction leans in close. 'Has he always been like this?' she asks quietly.

'You mean a massive twat?' I reply, abandoning all hope that he ever wanted to improve himself.

'Mm-hmm.'

'Yes, and increasingly so.'

Her eyes flash with understanding, as though a fugue has lifted. 'But when did *you* figure that out and how—'

'Hey, everyone,' says Harry, cutting Becca off. 'I hate to bust up this little party, but we still have a finale to shoot. Uh, Jack, a word?'

Jack, now looking sheepish, walks with Harry down to the lapping water where they put their heads together and talk in murmurs. After a moment, Jack lifts his head and catches my eye, giving me a quick smile before Harry back-hands him on the shoulder.

'Uh, Abby,' says Daniel, suddenly beside me (the stealthy bugger). 'It seems that you've done a very selfless and honourable thing.' My stomach clenches at the thought of where he's going with this.

'Er, thank you.'

'And does this mean that all those times you gave me a

serve and put me in my place——that was you playing the Villain?'

'No, no, Daniel, that was me being *me*.'

'I see,' he says, a ghastly twinkle in his eyes. 'Then I was right.'

'About?'

'*You*. You have an excellent character ...' Well, closer to the truth is that I *play* an excellent character. 'You're bright, you're selfless, and you will put me in my place when I need it.' He's peering me as though seeing me in a new light, and never has a series of compliments made me feel so uncomfortable.

'What are you saying?' I ask softly.

'I'm saying that I stand by my initial decision. I choose you. Harry! Can we start the cameras, please? I still choose Abby.'

'Gah!' Me again, my frustration with Daniel, this ridiculous situation, and this dreadful, stupid assignment spilling out into one guttural sound.

'Daniel, hear me when I say that you may choose me, but I do *not* choose you. We are not right for each other, we have less in common than you believe, and I find you to be pompous, condescending, narcissistic, and overly didactic! Do you understand? Are you hearing me?'

'You don't have to protect Becca anymore, Abby. I know you're just saying those things to save her from further humiliation.' I catch Becca's expression, her brow creasing in fury.

'Really? You're *so* certain?' I ask.

'I know it, darling Abby.' Being called 'darling' by Daniel is the final straw.

'Do you have it, the pin?' I ask him.

'The pin?'

'Yes, Daniel, the pin you intend to give me.'

He smiles, clearly thinking he's won, and retrieves it from his coat pocket. I'm vaguely aware that Tim is close by, a camera on his shoulder, but with what I'm about to do, this will not be usable footage.

'Here.' Daniel holds out the pin, reaching for the neckline of my gown.

'Thank you!' I say, snatching it from his hand. Then (with great difficulty in my heels), I stride across the sand to Jack.

'Abby? What are you doing?' Jack asks, his voice soft and a curious smile on his lips.

'Yeah, Abby, what gives?' asks Harry.

Ignoring Harry, I look up at Jack and smile. 'I'm fixing it,' I say, though I'm not wholly confident I am. 'Daniel,' I say, giving him a no-nonsense look, 'I don't want to be with you, because I've fallen for someone else. I've fallen for Jack.' I reach up and slide the silver stag-shaped pin onto Jack's T-shirt, being careful not to stab him with it. He's shaking his head, but his smile is still in place.

'Well, fuck,' says Harry behind me. 'Cut, Tim. We can't use any of this.' I hear the words but I don't *hear* them. I'm too caught up in the gorgeous Australian man and those gorgeous green eyes and those perfect, perfect lips. I want to kiss them, but we're interrupted.

'Oh, absolutely not! You've been dallying with one of the crew? The *crew*, Abby?' says Daniel, his disdain for 'lowly workers' blatant. 'Then you're right, you aren't the woman for me.'

'I said he was fickle,' I say quietly to Jack who sniggers.

'Abs?' Becca approaches. 'So …?' She wags a finger between Jack and me. 'Really?'

'Really.' I grin and she returns it.

'Oh, my god! See! I *knew* there was something up with you.'

'What do you mean?'

'No one meditates that much, Abby, not even the Dalai Lama!' Before I can register that I haven't quite pulled off my secret ops, she grabs my hand and squeezes, just like she used to. 'Oh, I'm so happy for you, Abby! You be good to this one,' she says to Jack and I try not to think about how he and I still haven't talked properly.

'So, are we filming this or not?' says Daniel from his position further up the beach. 'Becca, you coming?'

My eyes fly to Becca's and from the conspiratorial look she gives me, I know that we will now swap roles, with her protecting me, the show, and even Jack.

'Coming, Daniel,' she calls over her shoulder.

'Positions, everyone!' calls Harry. 'Gordo, get your arse down here.'

'You sure?' I ask her.

She nods at me. 'Absolutely. We need a finale, right?'

Harry inserts himself into the conversation. 'So, what are you thinking here, Becca?' he asks. I've known him long enough to catch the nervousness in his voice.

'Don't worry. I promise, I've got this.'

Harry looks doubtful and glances at Jack, who shrugs. 'What else are we gonna do?' he asks.

'Ah, *shit*,' says Harry. He turns and calls out to the crew, 'Okay, everyone, we're going again!' Turning back to Jack, he holds out his hand. 'Give me the fricking pin.' Jack slides it from his shirt and hands it to his brother. 'And get out of the shot, will ya, you two?'

'Oh, right, sorry,' I say.

'Sorry, bro,' says Jack as he takes my hand and leads me up the beach.

Becca takes her position facing Daniel, who tucks the pin back inside his tuxedo pocket. Gordo stands off to the side as Daniel smiles at Becca and Harry shouts, 'Action!'

Chapter Twenty-Five

The Stag in Sydney Recap: And that's a wrap!
by Anastasia Blabbergasted

In an absolute first for this recapper, I am flabbergasted! No one could have predicted we'd have such a dramatic finale to *The Stag in Sydney*, even me!

Our top two Does, once best of friends, have been cooling on each other for some time now, with the Becca–Abby 'wromance' going from winks and conspiratorial whispers to barely civil smiles. But pitted against each other in the finale, the two contenders for Bride forget all prior chumminess entirely, beginning with duelling confessionals!

Abby: 'Becca's *lovely*, but Daniel needs someone who won't let him walk all over them—someone like *me*.'

Me-ow! Abby's cocky confessional wraps up with the question, 'What specifically did Daniel say that makes you so confident he'll choose you?' to which she answers, 'That he will.'

Ah-hah! So, that's what she and Daniel were saying when they snuck off at the Botanic Gardens. At this stage in the episode, I'm putting all my money on Abby for the win.

But it seems that Becca should not be underestimated—not by me and certainly not by Abby!

Becca: 'Abby may come across as kind and supportive, but she's a liar. She manipulates you into liking her, then stabs you in the back. Daniel is not going to choose someone like that.'

Touché, Becca! What a formidable sparring partner you're proving to be. And, as we've seen from Abby's behaviour over the past few episodes, Becca is bang on with her accusations. But will Abby get her just desserts?

This is where the episode gets *really* interesting in a plot twist *so* extreme, M. Night Shyamalan just phoned and asked the producers for a consult on his next script.

Becca's confessional wraps up with: 'Anyway, Daniel told me he's choosing me.'

Now, I am no mathematician but one man divided by two women equals *disaster!* Or, in some states in the US, polygamy. Seeing as this is Sydney and not Utah, 'disaster' it is!

Time for the Pin Ritual to end all Pin Rituals!

There he is, our Staggy, Daniel, handsome in that two-button, slim lapel tuxedo, the late afternoon Australian sun glinting off his flawless blonde hair. Daniel awaits his first Doe, Gordo looking on benevolently. And there she is, our Abby, splendid in a flowing red gown that shows off her curvaceous figure. She walks slowly down the path to Daniel, who's grinning ~~like an idiot~~ proudly, almost like an expectant groom.

On the beach, pinpoints of light dancing on the water behind them and gentle waves lapping against the shore, they face each other. Daniel, suddenly a man of few words, takes the much-coveted pin from his pocket and reaches towards Abby's neckline. 'Abby will you wear this pin?'

I am on the edge of my sofa with anticipation——this is exactly what Abby hoped for *and* she's the first Dark Horse to *ever* become the Bride.

'I'm sorry, Daniel, I cannot accept your pin.'

WHAT?

'You see, I know how torn you are. You've told both me *and* Becca that you've chosen us.'

Daniel blinks and gawps—a goldfish out of water—then recovers. 'I want to be with you.'

'You may, but you also want to be with Becca and I can't be with someone who's unsure of his feelings.'

'I choose you. You're bright, you're selfless, and you will put me in my place when I need it.'

'I'm sorry, Daniel. I cannot accept. But I wish you every happiness.' And with that, Abby retreats into the Manor. Stag lovers, when have we *ever* seen a Doe say 'no' in the finale?! Well, I can tell you that and it's never!

Poor Daniel! But he won't be forlorn for much longer, as here comes the lovely Becca. As far as consolation prizes go, she far exceeds a kitchen appliance and doesn't she look a picture in that champagne-coloured dress—no doubt a signpost of celebrations to come.

Daniel, having recovered miraculously from Abby's

refusal of his pin, smiles winsomely at Becca as he takes her hands in his. Again, Gordo presides and I can't help wondering if we're about to witness a proposal *and* a wedding! (Surely, Gordo is ordained, right?)

Daniel finds his words again and extols Becca's virtues (which, for him, seem to start and stop with her looks) 'Becca, you are a beautiful woman, and I've had a lovely time getting to know you. This was not a difficult decision. I choose you.'

Not content with perching on the edge of the sofa, I am now seated on the floor directly in front of the television.

'I'm sorry, Daniel, but I can't be with you.'

WHAT IS HAPPENING, PLEASE?

Daniel has turned from a 'goldfish out of water' into an 'enormous bug-eyed fish out of water'——apologies, I know I could have conducted an online search for the name of said fish, but I am too flabbergasted!

'What do you mean?' he asks after gawping for (it certainly feels like) several minutes.

Becca's reply will be indelibly inked on my mind. 'I heard you with Abby, Daniel, and I don't want her sloppy seconds. I'm worth more than that. *Much* more. More than you could ever offer me.'

I could turn off the episode here and be completely happy—no, that's not the right word. Elated. Empowered. Breaking into 'I AM WOMAN!' at full voice.

But before I can reach for the remote, Daniel does something *very* un-suave and not remotely sophisticated. He storms off in a colossal toddler-style huff. I listen for a slamming door, but it doesn't come – though, those bifold glass doors *are* quite difficult to close.

And now for one last treat from the producers. In lieu of a *romantic* happily ever after, we get a 'wromantic' one with Becca and Abby reconciling on the beach. 'Please forgive me for being such a massive cow,' wails Abby, redeeming herself in *my* eyes if not Becca's. 'I got all caught up in it and forgot who I was.' *Aww.*

Becca hugs her, calls her a 'dag' (another not-so-charming expression from the Australians), and the music swells as our top two Does are silhouetted against a stunning Sydney sky at sunset.

'Well, what do you think?' asks Jack.

Jack, Harry, Becca, and I are in the Control Room and we've just finished watching the final cut of the finale. After Becca's refusal, which was included in the episode verbatim, Daniel did storm off. Apparently, not staying for a final confessional was a breach of contract, and Jack got him to agree to the storyline that the four of us pieced together after the shoot.

We reshot Becca's confessional, so I could be seen in the background, and if viewers bother to go back to the Daniel–Abby scene, they'll see Becca hiding behind a tree over my shoulder. We filmed me walking down to the beach, then back up to the Manor, and the rest of the Pin Ritual was edited together from existing footage.

And, of course, Becca and I happily filmed our reconciliation on the beach. Although we'd worked out a loose script ahead of time, I meant every word I said—about Becca and how much I adore her and value our friendship, but also about me.

I *had* forgotten who I was—only not during the filming of *The Stag* but a long time ago. I've spent the last several years hiding in my little flat, writing under a pen name, barely raising my head, let alone going out into the world and getting amongst it. How am I supposed to become a real journalist, someone with something to say, if all my experiences are vicarious? Sure, online research is a start, but if I really want to establish myself in the profession, I need to leave the flat.

'It's brilliant,' I say to Jack, right as Becca says, 'Awesome. You guys did a great job.' She's right. No doubt, this finale will drive ratings through the roof—even Roberta couldn't fault it. I'm also betting that Prue will love my final recap and perhaps, one day, forgive me for abandoning my exposé.

'Hey, it was your quick thinking that saved us,' Harry says to Becca. 'God, I was packing myself when Abby pulled that stunt—sorry, Abby, but I was.'

'No, absolutely justified.'

Jack reaches for my hand and I grasp his. 'You were both terrific,' he says. 'Look, this is "reality TV"' —he waggles a finger for the air quotes— 'and over the years, we've reshot dozens of scenes, right Harry?'

'Oh, yeah—*and* there's the creative editing.' They chuckle.

'But don't you reckon this is our best effort?' continues Jack.

'Aw, yeah, for sure, no question. *And*, with any luck, one of our last, eh?' The brothers exchange a hopeful look. 'So, whaddya reckon, cause for a celebration?' asks Harry as he stands and stretches his arms above his head. I catch Becca staring at Harry's T-shirt straining against his biceps and wonder if something might spark between them.

'I'll see what's in the fridge,' says Harry, opening the door.

'I'll help you,' says Becca. This time, Jack and I share a look and when the door closes behind them, he turns in his chair to face me, our knees touching.

'You're amazing,' he says to me quietly, his gaze intense.

'*I* am?' I don't typically fish for compliments but, right

now, I'm all kinds of interested in exactly how amazing I am.

'Yeah, you and Becca—you saved our arses.' Oh, he's talking about the show.

'Well, you're welcome.' I hope I've tempered my tone enough to disguise my disappointment.

'And *you* are amazing, Abby. Just you.'

'Oh.'

'You're beautiful, you're clever, you're funny …' his voice gets quieter as his lips get closer to mine. 'Thoughtful, talented, and *extremely* sexy.' Disappointment has left the building!

'As much as I enjoy being told how wonderful I am, will you please kiss me?'

His chuckle tickles my lips as he touches those perfect, perfect lips to mine. *This* kiss is the best kiss in the history of the universe, eclipsing all other kisses we've shared—all other kisses that anyone has ever shared! His lips are soft and full and they move against mine, fervent and hungry, as though tasting me is knowing me. His tongue touches mine, our breath mingles and—

'Oh, my god, you two! I mean it, get a fricking room.' Harry—*again*. We spring apart—*again*. And Jack releases a string of obscenities at his brother.

'Fine! I'm going. I just wanted to tell you we've opened a bottle of bubbly.'

'Out!' Jack bellows, his commanding tone doing wonders for my insides. 'Sorry about that,' he says when the door closes for the second time.

I giggle. 'It's fine. But I am very much looking forward to

not being in the Manor, just being …' I trail off, reality intruding on my Manor bubble.

'Just being together, alone?' I nod, my recently warmed insides turning squidgy with nerves—the bastards. 'That's what I want too, Abby.'

'Really? But what can even hap—' God, I can't even say it. I stare hard at an errant paperclip on the floor.

'Hey, look at me.' I do, reluctantly. This is suddenly all too serious—another bubble in our land of make-believe bursting in the glaring light of reality. 'I'm not a cad, Abby. I don't scout my own shows for women to sleep with. I've *never* done that.'

'*No!* I would never think that of you.' It's true. I've never thought that Jack was a player. It's just … what can possibly come of this?

'Good, because you know how you told Daniel that you'd fallen for me?' How could I forget? Not only was it out of my mouth before I could even consider the implications, I've replayed it in my mind a thousand times since. I nod again. 'Man, that was … that was awesome.' It was? 'I mean, yeah, we've been sneaking around and Harry's been on my arse to stop watching you all the time—he said it was becoming really obvious—but I didn't know if it was just me or …'

'If I felt the same,' I say, finishing his thought. So, we'd both been uncertain.

'Yes, exactly. So, when you said that … Abby, I'm *crazy* about you. And I know we live in different countries, but we're both able to work from anywhere, right? I mean, I can look for gigs in the UK, you can come here and write, and when Harry and I start our production company ... well, we can figure that out then.'

'You've given this a lot of thought.'

'Of course I have, Abby!' he says, grinning.

Then my monkey mind settles on one thought: *Jack wants to be with me. Jack wants to be with me.'*

~~Flirtation. Fling. Crush. Bit of crumpet on the side.~~

No.

A proper, grown-up relationship with a proper, grown-up man, a man who champions my aspirations, who sees me as I really am, who does wonders to my insides just with a look, and who thinks I'm brilliant and beautiful. Oh, tick, tick, tick! Thank you, karma, or Cadmus, or the universe! Whoever or whatever, *thank you*!

'It's been really fricking hard keeping my mind on the show—another reason Harry's shitty with me. Seriously, I owe him big time! And he will *never* let me forget it.' We share another laugh, mine steeped in relief and joy and a myriad of other emotions. 'But let's forget about all that—for now, anyway.'

The timbre of his voice drops, and I'm suddenly aware of how firm his hands are on my thighs as they pull me closer to him. 'What do you say we have a celebratory drink with Harry and Becca, then I take you home to my place?' he asks quietly, almost shyly.

I stare into those vibrant green eyes, my insides ablaze with delicious tingles. 'Oh, I'd absolutely love that.'

A mix of elation and lust flashes across his face in an instant as he grins at me. 'Awesome.' He smacks a kiss on my lips, stands and reaches for my hand. 'Come on.'

'Wait. Just us, though, right? Not Harry? I mean, I know he lives there too …'

'Oh, no. My brother can find somewhere else to sleep tonight. Hell, we've got this place for a couple more days. He can stay here for all I care.'

'Perfect,' I say, grinning and taking his hand.

The Stag in Sydney: Where are they now?
by Anastasia Blabbergasted

Well, well, well. It has been several months now since the finale of the most twisty-turny season in *The Stag's* history and this recapper has only just recovered from that vertiginous ride. Here's hoping you have too, as *Isle of Passion* and *I'm Super Famous, I Want Out* are just around the corner.

For this special 'Where are they now?' recap, I sent my spies to the corners of not only Britain, but Australia and they found some particularly juicy titbits about the cast *and* crew. And, of course, I consider it my civic duty to pass those along to you.

Let's start with a season favourite, the delightful **Kaz**. Our feisty redhead returned to Perth well rested after

~~her holiday~~ she was booted off the show, and on her very first day at a new building site, met the affable Carl—foreperson, single father, and a damned nice fellow to boot. They have been dating ever since, and Kaz gets along famously with his two littlies, twins Carla and Darla, or as she calls them, Carls and Darls.

Wannabe actress **Justine** got her much hoped for ratings boost from appearing on *The Stag* and signed with a mid-sized talent agency in Sydney. She was last seen draped across a rather luxurious sports car at the annual Sydney Car Show, saying that the gig was a steppingstone to something grander—no doubt she's on track to replace Cate Blanchett in *Medea*. Her relationship with camera operator, Tim, burned brightly for approximately three-and-a-half weeks before they realised that the only thing they had in common was a strong physical attraction to the other.

Daphne, British blue blood and thawed ice queen, returned to England more determined than ever to escape the stifling clutches of her family and their failing fortune. She has recently taken on a role at a not-for-profit that supports girls' education in developing nations, putting all that volunteering experience (literally) to work. She's just moved into a modest flat in Crouch End and Daphne 2.0 has been known to leave the flat wearing *jeans* (imagine that!) and sans her (formerly) ubiquitous string of pearls.

Our **Stevie** landed in Adelaide just in time to (generously) collect her girlfriends from the airport post their trip to Thailand and, though she still regrets the decision to forego the holiday to appear on *The Stag*, she remains close to Abby, Daphne, Becca, and Kaz, catching up with them regularly on WhatsApp. She remains single but hopeful that she will meet someone special when 'the universe decides she's ready'. I hope so, as the universe certainly wasn't playing fair when it shoved Daniel in her path. Still, it's a testament to her strength of character that she wasn't permanently ruined for love by her time spent with Staggy.

Speaking of …

It's rumoured—and my spies had to dig deep into the muck to find this juicy gossip—that **Daniel** has become a frequenter of nightclubs where he's amassed a bevvy of ~~hangers on~~ beauties, average age 21.3. No longer on the search for a wife—being turned down by both Abby and Becca must have dented his ego irreparably—Daniel has instead opted to relive his salad days, jumping from one (brief) affair to the next. I wonder where that leaves his plans for the wildlife sanctuary he seemed so keen on. Not to worry, Daniel. No doubt lavishing the young women of London's club scene with tawdry trinkets is just as worthy a cause as saving endangered animals from poachers.

Beautiful **Becca** is wrapping up her final year of studies and about to head into the world of Data Science (whatever that may be, as even after having it explained to me, it still sounds like a made up profession). After she awakened from a weeks' long stupor, realising during the show's finale that she was *not* in love with Daniel the Dick (as Kaz so eloquently called him) after all, she shifted her amorous attentions onto the show's director, Handsome Harry. Harry, being one of those men who is oblivious when a woman is (quite obviously) attracted to him took a while to twig. But eventually it occurred to him that frequent flirtatious texts from a beautiful woman were, in fact, a clue that she might actually *like* him. He asked her out and they have now been dating for some time. He even introduced her to his parents recently, proving that good things do come to those who wait (and persist).

I smile to myself as I write that last part. Harry really was so dim. I finally had to ask Jack to tell him to stop being such an idiot and ask Becca out. They are so adorable together, and it has been one of the loveliest parts of the last few months—the four of us spending time together. That's right. I not only have a boyfriend and a new girlfriend, but a (sort-of) brother too.

It's been a bit manic, though, all this back and forth. I spent an extra couple of weeks in Sydney after the show finished filming, getting to know 'Jack's Sydney' as well as the man himself, and then I flew home to see Mum, Lisa, and Aunty Lo. I'd missed them so much.

Jack wasn't far behind me, as he wanted to meet Mum face to face and see my little corner of the world. It's funny how what I thought was an incredibly small existence turned out to be so much more when there was someone to share it with.

And Jack was (as expected) a hit with my family. Aunty Lo took one look at him and said in an incredibly loud stage whisper, 'Ooh, he's bit of all right.' I would have died of embarrassment on the spot if Jack hadn't handled it like a pro. 'Now, now, Lois, I know you're the naughty one in the family and as tempting as that may be, I only have eyes for Abby.' She swatted him and giggled like a schoolgirl. Lise pulled me aside later that evening. 'Oh, Abs, he's just brilliant. I'm so happy for you.'

And most importantly, Mum absolutely loves him. When I got home, she went on and on about how lovely he was to her when she was filming her part as Doe Abby's mum. 'You should have seen the enormous flower arrangement he sent as a thank you, Abigail. It was so large, I couldn't see your Aunty Lo on the other side of the kitchen table!' Meeting him in person and spending time with him really sealed the deal. I almost suspect Mum would trade me for Jack if she were forced to choose between us.

Tomorrow I fly out to Sydney—this time for three months, as I've teed up a job at a women's magazine. Actually, it was Prue who set it up—pushing that little bird out of the nest, as promised. I'll be a guest feature writer and if the stint goes well, it could become permanent. Me—a staff writer at a proper magazine! Though, I think I might miss writing as Anastasia. She really is a fun part to play.

That's why I've written this recap. It's just for me, of course—it could never see the light of day.

My phone chimes with a message alert and seeing Jack's name on the screen, I smile.

Fly safe gorgeous. I can't wait to see you. J xxxxx

Likewise, Mr Freeman. Likewise.

Oh, and just one more thing—an end cap to my final recap.

And what about everyone's favourite Dark Horse, Abby?

Well, first off, she should be applauded and lauded for managing to leave Stag Manor with her secret identity intact—huzzah! I am in awe that she pulled it off, as there were more than a few nerve-wracking moments that had this recapper biting her proverbials.

But best of all … not only did Abby find life-long friendship amongst the cast and crew and her Happily Ever After with the lovely (and gorgeous) Jack, she found one with herself. I can only *imagine* what incredible things she will do next.

Cast of Characters

London

Abigail 'Abby' Jones (a.k.a. Anastasia Blabbergasted), our heroine
Lisa, Abby's best friend since college
Mum, Abby's mother
Prue, Abby's editor at *Feed Your Mind*
Jack, producer of *The Stag*
Roberta, executive producer of *The Stag*
Nadia, beauty therapist and makeup artist (makeover team)
Günter, hair stylist (makeover team)
Caitriona, clothing stylist (makeover team)
Aunty Lo, Abby's mum's best friend and Abby's unofficial aunty
Ian, Lisa's running partner and crush
Angus, Abby's ex-boyfriend

Sydney

Harry, Jack's younger brother and director of *The Stag in Sydney*

Carlie, crewmember on *The Stag in Sydney*

Tim, camera operator for *The Stag in Sydney*

Silvia, editor of *The Stag in Sydney*

Cast of The Stag in Sydney

Gordo, the host

Daniel, the Stag – a British banker (wanker)

The Australian Does

Becca (potential Bride) – from Sydney, Abby's best friend in the Manor

Kaz (Dark Horse) – from Perth, has a shock of red hair, friends with Abby and Becca

Justine (potential Bride) – from Sydney, a wannabe actress

Kylie (Villain) – from Queensland, has platinum-blonde hair, one half of the 'Cruella Sisters'

Merrin (Miscellaneous) – a cat lover from Tasmania

Laura (Filler) – loves all things country music, from Tamworth

Stevie (Interloper) – from Adelaide, a psychologist, resembles Karlie Kloss

The British Does

Daphne (potential Bride) – titled, posh, and snobby
Tabitha (Filler)
Ellie (Dark Horse) – brought a ventriloquist's dummy of
herself to the Manor
Tara (Villain) – from the East End of London, has jet-black
hair, one half of the 'Cruella Sisters'
Elizabeth (Miscellaneous) – a shy and quiet Reception
teacher from Devon, friends with Abby
Abby (Dark Horse) – a.k.a. our heroine and 'Doe Abby'

Acknowledgments

As we all know, 2020 was an incredibly trying year across the world (and 2021 has already had its challenges too), but something that came from that difficult time—when my home city of Melbourne was strictly locked down for the better part of the year—was this book.

The idea came from a sweepstake at work. *The Bachelor* (or Bacchie, as we call it in Australia) was starting and for some mid-pandemic light relief, my colleagues created a sweepstake, with the pot going to whoever drew the winning Bachelorette. To add to the experience, I started writing recaps of each episode—snarky, funny recaps—which I would post in our group chat the morning after each episode aired.

I mentioned the recaps to a close author friend, Andie Newton, one of my fellow Renegades. She asked to read one and immediately replied with, 'This needs to be a book.' I couldn't imagine how a recap could turn into a book, but she came back with, 'Write the story about the woman who writes the recaps.' Genius. I bounced ideas off her and the other Renegades, Nina Kaye and Fiona Leitch, sent a sample chapter to my agent, Lina Langlee, and we pitched it to my editor at One More Chapter. Once I had the 'thumbs up' from my publisher, I researched, researched, researched—meaning I watched every episode of *The Bachelor* and continued to write my recaps. When the season was over, I sat down and wrote this book.

An enormous thank you, Andie, for sparking the original idea and for being a brilliant sounding board in the planning stages. For a historical fiction author, you certainly have excellent ideas for romcoms. Thank you also to Nina and Fi, who have been right there with me throughout the entire authoring process and particularly for answering my endless 'Does this sound British enough?' questions. And thank you to Fi and Andie for being early readers and giving me (incredibly) helpful feedback.

Thank you also to my lovely colleagues (and work friends) who ran the sweepstake, LOLed at my recaps (which spurred me on), and encouraged me, especially Carla, Natalie, Amanda, Dee, Shileen, Sam, and Keely.

A huge shout out to my wonderful editors. Hannah Todd was still at One More Chapter when we pitched this book. Hannah, thank you for advocating for me and *The Dating Game*—I so appreciate it—and thank you for all I learnt from you while working on my first four books.

To Jennie Rothwell, although you are new to One More Chapter, I already know that we are going to be a great team. Your inciteful feedback and your vision for this book have elevated my writing and I so look forward to working with you on my next books with One More Chapter. And speaking of … thank you so much to the incredibly hardworking team at One More Chapter, especially Charlotte Ledger and Bethan Morgan for being champions of my writing and for working so hard through the toughest of times.

A big thank you to my (fabulous, talented, and dedicated) agent, Lina Langlee of The North Literary Agency. I so appreciate the leap of faith you took with me on this book, and your early feedback was instrumental in setting me up for success. And another big thank you to Julie Fergusson, also of The North, who stepped in while Lina was on maternity leave. Thank you for your expert guidance and unwavering support to help me get this book across the line.

As always, I am grateful to my fellow authors for their support, their empathy, their trust, and their inspiring work. It is an honour and a privilege to be part of your community and I am constantly in awe of how generous you are and of your incredible work. A special mention and thank you to the volunteers who run our associations, the Romance Novelists Association (UK) and the Romance Writers Association (AU) for continuing to support and elevate the Romance genre. And thank you to my fellow #AusWritesers and #6amAusWrites-ers—I love our catchups on the socials and sometimes even in person!

A special thank you to Julie Houston, who provided the cover quote for this book. Julie, I admire you as a writer, but also as a person—you are so generous, thoughtful, and talented. Thank you for taking time out of your incredibly busy schedule to read my book. It means the world to me that you loved it.

And when I cheekily asked some other fellow romance authors if they'd like to do an early read, they all said yes! Thank you, Jessica Redland, Katie Ginger, Lucy Knott (and Kelly too), Rachael Stewart, Kiley Dunbar, and debut novelist and writing community maven, Anita Faulkner. I am also grateful to belong to the incredibly supportive (and aptly named) Author Support Network.

Thank you also to the reading and reviewing community—the bloggers, podcasters, and reviewers who generously share their thoughts on reading and books—especially to the community of Chick Lit and Prosecco (particularly for supporting my cover reveal and the lead up to publication day); the Australian Romance Readers Association (particularly you, Debbie, for all your incredible work); Australian Book Lovers (Darren and Veronica) who have generously hosted me on their podcast twice; Kim the Bookworm (Kim Nash) for inviting me on Book Chat with Kim—you are not only a wonderful author in your own right, but a terrific supporter of our community; and to the Australian Writers Centre for hosting me on their podcast, 'So You Want to Be a Writer?' (thank you, Valerie and Allison). And I have worked with the wonderful Rachel Gilbey several times—Rachel, it is a pleasure to work with you and thank you for all you do to organise such incredible book blog tours.

I always rely heavily on the support of my close friends and family, and my partner, Ben, to get through each stage of launching a book—from conception to publication and beyond. Ben, thank you for understanding that even minor milestones should be celebrated (and usually with bubbles). Thank you to my sis, Victoria, my mum, Lee, and dear friends, Lindsey, Jen, and Kate, for being early readers of this book and supporting and encouraging me. Thank you to the best, most supportive and loving parents and family a woman could ask for—your unwavering support is such a large part of why I get to do this wondrous thing, be an author. A special shout out to my Aunties, Linda, Candyce, Fran, Carmel, Karen, and Jenny. I am so fortunate to have such incredible role models in my life.

And lastly, thank you, dear reader, for coming on this fun and fabulous journey with me, Abby, and the gang. I hope you had a blast!